Also by Sara Paretsky
Published by Ballantine Books.

INDEMNITY ONLY
KILLING ORDERS
BITTER MEDICINE

DEADLOCK

A V.I. Warshawski Mystery

Sara Paretsky

BALLANTINE BOOKS • NEW YORK

For Lucella Wieser, a lady who sailed these seas
with wit and great courage for over a hundred and six
years.

The Canada Steamship Line very generously allowed me to get a firsthand look at a Great Lakes freighter in operation during the fall of 1980. Captain Bowman, master of their 720-foot self-unloading vessel, the *J. W. McGiffin*, invited me to sail with him from Thunder Bay through the Soo locks to the Welland Canal. He gave me run of the ship, from the bridge to the holds. Chief Engineer Thomas Taylor took me through the engine room and explained the intricacies of the self-unloader. I wish I could have put his humor and his love of machines into this story. However, no resemblance is intended between any of the officers or crew of the *McGiffin* and those of the ships in this novel. Nor are the operations of Grafalk Steamship or the Pole Star Line meant to resemble Canada Steamship in any way.

A former naval person who advised me on ships and maritime law and customs also has my heartfelt thanks.

1 * A Hero's Death

More than a thousand people attended Boom Boom's funeral. Many of them were children, fans from the suburbs and the Gold Coast. A handful came from Chicago's depressed South Side where Boom Boom had learned to fight and skate. He was a wing with the Black Hawks until he shattered his left ankle hang-gliding three years earlier. And before Wayne Gretzky came along, he'd been the game's biggest hero since Bobby Hull.

He underwent surgery for the ankle three times, refusing to admit he couldn't skate anymore. His doctors hadn't even wanted to attempt the third operation, but Boom Boom bowed to reality only when he could find no one to perform a fourth. After that he drifted through a series of jobs. A lot of people were willing to pay him to generate customers and goodwill, but Boom Boom was the kind of person who had to be doing, had to sink his teeth into—whatever it was.

He finally ended up with the Eudora Grain Company, where his father had been a stevedore during the thirties and forties. It was their regional vice-president, Clayton Phillips, who found Boom Boom's body floating close to the wharf last Tuesday. Phillips tried calling me since Boom Boom's employment forms listed me as his nearest relative. However, I was out of town on a case that took me to Peoria for three weeks. By the time the police located me one of Boom Boom's mother's numerous sisters had identified the body and begun arranging a big Polish funeral.

Boom Boom's father and mine were brothers, and we'd grown up together in South Chicago. We were both only children and were closer than many brothers and sisters. My Aunt Marie, a good Polish Catholic, had produced endless babies, dying in her twelfth attempt. Boom Boom was the fourth, and the only one who lived more than three days.

He grew up playing hockey. I don't know where he got the craze or the skill but, despite Marie's frenzy over the danger, he spent most of his childhood thinking up ways to play without her knowing. A lot of them involved me—I lived six blocks away, and a visit to Cousin Vic was often a cover for a few precious hours with the puck. In those days all the hockey-mad kids adulated Boom-Boom Geoffrion. My cousin copied his slap shot slavishly; to please him the other boys took to calling him "Boom Boom" and the nickname stuck. In fact when the Chicago police found me at my Peoria hotel and asked if I was Bernard Warshawski's cousin it took me a few seconds to realize who they meant.

Now I sat in the front pew at St. Wenceslas Church with Boom Boom's moist, indistinguishable aunts and cousins. All in black, they were offended by my navy wool suit. Several took the trouble to tell me so in loud whispers during the prelude.

I fixed my eyes on the imitation Tiffany windows, depicting in garish colors highlights in the life of St. Wenceslas, as well as the Crucifixion and the wedding at Cana. Whoever designed the windows had combined Chinese perspective with a kind of pseudocubism. As a result, jugs of water spouted from peoples' heads and long arms stretched menacingly from behind the cross. Attaching people to their own limbs and sorting out who was doing what to whom kept me fully occupied during the service and gave me—I hope—a convincing air of pious absorption.

Neither of my parents had been religious. My Italian mother was half Jewish, my father Polish, from a long line of skeptics. They'd decided not to inflict any faith on me, although my mother always baked me little *orecchi d'Aman* at Purim. The violent religiosity of Boom Boom's mother and the cheap plaster icons in her house always terrified me as a child.

My own taste would have been for a quiet service at a nondenominational chapel, with a chance for Boom Boom's old teammates to make a short speech—they'd asked to, but the aunts had turned them down. I certainly would not have picked this vulgar church in the old neighborhood, presided over by a priest who had never met my cousin and talked about him now with hypocritical fulsomeness.

However, I left the funeral arrangements to his aunts. My cousin named me his executor, a duty that was bound to absorb a lot of energy. I knew he would not care how he was buried, whereas the little excitement in his aunts' lives came from weddings and funerals. They made sure we spent several hours over a full-blown mass for the dead, followed by an interminable procession to the Sacred Heart cemetery on the far South Side.

After the interment Bobby Mallory fought through the crowd to me in his lieutenant's dress uniform. I was on my way to Boom Boom's Aunt Helen, or maybe his Aunt Sarah, for an afternoon of piroshkis and meatballs. I was glad Bobby had come: he was an old friend of my father's from the Chicago Police Department, and the first person from the old neighborhood I really wanted to see.

"I was real sorry about Boom Boom, Vicki. I know how close you two were."

Bobby's the only person I allow to call me Vicki. "Thanks, Bobby. It's been tough. I appreciate your coming."

A chilly April wind ruffled my hair and made me shiver in my wool suit. I wished I'd worn a coat. Mallory walked with me toward the limousines carrying the fifty-three members of the immediate family. The funeral would probably eat fifteen thousand out of the estate, but I didn't care.

"Are you going to the party? May I ride with you? They'll never miss me in that crowd."

Mallory agreed good-naturedly and helped me into the back seat of the police limo he'd commandeered. He introduced me to the driver. "Vicki, Officer Cuthbert was one of Boom Boom's many fans."

"Yes, miss. I was real sorry when Boom . . . sorry, when your cousin had to stop playing. I figure he could've beat Gretzky's record easy."

"Go ahead and call him Boom Boom," I said. "He loved the name and everyone used it . . . Bobby, I couldn't get any information out of the guy at the grain company when I phoned him. How did Boom Boom die?"

He looked at me sternly. "Do you really need to know that, Vicki? I know you think you're tough, but you'll be happier remembering Boom Boom the way he was on the ice."

I pressed my lips together; I wasn't going to lose my temper at Boom Boom's funeral. "I'm not indulging an appetite for gore, Bobby. I want to know what happened to my cousin. He was an athlete; it's hard for me to picture him slipping and falling like that."

Bobby's expression softened a bit. "You're not thinking he drowned himself, are you?"

I moved my hands indecisively. "He left an urgent message for me with my answering service—I've been out of town, you know. I wondered if he might've been feeling desperate."

Bobby shook his head. "Your cousin wasn't the kind of man to throw himself under a ship. You should know that as well as I do."

I didn't want a lecture on the cowardice of suicide. "Is that what happened?"

"If the grain company didn't let you know, they had a reason. But you can't accept that, can you?" He sighed. "You'll probably just go butting your head in down there if I don't tell you. A ship was tied up at the dock and Boom Boom went under the screw as she pulled away. He was chewed up pretty badly."

"I see." I turned my head to look at the Eisenhower Expressway and the unpainted homes lining it.

"It was a wet day, Vicki. That's an old wooden dock— they get very slippery in the rain. I read the M.E.'s report myself. I think he slipped and fell in. I don't think he jumped.''

I nodded and patted his hand. Hockey had been Boom Boom's life and he hadn't taken easily to forced retirement. I agreed with Bobby that my cousin wasn't a quitter, but he'd been apathetic the last year or so. Apathetic enough to fall under the propeller of a ship?

I tried to push the thought out of my mind as we pulled up in front of the tidy brick ranch house where Boom Boom's Aunt Helen lived. She had followed a flock of other South Chicago Poles to Elmwood Park. I believe she had a husband around someplace, a retired steelworker, but, like all the Wojcik men, he stayed far in the background.

Cuthbert let us out in front of the house, then went off to park the limo behind a long string of Cadillacs. Bobby accompanied me to the door, but I quickly lost sight of him in the crowd.

The next two hours put a formidable strain on my frayed temper. Various relatives said it was a pity Bernard insisted on playing hockey when poor dear Marie hated it so much. Others said it was a pity I had divorced Dick and didn't have a family to keep me busy—just look at Cheryl's and Martha's and Betty's babies. The house was swarming with children: all the Wojciks were appallingly prolific.

It was a pity Boom Boom's marriage had only lasted three weeks—but then, he shouldn't have been playing hockey. Why was he working at Eudora Grain, though? Breathing grain dust all his life had killed his father. Still, those Warshawskis never had much stamina anyway.

The small house filled with cigarette smoke, with the heavy smell of Polish cooking, with the squeals of children. I edged my way past one aunt who said she expected me to help wash up since I hadn't handled any of the preparation. I had vowed that I would not say anything over the baked meats beyond "Yes," "No," and "I don't know," but it was getting harder.

Then Grandma Wojcik, eighty-two, fat, dressed in shiny black, grabbed my arm in a policeman's grip. She looked at me with a rheumy blue eye. Breathing onions, she said, "The girls are talking about Bernard."

The girls were the aunts, of course.

"They're saying he was in trouble down at the elevator. They're saying he threw himself under the ship so he wouldn't be arrested."

"Who's telling you that?" I demanded.

"Helen. And Sarah. Cheryl says Pete says he just jumped in the water when no one was looking. No Wojcik ever killed himself. But the Warshawskis . . . Those Jews. I warned Marie over and over."

I pried her fingers from my arm. The smoke and noise and the sour cabbage smell were filling my brain. I put my head down to look her in the eyes, started to say something rude, then thought better of it. I fought my way through the smog, tripping over babies, and found the men hovering around a table filled with sausages and sauerkraut in one corner. If their minds had been as full as their stomachs they could have saved America.

"Who are you telling that Boom Boom jumped off the wharf? And how the hell do you know, anyway?"

Cheryl's husband Pete looked at me with stupid blue eyes. "Hey, don't lose your pants, Vic. I heard it down at the dock."

"What trouble was he in at the elevator? Grandma Wojcik says you're telling everyone he was in trouble down there."

Pete shifted a glass of beer from one hand to the other. "It's just talk, Vic. He didn't get along with his boss. Someone said he stole some papers. I don't believe it. Boom Boom didn't need to steal."

My eyes fogged and I felt my head buzzing. "It's not true, goddamn you! Boom Boom never did anything cheap in his life, even when he was poor."

The others stared at me uneasily. "Take it easy, Vic," one said. "We all liked Boom Boom. Pete said he didn't believe it. Don't get so wild over it."

He was right. What was I doing, anyway, starting a scene at the funeral? I shook my head, like a dog coming out of water, and pushed back through the crowd to the living room. I made my way past a Bleeding Heart of Mary taste-fully adorning the front door and went out into the chilly spring air.

I opened my jacket to let the cool air flow through me and cleanse me. I wanted to go home, but my car was at my apartment on Chicago's North Side. I scanned the street: as I'd feared, Cuthbert and Mallory had long since disap-peared. While I looked doubtfully around me, wondering whether I could find a cab or possibly walk to a train station in high heels, a young woman joined me. She was small and tidy, with dark hair falling straight just below her ears, and honey-colored eyes. She wore a pale gray silk shantung suit with a full skirt and a bolero jacket fastened by large mother-of-pearl buttons. She looked elegant, perfect, and vaguely familiar.

"Wherever Boom Boom is, I'm sure he'd rather be there than here." She jerked her head toward the house and gave a quick, sardonic smile.

"Me too."

"You're his cousin, aren't you . . . I'm Paige Carring-ton."

"I thought I recognized you. I've seen you a few times, but only on stage." Carrington was a dancer who had cre-ated a comic one-woman show with the Windy City Ballet-works.

She gave the triangular smile audiences loved. "I've been seeing a lot of your cousin the last few months. We kept it quiet because we didn't want Herguth or Greta splashing it around the gossip columns—your cousin was news even when he stopped skating."

She was right. I was always seeing my cousin's name in print. It's funny being close to someone famous. You read a lot about them, but the person in print's never the one you know.

"I think Boom Boom cared more for you than anyone." She frowned, thinking about the statement. Even her frown was perfect, giving her an absorbed, considering look. Then she smiled, a bit wistfully. "I think we were in love, but I don't know. I'll never be sure now."

I mumbled something soothing.

"I wanted to meet you. Boom Boom talked about you all the time. He loved you very much. I'm sorry he never introduced us."

"Yes. I hadn't seen him for several months. . . . Are you driving back to the city? Can I beg a ride? I had to come out with the procession and my car is on the North Side."

She pushed back the white silk cuff emerging from her jacket sleeve and looked at her watch. "I have to be at a rehearsal in an hour. Okay if I drop you downtown?"

"That'd be great. I feel like Br'er Rabbit out here in suburbia—I need to get back to my brier patch."

She laughed at that. "I know what you mean. I grew up in Lake Bluff myself. But now when I go out there to visit I feel like my oxygen's been cut off."

I looked at the house, wondering if I should make a formal farewell. Good manners certainly dictated it, but I didn't want a fifteen-minute lecture on why I should clean up both the dishes and my life. I shrugged and followed Paige Carrington down the street.

She drove a silver Audi 5000. Either the Windy City Balletworks paid better than the average struggling theater or the Lake Bluff connection supplied money for shantung suits and foreign sports cars.

Paige drove with the quick, precise grace that characterized her dancing. Since neither of us knew the area, she made a few wrong turns in the rows of identical houses before finding an access ramp to the Eisenhower.

She didn't say much on the ride back to town. I was quiet too, thinking about my cousin and feeling melancholy—and guilty. That was why I'd had a temper tantrum with those stupid, hulking cousins, I realized. I hadn't kept up with Boom Boom. I knew he was depressed but I hadn't kept in touch. If only I'd left my Peoria number with my answering service. Was he sick with despair? Maybe he'd thought love would cure him and it hadn't. Or maybe it was the talk on the docks that he'd stolen some papers—he thought I could help him combat it, like the thousand other battles we'd fought together. Only I wasn't there.

With his death, I'd lost my whole family. It's true my mother had an aunt in Melrose Park. But I'd rarely met her, and neither she nor her fat, self-important son seemed like real relations to me. But Boom Boom and I had played, fought, protected each other. If we hadn't spent much time together in the last ten years, we'd always counted on the other being around to help us out. And I hadn't helped him out.

As we neared the I-90/94 interchange rain started spattering the windshield, breaking into my fruitless reverie. I realized Paige was glancing at me speculatively. I turned to face her, eyebrows raised.

"You're Boom Boom's executor, aren't you?"

I assented. She drummed her fingers on the steering wheel. "Boom Boom and I—never got to the stage of exchanging keys." She gave a quick, embarrassed smile. "I'd like to go to his place and get some things I left there."

"Sure. I was planning on being there tomorrow afternoon for a preliminary look at his papers. Want to meet me there at two?"

"Thanks. You're sweet . . . Do you mind if I call you Vic? Boom Boom talked about you so much I feel as though I know you."

We were going under the post office, where six lanes had been carved out of the building's foundations. Paige gave a satisfied nod. "And you must call me Paige." She changed lanes, nosed the Audi around a garbage truck, and turned left on Wabash. She dropped me at my office—the Pulteney Building on the corner of Wabash and Monroe.

Overhead an el train thundered. "Good-bye," I yelled above the din. "See you tomorrow at two."

2 * Love's Labors Lost

The Hawks had paid Boom Boom a lot of money to play hockey. He'd spent a fair amount of it on a condo in a slick glass building on Lake Shore Drive north of Chestnut Street. Since he bought it five years ago I'd been there a number of times, often with a crowd of drunken friendly hockey players.

Gerald Simonds, Boom Boom's lawyer, gave me the building keys, along with those to my cousin's Jaguar. We spent the morning going over Boom Boom's will, a document likely to raise more uproar with the aunts—my cousin left the bulk of his estate to various charities and to the Hockey Widows Pension Fund; no aunts were mentioned. He left me some money with a request not to spend it all on Black Label. Simonds frowned disapprovingly as I laughed. He explained that he had tried to keep his client from inserting that particular clause, but Mr. Warshawski had been adamant.

It was about noon when we finished. There were a couple of things I could have done in the financial district for one of my clients but I just didn't feel like working. I didn't have any interesting cases going at the moment—just a couple of processes to serve. I was also trying to track down a man who had disappeared with half the assets in a partnership, including a forty-foot cabin cruiser. They could all wait. I retrieved my car, a green Mercury Lynx, from the Fort

Dearborn Trust's parking lot and headed over to the Gold Coast.

Like most posh places, Boom Boom's building had a doorman. A pudgy, middle-aged white man, he was helping an old lady out of her Seville when I got there, and didn't pay much attention to me. I fumbled with the keys, trying to find the one that opened the inner door.

Inside the lobby, a woman got off the elevator with a tiny poodle, its fluffy white hair tied in blue ribbons. She opened the outer door, and I went inside, giving the dog a commiserating look. The dog lurched at its rhinestone-studded leash to smell my leg. "Now, Fifi," the woman said, pulling the poodle back to her side. Dogs like that aren't supposed to sniff at things or do anything else to remind their owners they're animals.

The inner lobby wasn't big. It held a few potted trees, two off-white couches where residents could chat, and a large hanging. You see these hangings all over the place, at least in this kind of building: they're woven, usually with large knots of wool sticking out here and there and a few long strands trailing down the middle. While I waited for an elevator I studied this one without enthusiasm. It covered the west wall and was made from different shades of green and mustard. I was just as glad I lived in a tired three-flat with no neighbors like Fifi's owner to decide what should hang in the lobby.

The elevator opened quietly behind me. A woman my age came out dressed for running, followed by two older women on their way to Saks, debating whether to eat lunch at Water Tower on the way over. I looked at my watch: twelve forty-five. Why weren't they at work on a Tuesday? Perhaps like me they were all private investigators taking time off to handle a relative's estate. I pressed 22 and the elevator carried me up swiftly and noiselessly.

Each floor of the thirty-story condo had four units. Boom Boom had paid over a quarter of a million to get one in the northeast corner. It contained just about fifteen hundred square feet—three bedrooms, three baths, including one with a sunken tub off the master bedroom—and a magnificent view of the lake from the north and east sides.

I opened the door to 22C and went through the hallway to the living room, my feet soundless in the deep pile of the wall-to-wall carpeting. Blue print drapes were pulled away from the glass forming the room's east wall. The panoramic view drew me—lake and sky forming one giant gray-green ball. I let the vastness absorb me until I felt a sense of peace. I stood so a long moment, then realized with a start of resentment that I wasn't alone in the apartment. I wasn't sure what alerted me; I concentrated hard for several minutes, then heard a slight rasping noise. Paper rustling.

I moved back to the entryway. This led to a hall on the right where the three bedrooms and the master bath were. The dining room and kitchen were off a second, smaller hallway to the left. The rustling had come from the right, the bedroom side.

I'd worn a suit and heels to see Simonds, clothing totally unsuitable for handling an intruder. I quietly opened the outside door to provide an escape route, slipped off my shoes, and left the handbag next to a magazine rack in the entryway.

I went back into the living room, listening hard, looking for a potential weapon. A bronze trophy on the mantelpiece, a tribute to Boom Boom as most valuable player in a Stanley Cup victory. I picked it up quietly and moved cautiously down the hallway toward the bedrooms.

All the doors were open. I tiptoed to the nearest room, which Boom Boom had used as a study. Flattening myself against the wall, bracing my right arm with the heavy trophy, I stuck my head slowly into the open doorway.

Her back to me, Paige Carrington sat at Boom Boom's desk sorting through some papers. I felt both foolish and angry. I retreated up the hall, put the trophy down on the magazine table, and slipped into my shoes. I walked back to the study.

"Early, aren't you? How did you get in?"

She jumped in the chair and dropped the papers she was holding. Crimson suffused her face from the neck of her open shirt to the roots of her dark hair. "Oh! I wasn't expecting you until two."

"Me either. I thought you didn't have a key."

"Please don't get so angry, Vic. We had an extra rehearsal called for two o'clock, and I really wanted to find my letters. So I persuaded Hinckley—he's the doorman—I persuaded him to come up and let me in." For a minute I thought I saw tears in the honey-colored eyes, but she flicked the back of her hand across them and smiled guiltily. "I hoped I'd be gone before you showed up. These letters are terribly, terribly personal and I couldn't bear for anyone, even you, to see them." She held out her right hand beseechingly.

I narrowed my eyes at her. "Find anything?"

She shrugged. "He may just not have kept them." She bent over to pick up the papers she'd scattered at my entrance. I knelt to help her. It looked like a stack of business letters—I caught Myron Fackley's name a couple of times. He'd been Boom Boom's agent.

"I've only been through two drawers, and there are six others with papers in them. He saved everything, I think—one drawer is stuffed full of fan letters."

I looked at the room with jaundiced eyes. Eight drawers full of papers. Sorting and cleaning have always been my worst skills on aptitude tests.

I sat on the desk and patted Paige's shoulder. "Look. This is going to be totally boring to sort through. I'm going to have to examine even the stuff you've looked at because I have to see anything that might affect the estate. So why don't you leave me to it? I promise you if I see any personal letters to Boom Boom I won't read them—I'll put them in an envelope for you."

She smiled up at me, but the smile wobbled. "Maybe I'm just being vain, but if he saved a bunch of letters from kids he never met I thought he'd keep what I wrote him." She looked away.

I gripped her shoulder for a minute. "Don't worry, Paige. I'm sure they'll turn up."

She sniffed a tiny, elegant sniff. "I think I'm just fixating on them because they keep me from thinking, 'Yes, he's really . . . gone.' "

"Yeah. That's why I'm cursing him for being such a damned pack rat. And I can't even get back at him by making him *my* executor."

She laughed a little at that. "I brought a suitcase with me. I might as well pack up the clothes and makeup I left over here and get going."

She went to the master bedroom to pull out her things. I puttered around aimlessly, trying to take stock of my task. Paige was right: Boom Boom had saved everything. Every inch of wall space was covered with hockey photographs, starting with the peewee team my cousin belonged to in second grade. There were group photos of him with the Black Hawks, locker-room pictures filled with champagne after Stanley Cup triumphs, solo shots of Boom Boom making difficult plays, signed pictures from Esposito, Howe, Hull—even one from Boom-Boom Geoffrion inscribed, "To the little cannon."

In the middle of the collection, incongruous, was a picture of me in my maroon robes getting my law degree from the University of Chicago. The sun was shining behind me and I was grinning at the camera. My cousin had never gone to college and he set inordinate store by my education. I frowned at this younger, happy V. I. Warshawski and went into the master bedroom to see if Paige needed any help.

The case sat open on the bed, clothes folded neatly. As I came in she was rummaging through a dresser drawer, pulling out a bright red pullover.

"Are you going through all his clothes and everything? I think I've got all my stuff, but let me know if you find anything—size sixes are probably mine, not his." She went into the bathroom where I heard her opening cabinets.

The bedroom was masculine but homey. A king-size bed dominated the middle of the floor, covered with a black and white quilt. Floor-length drapes in a heavy off-white cloth were pulled back, showing the lake. Boom Boom's hockey stick was mounted over the severe walnut bureau. A purple and red painting provided a splash of color and a couple of rugs picked it up again in the same red. He'd avoided the mirrors that so many bachelors think make the complete singles apartment.

A bedside table held a few magazines. I sat on the bed to see what my cousin had read before going to sleep—*Sports Illustrated, Hockey World,* and a densely printed paper called *Grain News.* I looked at this with interest. Published in Kansas City, it was filled with information about grain—the size of various crops, prices on different options exchanges, rates for shipping by rail and boat, contracts awarded to different transporters. It was pretty interesting if grain was important to you.

"Is that something special?"

I'd gotten so absorbed I hadn't noticed Paige come out of the bathroom to finish her packing. I hesitated, then said, "I've been worried about whether Boom Boom went under that propeller—deliberately. This thing"—I waved the paper at her—"tells you everything you'd ever want to know about grains and shipping them. It apparently comes out twice a month, weekly during the harvest. If Boom Boom was involved enough at Eudora Grain to study something like this, it gives me some reassurance."

Paige looked at me intently. She took *Grain News* and flipped through it. Looking at the pages, she said, "I know losing hockey upset him—I can imagine how I'd feel if I couldn't dance, and I'm not nearly as good a ballerina as he was a hockey player. But I think his involvement with me—kept him from being too depressed. I hope that doesn't offend you."

"Not at all. If it's true, I'm pleased."

Her thin, penciled brows rose. "*If* it's true? Do you mind explaining that?"

"Nothing to explain, Paige. I hadn't seen Boom Boom since January. He was still fighting the blues then. If knowing you helped him out of the depths, I'm glad. . . . There was some talk at the funeral about his being in trouble down at Eudora Grain—I guess there's a rumor going around that he stole some papers. Did he say anything about that to you?"

The honey-colored eyes widened. "No. Not a word. If people were talking about it, it must not have bothered him enough to mention it; we had dinner the day before he died. I wouldn't believe it, anyway."

"Do you know what he wanted to talk to me about?"

She looked startled. "Was he trying to get in touch with you?"

"He left an urgent message for me with my answering service, but he didn't say what it was about. I wondered: if there was some story going around the docks maybe he wanted my professional help."

She shook her head, fiddling with the zipper on her purse. "I don't know. He seemed fine Monday night. Look—I've got to get going. I'm sorry if I upset you earlier, but I have to run now."

I walked back to the front door with her and shut it behind her—I'd forgotten to close it when I came back for my shoes earlier. I also fastened the deadbolt. I was damned if the doorman was going to let in anyone else without telling me—at least not while I was in the apartment.

Before getting down to the dispiriting task of sorting my cousin's papers I took a quick look around. Unlike me, he was—had been—phenomenally tidy. If I'd been dead for a week and someone came into my place, they'd find some nasty surprises in the sink and a good layer of dust, not to mention an array of clothes and papers in the bedroom.

Boom Boom's kitchen was spotless. The refrigerator was clean inside as well as out. I went through it and got rid of vegetables which were going bad. Two gallons of milk went down the sink—I guess he never got out of the habit of drinking it, even when he wasn't training any longer. Tidy, tidy. I'd often said the same thing to Boom Boom, teasing him. Remembering those words made my stomach turn over, as if the air had been sucked out from underneath it. It's like that when someone you love dies. I'd been through it with my parents, too. Little things keep reminding you and it takes awhile before the physical pain goes out of the memory.

I went back to the study and made an organized attack on

the drawers. Left to right, top to bottom. If it has to be done, do it thoroughly so there's no need to take extra time backtracking. Fortunately, my cousin was not only a pack rat, he was also organized. The eight drawers all had neatly labeled file folders.

The top left held fan mail. Given the size of the turnout at the funeral, I shouldn't have been surprised to see how many letters people sent him. He still got three or four a week in labored boyish handwriting.

Dear Boom Boom Warshawski,
   I think you're the greatest hockey player in the universe. Please send me your picture.

                                    Your friend,
                                    Alan Palmerlee

P.S. Here is a picture of me playing wing for the Algonquin Maple Leafs.

Across each letter was a neatly written note indicating the date and the reply—"March 26, sent signed picture" or "Called Myron. Asked him to arrange speaking date." A lot of high schools wanted him to speak at graduation or at sports banquets.

The next drawer contained material relating to Boom Boom's endorsement contracts. I'd have to go over these with Fackley and Simonds. My cousin had done some TV spots for the American Dairy Association. Maybe that explained his milk—if you advertise it, you have to drink it. There was also the Warshawski hockey stick, a warm-up jersey, and an ice-skate endorsement.

At five o'clock I rummaged through the spotless kitchen and found a can of coffee and an electric percolator. I made a pot and carried it back into the study with me. At eight-thirty I located Boom Boom's liquor supply in a carved Chinese chest in the dining room and poured myself a Chivas—not my first choice in scotch but an adequate substitute for Black Label.

By ten o'clock I was surrounded by stacks of papers—a

pile for Fackley, the agent. One for the attorney, Simonds. Quite a few for the garbage. A few things of sentimental value to me. One or two that might interest Paige. Some memorabilia for the Hockey Hall of Fame in Eveleth, Minnesota, and some other items for the Black Hawks.

I was tired. My olive silk blouse had a smear of greasy dust across the front. My nylons were full of runs. I was hungry. I hadn't found Paige's letters. Maybe I'd feel better after some food. At any rate, I'd been through all the drawers, including the ones in the desk. What had I really expected to find?

Abruptly I stood and skirted the mounds of paper to get to the telephone. I dialed a number I knew by heart and was relieved to hear it answered on the third ring.

"This is Dr. Herschel."

"Lotty: it's Vic. I've been sorting through my cousin's papers and gotten myself thoroughly depressed. Have you eaten?"

She had had dinner several hours ago but agreed to meet me at the Chesterton Hotel for coffee while I got something to eat.

I washed up in the master bathroom, looking enviously at the sunken tub with its whirlpool attachment. Relief for my cousin's shattered ankle. I wondered if he'd bought the condo for the whirlpool. It would be like Boom Boom, tidy in details but not very practical.

On my way out I stopped to talk to the doorman, Hinckley. He was long gone for the day. The man on duty now was more of a security guard. He sat behind a desk with TV consoles on it—he could see the street or the garage or look at any of the thirty floors. A tired old black man with tiny wrinkles that showed only when I got close to him, he looked at me impassively as I explained who I was. I showed him my power of attorney from Simonds and told him I would be coming around until my cousin's affairs were straightened out and the unit was sold.

He didn't say anything. He didn't blink or move his head, just looked at me through expressionless brown eyes whose irises were stained yellow with age.

I could feel my voice rising and checked it. "The man on duty this afternoon let someone into the apartment. Can you please see that no one goes in unless I accompany him or her?"

He continued to stare at me with unblinking eyes. I felt anger flush my face. I turned and left him sitting under the mustard-colored weaving.

3 ＊ Reflections

"What were you looking for?" Lotty sat drinking coffee, her sharp black eyes probing me, but with affection.

I took a bite of my sandwich. "I don't know. I guess I've been a detective too long—I keep expecting to find secrets in people's desks."

We were sitting in the Dortmunder Restaurant in the basement of the Chesterton Hotel. I had picked a half bottle of Pomerol from the wine bins that lined the walls and was drinking it with a sandwich—Emmenthaler on thin, home-made rye bread. Service is slow at Dortmunder's—they're used to the old ladies who live in the hotel whiling away an afternoon over a cup of coffee and a single pastry.

"My dear, I don't want to press you if you don't want to think about it. But you never sort papers. Even for your cousin you would give them to the attorney unless you were looking for something. So what you were looking for was very important to you, right?"

Lotty is Austrian. She learned English in London where she spent her adolescence, and a trace of a Viennese accent underlies the English inflection of her sharp, crisp words. We've been friends for a long time.

I finished my sandwich and drank some more wine, then held the glass, turning it to catch the light. I stared into the ruby glow and thought. Finally I put the glass down.

"Boom Boom left an urgent message with my answering service. I don't know if he was just terribly depressed or in some trouble at Eudora Grain, but he never left that kind of message for me before." I stared again at the wine. "Lotty, I was looking for a letter that said, 'Dear Vic, I've been accused of stealing some papers. Between that and losing my ankle I'm so blue I can't take it anymore.' Or 'Dear Vic—I'm in love with Paige Carrington and life is great.' She says he was and maybe so— but she's so—so, oh, sophisticated, maybe. Or perfect—it's hard for me to picture him in love with her. He liked women who were more human."

Lotty set down her coffee cup and put her square, strong fingers over mine. "Could you be jealous?"

"Oh, a little. But not so much that it would distort my judgment. Maybe it's egocentrism, though. I hadn't called him for two months. I keep going over it in my head—we'd often let months go by without being in touch. But I can't help feeling I let him down."

The hold on my fingers tightened. "Boom Boom knew he could count on you, Vic. You have too many times to remember when that was so. He called you. And he knew you'd come through, even if he had to wait a few days."

I disengaged my left hand and picked up my wineglass. I swallowed and the tightness in my throat eased. I looked at Lotty. She gave an impish smile.

"You are a detective, Vic. If you really want to be totally sure about Boom Boom, you could try investigating what happened."

4 ✳ On the Waterfront

The Eudora Grain Company elevator lay in the labyrinth that makes up the Port of Chicago. The Port lines six miles of the Calumet River as it snakes south and west from its mouth near 95th Street. Each elevator or plant along the river has its own access road, and none of them is clearly marked.

I covered the twenty miles from my North Side apartment to 130th Street in good time, reaching the exit by eight o'clock. After that I got lost trying to make my way past the Calumet River, some steel mills, and a Ford assembly plant. It was nine-thirty before I found Eudora Grain's regional office.

Their regional headquarters, a modern, single-story block, lay next to a giant elevator on the river. The elevator loomed behind the building at right angles, two sections of massive tubes, each containing perhaps a hundred ten-story-high cylinders. The sections were split by a slip where a boat could tie up. On the right side, railway tracks ran into a shed. A few hopper cars were there now and a small group of hard-hatted men were fixing one onto a hoist. I watched, fascinated: the car disappeared up inside the elevator. On the far left side I could see the tip of a ship poking out—someone was apparently taking on a load of grain.

The building had a modern lobby with wide windows opening onto the river. Pictures of grain harvests—combines sweeping through thousands of acres of golden wheat,

21

smaller versions of the mammoth elevator outside, trains taking on their golden hoard, boats unloading—covered the walls. I took a quick glance around, then approached a receptionist behind a marble counter set in the middle of the room. She was young and eager to help. After a spirited interchange with his secretary, she located the regional vice-president, Clayton Phillips. He came out to the foyer to meet me.

Phillips was a wooden man, perhaps in his early forties, with straw-colored hair and pale brown eyes. I took an immediate dislike to him, perhaps because he failed to offer me any condolences for Boom Boom, even when I introduced myself as his closest relative.

Phillips dithered around at the thought of my asking questions at the elevator. He couldn't bring himself to say no, however, and I didn't give him any help. He had an irritating habit of darting his eyes around the room when I asked him a question, instead of looking at me. I wondered if he found inspiration from the photographs lining the foyer.

"I don't need to take any more of your time, Mr. Phillips," I finally said. "I can find my own way around the elevator and ask the questions I want on my own."

"Oh, I'll come with you, uh—uh—" He looked at my business card, frowning.

"Miss Warshawski," I said helpfully.

"Miss Warshawski. The foreman won't like it if you come without an introduction." His voice was deep but tight, the voice of a tense man speaking from the vocal cords rather than through the nasal passages.

Pete Margolis, the elevator foreman, didn't seem happy to see us. However, I quickly realized his annoyance was directed more at Phillips than at me. Phillips merely introduced me as "a young lady interested in the elevator." When I gave Margolis my name and told him I was Boom Boom's cousin, his manner changed abruptly. He wiped a dirty paw on the side of his overalls and shook hands with me, told me how sorry he was about my cousin's accident, how much the men liked him, and how badly the company would miss him. He dug out a hard hat for me from under a pile of papers in his minuscule office.

Paying little attention to Phillips, he gave me a long and detailed tour, showing me where the hopper cars came in to dump their loads and how to operate the automatic hoist that lifted them into the heart of the elevator. Phillips trailed along, making ineffectual comments. He had his own hard hat, his name neatly lettered across the top, but his gray silk summer suit was totally out of place in the dirty plant.

Margolis took us up a long flight of narrow stairs that led into the interior of the elevator, perhaps three stories up. He opened a fire door at the top, and noise shattered my eardrums.

Dust covered everything. It swirled through the air, landing in layers on the high steel beams, creating a squeaky film on the metal floor. My toes quickly felt greasy inside their thick cotton socks. My running shoes skidded on the dusty floor. Under the ill-fitting, heavy hard hat, my hair became matted and sticky.

We stood on a catwalk looking down on the concrete floor of the elevator. Only a narrow waist-high handrail stood between me and an unpleasant crash onto the conveyor belts below. If I fell, they'd have to change the sign posted in the doorway: 9,640 man-hours without an accident.

Pete Margolis stood at my right side. He grabbed my arm and gesticulated with his free hand. I shook my head. He leaned over next to my right ear. "This is where it comes in," he bellowed. "They bring the boxcars up here and dump them. Then it goes by conveyor belt."

I nodded. A series of conveyor belts caused much of the clanking, shattering noise, but the hoist that lifted boxcars ninety feet in the air as though they were toys also contributed to the din. The belts ferried grain from the towers where boxcars dumped it over to chutes that spilled it into cargo holds of ships moored outside. A lot of grain dust escaped in the process. Most of the men on the floor wore respirators, but few seemed to have any ear protection.

"Wheat?" I screamed into Margolis's ear.

"Barley. About thirty-five bushels to the ton."

—

He shouted something at Phillips and we went on across the gangway outside, to a narrow ledge overlooking the water. I gulped in the cold April air and let my ears adjust to the relative quiet.

Below us sat a dirty old ship tied to the dock by a series of cables. She was riding above her normal waterline, where the black paint on the hull gave way abruptly to a peeling greenish color. On her deck, more men in hard hats and dirty boiler suits were guiding three massive grain chutes with ropes, filling the holds through some twelve or fourteen openings in the deck. Next to each opening lay its lid— "hatch cover," Phillips told me. A mass of coiled ropes lay near the back end, our end, where the pilothouse stood. I felt slightly dizzy. I grew up in South Chicago where steel mills dot the lake, so I've seen plenty of Great Lakes freighters close up, but they always give me the same feeling— stomach contractions and shivers up the spine. Something about the hull thrusting invisibly into black water.

A cold wind whipped around the river. The water was too sheltered here for whitecaps, but grain dust blew up at us, mixed with cigarette wrappers and potato chip bags. I coughed and turned my head aside.

"Your cousin was standing at the stern." I followed Phillips's pointing finger. "Even if someone were leaning forward they wouldn't have been able to see him from up here."

I tried, but the angle of the elevator cut off the view part way along the pilothouse. "What about all those people on deck? And there're a couple down there on the ground."

Phillips swallowed a superior smile. "The *O. R. Daley's* tied up now and loading. When the ship is casting off all the elevator people are gone and everyone connected with the ship has an assignment. They wouldn't pay much attention to a guy on the wharf."

"Someone must have seen him," I said stubbornly. "What about it, Mr. Margolis? Any problem with you if I talk to the men on the elevator?"

Margolis shrugged. "Everyone liked your cousin, Miss Warshawski. If they'd seen anything they'd have come for-

ward with it by now . . . But if you think it'll do some good
I don't mind. They'll break for lunch in two shifts starting in
twenty-five minutes."

I scanned the wharf. "Maybe you could show me exactly
where my cousin went in."

"We don't really know," Phillips responded, his deep
voice trying to hide impatience. "But if it will make you feel
better in some way . . . Pete, maybe you could take Miss
Warshawski down."

Margolis looked back at the elevator, hesitated, then reluctantly agreed.

"This isn't the ship that was here then, is it?"

"No, of course not," Phillips said.

"Know which one was?" I asked.

"There's no way of knowing that," Phillips said, just as
Margolis said, "The *Bertha Krupnik*."

"Well, maybe you're right." Phillips gave a strained
smile. "I keep forgetting that Pete here has the day-to-day
details of this operation at his fingertips."

"Yup. It was supposed to be the *Lucella Wieser*. Then
she had that accident—water in the hold or something—and
they brought up three old tubs to take her load. The *Bertha*
was the last of 'em. Pilot's an old friend of mine. He like
to've lost his lunch when he heard about Boom Boom . . .
your cousin, I mean. He was a hockey fan himself."

"Where's the *Bertha Krupnik* now?"

Margolis shook his head. "No way of knowing that.
She's one of Grafalk's, though. You could ask them. Their
dispatcher would know." He hesitated a minute. "You
might want to check with the *Lucella*. She was tied up over
there." He pointed across the old boat at our feet to another
pier about two hundred yards away. "They moved her over
out of the way while they cleaned out her holds. She moved
out yesterday or the day before." He shook his head.
"Don't think anyone's going to be able to tell you anything,
though. You know what people are like. If they'd seen your
cousin go in they'd have said something fast enough at the
time."

Unless they were embarrassed at not doing anything to help, I thought. "Where's Grafalk's office?"

"Do you really want to go there, Miss Warshawski?" Phillips asked. "It's not the kind of place you should just go into without some sort of credential or justification."

"I have a credential." I fished my private investigator's license out of my wallet. "I've asked a lot of people a lot of questions based on this."

His wooden expression didn't change, but he turned red to the roots of his pale blond hair. "I think I should go over with you and introduce you to the right person."

"You want to swing by the *Lucella* with her, too, Mr. Phillips?" Margolis asked.

"Not particularly. I'm running late as it is. I'll have to go back to your office, Pete, and call Rodriguez from there."

"Look, Mr. Phillips," I put in, "I can take care of myself perfectly well. I don't need you to interrupt your schedule to ferry me around."

He assured me it was no problem, he really wanted to do it if I thought it was necessary. It occurred to me he might be worrying that I would turn up some witness suggesting that Eudora Grain had been negligent. In any case, he could smooth my path at Grafalk's, so I didn't mind his tagging along.

While he went back through the elevator to use the phone, Margolis took me down a narrow iron ladder to the wharf. Close up, the ship looked even dirtier. Heavy cables extended from the deck and tied her up fast to large knobs sticking out of the concrete wharf. Like the ship, the cables were old, frayed, and none too clean. As Margolis led me to the rear of the *O. R. Daley*, I notice how badly the paint had cracked above the waterline. "*O. R. Daley*. Grafalk Steamship Line. Chicago." was painted in chipped white letters near the back.

"Your cousin was probably standing here." The concrete had ended, replaced by faded wood planks. "It was a sloppy day. We had to stop loading every few hours, cover the hatches, and wait for the rain to end. Very long job. Anyway, wood like this—real old, you know—gets very slip-

pery when it's wet. If Boom Boom—your cousin, I mean—
was leaning over to see something, he might've just slipped
and fallen right in. He did have that bad leg."

"What would he be leaning over to look at, though?"

"Anything. He was an inquisitive guy. Very interested in
everything and anything about the ships and the business.
Between you and me, he got on Phillips's nerves a bit." He
spat expertly into the water. "But, what I hear, Argus got
him this job and Phillips didn't like to stand up to him."

David Argus was chairman of Eudora Grain. He'd flown
in from Eudora, Kansas, to attend Boom Boom's funeral
and had made a hundred-dollar donation to a children's
home in Boom Boom's name. He hadn't gone to the post-
funeral party, lucky devil, but he'd shaken my hand briefly
after the ceremony, a short, stocky guy in his sixties who exuded a blast-furnace personality. If he had been my cousin's
patron, Boom Boom was well protected in the organization.
But I couldn't believe Boom Boom would abuse the relationship, and said so.

"Naw, nothing like that. But Phillips didn't like having a
young guy around that he had to look after. Nope, Boom
Boom worked real hard, didn't ask for any special favors the
way he might've, being a star and all. I'd say the fellows
liked him pretty well."

"Someone was telling me there was a lot of talk down
here about my cousin—that he might have committed suicide." I looked at the foreman steadily.

He gave a surprised grimace. "Not so far as I know. I
haven't heard anything. You could talk to the men. But, like
I say, I haven't heard anything."

Phillips walked toward us dusting his hands. Margolis
jerked his head toward Phillips. "You going with him?
Want to come back later to talk to the men?"

We settled on ten the next morning, break time for the
morning shift. Margolis said he would talk to them in the
meantime, but he really thought if anyone had seen anything
he would have volunteered it. "An accident always gets a
lot of talk. And Warshawski, being a celebrity and all,

everyone who knew anything was mouthing off. I don't think you'll find out anything.''

Phillips came up to us. "Are you ready? I've talked to the dispatcher at Grafalk's. They're very reluctant to let you know where the *Bertha Krupnik* is, but they'll talk to you if I bring you over.'' He looked self-consciously at his watch.

I shook hands with Margolis, told him I'd see him in the morning, and followed Phillips on down the pier and around the back of the elevator. We picked our way across the deeply pocked yard, stepping over strips of rusted metal, to where Phillips's green Alfa sat, sleek and incongruous between an old Impala and a rusty pickup. He put his hard hat carefully on the back seat and made a great show of starting the car, reversing it between ruts and sliding to the yard entrance. Once we'd turned onto 130th Street and were moving with the traffic I said, ''You're clearly annoyed about chauffeuring me around the Port. It doesn't bother me to barge in on people without an escort—just as I did on you this morning. Why do you feel you have to come with me?''

He shot a quick glance at me. I noticed his hands gripping the wheel so tightly that the knuckles showed white. He didn't say anything for a few minutes and I thought perhaps he was going to ignore me altogether. Finally he said in his deep, tight voice, ''Who asked you to come down to the Port?''

''No one: I came on my own. Boom Boom Warshawski was my cousin and I feel an obligation to find out the circumstances surrounding his death.''

''Argus came to the funeral. Did he suggest there was anything wrong?''

''What are you trying to tell me, Phillips? Is there some reason to think that my cousin's death was not an accident?''

''No. No,'' he repeated quickly. He smiled and suddenly looked more human. ''He came down here on Thursday—Argus did—and put us through the wringer on safety at the elevators. He took a personal interest in your cousin and he was very upset when he died. I just wondered if he'd asked you to investigate this as part of your professional function rather than as Warshawski's cousin.''

"I see . . . Well, Mr. Argus didn't hire me. I guess I hired myself." I thought about explaining my personal concern but my detective training made me cautious. Rule number something or other—never tell anybody anything unless you're going to get something better in return. Maybe someday I'd write up a *Manual for the Neophyte Detective*.

We were driving past the elevators lining the Calumet River and the entrance to the main Port. Large ships loomed everywhere, poking black smokestacks between gray columns of grain and cement elevators. Little trees struggled for life in patches of earth between railroad tracks, slag heaps, and pitted roadbeds. We passed a dead steel mill, a massive complex of rust-red buildings and railway junctions. The cyclone fence was padlocked shut at the entrance: the recession having its impact—the plant was closed.

The headquarters for the Port of Chicago were completely rebuilt a few years ago. With new buildings, modern docks, and a well-paved road the place looked modern and efficient. Phillips stopped at a guard station where a city cop looked up from his paper and nodded him in. The Alfa purred across smooth tarmac and we stopped in a slot labeled EUDORA GRAIN. We locked the doors and I followed Phillips toward a row of modern buildings.

Everything here was built on a giant scale. A series of cranes towered over the slips for the ships. Giant teeth hovered over one huge vessel and easily lifted the back of a fifty-ton semi from a stack and lowered it onto a waiting truck bed. Some ten ships were docked here at the main facility, flying the flag of many nations.

All the Port buildings are constructed from the same tan brick, two stories high. The Grafalk Steamship Line offices occupied all of one of the larger blocks halfway along the wharf. A receptionist, middle-aged and pleasant, recognized Phillips by sight and sent us on back to see Percy Mac-Kelvy, the dispatcher.

Phillips was clearly a frequent visitor. Greeting various people by name, he led me through a narrow hall which crossed a couple of small rooms. We found the dispatcher in an office crammed with paper. Charts covered every wall

and stacks of paper hid the desk, three chairs, and a good
deal of the floor. A rumpled man in his mid-forties, wearing
a white shirt long since wrinkled for the day, MacKelvy was
on the phone when we came in. He took a cigar out of his
mouth long enough to say hello.

He grunted into the phone, moved a red tack on a chart of
the lakes at his right hand, punched a query into a computer
terminal next to the phone, and grunted again. Finally he
said, "Six eighty-three a ton. Take it or leave it . . . Pick
up on the fourth, six eighty-two . . . Can't bring it any
lower than that . . . No deal? Maybe next time." He hung
up, added a few numbers to the terminal, and snatched up a
second phone which had started to ring. "This is a zoo," he
said to me, loosening his tie further. "MacKelvy . . .
Yeah, yeah." I watched as he followed a similar sequence
with chart, tacks, and computer.

When he hung up he said, "Hi, Clayton. This the lady
you mentioned?"

"Hi," I said. "I'm V. I. Warshawski. My cousin Bernard Warshawski was killed last Monday when he fell under
the *Bertha Krupnik*'s propeller."

The phone was ringing again. "Yeah? MacKelvy here.
Yeah, hold on just a second . . . You figuring the *Bertha*
was at fault somehow?"

"No. I have some personal concerns as my cousin's executor. I'd like to know if anyone saw the accident. Phillips
here says you can tell me when the *Bertha* might be expected, either back here, or at some port where I could go
talk to the crew."

"Hi, Duff," he spoke into the phone. "Sulphur from
Buffalo? Three eighty-eight a ton, pick up on the sixth, de-
liver to Chicago on the eighth. You got it." He hung up.
"What's the scoop, Clayton? She likely to sue?"

Phillips was standing as far from the desk as possible in
the crowded room. He stood very still as if to make himself
psychologically as well as physically remote. He shrugged.
"David has expressed some interest."

"What about Niels?"

"I haven't discussed it with him."

I put my hands on the mass of papers and leaned across the desk as the phone rang again.

"MacKelvy here . . . Hi, Gumboldt. Hold on a sec, will you?"

"Mr. MacKelvy, I'm not a hysterical widow trying to get financial restitution from the easiest possible source. I'm trying to find anyone who might have seen my cousin in the last minutes of his life. We're talking about an open dock at ten in the morning. I can't believe not a living soul saw him. I want to talk with the crew on the *Bertha* just to make sure."

"Yeah, Gum? Yeah . . . yeah . . . Toledo on the sixteenth? How about the seventeenth? Can't help ya, fella. Night of the sixteenth? Say two-three in the morning? . . . Okay, fella, some other time." He shook his head worriedly. "Business is rotten. The steel slump's killing us and so are the thousand-footers. Thank God, Eudora's still shipping with us."

The constant interruptions were getting on my nerves. "I'm sure I can find the *Bertha Krupnik*, Mr. MacKelvy. I'm a private investigator and I'm used to tracking things down. An active ship on the Great Lakes can't be that difficult to locate. I'm just asking you to make it easier."

MacKelvy shrugged. "I'll have to talk to Niels. He's coming down here for lunch, Miss—who'd you say?—and I'll check with him then. Stop back here around two. Right, Clayton?"

The phone rang again. "Who's Niels?" I asked Phillips as we walked out of the office.

"Niels Grafalk. He owns Grafalk Steamship."

"Want to give me a lift back to your office? I can pick up my car there and leave you to your meetings."

His pale eyes were darting around the hall, as if looking for someone or trying to get help from someplace. "Uh, sure."

We were in the front office, Phillips saying good-bye to the receptionist, when we heard a tremendous crash. I felt a shudder through the concrete floor and then the sound of glass breaking and metal screaming. The receptionist got out of her chair, startled.

"What was that?"

A couple of people came into the reception room from inside the building. "An earthquake?" "Sounds like a car crash." "Was the building hit?" "Is the building falling over?"

I went to the outer door. Car crash? Maybe, but a damned big car. Maybe one of those semis they'd been loading?

Outside a large crowd was gathering. A siren in the distance grew louder. And at the north end of the pier a freighter stood, nose plowed into the side of the dock. Large chunks of concrete had broken in front of it like a metal road divider before a speeding car. Glass fragments broke loose from the sides of the ship as I moved with the crowd to gawk. A tall crane at the edge of the wharf twisted and slowly fell, crumpling on itself like a dying swan.

Two police cars, blue lights flashing, squealed to a stop as close to the disaster as possible. I jumped to one side to avoid an ambulance wailing and honking behind me. The crowd in front of me parted to let it through. I followed quickly in its wake and made it close to the wreck.

A crane and a couple of forklift trucks had been waiting at dockside. All three were thoroughly chewed up by the oncoming freighter. The police helped the ambulance driver pry one of the forklift drivers out of the mess of crumpled steel. An ugly sight. The crowd—stevedores, drivers, crew members—watched avidly. Disasters are good bowling-league conversation pieces.

I turned away and found a man in a dirty white boiler suit looking at me. His face was sunburned dark red-brown and his eyes were a deep bright blue. "What happened?" I asked.

He shrugged. "Ship rammed the dock. My guess is they were bringing it in from the engine room and someone went full ahead instead of full astern."

"Sorry, I'm a stranger here. Can you translate?"

"Know anything about how you steer a ship?"

I shook my head.

"Oh. Well, it's hard to explain without showing you the controls. But basically you have two levers, one for each screw. Now if you're out at sea you steer by turning the wheel. But coming into the dock, you use the levers. Putting one full ahead and one full astern—toward the back, that is—will swing you to the right or the left, depending on which one you move which way. Putting both of them full astern is like putting your car in reverse. Slows the ship way down and brings you gently up against the wharf. It looks like some poor bastard thought that was what he was doing but went full ahead instead.''

"I see. It seems strange that a little thing like that could cause so much damage.''

"Well, if you drove your car at the pier—assuming you could get down in the water and do it—you'd be chewed up and the concrete walls would laugh at you. But your car—what kind do you drive?—about a ton and two hundred horsepower? Now that thing has twelve thousand horse-power and weighs about ten thousand tons. They did the equivalent of flooring her accelerator and that's the result.''

Someone had rigged a ladder up to the front of the ship. A couple of crew members, rather shaky, came down onto the pier. I felt a hand on my shoulder and jerked around. A tall man with a sunburned face and a magnificent shock of white hair shouldered past me. "Excuse me. Out of the way, please.''

The police, who were keeping everyone else back from the forklift trucks and the ladder, let the white-haired man through without a question.

"Who's that?'' I asked my informative acquaintance. "He looks like a Viking.''

"He is a Viking. That's Niels Grafalk. He owns this sorry hunk of steel . . . Poor devil!''

Niels Grafalk. I didn't think the timing was too hot to go swarming up the ladder after him in search of the *Bertha Krupnik*. Unless . . .

"Is this the *Bertha Krupnik*?''

"No,'' my friend answered. "It's the *Leif Ericsson*. You got some special interest in the *Bertha*?''

"Yeah, I'm trying to find out where she is. I can't get MacKelvy—d'you know him?—to let the information loose

without Grafalk's say-so. You wouldn't know, would
you?''

When my acquaintance wanted to know the reason, I felt
an impulse to shut up and go home. I couldn't think of anything much stupider than my obsession about Boom Boom
and his accident. Obviously, from the crowd converging
here, disaster brought a lot of people to the scene. Margolis
had been right: if the men at the elevator knew anything
about Boom Boom's death, they would have been talking
about it. It was probably high time to return to Chicago and
serve some processes to their reluctant recipients.

My companion saw my hesitation. "Look—it's time for
lunch. Why don't you let me take you over to the Salle de la
Mer—it's the private club for owners and officers here. I just
need to shed this boiler suit and get a jacket.''

I looked at my jeans and running shoes. "I'm hardly
dressed for a private club.''

He assured me they didn't care about what women
wore—only men have to observe clothing rules in the modern restaurant. He left me to watch the debacle at the pier for
a few minutes while he went to change. I was wondering
vaguely what had happened to Phillips when I saw him picking his way tentatively through the crowd to the *Leif
Ericsson*. Something in his hesitant manner irritated me profoundly.

5 ∗ A Glass in the Hand

"I'm Mike Sheridan, chief engineer on the *Lucella Wieser*."

"And I'm V. I. Warshawski, a private investigator."

The waiter brought our drinks, white wine for me and vodka and tonic for Sheridan.

"You're related to Boom Boom Warshawski, aren't you?"

"I'm his cousin . . . You connected with the *Lucella Wieser* that was across from the *Bertha Krupnik* when he fell under the propeller last week?"

He agreed, and I commented enthusiastically on what a small world it was. "I've been trying to find someone who might have seen my cousin die. To tell you the truth, I think it's pretty hopeless—judging by the crowd that wreck out there drew." I explained my search and why the *Lucella* was included in it.

Sheridan drank some vodka. "I have to admit I knew who you were when you were standing on the wharf. Someone pointed you out to me and I wanted to talk to you." He smiled apologetically. "People gossip a lot in a place like this . . . Your cousin was coming over to talk to John Bemis, the *Lucella*'s captain, that afternoon. He claimed to know something about an act of vandalism that kept us from loading for a week. In fact that's why we were tied up across the way: we were supposed to be taking on grain at that Eudora elevator, but we ended up with water in our holds. We

35

had to dry them out and get Board of Health clearance again before we could load."

"You mean someone deliberately put water in your holds? That was the vandalism?"

He nodded. "We assumed it was done by a disgruntled crewman. We asked him to leave the ship. He didn't raise a fuss about it so I think we were right. But your cousin sounded serious, and of course Bemis wanted to talk to him. You wouldn't know anything about what was on his mind, would you?"

I shook my head. "That's part of my problem. I hadn't seen Boom Boom for two or three months before he died. To tell you the truth, I was mostly worried that he might have— well, let himself fall because he was terribly depressed about not being able to skate or play hockey any more. But, from what you're saying and what Pete Margolis at the elevator said, he'd gotten pretty involved in what was going on down here, not depressed at all. I'd sure like to know, though, if anyone on the *Bertha* or the *Lucella* saw the accident first-hand."

Sheridan shook his head. "It's true we were tied up across the way, but the *Bertha Krupnik* lay between us and the wharf. I don't think anyone on the *Lucella* could have seen anything."

The waiter came back to take our orders; we told him we needed a few minutes to study the menu. He was back again within thirty seconds, coughing apologetically.

"Mr. Grafalk wants to know if you and the lady would join him and Mr. Phillips at his table."

Sheridan and I looked at each other in surprise. I hadn't noticed either of them come in. We followed the waiter across the rose and purple carpet to a table in the corner on the other side. Grafalk stood up to shake hands with Sheridan.

"Thanks for interrupting your lunch to join us, Mike." To me he added, "I'm Niels Grafalk."

"How do you do, Mr. Grafalk. I'm V. I. Warshawski."

Grafalk wore a soft tweed jacket, tailored to fit his body, and an open-necked white shirt. I didn't have to know he was born with money to feel that he was a man used to controlling things around him. He exuded a seafaring atmosphere, his hair bleached white, his face red with wind and sunburn.

"Phillips here told me you were asking some questions of Percy MacKelvy. Since I'm on the spot, maybe you can tell me why you're interested in Grafalk Steamship."

I embarked on a story which by now seemed very threadbare. "Mr. MacKelvy thought he ought to check with you before he told me where the *Bertha Krupnik* is," I finished.

"I see." Grafalk looked at me sharply. "Phillips told me you were a private investigator. I thought maybe you'd decided to do some snooping around my company."

"When people meet a policeman unexpectedly they often feel guilty: nameless crimes rise up to confront them. When they meet a private investigator they usually feel defensive: don't come snooping around me. I'm used to it," I said.

Grafalk threw his head back and let out a loud crack of laughter. Sheridan gave me a sardonic smile but Phillips looked as strained as ever.

"If you have a minute after lunch, walk back with me to the office—I'll get Percy to cough up the *Bertha*'s whereabouts for you."

The waiter came to take our order. I asked for a whole artichoke stuffed with shrimp. Grafalk chose grilled lake trout, as did Phillips. Sheridan ordered a steak. "When you spend nine months of your life on the water, beef has a solid, earthy appeal."

"So tell me, how does a young woman like you get involved in a career as a detective? You work for a firm or for yourself?"

"I've been in business for myself for about six years. Before that I was an attorney with the Public Defender in Cook County. I got tired of seeing poor innocent chumps go off to Stateville because the police wouldn't follow up our investigations and find the real culprits. And I got even more tired of watching clever guilty rascals get off scot-free because they could afford attorneys who know how to tap-dance

around the law. So I thought—à la Doña Quixote perhaps—
that I'd see what I could do on my own about the situation."

Grafalk smiled with amusement over a glass of Niersteiner gutes Domthal. "Who usually hires you?"

"I do a certain amount of financial crime—that's my spe-
cialty. The Transicon Company; that business last year with
Ajax Insurance and the Knifegrinders . . . I just finished a
job involving computer fraud in wire transfers at a small
bank in Peoria. I fill in the gaps tracking down missing witnesses and serving subpoenas on people anxious to avoid a
day in court."

Grafalk was watching me with the same amused smile—
wealthy man enjoying the foibles of the middle class: what
do the simple folk do if they don't own a steamship company? The smile grew rigid. He was looking at someone behind me whom he apparently didn't want to see. I turned as a
stocky man in a gray business suit walked up to the table.

"Hello, Martin."

"Hello, Niels. . . . Hi, Sheridan. Niels trying to enlist
your help with the *Ericsson*?"

"Hi, Martin. This is V. I. Warshawski. She's Boom
Boom Warshawski's cousin—down here asking us all a few
questions about his death," Sheridan said.

"How do you do, Miss Warshawski. I was very sorry
about the accident to your cousin. None of us knew him
well, but we all admired him as a hockey player."

"Thanks," I said.

He was introduced as Martin Bledsoe, owner of the Pole
Star Line, which included the *Lucella Wieser*. He took a vacant chair between Sheridan and Phillips, asking Grafalk after he sat down if it was okay to join us.

"Glad to have you, Martin," the Viking said warmly. I
must have imagined the strain in his smile a few minutes before.

"Sorry about the *Ericsson*, Niels. Hell of a mess out
there. You figure out what happened?"

"Looked to me like she ran into the dock, Martin. But
we'll know for sure after we've made a complete investigation."

I suddenly wondered what Grafalk was doing eating a leisurely lunch when he had several hundred thousand dollars' worth of damage sitting outside.

"What happens in a case like this?" I asked. "Do you have insurance to cover your hull damage?"

"Yes." Grafalk grimaced. "We have coverage for everything. But it'll boost my premium by a good deal. . . . I'd rather not think about it right now, if you don't mind."

I changed the subject by asking him some general questions about shipping. His family owned the oldest company still operating on the Great Lakes. It was also the biggest. An early ancestor from Norway had started it in 1838 with a clipper that carried fur and ore from Chicago to Buffalo. Grafalk became quite enthusiastic, recounting some of the great ships and shipwrecks of the family fleet, then caught himself up apologetically. "Sorry—I'm a fanatic on shipping history . . . My family's been involved in it for so long . . . Anyway, my private yacht is called the *Brynulf Nordemark* in memory of the captain who went down so gallantly in the disaster of 1857."

"Grafalk's a fantastic sailor in his own right," Phillips put in. "He keeps two sailboats—his grandfather's old yacht and a racing boat. You sail in the Mackinac race every year, don't you Niels?"

"I've only missed two since graduating from college— that probably happened before you were born, Miss Warshawski."

He'd been to Northwestern, another family tradition. I vaguely remembered a Grafalk Hall on the Northwestern campus and the Grafalk Maritime Museum next to Shedd Aquarium.

"What about the Pole Star Line?" I asked Bledsoe. "That an old family company?"

"Martin's a Johnny-come-lately," Grafalk said lightly. "How old's PSL now? Eight years?"

"I used to have Percy MacKelvy's job," Bledsoe said. "So Niels remembers every day since my desertion."

"Well, Martin, you were the best dispatcher in the industry. Of course I felt deserted when you wanted to go into competition against me . . . By the way, I heard about the sabotage on the *Lucella*. That sounded like an ugly incident. It was one of your crew members?''

Waiters were bringing our entrees. Even though they slid the plates in front of us, barely moving the airwaves, it was enough of a distraction that I missed Bledsoe's facial reaction.

''Well, the damage was minor, after all,'' he said. ''I was furious at the time, but at least the ship is intact: it'd be a pain in the ass to have to spend the main part of the season patching the *Lucella*'s hull.''

''True enough,'' Grafalk agreed. ''You do have two smaller ships, though, don't you?'' He smiled at me blandly. ''We have sixty-three other vessels to pick up any slack the *Ericsson*'s incapacitation has caused.''

I wondered what the hell was going on here. Phillips was sitting stiffly, not making any pretense of eating, while Sheridan seemed to be casting about for something to say. Grafalk ate some minced vegetables and Bledsoe attacked his broiled swordfish with gusto.

''And even though my engineer really screwed up down there, I'm convinced that the guy just got overexcited and made a mistake. It's not like having deliberate vandalism among the crew.''

''You're right,'' Bledsoe said. ''I did wonder if this was part of your program to junk your 360-footers.''

Grafalk dropped his fork. A waiter moved forward and wafted a new one to the table. ''We're satisfied with what we've got out there,'' Grafalk said. ''I do hope you've isolated *your* trouble, though, Martin.''

''I hope so too,'' Bledsoe said politely, picking up his wineglass.

''It's so distressing when someone in your organization turns out to be unreliable,'' Grafalk persisted.

''I wouldn't go that far,'' Bledsoe responded, ''but then I've never shared the Hobbesian view of the social contract with you.''

Grafalk smiled. ''You'll have to explain that one to me,

Martin.'' He turned to me again. ''At Martin's school they went in for a lot of memorizing. I had an easier time, being a gentleman: we weren't expected to know anything.''

I was starting to laugh when I heard glass shatter. I turned with the rest to stare at Bledsoe. He had crushed his wineglass in his hand and the clear shards sticking out of his palm were rapidly engulfed in red. As I leaped to my feet to send for a doctor I wondered what all that had been about. Of all the remarks exchanged, Grafalk's last one had been the least offensive. Why had it produced such an extraordinary reaction?

I sent a very concerned maître d'hôtel to call an ambulance. He confided in a moment of unprofessional panic that he knew he should never have allowed Mr. Bledsoe to join Mr. Grafalk. But then—Mr. Bledsoe was not a gentleman, he had no sensitivity, one could not keep him from barging in where he did not belong.

Quiet panic prevailed at our table. The men stared helplessly at the pool of red growing on the tablecloth, on Bledsoe's cuff, on his lap. I told them an ambulance was coming and meanwhile we should probably try to get as much glass as possible out of his hand. I sent the waiters for another ice bucket and began packing Bledsoe's hand with ice and some extra napkins.

Bledsoe was in pain but not in danger of fainting. Instead he was cursing himself steadily for his stupidity.

''You're right,'' I said. ''It was damned stupid. In fact I don't know when I've ever seen anything to compare with it. But fretting over it won't alter the past, so why don't you concentrate on the present instead?'' He smiled a bit at that and thanked me for my help.

I glanced briefly at Grafalk. He was watching us with a strange expression. It wasn't pity and it wasn't satisfaction. Speculative. But what about?

6 ✳ A Capital Ship

After the ambulance carted Bledsoe away, everyone returned to lunch a little furtively, as though eating were in bad taste. The headwaiter cleared Bledsoe's place with palpable relief and brought Grafalk a fresh bottle of Niersteiner gutes Domthal—"with our compliments, sir."

"They don't like your boss here," I said to Sheridan.

The chief engineer shrugged. "The maître d' is a snob. Martin's a self-made man and that offends him. Niels here brings class to his joint. Martin slashes his hand open and Niels gets a free bottle of wine so he won't be offended and drop his membership."

Grafalk laughed. "You're right. The most insufferable snobs are the hangers-on to the rich. If we lose our glamour, they lose the basis for their existence."

While we talked Phillips kept darting glances at his watch and muttering, "Uh, Niels," in his tight voice. He reminded me of a child tugging at its mother's skirts while she's absorbed in conversation—Grafalk gave him about the same amount of attention. Finally Phillips stood up. "Uh, Niels, I'd better leave now. I have a meeting with, uh, Rodriguez."

Grafalk looked at his watch. "We'd all better be going, I guess. Miss Warshawski, let me take you over to Percy MacKelvy and get the *Bertha Krupnik*'s location for you." He got a bill from the waiter and signed it without looking at the amount, politely waiting for me to finish. I dug the heart out of my artichoke and cut it into four pieces, savoring each one, before putting my napkin to one side and getting up.

Phillips lingered with us in the doorway, despite his meeting. He seemed to be waiting for some sign from Grafalk, a recognition of who he was, perhaps, that would enable him to leave in peace. The power of the rich to bestow meaning on people seemed as though it might work with Phillips.

"Don't you have a meeting, Clayton?" Grafalk asked.

"Uh, yes. Yes." Phillips turned at that and walked back across the tarmac to his Alfa.

Sheridan accompanied me over to Grafalk's office. "I want you to come back to the *Lucella* and talk to Captain Bemis when you're finished here," he said. "We need to know if you can tell us anything about what your cousin wanted to say."

I couldn't, of course, but I wanted to know what they could tell me about Boom Boom, so I agreed.

Our visit to Grafalk's office was interrupted by reporters, a television crew, and an anxious phone call from the chairman of Ajax Insurance, which covered Grafalk Steamship.

Grafalk handled all of these with genial urbanity. Treating me like a treasured guest, he asked the NBC television crew to wait while he answered a question for me. He took the call from Ajax chairman Gordon Firth in MacKelvy's office.

"Just a minute, Gordon. I have an attractive young lady here who needs some information." He put Firth on hold and asked MacKelvy to dig up the *Bertha*'s location. She was making a tour of the Great Lakes, picking up coal in Cleveland to drop in Detroit, then steaming up to Thunder Bay. She'd be back in Chicago in two weeks. MacKelvy was to instruct the captain to place himself and the crew at my disposal. Grafalk brushed my thanks aside: Boom Boom had been an impressive young man, just the kind of person the shipping industry needed to attract. Whatever they could do to help, just let him know. He returned to Firth and I found my way out alone.

Sheridan had waited for me outside, away from the reporters and television crews. As I came out a cameraman thrust a microphone under my nose. Had I seen the disaster, what did I think of it—all the inane questions television reporters ask in the wake of a disaster. "Unparalleled tragedy," I said. "Mr. Grafalk will give you the details."

Sheridan grinned as I ducked away from the mike. "You're quicker on your feet than I am—I couldn't think of a snappy remark on the spur of the moment."

We walked down the pier to the parking lot where his Capri sat. As he backed it out of the lot he asked if Grafalk had told me what I wanted to know.

"Yeah. He was pretty gracious about it." Overwhelmingly gracious. I wondered if he were bent on erasing any unfavorable ideas I might have picked up as a result of his interchange with Bledsoe. "Why did Grafalk's remark about where Bledsoe went to school upset him so much?" I asked abruptly.

"Was that what set him off? I couldn't remember."

"Grafalk said: 'At Martin's school they went in for a lot of memorizing.' Then something about *his* being a gentleman and not needing to know anything. Even if Bledsoe went to some tacky place like West Schaumburg Tech, that's scarcely a reason to shatter a wineglass in your fist."

Sheridan braked at a light at 103rd and Torrence. A Howard Johnson's on our left struggled ineffectually with prairie grass and a junkyard. Sheridan turned right. "I don't think Martin went to school at all. He grew up in Cleveland and started sailing when he was sixteen by lying about his age. Maybe he doesn't like a Northwestern man reminding him he's self-educated."

That didn't make sense—self-educated people are usually proud of the fact. "Well, why is there so much animosity between him and Grafalk?"

"Oh, that's easy to explain. Niels looks on Grafalk Steamship as a fiefdom. He's filthy rich, has lots of other holdings, but the shipping company's the only thing he cares about. If you work for him, he thinks it's a lifelong contract, just like a baron swearing loyalty to William the Conqueror or something.

"I know: I started my career at Grafalk. He was sore as

hell when I left. John Bemis too—the captain of the *Lucella*. But our going never bugged him when we left the way it did with Martin. He regarded that as the ultimate betrayal, maybe because Martin was the best dispatcher on the lakes. Which is why Pole Star's done as well as it has. Martin has that sixth sense that tells him what fraction of a dollar he can offer to be the low bidder and still make a profit.''

We were pulling into the yard of another elevator. Sheridan bumped the car across the ruts and parked behind a weather-beaten shed. Four hopper cars were being maneuvered on the tracks in front of us onto the elevator hoist. We picked our way around them, through the ground floor of the giant building, and out to the wharf.

The *Lucella* loomed high above us. Her red paint was smooth and unchipped. She made the other ships I'd seen that day look like puny tubs. A thousand feet long, her giant hull filled the near horizon. I felt the familiar churning in my stomach and shut my eyes briefly before following Sheridan up a steel ladder attached to her side.

He climbed briskly. I followed quickly, putting from my mind the thought of the black depths below, of the hull thrusting invisibly into murky water, of the sea, alive and menacing.

We met Captain Bemis in the mahogany-paneled bridge perched on top of the pilothouse. Through glass windows encircling the bridge we could see the deck stretching away beneath us. Men in yellow slickers were washing out the holds with high-pressure hoses.

Captain Bemis was a sturdy, short man, barely my height. He had steady gray eyes and a calm manner—useful, no doubt, in a high sea. He called down to the deck on a walkie-talkie to his first mate, asking him to join us. A yellow-slickered figure detached itself from the group on deck and disappeared into the pilothouse.

''We're very concerned about this vandalism to the *Lucella*,'' Bemis told me. ''We were sorry when young Warshawski died. But we'd also like to know what it was he had to say.''

I shook my head. ''I don't know. I hadn't talked to Boom

Boom for several months . . . I was hoping he might have said something to you that would give me a clue about his state of mind.''

Bemis gave a frustrated sign. ''He wanted to talk to us about this business with the holds. Sheridan told you about that? Well, Warshawski asked if we'd found the culprit. I told him yes. He said he thought there might be more to it than just a dissatisfied seaman. He had some additional checking to do, but he wanted to talk to me the next day.''

The first mate came onto the bridge and Bemis stopped talking to introduce me. The mate's name was Keith Winstein. He was a wiry young man, perhaps thirty years old, with a shock of curly black hair.

''I'm telling her about the business with young Warshawski,'' Bemis explained to the mate. ''Anyway, Keith here and I waited on the bridge until five on Tuesday, hoping to talk to him. Then we got the news that he'd died.''

''So no one here saw him fall!'' I exclaimed.

The first mate shook his head regretfully. ''I'm sorry, but we didn't even realize there'd been an accident. We were tied up across the way, but none of our men was on deck when the ambulance came.''

I felt a sharp twist of disappointment. It seemed so—so unfair that Boom Boom could slide out of life without one person to see him do it. I tried to concentrate on the captain and his problem, but none of it seemed important to me. I felt stupid, as though I'd wasted a day. What had I expected to find out, anyway? Rushing around the wharf, playing detective, just to avoid admitting that my cousin was dead.

I suggested to Bemis and Winstein that they find the man they'd fired and question him more thoroughly, then pleaded a meeting in the Loop and asked the chief engineer to drive me back to the Eudora Grain parking lot. I picked up my Lynx there and headed north.

7 * Watchman, Tell Us of the Night

My apartment is the large, inexpensive top of a three-flat on Halsted, north of Belmont. Every year the hip young professionals in Lincoln Park move a little closer, threatening to chase me farther north with their condominium conversions, their wine bars, and their designer running clothes. So far Diversey, two blocks south, has held firm as the dividing line, but it could go any day.

I got home around seven, exhausted and confused. On the long drive back, snarled in commuter traffic for two hours, I'd wrestled with my depression. By the time I parked in front of my gray stone building the gloom had lifted a bit. I began wondering about some of the strange behavior down at the Port.

I poured myself a solid two fingers of Black Label and ran a bath. When you thought about it, it was very odd that Boom Boom had called the captain, made an appointment to discuss vandalism, and then died. It hadn't even occurred to me to ask Bemis or Winstein about the papers Boom Boom might have stolen.

It sounded as though Boom Boom might have been playing detective. Maybe that was why he was calling me—not out of despair but for a professional consultation. What had he discovered? Something worth my finding out too?

Was I still looking for some deeper importance to his death than an accident, or was there something to know?

I sipped my whiskey. I couldn't sort my feelings out enough to tell. It was incredible to me that someone might kill Boom Boom to keep him from talking to Bemis. Still. What about the tension between Grafalk and Bledsoe? Boom Boom's death following so quickly after his phone call to Bemis? The accident today at the wharf?

I got out of the tub and wrapped myself in a red bath sheet and poured another slug of scotch. There were enough odd actions down at the Port that it would be worth my asking a few more questions. Anyway, I thought, tossing off the whiskey, so what if I work out my grief by carrying out an investigation? Is that any stupider than getting drunk or whatever else people do when someone they love dies?

I put on a pair of clean jeans and a T-shirt and wandered out to the kitchen. A depressing sight—pans stacked around the sink, crumbs on the table, an old piece of aluminum foil, cheese congealed on the stove from a pasta primavera I'd made a few nights ago. I set about washing up—there are days when the mess hits you so squarely that you can't add to it.

The refrigerator didn't have much of interest in it. The wooden clock by the back door said nine—too late to go out for dinner, as tired as I was, so I settled for a bowl of canned pea soup and some toast.

Over another scotch I watched the tail end of a depressing Cubs defeat in New York—their eighth in a row. The New Tradition takes hold, I thought gloomily, and went to bed.

I woke up around six to another cold cloudy day. The first week in May and the weather was like November. I put on my long running pants and conscientiously did five miles around Belmont Harbor and back. I'd been using Boom Boom's death as an excuse for indolence and the run left me panting more than it should have.

I drank orange juice, showered, and had some fresh-ground coffee with a hard roll and cheese. It was seven-thirty. I was due at Eudora Grain in three hours to talk to the men. In the interim I could go back for a quick scan of Boom

Boom's belongings. I'd been looking for something personal on my previous visit, something that might indicate his state of mind. This time I'd concentrate on something that indicated a crime.

A small trickle of beautifully suited lawyers and doctors oozed from the 210 East Chestnut building. They had the unhealthy faces of people who eat and drink too much most of the time but keep their weight down through strenuous diets and racquetball in between. One of them held the door without really noticing me.

Up in Boom Boom's condo I stopped again for a few minutes to look at the lake. The wind whipped whitecaps up on the green water. A tiny red sliver moved on the horizon, a freighter on its journey to the other side of the lakes. I stared for a long time before bracing my shoulders and heading to the study.

An appalling sight met me. The papers I had left in eight discrete piles were thrown pell-mell around the room. Drawers were open-ended, pictures pulled from the wall, pillows torn from a daybed in the corner and the bedding strewn about.

The wreckage was so confused and so violent that the worst abomination didn't hit me for a few seconds. A body lay crumpled in the corner on the far side of the desk.

I walked gingerly past the mess of papers, trying not to disturb the chaos lest it contain any evidence. The man was dead. He held a gun in his hand, a Smith & Wesson .358, but he'd never used it. His neck had been broken, as nearly as I could tell without moving the body—I couldn't see any wounds.

I lifted the head gently. The face stared at me impassively, the same expressionless face that had looked at me two nights ago in the lobby. It was the old black man who'd been on night duty. I lowered his head carefully and sprinted to Boom Boom's lavish bathroom.

I drank a glass of water from the bathroom tap and the heaving subsided in my stomach. Using the phone next to the king-size bed to call the police, I noticed that the bedroom had come in for some minor disruption. The red and purple painting on the wall had been taken down and the magazines thrown to the floor. Drawers stood open in the polished walnut dresser and socks and underwear were on the floor.

I went through the rest of the apartment. Someone had clearly been looking for something. But what?

The night guard's name had been Henry Kelvin. Mrs. Kelvin came with the police to identify the body, a dark, dignified woman whose grief was more impressive for the restraint with which she contained it.

The cops who showed up insisted on treating this as an ordinary break-in. Boom Boom's death had been widely publicized. Some enterprising burglar no doubt took advantage of the situation; it was unfortunate that Kelvin had surprised him in the act. I kept pointing out that nothing of value had been taken but they insisted that Kelvin's death had frightened off the intruders. In the end I gave up on it.

I called Margolis, the elevator foreman, to explain that I would be delayed, perhaps until the following day. At noon the police finished with me and took the body away on a stretcher. They were going to seal the apartment until they finished fingerprinting and analyzing eveything.

I took a last look around. Either the intruders had found what they came for, or my cousin had hidden what they were looking for elsewhere, or there was nothing to find but they were running scared. My mind flicked to Paige Carrington. Love letters? How close had she been to Boom Boom, really? I needed to talk to her again. Maybe to some of my cousin's friends as well.

Mrs. Kelvin was sitting stiffly on the edge of one of the nubby white sofas in the lobby. When I got off the elevator she came over to me.

"I need to talk to you." Her voice was harsh, the voice of someone who wanted to cry and was becoming angry instead.

"All right. I have an office downtown. Will that do?"

She looked around the exposed lobby, at the residents staring at her on their way to and from the elevator, and agreed. She followed me silently outside and over to Delaware, where I'd found a place to squeeze my little Mercury. Someday I'd have enough money for something really wonderful, like an Audi Quarto. But in the meantime I buy American.

Mrs. Kelvin didn't say anything on the way downtown. I parked the car in a garage across from the Pulteney Building. She didn't spare a glance for the dirty mosaic floors and the pitted marble walls. Fortunately the tired elevator was functioning. It creaked down to the ground floor and saved me the embarrassment of asking her to climb the four flights to my office.

We walked to the east end of the hall where my office overlooks the Wabash Avenue el, the side where cheap rents are even lower because of the noise. A train was squeaking and rattling its way past as I unlocked the door and ushered her to the armchair I keep for visitors.

I took the seat behind my desk, a big wooden model I picked up at a police auction. My desk faces the wall so that open space lies between me and my clients. I've never liked using furniture for hiding or intimidating.

Mrs. Kelvin sat stiffly in the armchair, her black handbag upright in her lap. Her black hair was straightened and shaped away from her long face in severely regimented waves. She wore no make-up except for a dark orange lipstick.

"You talked to my husband Tuesday night, didn't you?" she finally said.

"Yes, I did." I kept my voice neutral. People talk more when you make yourself part of their scenery.

She nodded to herself. "He came home and told me about it. This job was pretty boring for him, so anything out of the way happened, he told me about it." She nodded again. "You young Warshawski's executor or something, that right?"

"I'm his cousin and his executor. My name is V. I. Warshawski."

"My husband wasn't a hockey fan, but he liked young Warshawski. Anyway, he came home Tuesday night—yesterday morning that would be—and told me some uppity white girl was telling him to look after the boy's apartment. That was you.'' She nodded again. I didn't say anything.

"Now Henry did not need anybody telling him how to do his job.'' She gave an angry half sob and controlled herself again. "But you told him special not to let anyone into your cousin's apartment. So you must have known something was going on. Is that right?''

I looked at her steadily and shook my head. "The day man, Hinckley, had let someone into the apartment without my knowing about it ahead of time. There were things there that some crazy fan would find valuable—his hockey stick, stuff like that—and legal documents I didn't want anyone else going through.''

"You didn't know someone was going to break in like that?''

"No, Mrs. Kelvin. If I'd had any suspicion of such a thing I would have taken greater precautions.''

She compressed her lips. "You say you had no suspicion. Yet you took it upon yourself to tell my husband how to do his job.''

"I didn't know your husband, Mrs. Kelvin. I'd never met him. So I couldn't see whether he was the kind of person who took his work seriously. I wasn't trying to tell him how to do his job, just trying to safeguard the interests my cousin left to my charge.''

"Well, he told me, he said, 'I don't know who that girl'— that's you—'thinks is going to try to get into that place. But I got my eye on it.' So he plays the hero, and he gets killed. But you say you weren't expecting anything special.''

"I'm sorry,'' I said.

"Sorry doesn't bring the dead back to life.''

After she left I sat for a long time without doing anything. I did feel in a way as though I had sent the old man to his death. He got my goat Tuesday, acting like I was a talking elevator door or something. But he'd taken what I said seriously—more seriously than I had. He must have kept a close watch on the twenty-second floor from his TV console and seen someone go into my cousin's place. Then he'd gone up after him. The rest was unpleasantly clear.

It was true I'd had no reason to think anyone would be going into Boom Boom's apartment, let alone be so desperate to find something he'd kill for it. Yet it had happened, and I felt responsible. It seemed to me I had a murdered man's death to investigate.

Paige Carrington's answering service took my phone call. I didn't leave a message but looked up the address for the Windy City Balletworks: 5400 N. Clark. I stopped on the way for a sandwich and a Coke.

The Balletworks occupied an old warehouse between a Korean restaurant and a package goods store. The warehouse was dingy on the outside but had been refinished within. An empty hallway with a clapboard box office was lined with pictures of the Windy City ballerinas in various roles. The company did some standard pieces, including a lot of Balanchine, but it also experimented with its own choreography. Paige was on the wall as a cowgirl in *Rodeo*, as Bianca in *Taming of the Shrew*, and in her own light comic role in *Clark Street Fantasy*. I'd seen that piece twice.

The auditorium was to the left. A little sign outside it announced that a rehearsal was in progress. I slipped in quietly and joined a handful of people seated in the house. Onstage someone was clapping her hands and calling for quiet.

"We'll take it from the scherzo entrance again. Karl, you're coming in a second behind the beat. And, Paige, you want to stay downstage until the *grand jeté*. Places, please."

The dancers wore a motley collection of garments, their legs covered with heavy warmers to prevent muscle cramps. Paige had on a bronze leotard with matching leg warmers. Her dark hair was pulled back from her face in a pony tail. She looked about sixteen from where I sat.

Someone operated a fancy tape deck in front of the stage. The music began. The piece was a jarring modern one and the choreography matched it, a dance on the depravity of modern urban life. Karl, entering on time in what was apparently the scherzo movement—hard to tell amidst all the wailing and jangling—seemed to be dying of a heroin overdose. Paige arrived on the scene seconds ahead of the narc squad, watched him die, and departed. I didn't pick all that up right away, but I got to see the thing six times before the director was satisfied with it.

A little after five the director dismissed the troupe, reminding them that they had a rehearsal at ten in the morning and a performance at eight the next night. I moved up front with the other members of the audience. We followed the dancers backstage; no one questioned our right to be there.

Following the sound of voices, I stuck my head into a dressing room. A young woman pulling a leotard from her freckled body asked me what I wanted. I told her I was looking for Paige.

"Oh, Paige . . . She's in the soloists' dressing-room—three doors down on your left."

The soloists' dressing-room door was shut. I knocked and entered. Two women were there. One of them told me Paige was taking a shower and asked me to wait in the hall—there wasn't an inch of extra room in the place.

Presently Paige herself came down the hall from the shower, muffled in a white terry-cloth robe with a large white towel wrapped around her head.

"Vic! What are you doing here?"

"Hi, Paige. I came to talk to you. When you're dressed I'll take you out for coffee or gin or whatever you drink this time of day."

The honey-colored eyes widened slightly: she wasn't used to being on the receiving end of orders, even when given in a subtle way. "I'm not sure I have time."

"Then I'll talk to you while you get dressed."

"Is it that important?"

"It's extremely important."

She shrugged. "Wait for me here. I'll only be a few minutes."

The few minutes stretched into forty before she reappeared. The other two women came out together, carrying on a vigorous conversation about someone named Larry. They glanced at me and one of them broke off to say, "She's about halfway through her makeup," as they passed.

Paige presently emerged in a gold silk shirt and white full skirt. She wore a couple of thin gold chains at her throat with little diamond chips in them. Her makeup was perfect—rusty tones that looked like the delicate flush of Mother Nature—and her hair framed her face in a smooth pageboy.

"Sorry to keep you waiting—it always takes longer than I think it will—and the more I try to hurry the longer it seems to take."

"You people work up a good sweat. What was that you were rehearsing this afternoon? It looked pretty grim."

"It's one of Ann's flights—Ann Bidermyer, the director, you know. *Pavane for a Dope Dealer*. Not in the best taste but it's a good role. For Karl too. Gives us both a great chance to show off. We open with it tomorrow. Want to see it? I'll get them to leave a ticket for you at the box office."

"Thanks . . . Any place around here to talk, or do we need to head farther south?"

She considered. "There's a little coffee shop around the corner on Victoria. It's a hole in the wall but they have good cappuccino."

We went out into the brisk spring evening. The coffee shop seated only six people at tiny round tables on spindly cast-iron chairs. They sold fresh coffee beans, a vast assortment of tea, and a few homemade pastries. I ordered espresso and Paige had English Breakfast tea. Both came in heavy porcelain mugs.

"What were you looking for in my cousin's apartment?"

Paige drew herself up in her chair. "My letters, Vic. I told you that."

"You're not the kind of person who embarrasses easily—I just can't picture you getting that worked up about some letters, even if they are personal . . . Come to think of it, why would two people in the same city write each other anyway?"

She flushed below the rouge. "We were on tour."

"How did you meet Boom Boom?"

"At a party. A man I know was thinking about buying a share in the Black Hawks and Guy Odinflute invited some of the players. Boom Boom came." Her voice was cold.

Odinflute was a North Shore tycoon with a flair for business matchmaking. He'd be the ideal person to bring together buyers and sellers of the Black Hawks.

"When was that?"

"At Christmas, Vic, if you must know."

I'd seen Boom Boom a couple of times during the winter and he'd never mentioned Paige. But was that so strange? I never told him who I was dating either. When he got married, at twenty-four, I first met his wife a few weeks before the wedding. That was a little different—he'd been slightly ashamed to introduce me to Connie. When she left him three weeks later and received an annulment, he'd gotten gloriously drunk with me, but still hadn't really talked about it. He kept his private life emphatically private.

"What are you thinking, Vic? You look very hostile, and I resent it."

"Do you? Henry Kelvin was killed last night when some people broke into Boom Boom's place. They tore it apart. I want to know if they were looking for the same thing you were. And if so, what?"

"Henry? The night watchman? Oh, I'm *so* sorry, Vic. Sorry to get mad at you, too. If you'd only told me, instead of playing games with me . . . Was anything stolen? Could it have been a robbery?"

"Nothing was taken, but the place was sure chewed up pretty thoroughly. I think I saw everything Boom Boom had in his files and I can't imagine what value any of it would have to anyone besides a hockey memorabilia collector."

She shook her head, her eyes troubled. "I don't know either. Unless it was a robbery. I know he kept some share certificates there, even though I kept telling him to put them in a safe deposit box. He just couldn't be bothered with stuff like that. Were those gone?"

"I didn't see them when I was there on Tuesday. Maybe he did take them to a bank." Another point to check with the lawyer Simonds.

"They were probably the most valuable things in the place, barring that antique chest in the dining room. Why don't you try to locate them?" She put her hand on my arm.

"I know it sounds crazy about the letters. But it's true. In fact I'll show you the one your cousin wrote me while we were away, if that's what it will take to convince you." She rummaged in her large handbag and unzipped a side compartment. She pulled out a letter, still in its typed envelope, addressed to her at the Royal York Hotel in Toronto. Paige unfolded the letter. I recognized my cousin's tiny, careful handwriting at once. It began, "Beautiful Paige." I didn't think I should read the rest.

"I see," I said. "I'm sorry."

The honey-colored eyes looked at me reproachfully and with a hint of coldness. "I'm sorry, too. Sorry that you couldn't trust what I said to you."

I didn't say anything. I didn't doubt Boom Boom had sent the letter—his handwriting was unmistakable—but why was she carrying it around in her handbag ready to show to anyone?

"I hope you're not jealous of me for being Boom Boom's lover."

I grinned. "I hope not too, Paige." Of course, that might explain my suspicions. Maybe to Paige at any rate.

We took off shortly after that, Paige to an unknown destination and I for home. What a thoroughly dispiriting day. Kelvin dead, the encounter with Mrs. Kelvin, and an unsatisfactory meeting with Paige. Maybe I was just a tiny bit jealous. If you were going to fall in love, Cousin, did it have to be with someone that perfect?

I couldn't figure out where Boom Boom would have kept his most private papers. He didn't have a safe deposit box. Simonds, his attorney, didn't have any secret documents. Myron Fackley, his agent, didn't have any. I didn't. If Paige was right about the stock certificates, where were they? Whom had Boom Boom trusted besides me? Perhaps his old teammates. I'd call Fackley tomorrow and see if he could put me in touch with Pierre Bouchard, the guy Boom Boom was closest to.

I took myself out to dinner at the Gypsy, a pleasant, quiet restaurant farther south on Clark. After the frustrating day I'd had I was due some peace and quiet. Over calf's liver with mustard sauce and a half bottle of Barolo I made a list of things to do. Find out something about Paige Carrington's background. Get Pierre Bouchard's phone number from Fackley. And get back down to the Port of Chicago. If Henry Kelvin's death and Boom Boom's were connected, the link lay in something my cousin had learned down there.

This was one of the rare occasions when I wished I had a partner, someone who could dig into Paige's background while I disguised myself as a load of wheat and infiltrated Eudora Grain.

I paid the bill and headed for home and a free phone. Relatively free. Murray Ryerson, crime reporter for the *Herald-Star*, had left for the night. They took a message from me at the city desk. I also left my name and number on Fackley's phone machine. There was nothing more I could do tonight, so I went to bed. A life of nonstop thrills.

8 ✳ Learning the Business

I tried Murray again in the morning after my run. I was getting up too early these days—the star reporter hadn't arrived for work yet. I left another message and got dressed: navy linen slacks, a white shirt, and a navy Chanel jacket. A crimson scarf and low-heeled navy loafers completed the ensemble. Tough but elegant, the image I wanted to get across at Eudora Grain. I tossed an outsize shirt and my running shoes into the back seat to wear at the elevator—I wasn't going to ruin any good clothes down there.

Margolis was waiting for me. As the men came off shift for their morning break I talked to them informally in the yard. Most were pretty cooperative: seeing a detective, even a lady detective, relieved the monotony of the day. None of them had seen anything of my cousin's death, however. One of them suggested that I talk to the men on the *Lucella*. Another said I ought to speak to Phillips.

"He hanging around here? I don't remember that," a short fellow with enormous forearms said.

"Yup. He was here. He come through with Warshawski and told Dubcek here to put on his earmuffs."

They debated the matter and finally agreed that the speaker was right. "He stuck pretty close to Warshawski. Don't know how he missed him out there on the wharf. Guess he was in with Margolis."

I asked about the papers Boom Boom was supposed to have stolen. They were reticent but I finally pried out the information that Phillips and Boom Boom had had a terrible argument about some papers. That Phillips had accused my cousin of stealing? I asked. No, someone else said—it was the other way around. Warshawski had accused Phillips. None of them had actually heard the argument—it was just a rumor.

That seemed to be that. I checked back with Margolis. Phillips had been with him at what might have been the critical time. After the *Bertha Krupnik* pulled away he had asked impatiently for Warshawski and had gone out to the wharf to get him and found him floating off the pier. They'd hauled Boom Boom up right away and given first aid, but he had been dead for twenty minutes or more.

"You know anything about the water in the holds of the *Lucella*?"

Margolis shrugged. "Guess they found the guy who did it. She was tied up here, waitin' to load, when it happened. They pulled off the hatch covers and started to pour into the central hold when someone saw there was water in the thing. So they had to move her off and clean 'em out. Quite a mess, by the time they got twenty thousand bushels in there."

"My cousin didn't discuss it with you?"

Margolis shook his head. "Course, we didn't talk too much. He'd ask me about the load and we'd chat about the Hawks's chances but that'd be about it."

He kept looking at the elevator as we were talking and I realized I was keeping him from his job. I couldn't think of anything else to ask. I thanked him for his time and took off for Eudora Grain's regional headquarters.

The receptionist vaguely remembered me from the other day and smiled at me. I reminded her who I was and told her that I had come to go through my cousin's papers to see if he'd left anything personal down there.

She spoke to me between phone calls. "Why, certainly. We all liked Mr. Warshawski very much. It was a terrible thing that happened to him. I'll just get his secretary to come out and get you . . . I hope you weren't planning to see Mr. Phillips, because he's out of the office right now . . . Janet, Mr. Warshawski's cousin is here. She wants to look at his papers. Will you come out for her?. . . Good morning, Eudora Grain. One moment, please . . . Good morning, Eudora Grain . . . Won't you sit down, Miss Warshawski? Janet will be right here." She went back to her waiting calls and I flipped through the *Wall Street Journal* lying on the table in the waiting area.

Janet proved to be a woman at least twenty years my senior. She was quiet and well put together in a simple shirtwaist dress and canvas wedgies. She didn't wear makeup or stockings—no one down in the Port dressed up as much as they do in the Loop. She told me she had come to the funeral and she was sorry she hadn't talked to me then, but she knew what funerals were like—you had enough to do with your own relations without a lot of strangers bothering you.

She took me back to Boom Boom's office, a cubbyhole, really, whose walls were glass from waist-height up. Like the Grafalk dispatcher MacKelvy's, it had charts of the lakes covering all the walls. Unlike MacKelvy's, it was extremely tidy.

I flipped through some reports lying on his desk top. "Can you tell me what Boom Boom was doing?"

She stood in the doorway. I gestured to one of the vinyl-covered chairs. After a minute's hesitation she turned to a woman in the outer area behind us. "Can you take my calls, Effie?" She sat down.

"Mr. Argus brought him in here just out of sympathy at first. But after a few months everyone could see your cousin was really smart. So Mr. Argus was having Mr. Phillips train him. The idea was he would be able to take over one of the regional offices in another year or so—probably Toledo, where old Mr. Cagney is getting ready to retire."

Secretaries always know what is going on in an office. "Did Phillips know Boom Boom was being groomed? How did he feel about it?"

She looked at me consideringly. "You don't look much like your cousin, if you don't mind my saying so."

"No. Our fathers were brothers, but Boom Boom and I both took after our mothers in appearance."

"But you're very like him around the eyes . . . It's hard to tell how Mr. Phillips feels about anything. But I'd say he was glad your cousin was going to be off his hands before long."

"Did they fight?"

"Oh no. At least not so that anyone here would know about it. But your cousin was an impatient person in a lot of ways. Maybe playing hockey made him want to do everything faster than Mr. Phillips is used to—he's more the deliberate type." She hesitated and my stomach muscles tightened: she was about to say something important if she didn't think it would be indiscreet. I tried to make my eyes look like Boom Boom's.

"The thing is, Mr. Phillips didn't want him so involved in the shipping contracts. Each regional vice-president sort of owns his own contracts, and Mr. Phillips seemed to think if Mr. Warshawski got too involved with the customers he might be able to shift some of them to Toledo with him."

"So did they argue about the contracts? Or the customers?"

"Now if I tell you this, I don't want you getting me in trouble with Mr. Phillips."

I promised her her secret was safe.

"You see, Lois—Mr. Phillips's secretary—doesn't like anyone touching the contract files." She looked over her shoulder, as though Lois might be standing there listening. "It's silly, really, because all the sales reps have to use them. We all have to be in and out of them all day long. But she acts like they're—they're diamonds or something. So if you take them you're supposed to write a note on her desk saying which ones you've taken and then let her know when you bring them back."

The boss's secretary has a lot of control in an office and often exercises it through petty tyrannies like these. I murmured something encouraging.

"Mr. Warshawski thought rules like that were pretty stupid. So he'd just ignore them. Lois couldn't stand him because he didn't pay any attention to anything she said." She smiled briefly, a tender, amused smile, not spiteful. Boom Boom must have livened up the place quite a bit. Stanley Cup winners don't get there by too scrupulous attention to rules. Lois's petty ways must have struck him as some kind of decrepit penalty box.

"Anyway, the week before he died, Mr. Warshawski pulled several months of contracts—all last summer's, I think—and took them home with him. If Lois found out she'd really get me in trouble, because he's gone and I was his secretary and she'd have to blame someone."

"Don't worry: I won't tell anyone you told me. What did he do with them?"

"I don't know. But I do know he took a couple of them in with him to see Mr. Phillips late Monday night."

"Did they have any kind of argument?"

She shrugged helplessly. "I don't know. We were all on our way out the door when he went in. Even Lois. Not that she'd say if she knew."

I scratched my head. That was probably the origin of the rumors about Boom Boom stealing papers and fighting with Phillips. Maybe my cousin thought Phillips was enticing customers from the ancient Mr. Cagney in Toledo. Or that Phillips hadn't been telling him everything he needed to know. I wondered if I'd be able to understand a shipping contract if I saw one.

"Any chance I could look at the files my cousin took home with him?"

She wanted to know why. I looked at her kind, middle-aged face. She had been fond of Boom Boom, her young boss. "I'm not satisfied with the accounts I've heard of my cousin's death. He was an athlete, you know, despite his bad ankle. It would take more than a slippery wharf to get him into the lake. If he'd had a fight with Phillips over something important, he might have been mad enough to get careless. He had quite a temper, but he couldn't fight Phillips with fists and sticks the way he could the Islanders."

She pursed her mouth up, thinking it over. "I don't think he was angry the morning he died. He came here before going over to the elevator, you know, and I'd say his mood was—excited. He reminded me of my little boy when he's just pulled off some big stunt on his dirt bike."

"The other thing I'm wondering is if someone might have pushed him in."

She gulped once or twice at that. Why would someone push a nice young man like Mr. Warshawski to his death? I didn't know, I told her, but it was possible those files might give me some kind of clue. I explained to her that I was a private investigator by profession. That seemed to satisfy her: she promised to hunt them up for me while Lois was at lunch.

I asked her if there were anyone else in the office with whom Boom Boom might have quarreled. Or, failing that, whom he might have been close to.

"The people he worked with most were the sales reps. They do all the buying and selling. And of course Mr. Quinchley, who handles the Board of Trade on his computer."

She gave me names of some of the likelier prospects and went back to her desk. I went out to the pit to see if I could find Brimford or Ashton, two of the reps Boom Boom had usually worked with. They were both on the phone, so I wandered around a bit, getting covert stares. There were some half dozen typists handling correspondence, bills, contracts, invoices, who knows what else. A few cubbyholes like Boom Boom's were stuck along the windows here and there. One of them held a man sitting at a computer terminal—Quinchley, hard at work with the Board of Trade.

Phillips's office was in the far corner. His secretary, a woman about my age with a bouffant hairdo I'd last seen in seventh grade, was over interrogating Janet. What does that cousin of Warshawski's want now? I grinned to myself.

Ashton hung up his phone. I stopped him as he started dialing again and asked if he'd mind talking to me for a few minutes. He was a heavyset guy in his middle or late forties; he followed me goodnaturedly into Boom Boom's cubicle. I explained again who I was and that I was trying to find out more about Boom Boom's job and whether he had tangled with anyone in the organization.

Ashton was friendly, but he didn't want to commit himself to anything. Not with a strange woman, anyway. He agreed with Janet's description of my cousin's job. He liked Boom Boom—he livened the place up quite a bit, and he was smart, too. Didn't try to trade on his relations with Argus. But as to whether he quarreled with anyone—he didn't think so, but I'd have to talk to Phillips about that. How had Boom Boom and Phillips gotten along? Again, I'd have to ask Phillips, and that was that.

By the time we finished, the other guy, Brimford, had taken off. I shrugged. I didn't think talking to him would help me any. Going through Boom Boom's tidy, well-sorted drawers, I quickly realized he could have had a dozen dangerous documents connected with the shipping industry and I wouldn't know it. He had lists of farmers supplying Eudora Grain, lists of Great Lakes carriers, lists of rail carriers and their jobbers, bills of lading, reports of loads, by date, back copies of *Grain News*, weather forecasts . . . I flipped through three drawers with neatly labeled files. They were all organized topic by topic but none of it meant anything to me. Other than that Boom Boom had gotten totally immersed in a very complicated business.

I shut the file drawers and rummaged through the top of the desk, where I found pads of paper covered with Boom

Boom's meticulous handwriting. The sight of it suddenly made me want to cry. Little notes he had written to himself to remind him of what he'd learned or what he had to do. Boom Boom planned everything very carefully. Maybe that was what gave him the energy to be so wild on the ice—he knew he had his life in shape behind him.

His desk diary was filled in with appointments. I copied the names he'd entered in the last few weeks of his life. He'd seen Paige on Saturday and again on Monday night. For Tuesday, April 27, he had written in John Bemis's name and Argus with a question mark. He wanted to talk to Bemis on the *Lucella* and then—depending on what was said—he would call Argus? That was interesting.

Flipping through the pages, I noticed that he'd taken to circling some of the dates. I sat up in my chair and started through the diary page by page. Nothing in January, February, or March, but three dates in April—the twenty-third, the sixteenth, and the fifth. I turned back to the front cover, which displayed a 1981 and 1983 calendar along with 1982 at a glance. He had circled twenty-three days in 1981 and three in 1982. In 1981 he'd started with March 28 and ended with November 13. I put the diary in my handbag and looked through the rest of the office.

I'd covered about everything there was—unless I looked at each sheet of paper—when Janet reappeared. "Mr. Phillips has come in and he'd like to see you." She paused. "I'll leave those files in here for you before you go . . . You won't say anything to him, will you?"

I reassured her and went over to the corner office. It was a real office—the heart of the castle, guarded by a frosty turnkey. Lois looked up briefly from her typing. Efficiency personified. "He's expecting you. Go on in."

Phillips was on the phone when I went in. He covered the mouthpiece long enough to ask me to sit down, then went on with his conversation. His office contrasted with the utilitarian furnishings elsewhere in the building. Not that they were remarkably ornate, but they were of good quality. The furniture was made out of real wood, perhaps walnut, rather than pressed board coated with vinyl. Thick gray carpeting covered the floor and an antique clock adorned the wall facing the desk. A view of the parking lot was mercifully shrouded by heavy drapes.

Phillips himself was looking handsome, if a trifle heavy and stiff, in a pale blue woolen suit. A darker blue shirt with his initials on the pocket set off the suit and his fair hair to perfection. He must make a good packet: the way he dressed, that Alfa—a fourteen-thousand-dollar car, and it was a new one—the antique clock.

Phillips disengaged himself from the phone call. He smiled woodenly and said, "I was a little surprised to see you down here this morning. I thought we'd taken care of your questions the other day."

"I'm afraid not. My questions are like Hydra's heads—the more you lop off the more I have to ask."

"Well, uh, I hear you've been going around bothering the folks here. Girls like Janet have their jobs to do. If you have questions, could you bring them to me? I'd sure appreciate that, and we wouldn't have to interrupt the other folks' work out there."

I felt he was trying too hard for a casual approach. It didn't fit his perfect tailoring or his deep, tight voice.

"Okay. Why was my cousin discussing last summer's shipping contracts with you?"

A tide of crimson washed through his face and receded abruptly, leaving a row of freckles standing out on his cheekbones. I hadn't noticed those before.

"Contracts? We weren't!"

I crossed my legs. "Boom Boom made a note of it in his desk diary," I lied. "He was very meticulous, you know: he wrote down everything he did."

"Maybe he did discuss them with me at some point. I don't remember everything we talked about—we were together a great deal. I was training him, you know."

"Maybe you can remember what he discussed with you the night before he died if it wasn't the contracts. I understand he stayed late to meet with you." He didn't say anything. "That was last Monday night, if you've forgotten. April 26."

"I haven't forgotten when your cousin died. But the only reason we stayed late was to go over some routine items we didn't have time for during the day. In my position I'm often tied up for hours at a time. Lois tries to help me keep on top of my calendar but it isn't always possible. So Warshawski and I would stay late to go over questions that we couldn't get to earlier."

"I see." I had promised Janet I wouldn't get her in trouble, so I couldn't tell him I had a witness who'd seen Boom Boom with the files. She was the only person who could have told me—Lois would't have any trouble figuring that out.

Phillips was looking more relaxed. He stuck a cautious finger behind his collar and eased his tie a bit. "Anything else?"

"Are your sales reps paid on commission?"

"Sure. That's the best way to keep them active."

"What about you?"

"Well, we officers don't have access to direct sales, so it wouldn't be a very fair system."

"But the pay is good."

He looked at me with something approaching shock: well-behaved Americans don't discuss their salaries.

"Well, you've got a nice car, nice clothes, nice clock. I just wondered."

"It's none of your damned business. If you don't have anything further to say, I have a lot of work to do and I need to get to it."

I got up. "I'll just be taking my cousin's personal items home with me."

He started dialing. "He didn't leave any, so I expect you not to take anything away with you."

"You went through his desk, Phillips? Or did the all-efficient Lois?"

He stopped mid-dial and turned very red again. He didn't say anything for a second, his pale brown eyes darting around the room. Then he said with an assumption of naturalness, "Of course we went through his papers. We didn't know if he was in the middle of anything critical that someone else would have to take over."

"I see." I went back toward Boom Boom's cubbyhole. No one was on the floor. A black and white institutional clock above the far entrance said twelve-thirty. They must all be at lunch. Janet had left a neatly wrapped package on the desk with my name on it, or rather, as she had forgotten my name, "Mr. Warshawski's cousin." Beneath it she'd written: "Please (heavily underscored) return as early as possible." I scooped it up and walked out the door. Phillips didn't try to stop me.

9 ✳ Just Another Dead Black

Interstate 94 back to the city was clear that time of day. I made it to my office around one-thirty and checked in with my answering service. Murray had returned my call. I got back to him immediately.

"What's up, Vic? You got something on the Kelvin death for me?"

"Not a sniffle. But I'm hoping you might oblige a lady and get one of your society people to do a little digging for me."

"Vic, any time you want something like that, it's usually a cover-up for some big story you don't let us in on until after it's over."

"Murray! What a remark. How about Anita McGraw? How about Edward Purcell? And John Cotton? Weren't those good stories?"

"Yeah, they were. But you led me around in circles first. You got something hot on Kelvin?"

"Well, maybe, in a way. I want some background on Paige Carrington."

"Who's she?"

"She's a dancer. And she was hanging out with my cousin before he died. She was looking for some love letters in his condo the other day. Then Kelvin got knocked off. Whoever did it searched the place pretty thoroughly. It makes me nervous—I'd like to find out something about her background, and I also wondered if any of your gossip people—Greta Simon, for example—had sniffed out the relationship between her and Boom Boom."

"Oh yeah. Boom Boom Warshawski was your cousin. I should have guessed. You're the only two Warshawskis I ever heard of. I was sorry to hear he died: I was quite a fan of his . . . Nothing fishy about his death, is there?"

"Not as far as I know, Murray. He seems to have slipped on some wet planks and gone under the screw of a lakes freighter."

"Ouch. Jesus! Hard to imagine someone as agile as Boom Boom doing something like that . . . Look, as an old fan of his, I'll be glad to help you out. But I've got dibs if anything turns up. Paige Carrington . . . What's her father's name?"

"I don't know. She did mention something about growing up in Lake Bluff."

"Okay, Vic. I'll call you in two-three days."

I unwrapped Janet's tidy package and pulled out the papers. Three big accordion files marked June, July, and August were filled with hundreds of flimsies, each a carbon of a computer printout. Before going through them I went downstairs to Johnnie's Steak Joynt, where I had a Fresca and a gyros sandwich. Thumbing through the *Herald-Star*, I saw a notice about Kelvin's wake. It was today, starting at four, in a funeral home on the South Side. Maybe I should go.

Back in my office I cleared off the desk top by putting everything into the bottom drawer and spread the files out in front of me. They were computer reports, all arranged in the same way. Each showed a transaction date, a point of origin, a destination, a carrier, volume, weight, type, cost per bushel, and date of arrival. They reflected Eudora Grain's shipments of grain over a three-month period. They weren't legal documents but records of legal transactions. Each report was actually titled "Contract Verification Form."

I scratched my head but started reading through them. Some showed more than one carrier, many three or four. Thus, I'd find Thunder Bay to St. Catharines on June 15 via GSL, canceled, via PSL, canceled, and finally picked up by a third carrier at a different rate. I should have brought my cousin's list of the Great Lakes steamship lines. I frowned. PSL might be Bledsoe's outfit, the Pole Star Line. GSL was perhaps Grafalk Steamship. But there were dozens of initials. I'd need a guide.

I looked at Boom Boom's diary and pulled the forms that matched the dates he'd marked for last summer. There were fourteen for those three days. Since the forms were all in date order it was easy to pick out the ones I wanted, although frequently there was more than one report for each date. There were thirty-two records altogether. Twenty-one were multiple-contract shipments, eight of which ended up with GSL. Of the other eleven, five were with GSL. What did that mean? If GSL was Grafalk's line, Eudora did a lot of business with him. But he had told me he had the biggest fleet on the lakes, so that wasn't too surprising. PSL had lost seven shipments to GSL but had gotten two of its own in August. Their August rates were lower than the June rates; that might be the reason.

I looked at my watch. It was almost three o'clock. If I was going to Kelvin's wake I'd have to go home and put on a dress. I gathered up all the files and took them to an office service shop on the building's fifth floor where they do clerical jobs for one-person offices like mine. I asked them to make me a copy of each of the forms and refile them in date order. The man behind the counter was pleased but someone in the background groaned.

I drove home and changed quickly into the navy suit I'd worn to Boom Boom's funeral. I made good time going back south—it was only four-thirty when I got to the funeral home. A tan brick bungalow at 71st and Damen with a tiny lawn manicured within an inch of the ground had been converted to a funeral parlor. A vacant lot on its south side was packed with cars. I found a place for the Lynx on 71st Place and went into the home. I was the only white person there.

Kelvin's body was displayed in an open casket surrounded with waxy lilies and candles. I made the obligatory stop to look. He was laid out in his best suit; his face in repose had the same unresponsive stare I'd encountered Tuesday night.

I turned to condole with the family. Mrs. Kelvin was standing in quiet dignity, wearing a black wool dress and surrounded by her children. I shook hands with a woman my own age in a black suit and pearls, two younger men, and with Mrs. Kelvin.

"Thank you for coming down, Miss Warshawski," the widow said in her deep voice. "These are my children and my grandchildren." She gave me their names and I told them how sorry I was.

The little room was crowded with friends and relations, heavy-bosomed women clutching handkerchiefs, dark-suited men, and preternaturally quiet children. They moved a little closer to the grieving family as I stood there—protection against the white woman who drove Kelvin to his death.

"I was a little hasty in how I spoke to you yesterday," Mrs. Kelvin said. "I believed you must have known something was going to happen in that apartment."

There was a little murmur of assent from the group behind me.

"I still think you must have known something was going on. But blaming people won't bring my husband back to life." She gave the ghost of a smile. "He was a very stubborn man. He could have called for help if he knew someone was going into that place—he should have called for help, called the police." Again the murmur of assent from the people around her. "But once he knew someone was breaking in, he wanted to handle it by himself. And that's not your fault."

"Do the police have any leads?" I asked.

The young woman in the black suit gave a bitter smile. Daughter or daughter-in-law—I couldn't remember. "They aren't going to do anything. They have the pictures, the film from the TV consoles Daddy watched, but the killers had their faces and hands covered. So the police say if no one can recognize them there's nothing they can do."

Mrs. Kelvin spoke sadly. "We keep telling them there was something going on in that apartment—we keep telling them that you knew about it. But they aren't going to do anything. They're just treating it like another black killing and they aren't going to do a thing."

I looked around at the group. People were watching me steadily. Not exactly with hostility—more as though I was some unpredictable species, perhaps an ibex.

"You know my cousin died last week, Mrs. Kelvin. He fell from a wharf under the screw of a freighter. There were no witnesses. I'm trying to find out whether he fell or was pushed. Your husband's death makes me think he was pushed. If I can find out for sure and find out who did it, they'll probably be the same people who killed Mr. Kelvin. I know catching the murderer is a small consolation in the midst of great grief, but it's the best I can offer—for myself as well as you."

"Little white girl going to succeed where the police failed." The person behind me spoke softly but audibly and a few people laughed.

"Amelia!" Mrs. Kelvin spoke sharply. "No need to be rude. She's trying to be kind."

I looked around coolly. "I'm a detective and I have a pretty good record." I turned back to Mrs. Kelvin. "I'll let you know what I find out."

I shook her hand and left, heading back to the Dan Ryan and the Loop. It was after five and traffic scarcely moved. Fourteen lanes and all of it bumper-to-bumper within high concrete walls. Truck exhaust mingled with the damp still air. I shut the windows and wriggled out of my jacket. It was chilly on the lakefront but muggy in the expressway's canyon.

I inched my way downtown and oozed off the expressway at Roosevelt Road. Main police headquarters are at State and Roosevelt, a good location, close to a lot of crime. I wanted to see if anyone there would give me any information about Kelvin.

My dad had been a sergeant, working mostly out of the Twenty-First District on the South Side. The brick building on 12th Street brought on a twinge of nostalgia—it had the same linoleum, the same cinder-block walls with yellow paint peeling away. A few harassed, overweight men behind the desk were processing everyone from drivers putting up bond for their licenses to women trying to see men brought in on assault charges. I waited my turn in line.

The desk officer I finally spoke to called inside on a microphone. "Sergeant McGonnigal, lady here to see you on the Kelvin case."

McGonnigal came out a few minutes later, big, muscular, wearing a rumpled white shirt and brown slacks. We'd met a couple of years back when he was on the South Side and he remembered me immediately.

"Miss Warshawski. Nice to see you." He ushered me back through the linoleum corridors to a tiny room he shared with three other men.

"Nice to see you, Sergeant. When were you transferred downtown?"

"Six, seven months ago. I got assigned to the Kelvin case last night."

I explained that the murder had taken place in my cousin's apartment and that I wanted to know when I could get back in and straighten out his papers. McGonnigal expressed the usual regrets at Boom Boom's death—he'd been a fan, et cetera, and said they were almost finished with the apartment.

"Did you turn up anything? I understand the TV films showed two men going in. Any fingerprints?"

He grimaced. "They were too smart for that. We did find a footprint on the papers. One of them wears size twelve Arroyo hiking boots. But that doesn't tell us much."

"What killed Kelvin? He wasn't shot, was he?"

He shook his head. "Someone gave him an almighty hard blow to the jaw and broke his neck. May only have meant to knock him out. Jesus! What a fist. Doesn't tie in to any of our known B & E men."

"You think this is a straight break and entry job?"

"What else would it be, Miss Warshawski?"

"Nothing of value was taken. Boom Boom had a stereo, some fancy cuff links and stuff, and it was all there."

"Well, figure the guys are surprised by Kelvin. Then they see they've killed him rather than just stunning him like they intended. So they get nervous and leave. They don't know whether someone else is going to come up looking for the guy if he doesn't come back in so many minutes."

I could see his point. Maybe I was making a mountain out of a molehill. Maybe I was upset by my cousin's death and I wanted to blow it up into something bigger than an accident.

"You're not trying to get involved in this, are you?"

"I am involved, Sergeant: it happened in my cousin's apartment."

"The lieutenant is not going to be happy if he hears you're trying to stir up this case. You know that."

I knew that. The lieutenant was Bobby Mallory and he did not like me to get involved in police work, especially murder cases.

I smiled. "If I stumble across anything looking through my cousin's affairs, I don't think that'll upset him too much."

"Just give us a chance to do our job, Miss Warshawski."

"I spoke with the Kelvin family this afternoon. They're not too sure you guys are really trying your hardest."

He slammed his palm on his desk top. The three other men in the room tried to pretend they were still working. "Now why the hell did you go talk to them? One of the sons came around here and gave me a snootful. We're doing our best. But, Christ, we haven't got a damned thing to start from other than two pictures no one can identify and a size twelve boot!"

He pulled a file savagely from a stack on his desk and yanked a photograph from it to toss at me. I picked it up. It was a still made from the TV film of the men going into Boom Boom's place. Two men, one in jeans and the other in chinos. They both wore corduroy sports jackets and had those Irish caps held up over their faces. McGonnigal handed me a couple of other stills. One showed them getting off the elevator—backward. Another showed them walking down the hall, crouched over to disguise their height. You could see their hands pretty clearly—they were wearing surgical gloves.

I gave the pictures back to McGonnigal. "Good luck, Sergeant. I'll let you know if I come across anything. . . . When can I get the keys to the place back?"

He said Friday morning and warned me to be very, very careful. The police are always telling me that.

10 ∗ Down the Hatches

From my apartment I tried Boom Boom's agent again, even though it was after six. Like me, Fackley worked unusual hours. He was in and answered the phone himself. I told him I wanted to get in touch with Pierre Bouchard, star forward for the Hawks and another of his clients. Fackley told me Bouchard was in his hometown, Quebec, playing in the Coeur d'Argent, a demonstration hockey tournament. Fackley gave me his Chicago phone number and agreed to see me the following Wednesday to go through Boom Boom's papers.

I tried phoning the Pole Star Line but no one answered. There wasn't much else I could do tonight. I called Lotty and we went out for dinner together and then to see *Chariots of Fire*.

The photocopies of Eudora Grain's shipping records were ready for me at ten the next morning. I stuck them in a large canvas shoulder bag. The originals I wrapped in heavy brown paper, taped securely. Starting to write Janet's name on top, I realized I didn't know her last name. Women exist in a world of first names in business. Lois, Janet, Mr. Phillips, Mr. Warshawski. That's why I use my initials.

I reached the Port before lunch and dropped the packet off with the receptionist at Eudora Grain, then swung around to the main entrance, where Grafalk and Bledsoe had their offices. The guard at the gate gave me some static about going in without a pass but I finally convinced him I needed to talk to someone at Pole Star and he let me have a two-hour permit.

The Pole Star Line occupied only two rooms in one of the large sand-colored buildings at the far end of the pier. Although much smaller than Grafalk's operation, their offices included the same organized chaos of computers, charts, and telephones. All were manipulated in an electronic symphony by one harassed but friendly young woman. She unplugged herself from the phone long enough to tell me that Bledsoe was at Elevator 9 with the *Lucella*. She sketched rough directions for me—it was back along the Calumet River several miles—and returned to a madly ringing phone.

Phillips came out of the Grafalk building as I passed it on the way to my car. He wasn't sure whether to recognize me or not, so I solved the problem by saying hello to him.

"What are you doing here?" he demanded.

"Signing up for a water ballet class. How about you?"

He turned red again. "I assume you're still asking questions about your cousin. More Hydra heads?"

I was surprised to find he could be whimsical. "I just want to clear all the bases—I still have to talk to the crew on the *Lucella* before she sails."

"Well, I think you'll find you've put a lot of energy into

something not worth the effort. It's to be hoped you find that out soon.''

"I'm moving as fast as I can. I figure water ballet can only help." He snorted and strode over to the green Alfa. As I was climbing into the Lynx I heard him roar past, spitting a little gravel.

Elevator 9 was not one of Eudora Grain's but belonged to the Tri-State Grain Co-op. A chain fence separated the elevator yard from the road. Train tracks ran through a gap in it and a small guardhouse with a heavy, red-faced man reading the *Sun-Times* stood at the entrance. The Lynx bounced along the ruts to the guardhouse, where Redface reluctantly put down his paper and asked me what I wanted.

"I need to talk to Martin Bledsoe or John Bemis."

He waved me in. It didn't seem like much of a security system to me. I drove on around the potholes and pulled up into a gravel yard. A couple of boxcars were slowly moving along the rail siding and I stood for a minute to watch the hoist carry them up inside the elevator and dump their loads. Amazing process, really. I could understand why my cousin had gotten so intrigued by it.

I skirted around the elevator to the wharf where the *Lucella* lay. She was enormous, and a sense of mystery and dread filled me. The giant lay momentarily still, held down by steel cables three inches thick—a huge amphibious spider immobile in the coils of its own web. But when she started to move, what things would stir in the depths beneath that gigantic keel? I looked at the black water absorbing the hull and felt sick and slightly dizzy.

Little flecks of grain dust swirled through the air and reached me where I stood behind her. No one knew I was here. I began to see how Boom Boom could have fallen in unnoticed. I shivered and moved forward to the scene of the action.

An extension ladder was attached high up on the ship, with feet reaching the dock. It was sturdy and I forgot about the dark water underneath as I climbed up.

Except for a faint sound from the elevator and the chaff blowing in my eyes, I hadn't noticed any activity down on the wharf. On deck was another story. It only takes twenty people or so to load a freighter but they were extremely busy.

Five giant chutes were poised over openings in the deck. Guided by three men pulling them around with ropes, they spilled grain into the holds in a series of vast waterfalls. I couldn't see all the way down the thousand-foot deck—a cloud of grain dust billowed up and obscured the bow from view.

I stood at the edge of a giant machine which seemed to be a long conveyor belt on a swivel, rather like a tank turret, and watched. The area beyond was posted HARD HATS ONLY.

No one noticed me for a few minutes. Then a whitened figure in a blue boiler suit came over to me. He took off his hard hat and I recognized the first mate, Keith Winstein. His curly black hair was powdered white below a line made by his hat.

"Hi, Mr. Winstein. I'm V. I. Warshawski—we met the other day. I'm looking for Mr. Bledsoe."

"Sure, I remember you. Bledsoe's up on the bridge with the captain. Want me to take you up? Or you want to watch some of this first?"

He dug out a battered hard hat for me from the supply room behind the tank turret—"self-unloader," he explained. It was attached to a series of conveyor belts in the holds and could unload the entire ship in under twenty-four hours.

Winstein led me along the port side away from the main activity with the chutes. The holds were about half full, he said; they'd be through in another twelve hours or so.

"We'll take this cargo to the entrance of the Welland Canal and unload it onto oceangoing ships there. We're too big for the Welland—the longest ships through there are the 740-footers."

The *Lucella* had five cargo holds underneath with some thirty-five hatches opening into them. The chutes moved among the hatches, distributing the load evenly. In addition to the men guiding the chutes, another man watched the flow of grain at each hold and directed those at the ropes among the various openings. Winstein went around and checked their work, then escorted me onto the bridge.

Bledsoe and the captain were standing at the front of the glass-enclosed room looking down at the deck. Bemis was leaning against the wheel, a piece of mahogany as tall as I am. Neither of them turned around until Winstein announced to the captain that he'd brought a visitor.

"Hello, Miss Warshawski." The captain came over to me in a leisurely way. "Come to see what a freighter looks like in action?"

"It's most impressive . . . I have a couple of questions for you, Mr. Bledsoe, if you have some time."

Bledsoe's right hand was swathed in bandages. I asked how it was doing. He assured me that it was healing well. "No tendons cut . . . What have you got for me?"

Bemis took Winstein off to one corner to inquire about progress below. Bledsoe and I sat at a couple of high wooden stools behind a large drafting table covered with navigation charts. I pulled the photocopies of the contract verification forms from my canvas bag, flicking off some pieces of chaff which had settled on them. Putting the papers on the drafting table, I leafed through them to find July 17, one of Boom Boom's circled dates.

Bledsoe took the stack from me and fanned it. "These are Eudora Grain's shipping contract records. How'd you come to have them?"

"One of the secretaries lent them to me. Captain Bemis told me you were the most knowledgeable person around on these sorts of deals. I can't follow them—I was hoping you'd explain them to me."

"Why not get Phillips to?"

"Oh, I wanted to go to the expert."

The gray eyes were intelligent. He smiled ironically. "Well, there's no great secret to them. You start off with a load at point A and you want to move it to point B. We shippers move any cargo, but Eudora Grain is concerned chiefly with grain—although they may have a bit of lumber and coal now. So we're talking about grain. Now, on this one, the order was first placed on July 17, so that's the initial transaction date.''

He studied the document for a few minutes. "We have three million bushels of soybeans in Peoria and we want to move them to Buffalo. Hansel Baltic is buying the shipment there and that's where our responsibility ends. So Phillips's sales reps start scurrying around trying to find someone to carry the load. GLSL. They start there—Great Lakes Shipping Line. They're charging four dollars and thirty-two cents a ton to carry it from Chicago to Buffalo and they need five vessels. With that big a load you'd normally bid it out among several carriers—I guess the rep was just being a little lazy on this one. Phillips has to bring it from Peoria by rail by the twenty-fourth of July and they'll get it to Buffalo on the thirty-first or earlier.

"Now, in our business, contracts are set up and canceled routinely. That's what makes it so confusing—and why the difference of a few cents is so important. See, here, later on the seventeenth, we offer to carry the load for four twenty-nine a ton. That was before we had the *Lucella*—we can go way under our old prices now because these thousand-footers are so much cheaper to operate.

"Anyway, then Grafalk came in on the eighteenth at \$4.30 a ton but a promise to get it there by the twenty-ninth. Cutting it pretty close, really—wonder if they made it.''

"So there's nothing out of the ordinary about this?''

Bledsoe studied it intently. "Not as far as I can tell. What made you think there would be?''

The chief engineer came in at that point. "Oh, hi there. What do you have?''

"Hi, Sheridan. Miss Warshawski's been going over Eudora's shipping orders. She thought something might be wrong with them.''

"No, not that. I just needed help understanding them. I've been trying to figure out what my cousin might have known that he wanted to tell Captain Bemis. So I went through his papers yesterday over at Eudora Grain, and I learned he'd been particularly interested in these documents right before he died. I wondered if the fact that all these Pole Star contracts ended up with Grafalk was important.''

Bledsoe looked at the documents again. ''Not especially. Either they underbid us or they were promising an earlier delivery date.''

''The other question I had was why Boom Boom was interested in certain dates this spring.''

''What dates this spring?'' Bledsoe asked.

''One was the twenty-third of April. I don't remember the others offhand.'' I had the diary in my canvas bag but I didn't want to show it to them.

Bledsoe and Sheridan looked at each other thoughtfully. Finally Bledsoe said, ''The twenty-third was the date we were supposed to load up the *Lucella*.''

''You mean the day you found water in the holds?''

Sheridan nodded.

''Maybe the other dates also were connected with shipping accidents. Is there a record of such things?''

Bledsoe's face twisted in thought. He shook his head. ''That's a pretty tall order. There are so many steamship lines and so many ports. The *Great Lakes Underwriter* discusses them if they've got anything to do with hull or cargo damage. That'd be the best place to start. Recent dates, one of us might be able to help you out.''

I was getting tired of all the legwork that didn't lead in any real direction. I supposed I could track down the *Great Lakes Underwriter* and look for accidents to ships, but what would that tell me? Had Boom Boom uncovered some criminal ring vandalizing freighters? Just knowing that accidents had occurred wouldn't tell me that.

Winstein had gone back down to the deck and Captain Bemis wandered over to join our group. ''No further accidents are going to strike this ship. I've arranged for a security patrol on deck when they finish loading for the day.''

Bledsoe nodded. ''I've been thinking maybe I'll sail out with you.'' He grinned. ''No aspersion on your management of the ship, John, but the *Lucella*'s precious to all of us. I want to see her get this load to St. Catharines.''

"No problem, Martin. I'll have the head cook get the stateroom ready."

"We don't run to people like stewards on freighters," Bledsoe explained to me. "The head cook takes responsibility for the captain's and the guest quarters. Everyone else fends for himself . . . What time do you figure to sail, John?"

The captain looked at his watch. "We've got about eleven more hours of loading, and Tri-State doesn't want to pay overtime unless it's just an hour or two. So any time after nineteen hundred hours tomorrow."

Bledsoe offered to give me a tour of the ship, if Bemis didn't object. The captain gave his permission with a tolerant smile. Sheridan followed us down the narrow wooden stairs. "I get to show off the engine room," he explained.

The bridge was perched on top of the pilothouse. There were four levels above deck, each smaller than the one below it. The captain and the chief engineer had their quarters on the third story, directly below the bridge. Sheridan opened his door so I could take a quick look inside.

I was surprised. "I thought everyone slept in narrow bunk beds with a tiny sink." The chief engineer had a three-room suite, with an outsize bed in the bedroom, and an office cluttered with paper and tools.

Bledsoe laughed. "That was true in Dana's day, but times have changed. The crew sleep six to a room but they have a big recreational lounge. They even have a Ping-Pong table, which provides its amusing moments in a high sea."

The other officers and the head cook shared the second floor with the stateroom. The galley and the dining rooms—the captain's dining room and crew's mess—were on the deck floor and the crew's quarters on the first floor below deck.

"We should have put the officers' quarters over the stern," Sheridan told Bledsoe as we went down below the water level to the engine room. "Even up where John and I are the engines throb horribly all night long. I can't think why we let them build the whole caboodle into the pilothouse."

We climbed narrow steel rungs set into the wall down to the belly of the ship where the engines lay. Bledsoe disappeared for this part of the tour. "Once the chief gets started on engines he keeps going for a month or two. I'll see you on deck before you leave."

"Engine room" was really a misnomer. The engines themselves were in the bottom of the ship, each the size of a small building, say a garage. Moving parts were installed around them on three floors—drive shafts two feet in diameter, foot-wide piston heads, giant valves. Everything was controlled from a small room at the entrance to the holds. A panel some six feet wide and three feet deep was covered with switches and buttons. Transformers, sewage disposal, ballast, as well as the engines themselves, were all operated from there.

Sheridan showed me the controls that could be used for moving the ship. "Remember when the *Leif Ericsson* ran into the dock the other day? I was telling you about the controls in the engine room. This one is for the port engine, this for the starboard." They were large metal sticks, easy to move, with clearly marked grooves—"Full ahead, Half ahead, Half astern, Full astern."

He looked at his watch and laughed. It was after five. "Martin's right—I'd stay down here all day. I keep forgetting not everyone shares my love of moving parts."

I assured him I'd found it fascinating. It was hard to figure out on one visit, but interesting. The engines were laid out sort of like a giant car engine, with every piece exposed so it could be cared for quickly. If you were a Lilliputian you would climb up and down a car engine just this way. Every piece would be laid out neatly, easy to get at, just impossible to move.

I went back up to the bridge to pick up my papers. While we'd been down with the engines, the loading had stopped for the day. I watched while a couple of small deck cranes lifted covers over the hatches.

"We won't bolt 'em down," Bemis said. "It's supposed to be clear tonight, for a miracle. I just don't want to take any chances with four million dollars' worth of barley."

Bledsoe came up to us. "Oh, there you are. . . . Look—I feel I owe you an apology for ruining lunch the other day. I wondered if I could persuade you to eat dinner with me. There's a good French restaurant about twenty minutes from here in Crown Point, Indiana."

I'd worn a black corduroy pantsuit that day and it was covered with fine particles of barley. Bledsoe saw me eye it doubtfully.

"It's not that formal a place—and there's some kind of clothesbrush in the stateroom if you want to brush your suit. You look great, though."

11 * Grounded

Dinner at Louis Retaillou's Bon Appétit was delightful. The restaurant took up the ground floor of an old Victorian house. The family, who all played a role in preparing and presenting the meal, lived upstairs. It was Thursday, a quiet night with only a few of the inlaid wooden tables filled, and Louis came out to talk to Bledsoe, who was a frequent guest. I had the best duckling I've ever eaten and we shared a respectable St. Estephe.

Bledsoe turned out to be an entertaining companion. Over champagne cocktails we became "Martin" and "Vic." He regaled me with shipping stories, while I tried to pry discreetly into his past. I told him a bit about my childhood on Chicago's South Side and some of Boom Boom's and my adventures. He countered with stories of life on Cleveland's waterfront. I talked about being an undergraduate during the turbulent Vietnam years and asked him about his education. He'd gone straight to work out of high school. With Grafalk Steamship? Yes, with Grafalk Steamship—which reminded him of the first time he'd been on a laker when a big storm came up. And so on.

It was ten-thirty when Bledsoe dropped me back at the *Lucella* to pick up my car. The guard nodded to Bledsoe without taking his eyes from a television set perched on a shelf above him.

"Good thing you have a patrol on the boat—anyone could get past this fellow," I commented.

Bledsoe nodded in agreement, his square face in shadow. "Ship," he said absently. "A boat is something you haul aboard a ship."

He walked over with me to my car—he was going back on board the *Lucella* for one last look around. The elevator and the boat—ship—beyond loomed as giant shapes in the dimly lit yard. I shivered a bit in my corduroy jacket.

"Thanks for introducing me to a great new restaurant, Martin. I enjoyed it. Next time I'll take you to an out-of-the-way Italian place on the West Side."

"Thanks, Vic. I'd like to do that." He squeezed my hand in the dark, started toward the ship, then leaned back into the car and kissed me. It was a good kiss, firm and not sloppy, and I gave it the attention it deserved. He mumbled something about calling when he got back to town and left.

I backed the Lynx out of the yard and onto 130th Street. Few cars were out and I had an easy time back to I-94. The traffic there was heavier but flowing smoothly—trailer trucks moving their loads at seventy miles an hour under cover of darkness, and the restless flow of people always out on nameless errands in a great city.

The night was clear, as the forecast had promised Bemis, but the air was unseasonably cool. I kept the car windows rolled up as I drove north, passing slag heaps and mobile homes huddled together under the shadow of expressway and steel mills. At 103rd Street the highway merged with the Dan Ryan. I was back in the city now, the Dan Ryan el on my left and a steep grassy bank on my right. Perched on top were tiny bungalows and liquor stores. A peaceful urban sight, but not a place to stop in the middle of the night. A lot of unwary tourists have been mugged close to the Dan Ryan.

I was nearing the University of Chicago exit when I heard a tearing in the engine, a noise like a giant can opener peeling a strip off the engine block. I slammed on the brakes. The car didn't slow. The brakes didn't respond. I pushed again. Still nothing. The brakes had failed. I turned the wheel to move toward the exit. It spun loose in my hand. No steering. No brakes. In the rearview mirror I could see the lights of a semi bearing down on me. Another truck was boxing me in on the right.

Sweat came out on my forehead and the bottom fell out of my stomach. I pumped gently on the brakes and felt a little response. Gently, gently. Switched on the hazard indicator, put the car in neutral, leaned on the horn. The Lynx was veering to the right and I couldn't stop it. I held my breath. The truck to my right pulled out of my way but the one behind me was moving fast and blaring on his horn.

"Goddamn you, move!" I screamed at him. My speedometer needle had inched down to thirty; he was going at least seventy. I was still sliding toward the right lane.

At the last second the semi behind me swerved to the left. I heard a horrible shattering of glass and metal on metal. A car spun into the lane in front of me.

I pumped the brakes but there was nothing left in them. I couldn't stop. I couldn't do anything. In the last seconds as the car in front of me flipped over I hunched down and crossed my hands in front of my face.

Metal on metal. Wrenching jolts. Glass shattering on the street. A violent blow on my shoulder, a pool of wet warmth on my arm. Light and noise shattered inside my head and then quiet.

My head ached. My eyes would hurt terribly if I opened them. I had the measles. That was what Mama said. I would be well soon. I tried calling her name; a gurgling sound came out and her hand was on my wrist, dry and cool.

"She's stirring."

Not Gabriella's voice. Of course, she was dead. If she was dead I couldn't be eight and sick with the measles. It hurt my head to think.

"The steering," I croaked, and forced my eyes open.

A blur of white figures hovered over me. The light stabbed my eyes. I shut them.

"Turn off the overhead lights." That was a woman's voice. I knew it and struggled to open my eyes again.

"Lotty?"

She leaned over me. "So, *Liebchen*. You gave us a few bad hours but you're all right now."

"What happened?" I could hardly talk; the words choked in my throat.

"Soon I'll tell you. Now I want you to sleep. You are in Billings Hospital."

The University of Chicago. I felt a small sting in my side and slept.

When I woke up again the room was empty. The pain in my head was still there but small and manageable. I tried to sit up. As I moved, the pain swept over me full force. I felt vilely ill and lay back down, panting. After an interval I opened my eyes again. My left arm was attached to the ceiling by a pulley. I stared at it dreamily. I moved my right fingers up the arm, encountering thick tape, then a cast. I poked the shoulder around the edges of the cast and gave a cry of unanticipated pain. My shoulder was either dislocated or broken.

What had I done to my shoulder? I frowned in concentration, making my headache worse. But I remembered. My car. The brakes failing. A sedan turning over in front of me? Yes. I couldn't remember the rest. I must have plowed right into it, though. Lucky to have my shoulder belt on. Could anyone in the sedan have lived through that?

I started feeling very angry. I needed to see the police. I needed to talk to everyone. Phillips, Bledsoe, Bemis, the guard at the Tri-State elevator.

A nurse came crisply into the room. "Oh, you're awake now. That's good. We'll take your temperature."

"I don't want my temperature taken. I want to see the police."

She smiled brightly and ignored me. "Just stick this under your tongue." She was poking a plastic-wrapped thermometer into my mouth.

My fury was mounting, fueled by the helplessness of lying there attached to the ceiling while being ignored.

"I can tell you what my temperature is: it's rising by the second. Will you kindly get someone to call the police for me?"

"Now let's calm down. You don't want to get excited: you've had some concussion." She forced the thermometer into my mouth and started counting my pulse. "Dr. Herschel will be by later and if she feels it's wise for you to start talking to people she'll let us know."

"Were there any other survivors?" I asked her over the thermometer.

"Dr. Herschel will tell you what you need to know."

I shut my eyes while she solemnly wrote my vital statistics into the chart. Patient continues to breathe. Heart operates. "What's my temperature?"

She ignored me.

I opened my eyes.

"What's my pulse?" No answer. "Come on, damn-it, it's my body—tell me what it's doing."

She left to spread the good news that the patient was alive and disagreeable. I shut my eyes and fumed. My body was still weak. I went back to sleep.

When I woke up the third time my mind had cleared. I sat up in bed, slowly and still painfully, and surveyed my body. One problem shoulder. Knees covered with gauze—doubtless badly scraped. Bruises on the right arm. There was a table at the bedside with a mirror on it. Also a telephone. If I'd been thinking instead of yapping earlier I would have realized that. I looked at my face in the mirror. An impressive bandage covered my hair. Scalp wound: that accounted for the headache, though I didn't remember hitting my head. My eyes were bloodshot but my face wasn't damaged, thank the Lord—I'd still be beautiful at forty.

I picked up the telephone and stuck it under my chin. I had to raise the bed to use it, since I couldn't prop the phone against my right shoulder while lying down as long as the left one was attached to the ceiling. Pain shot through my left shoulder as I moved but I ignored it. I dialed Mallory's office number. I had no idea what time it was, but my luck was in: the lieutenant was there.

"Vicki, you'd better not be calling to sweet-talk me. McGonnigal told me about you horning in on the Kelvin investigation. I want you out. O-U-T. It's just my bad luck it happened in Boom Boom's apartment."

Ah, Bobby. It did me good to hear him ranting. "Bobby, you'll never believe this, but I'm in the hospital."

There was silence on the other end as Mallory collected his thoughts.

"Yup. Down at Billings . . . Someone else wanted me out of this case, too, and they took out my brakes and steering while I was at the Port yesterday. If it was yesterday. What day is today?"

Bobby ignored the question. "Come on, Vicki—don't fool around with me. What happened?"

"That's why I'm calling you—I hope you can find out. I was coming home around ten-thirty, eleven, when the steering went and then the brakes, and I ended up running into a sedan. I think a Mack truck had hit it and knocked it into my lane."

"Oh, nuts, Vicki. Why can't you stay home and raise a family and just stay the heck out of this kind of mess?" Bobby doesn't believe in using bad language in front of women and children. And even though I refuse to do woman's work I count as a woman with him.

"I can't help it, Bobby; trouble follows me."

There was a snort at the other end.

"I'm lying here with a dislocated shoulder and a concussion," I said plaintively. "I can't do anything—get involved in a mess or raise a family—for a while, anyway. But I would like to know what happened to my car. Can you find out who scooped me off the Dan Ryan and see if they examined my car?''

Bobby breathed heavily for a few minutes. "Yeah, I guess I could do that. Billings, you say? What's the number?''

I looked at the phone and read him the number. I asked him again for the day. It was Friday, 6:00 P.M.

Lotty must have gone back to her clinic on the North Side. She's the person I list to call in case of emergencies and I guess she's my doctor, too. I wondered if I could persuade her to release me—I needed to get going.

A middle-aged nurse popped her head through the door. "How are we doing?''

"Some of us are doing better than others. Do you know when Dr. Herschel is coming back?''

"Probably around seven.'' The nurse came in to feel my pulse. If there isn't anything else to do, make sure the patient's heart is still beating. Gray eyes twinkled with meaningless jollity in her red face. "Well, we're certainly a lot stronger than we were a few hours ago. Is the shoulder giving us any pain?''

I looked at her sourly. "Well, it isn't giving me any—I don't know about you.'' I didn't want anyone throwing codeine or Darvon at me. Actually it was throbbing rather badly.

When she left I used the phone again to call Pole Star and ask for Bledsoe. The helpful woman in his office told me he was over at the *Lucella,* which had a ship-to-shore line. She gave me the number and told me how to get an operator to connect me. This was going to be complicated—I'd have to bill it to my office phone.

I was in the middle of giving the operator the dialing and billing instructions when my middle-aged nurse came back. "Now, we're not to do anything like this until Doctor says we're up to it.''

I ignored her.

"I'm sorry, Miss Warshawski: we can't have you doing anything to excite yourself.'' She pulled the phone from my outraged grasp. "Hello? This is Billings Hospital. Your party is not going to be able to complete the call at this time."

"How dare you? How dare you decide for me whether I can talk on the phone or not? I'm a person, not a sack of hospital clothes lying here."

She looked at me sternly. "The hospital has certain rules. One of them is to keep concussion and accident victims quiet. Dr. Herschel will let us know if you're ready to start phoning people yet."

I was wild with rage. I started to get out of bed to wrestle the phone from her, but the damned pulley kept me attached. "Quiet!" I shouted. "Who's getting me excited? You are, pulling that phone away!"

She unplugged it from the wall and walked away with it. I lay in bed panting with exhaustion and fury. One thing was clear—I couldn't wait for Lotty. After my breathing returned to normal I raised myself up again and inspected the pulley. It was holding my shoulder steady. Again I explored it with my right fingers, this time gingerly. The plaster was hard. Even if my shoulder was broken, the cast would keep it in place without traction. No reason I couldn't go home as long as I was careful.

I undid the wires with my right hand. My left shoulder relaxed against the bed with a spasm of pain so strong tears ran down my cheeks. After much ungainly fumbling with the bedclothes I managed to pull the left arm forward again. But helplessness compounded my frustration and I felt momentarily like abandoning the struggle. I shut my eyes and rested for ten minutes. A sling would solve my problems. I looked around doubtfully and finally found a white cloth on the bottom shelf of the bedside table. It took a lot of effort to move around and I was panting and red in the face by the time I managed to turn on my side, reach the cloth, and pull it up to bed level.

After a short rest I put one corner of the cloth in my mouth and slung it around my neck. Using teeth and my right hand, I rigged up a decent sling.

I staggered out of bed, trying not to move the left shoulder more than I had to, and opened the narrow lockers by the entrance. My clothes were in the second. The black pants were torn at the knees and the jacket was stiff with dried blood. Nuts. One of my favorite outfits. I pulled the pants on with one hand, ignoring underwear, and was trying to figure out what to do about the top when Lotty came in.

"Glad to see you're feeling better, my dear," she said dryly.

"The nurse said I shouldn't be excited. Since she was agitating me so much I thought I'd better get home where I can rest."

Lotty's mouth twisted in an ironic smile. She took my right elbow and shepherded me back to the bed. "Vic, you must stay here another day or two. You dislocated your shoulder. You must keep it still to minimize the tear on the muscles. That's the point of the traction. And you hit your head against the door as your car turned over. It's badly cut and you were unconscious for six hours. I'm not letting you take chances with your health."

I sat on the bed. "But, Lotty, I've got so many people to talk to. And the *Lucella* sails at seven—I'll miss them if I don't get through soon."

"I'm afraid it's after seven now . . . I'll get the phone back in and you can make your calls. But really, Vic, even with your constitution, you must keep this shoulder in a stationary position for two more days. Come."

Tears of frustration pricked my eyes. My head was throbbing. I lay back on the bed and let Lotty undress me and reattach my arm to the pulley. I hated to admit it, but I was glad to be lying down.

She went to the nurses' station and returned with the phone. When she saw me fumbling with the receiver she took it from me and placed the call herself. But the *Lucella* had already sailed.

12 ✱ Bedside Stories

The next day I entertained a stream of visitors. Charles Mc-
Cormick, a sergeant from the Traffic Division, came to report to me on the accident and to find out my version of what
had happened. I told him as much as I could remember. As I
suspected, the semi that was bearing down on me had hit a
car when it moved into the left lane. The sedan's driver had
been thrown into the windshield and killed. Two passengers
were on the critical list, one with spinal cord injuries. I must
have looked as horrified and guilty as I felt, for he tried to
reassure me.

"They weren't wearing seat belts. I'm not saying it
would have saved them, but it might have helped. It certainly saved your life when your car went over on its side.
We arrested the truck driver—not a scratch on him, of
course—reckless driving and involuntary manslaughter."

"Did you inspect my car?"

He looked at me curiously. "Someone had emptied all the
brake fluid for you. And cut through the power steering
cables. You had enough left to get you going, but moving
the wheel would have worked through the last bit of the
cables for you."

"How come I could stop at the lights down on 130th?"

"If you were braking gently, there was probably enough
fluid left in the lines to hold you. But if you slammed on the
brakes you wouldn't get anything . . . Now who would do a
thing like that? Where had you parked your car?"

I told him. He shook his head. "Lot of vandals down in the Port. You're lucky you got out of this alive."

"There's a feeble excuse for a guard down at the Tri-State yard. You might have somebody talk to him and see if he noticed anything."

McCormick said he'd think about it. He asked a few more questions and took off.

Someone brought in an enormous bouquet of spring flowers. The note read:

Vic:
   So sorry to read about your accident. Speedy recovery.

                                                    Paige

That was kind. Bobby Mallory's wife sent a plant. Murray Ryerson came in person, carrying a cactus. His idea of a joke. "Vic! You must have cat blood. Nobody ever gets hit by a semi and lives to tell it."

Murray is a big guy with curly reddish hair. He looks sort of like a Swedish Elliott Gould. His hearty voice and forty-six-inch shoulders contracted the hospital room into half its size.

"Hi, Murray. You read too many sensational newspapers. I wasn't hit by a semi—it got off my tail and ran into some other poor bastard."

He pulled a vinyl-covered chair over to the bedside and straddled it backward. "What happened?"

"Is this an interview or a sick visit?" I asked crossly.

"How about an interview in exchange for the story on Paige? Or are you up to that sort of thing?"

I brightened up considerably. "What'd you find out?"

"Ms. Carrington's a hardworking girl—excuse me, young woman. She has one older sister, no brothers. She had a scholarship at the American Ballet Theater when she was fifteen but wasn't good enough for them in the long haul. She lives in a condo on Astor Place. Father's dead. Mother lives in Park Forest South. Her family doesn't have a lot of money. She may have a rich friend helping her out, or the ballet people may pay her a lot—you'd have to sic a detective on her to find out for sure. Anyway, she's lived at the same place for several years now."

I wrinkled my face. "Park Forest South? She told me she grew up in Lake Bluff."

"Maybe she did. That's just where her mother lives . . . Anyway, about her and your cousin. There was some talk about her and Boom Boom the last month or so before he died. They didn't go to any of the celebrity hot spots, so it took Greta awhile to catch on—someone spotted her with him at the Stadium back in March. If it was serious they kept it mighty quiet. We talked to some of the other hockey players. They seemed to think she was pursuing him—he wasn't so involved."

I felt an ignoble twitch of pleasure at that.

"Your turn." Murray's blue eyes were bright with amusement. I told him everything I knew about the accident.

"Who emptied your brake fluid?"

"Police say it's vandals down at the Port."

"And you say?"

"I say it was whoever pushed my cousin under the *Bertha Krupnik.*" But that I said to myself. "Not a glimmer, Murray. I can't figure it out."

"Vic, with anyone else I'd believe it. But not with you. You got someone mad and they cut your power steering. Now, who?"

I shut my eyes. "Could have been Lieutenant Mallory—he wants me to keep my nose out of the Kelvin case."

"Someone at the Port."

"I'm an invalid, Murray."

"Someone connected with Kelvin."

"No comment."

"I'm going to follow you around, Vic. I want to see this thing happening before it happens."

"Murray, if you don't get out of here I'm going to sic the nurses on you. They're a very mean lot in this hospital."

He laughed and ruffled my hair. "Get well soon, Vic. I'd

miss you if you got to your ninth life . . . Just for laughs, I'm going to talk to your red-faced guard over at Tri-State Grain.''

I opened my eyes. ''If you find anything, you'd better let me know.''

''Read about it in the *Star,* Vic.'' He laughed and was gone before I could think of a snappy comeback.

After he left, quiet descended for a while. I raised the head of the bed and struggled to fix up the side table so that I could write. I'd never mangled an arm before and hadn't realized how hard it is to do things with one hand. Thank goodness for power steering, I thought, then remembered I didn't have a car, either. I called my insurance agent to report the loss. I hoped my policy covered vandalism.

I doodled around on a sheet of cheap hospital paper—a freighter bouncing through a high sea, a few crocodiles. Anyone down at the Port could have sabotaged my car. Phillips knew I was there—he'd seen me outside the Pole Star offices. He could have told Grafalk or anyone at Grafalk's—the dispatcher, for example.

I added a shark with rows of wild teeth, jaws big enough to swallow the freighter, and a few panicky fishes. Everyone at the *Lucella* knew I was there. That included Bledsoe. Trouble was, Bledsoe kissed well. Could anyone who kissed that well be evil enough to put my car out of commission? Still, the *Lucella* had a complete machine shop in the engine room. Sheridan or Winstein—even Bemis—could have taken care of my car while Bledsoe fed me dinner.

Then, take Phillips. He acted strange whenever I talked to him. Maybe he had fallen in love with me and couldn't articulate it, but I didn't think so. Also, Boom Boom and he argued over the contracts the day before my cousin's accident.

I drew a round ball and added a thatch of hair. That was supposed to be Phillips. I labeled it in case one of the nurses wanted to save the picture for her grandchildren. I should really talk to all of them—Grafalk, Phillips, Bemis, Sheridan, Bledsoe—and soon.

I looked balefully at my left shoulder. I couldn't do much while I lay here attached to my pulley. Still, what about those Eudora shipping contracts? Someone had rescued my canvas bag from the wreckage of the Lynx. It lay now on the lower shelf of the bedside table.

I lowered the bed, stuck my head over the side to fish the diary out of the bag, raised the bed again, and stared fixedly at the dates circled in the front of the book. I keep track of my period by circling the dates when I get it in my desk calendar, but that wouldn't be true in my cousin's case. I grinned to myself, picturing Boom Boom's reaction if I'd suggested that to him.

The dates might not track Boom Boom's menstrual cycle, but maybe they indicated some other periodic occurrence. I copied all of them down on a single sheet of paper. Some were two days apart, some seventeen, eleven, five—all prime numbers—nope, six, three, four, two again. They started at the end of March and ended in November, then started in April again.

That meant the Great Lakes shipping season. Elementary, my dear Warshawski. It began in late March or early April and ended around New Year's when ice built up too heavily on the upper lakes for anyone to want to go crashing around in them.

Eudora Grain operated all year round, of course, but they could only ship by water nine months of the year. So the case against Phillips had something to do with his shipping contracts. But what?

My head was starting to feel worse; I drank some water and lowered the bed to rest. I slept for a while. When I woke up a young man was sitting in the visitor's chair watching me with nervous concern. His smooth, round face with its broken nose and doggy brown eyes looked vaguely familiar. I collected myself.

"Pierre Bouchard! How nice to see you. Myron told me you were out of town."

He smiled and looked much more familiar—I had never seen him around Boom Boom without a smile. "Yes, well, I got back last night. And Anna pointed out the story of your accident in the paper." He shook his head woefully. "I am so sorry, Vic. First Boom Boom and now this."

I smiled awkwardly. "My shoulder will heal. And I know

you won't give me sympathy for a mere dislocated shoulder when you've had your leg tied up for weeks, and your nose broken three times—''

"Four," he corrected with a twinkle.

"So did Myron tell you I wanted to see you?"

"Myron? No. How could he when I have only just returned to Chicago? No, Vic. I came for your sake." He pulled a package from the floor and handed it to me.

I opened it up. Inside was a seal carved from the soapstone used by Eskimos. I was very touched and told him so.

"Well, in a hospital one gets tired of flowers all day long. I know. This little fellow was carved by Eskimos two-three hundred years ago. I hope he will bring you luck."

"Thank you, Pierre. I hope he will too. And he will always help me think of you."

He beamed. "Good, good—only don't let Anna hear you say that!" He paused a minute. "I came, too, on an errand of Boom Boom's. I have been in Quebec for two weeks—I flew down for the funeral, you know—then went right back there.

"Well, I got home last night and there was a letter waiting from him! He had mailed it the day before he died." He fumbled in the breast pocket of his tweedy brown jacket and pulled out the letter, which he handed to me.

Boom Boom was haunting me from the grave with his letters. Everyone was bringing me personal correspondence from him—why didn't he ever write me? I pulled the single white sheet from its envelope and read the small, neat handwriting.

Pierre

Anna tells me you're playing in the Coeur d'Argent. Break their heads for me, my friend. I thought I saw Howard the other day in very odd circumstances. I tried calling him but Elsie said he was in Quebec with you. Give me a ring when you get back and let me know.

Boom Boom

"Who's Howard? Howard Mattingly?"

Pierre nodded. Mattingly was a second-string wing.

"Elsie's his wife. Poor girl. If he told her he was going to the Coeur d'Argent she would believe him—just in order not to find out where he really was."

"So he wasn't in Quebec with you?"

He shook his head. "Always a new girl, Mattingly. Boom Boom never cared for him—he can't even play hockey. And he brags, you know."

The unforgivable male sin—bragging about your success with girls and on the ice—especially when neither was very admirable.

I looked at the letter again, dubiously. It seemed totally unrelated to the mess I was trying to sort out. But it had been important enough that my cousin called, then wrote Bouchard. It must mean something. I'd at least have to try to find out where Boom Boom had been the last few days before he died. The letter was dated the twenty-sixth. He'd died on the twenty-seventh. That meant going back maybe to the twenty-third—when the *Lucella* had taken water on in her holds. Could Mattingly have been involved in that? I started feeling overwhelmed by the enormous amount of work I had to do, and looked despairingly at my arm attached to the ceiling.

"Do you have a good photo of Mattingly?"

Bouchard fingered his chin. "Publicity picture. Myron could give me one."

"Could you get me half a dozen copies? I want to see if I can find anyone who can ID him in some out-of-the-way places that occur to me."

"Sure. Right away." He got up enthusiastically. Action. That's what hockey players thrive on. "Maybe you want me to take it around while you're lying here?"

"Let me think about it . . . I know who I need to talk to and you might not be able to get to them."

He took off in a cloud of antiseptic. I looked at my cousin's calendar again. On the twenty-third he'd seen Margolis. Must have been over at the elevator. On the twenty-fourth, a Saturday, he'd been with Paige. He hadn't written in any other appointments. On Monday he talked to MacKelvy, the dispatcher at Grafalk, and to two people whose names I didn't recognize. I'd show Mattingly's picture to Margolis. Maybe get Pierre to do that.

I looked at my watch, strapped awkwardly on my right wrist. Four-thirty—Paige was probably at the theater. I called, got her answering service, and left a message.

Lotty came in around five, noting the disarray of papers and bedclothes with her thick black eyebrows raised. "You're a terrible patient, my dear. They tell me you're rejecting all medication . . . Now I do not mind if you don't want the pain pills—that's your choice. But you must take the antibiotics. I don't want any secondary infection in the arm."

She straightened the mess around the bed with a few efficient motions. I like watching Lotty—she's so compact and tidy. She sat down on the bed. A nurse, bringing in a supper tray, pursed her lips in disapproval. No sitting on beds, but doctors are sacrosanct.

Lotty looked at the food. "Everything's boiled to death. Good—no digestive problems for you." She grinned wickedly.

"Pizza," I groaned. "Pasta. Wine."

She laughed. "Everything's coming along nicely. If you can stand it for one more day I'll take you home on Monday. Maybe spend a few days with me while you recover, okay?"

I looked at her through narrowed eyes. "I've got work to do, Lotty. I'm not going to lie in bed for two weeks waiting for these shoulder muscles to heal."

"Don't threaten me, Vic: I'm not one of these silly nurses. When have I ever tried to stop you from doing your job, even when you were being a pit dog?"

I struggled up. "Pit dog, Lotty? Pit dog! What the hell do you mean?"

"A dog that has to get down in the pit—the ring—and fight every damn person, even its friends."

I lay down again. "You're right, Lotty. Sorry. It's very kind of you to invite me home. I would appreciate that."

She brushed a kiss on my cheek and disappeared for a

while, coming back with a deep-dish onion and anchovy pizza. My favorite. "No wine while you're on antibiotics."

We ate the pizza and played gin. Lotty won. She whiled away a lot of World War II in London bomb shelters playing gin with the family who had taken her in. She almost always beats me.

Sunday morning I tried Paige again but she still wasn't home. Around noon, however, she showed up in person, looking beautiful in a green ruffled blouse and black and green Guatemalan skirt. She moved buoyantly into the room, smelling faintly of spring, and kissed me on the forehead.

"Paige! How nice to see you. Thanks so much for the flowers—they brighten the place up, as you can see."

"Vic, I was so sorry about the accident. But I'm glad you weren't hurt more seriously. My answering service said you were trying to get in touch with me—I thought I'd come in person and see how you're doing."

I asked how *Pavane for a Dope Dealer* was doing and she laughed and told me about the performance. We chatted for a few minutes, then I explained that I was trying to follow up on my cousin's movements the last few days before he died.

Her arched brows snapped together in momentary annoyance. "Are you still trailing him around? Don't you think it's time you let the dead bury the dead, Vic?"

I smiled with what calmness I could, feeling at a disadvantage with my hair unwashed and wearing a hospital gown. "I'm doing a favor for an old friend of Boom Boom's—Pierre Bouchard."

Yes, she'd met Pierre. He was a sweetheart. What did he want to know?

"If you'd seen Howard Mattingly recently."

An indefinable expression crossed her face. "I don't know who that is."

"He's one of the second-string players. Boom Boom didn't like him, so he might never have introduced you to him . . . Where did you two go on that last Saturday? Any place that he might have seen the guy?"

She shrugged and gave me a disdainful look, designed to

make me feel like a ghoul. I waited. "You're being extremely vulgar, Vic. That was my last private day with Boom Boom. I want to keep it to myself."

"You didn't see him Monday night?"

She turned red. "Vic! I know you're a detective, but this is excessive. You have a morbid interest in your cousin that's very unhealthy. I believe you can't stand the thought that he might have been close to any other woman but you!"

"Paige, I'm not asking you to tell me what kind of a lover Boom Boom was or to describe any intimate passages of your lives together. I just want to know what you did on Saturday and whether you saw him on Monday . . . Look, I don't want to turn this into a big, hostile ordeal. I like you. I don't want to start calling Ann Bidermyer and your mother and everyone you know to get a bead on you. I'm just asking you."

The honey-colored eyes filled with tears. "I liked you too, Vic. You reminded me of Boom Boom. But he was never so aggressive, even though he was a hockey player.

"We were sailing on Saturday. We got back at four so I could get to rehearsal. He may have stayed in Lake Bluff with the boat. I don't know. Monday night we had dinner at the Gypsy. I never saw him after that. Are you satisfied? Does that tell you what you have to find out? Or will you still be calling my mother and everyone else I know?"

She turned and left. My head was aching again.

13 * Sherry at Valhalla

Monday morning, Lotty removed the cast, pronounced the swelling down and healing well underway, and had me released from bondage. We went north to her tidy apartment.

Lotty drives her green Datsun recklessly, believing that all other cars will move out of the way. A dent in the right fender and a long scrape along the passenger door are testimony to the success of her approach. I opened my eyes on Addison—a mistake, since it was in time to see her swerve in front of a CTA bus to turn right onto Sheffield.

"Lotty, if you're going to drive like this, get a semi—the guy who's responsible for putting my shoulder in this sling walked away from the accident unscratched."

Lotty turned off the ignition and hopped out of the car. "Firmness is necessary, Vic. Firmness or the others will drive one from the streets."

It was hopeless; I gave up an unequal struggle.

We had stopped by my apartment to pick up clothes and a bottle of Black Label—Lotty doesn't keep whiskey in the house. I'd also taken my Smith & Wesson from a locked cupboard in the bedroom closet. Someone had tried to smash me to bits on the Dan Ryan. I didn't feel like roving the streets unprotected.

Lotty went to the clinic she operates nearby. I settled down in her living room with a telephone. I was going to talk to everyone who'd had a chance to take a crack at me.

My rage had disappeared as my head wound healed, but my sense of purpose was strengthened.

I reached the helpful young office manager at the Pole Star Line on the third ring. The news she gave me was not encouraging. The *Lucella Wieser* had delivered her load in Buffalo and was steaming to Erie to pick up coal bound for Detroit. After that she was booked on the upper lakes for some time—they didn't expect her in Chicago until the middle of June. They could help me set up a radio conversation if it was urgent. I couldn't see going over the issues I needed to cover by radio—I'd have to speak to the Pole Star contingent face to face.

Baffled there, I called down to Eudora Grain's office and asked for Janet. She came to the phone and told me she was sorry about my accident and glad I was feeling better. I asked her if she knew where Phillips lived—I might pay a surprise visit to his wife to find out what time her husband had come home the night of my accident.

Janet didn't know. It was up north someplace. If it was important, she could ask around and find out. It was important, I said, and gave her Lotty's number.

While I was waiting I got Howard Mattingly's number from Myron Fackley. Boom Boom told Pierre he'd seen Mattingly in a strange place. I was betting Mattingly was hanging around Lake Bluff when Boom Boom went sailing there with Paige the Saturday before he died. I wanted to find out.

Mattingly wasn't home, but his wife Elsie the Breathless, was. I reminded her we'd met at a number of hockey functions. Oh yes, she gasped, she remembered me.

"Boom Boom told me he'd seen your husband sailing on the twenty-third. Did you go with him?"

She hadn't gone out with Howard that day—she was pregnant and she got tired so easily. She didn't know if he'd been sailing or not—he certainly hadn't said anything about it. Yes, she'd tell Howard to call me. She hung up without asking why I wanted to know.

Lotty came home for lunch. I fixed sardines on toast with cucumber and tomato and Lotty made a pot of the thick Viennese coffee she survives on. If I drank as much of it as she does they'd have to pull me off the chandeliers. I had orange juice and half a sandwich. My head still bothered me and I didn't have much appetite.

Janet called from Eudora Grain after lunch. She'd pilfered the personal files while everyone was eating and gotten Phillips's address: on Harbor Road in Lake Bluff. I thanked her absently—a lot seemed to go on in Lake Bluff. Grafalk. Paige had grown up there. Phillips lived there. And Paige and Boom Boom had gone sailing there on the twenty-third of April. I realized Janet had hung up and that I was still holding the receiver.

I put it down and went into the guest room to dress for a trip to the northern suburbs. We were in the second week in May and the air was still cold. My dad used to say Chicago had two seasons: winter and August. It was still winter.

I put on the blue Chanel jacket with a white shirt and white wool slacks. The effect was elegant and professional. Lotty had given me a canvas sling to keep as much pressure off the shoulder as possible—I'd wear it up in the car and take it off when I got to Phillips's house.

Lotty's spare room doubles as her study and I rummaged in the desk for a pad of paper and some pens. I also found a small leather briefcase. I put the Smith & Wesson in there along with the writing equipment. Ready for any occurrence.

Until they processed my claim check, the Ajax Insurance Company provided me a Chevette with the stiffest steering I've ever encountered. I'd considered using Boom Boom's Jaguar but didn't think I could operate a stick shift one-handed. I was trying to get Ajax to exchange the Chevette for something easier to handle. In the meantime it was going to make getting around difficult.

Driving up the Edens to Lake Bluff was a major undertaking. Every turn of the wheel wrenched my healing shoulder and strained the muscles in my neck, also weak from the accident. By the time I pulled off the Tri-State Tollway onto Route 137, my entire upper back was aching and my professionally crisp white blouse was wet under the armpits.

At two-thirty on a weekday Lake Bluff was still. Just south of the Great Lakes Naval Training Station on Lake Michigan, the town is a tiny pocket of wealth. To be sure, there are small lots and eight-room ranch houses, but imposing mansions predominate. A weak spring sun shone on nascent lawns and the trees sporting their first pale green frills.

I turned south on Green Bay Road and meandered around until I found Harbor Road. As I suspected, it overlooked the lake. I passed an outsize red brick dwelling sprawled on a huge lot, perhaps ten acres, with tennis courts visible through the budding shrubs—they'd be hidden by midsummer when the plants were in full foliage. Three lots later I came to the Phillipses.

Theirs was not an imposing mansion, but the setting was beautiful. As I wrenched the Chevette up the drive I could see Lake Michigan unfold behind the house. It was a two-story frame structure, topped with those rough shingles people think imitate thatching. Painted white, with a silvery trim around the windows, it looked as if it might have ten rooms or so—a big place to keep up, but an energetic person could do it without help if she (or he) didn't work outside the home.

A dark blue Olds 88 sedan, new model, rested outside the attached three-car garage. It looked as if the lady of the house might be in.

I rang the front bell. After a wait the door opened. A woman in her early forties, dark hair cut expensively to fall around her ears, stood there in a simple shirtwaist—Massandrea, it looked like. A good two hundred fifty dollars at Charles A. Stevens. Even though it was Monday afternoon at home, her makeup was perfect, ready for any unexpected visitors. Diamond drops hung from gold filigree attached to her ears.

She looked at me coldly. "Yes?"

"Good afternoon, Mrs. Phillips. I'm Ellen Edwards with Tri-State Research. We're doing a survey of the wives of important corporate executives and I wanted to talk to you. Do you have a few minutes this afternoon, or could we set a time when it would be convenient?"

She looked at me unblinkingly for a few minutes. "Who sent you?"

"Tri-State did. Oh, you mean how did we get your name? By surveying the biggest companies in the Chicago area—or divisions of big companies like Eudora Grain—and getting the names of their top men."

"Is this going to be published someplace?"

"We won't use your name, Mrs. Phillips. We're talking to five hundred women and we'll just do some composite profiles."

She thought about it and finally decided, grudgingly, that she would talk to me. She took me into the house, into a back room that gave a good view of Lake Michigan. Through the window I watched a tanned, well-muscled young man struggling with an eighteen-foot sailboat tied to a mooring about twenty yards from the shore.

We sat in wing chairs covered with needlepointed scenes in orange, blue, and green. Mrs. Phillips lighted a Kent. She didn't offer me one—not that I smoke, it just would have been good manners.

"Do you sail, Mrs. Phillips?"

"No. I never cared to learn. That's my son Paul. He just got home from Claremont for the summer."

"Do you have any other children?"

They had two daughters, both in high school. What were her own hobbies? Needlepointing, of course—the ugly chair covers were examples of her handiwork. And tennis, she adored tennis. Now that they belonged to the Maritime Country Club she could play year round with good professionals.

Had she lived in Lake Bluff long? The last five years. Before that they'd been in Park Forest South. Much closer to the Port, of course—but Lake Bluff was such a wonderful place to live. Such a good home for the girls, and, of course, for her.

I told her the main things we were interested in were the advantages and disadvantages of being a corporate spouse. So the advantages had to include life-style—right? Unless she or he had independent means to support it?

She gave a rather self-conscious laugh. "No, we're not like the—like some of the families around here. Every penny we spend Clayton earns. Not that some of these people aren't finding out what it's like to have to struggle a bit." She seemed about to expand on the statement but thought better of it.

"Most of the women we talk to find their husbands' schedules one of the biggest disadvantages—raising families alone, spending too much time alone. I imagine an executive like your husband puts in pretty long hours—and of course it's quite a drive from here down to the Port." The Tri-State Tollway to I-94 would be a smooth run, but he'd be doing it with the traffic as far as the Loop going in and starting at the Loop going home. Maybe ninety minutes if everything went well.

"What time does he usually get home?"

That varied, but generally by seven o'clock.

Paul had gotten the sails up and was untying the boat. It looked pretty big for one person to handle alone, but Mrs. Phillips didn't seem worried. She didn't even watch as the boat bobbed off into the lake. Maybe she had total confidence in her son's ability to handle the boat. Maybe she didn't care what he did.

I told her we'd just take a typical day in their lives together and go through it—say last Thursday. What time they had gotten up, what they had for breakfast, what she did with herself. What time her husband got home from work. I heard all the dreary details of a life without focus, the hours at the tennis club, at the beauty parlor, at the Edens Plaza Shopping Center, before I got the information I'd come for. Clayton hadn't gotten home that night until after nine. She remembered because she'd cooked a roast and finally she and the girls ate it without waiting for him. She couldn't remember if he seemed upset or tired or if his clothes were covered with grease.

"Covered with grease?" she echoed, astonished. "Why would your research firm want to know a thing like that?"

I'd forgotten who I was supposed to be for a minute. "I

wondered if you do your own laundry, or sent it out, or have a maid do it.''

"We send it out. We can't afford a maid." She gave a sour smile. "Not yet, anyway. Maybe next year."

"Well, thank you for your time, Mrs. Phillips. We'll mail you a copy of the report when we complete it. We'll be bringing it out later this summer.''

She took me back through the house. The furniture was expensive but not very attractive. Someone with more money than taste had picked it out—she, or Phillips, or the two of them together. As I said good-bye I idly asked who lived in the big brick place up the road, the one with the tennis courts.

An expression combining awe and envy crossed her well-made-up face. "That's the Grafalks. You ought to talk to her. Her husband owns one of the biggest firms in town, ships. They have maids and a chauffeur—the works.''

"Do you spend much time with them?''

"Oh well, they lead their lives, we lead ours. They sponsored us in the Maritime Club and Niels takes Paul and Clayton sailing with him sometimes. But *she's* pretty stand-offish. If you don't belong to the Symphony Board you aren't worth much to her." She seemed to feel she might have said too much, for she hastily changed the subject and said good-bye.

I backed the Chevette onto Harbor Road and drove past the Grafalks'. So that was where the Viking lived. A pretty nice spread. I stopped the car and looked at it, half tempted to go in and try my pitch on Mrs. Grafalk. As I sat, a Bentley nosed its way through the gates and turned onto the road. A thin, middle-aged woman with graying black hair was at the wheel. She didn't look at me as she came out—maybe they were used to gawkers. Or perhaps she wasn't the owner but just a visitor—a sister member of the Symphony Board.

Harbor Road turned west toward Sheridan a hundred yards beyond the Grafalk estate. The Bentley disappeared around the corner at a good clip. I put the Chevette into gear and was getting ready to follow when a dark blue sports car came around the bend. Going fifty or so, the driver turned left across my path. I braked hard and avoided a collision by inches. The car, a Ferrari, went on through the brick pillars lining the drive, stopping with a great squeal just clear of the road.

Niels Grafalk came up to the Chevette before I had time to disappear. I couldn't fool him with some tale about opinion polls. He was wearing a brown tweed jacket and an open-necked white shirt and his face was alive with anger.

"What the hell did you think you were doing?" he exploded at the Chevette.

"I'd like to ask you the same question. Do you ever signal before you turn?"

"What were you doing in front of my house anyway?" Anger had obscured his attention and he hadn't noticed who I was at first; now recognition mixed with the anger. "Oh, it's you—the lady detective. What were you doing—trying to catch my wife or me in an indiscreet position?"

"Just admiring the view. I didn't realize I needed life insurance to travel to the northern suburbs." I started once more to move the car up Harbor Road, but he stuck a hand through the open window and seized my left arm. It was attached at the top to my dislocated shoulder and his grasp sent a shudder of pain through both arm and shoulder. I stopped the car once more.

"That's right, you don't do divorces, do you?" His dark blue eyes were flooded with emotion—anger, excitement, it was hard to tell. He released my arm and I turned off the ignition. My fingers strayed to my left shoulder to rub it. I let them fall—I wasn't going to let him see he'd hurt me. I got out of the car, almost against my will, pulled by the force of his energy. That's what it means to have a magnetic personality.

"You missed your wife."

"I know—I passed her on the road. Now I want to know why you were spying on my property."

"Honest Injun, Mr. Grafalk—I wasn't spying. If I were, I wouldn't do it right outside your front door like that. I'd conceal myself and you'd never know I was here."

The blaze died down a bit in the blue eyes and he laughed.
"What were you doing here, then?"

"Just passing through. Someone told me you lived here
and I was gawking at it—it's quite a place."

"You didn't find Clayton at home, did you?"

"Clayton? Oh, Clayton Phillips. No, I expect he'd be at
work on a Monday afternoon, wouldn't he?" It wouldn't do
to deny I'd been at the Phillipses—even though I'd used a
fake name, Grafalk could check that pretty easily.

"You talked to Jeannine, then. What did you think of
her?"

"Are you interviewing her for a job?"

"What?" He looked puzzled, then secretly amused.
"How about a drink? Or don't private eyes drink on duty?"

I looked at my watch—it was almost four-thirty. "Let me
just move the Chevette out of the way of any further Lake
Bluff menaces. It isn't mine and I'd hate for something to
happen to it."

Grafalk was through being angry, or at least he had buried
his anger below the civilized urbanity I'd seen down at the
Port last week. He leaned against one of the brick pillars
while I hauled at the stiff steering and maneuvered the car
onto the grass verge. Inside the gates he put an arm around
me to guide me up the drive. I gently disengaged it.

The house, made from the same brick as the pillars, lay
about two hundred yards back from the road. Trees lined the
front on both sides, so that you had no clue to how big the
place really was as you approached it.

The lawn was almost completely green—another week
and they'd have to give it the season's first mowing. The
trees were coming into leaf. Tulips and jonquils provided
bursts of color at the corners of the house. Birds twittered
with the business of springtime. They were nesting on some
of the most expensive real estate in Chicago but they probably didn't feel snobbish toward the sparrows in my neighborhood. I complimented Grafalk on the grounds.

"My father built the place back in the twenties. It's a little
more ornate than we care for today—but my wife likes it, so
I've never done anything to change it."

We went in through a side door and back to a glassed-in porch overlooking Lake Michigan. The lawn sloped down steeply to a sandy beach with a little cabana and a couple of beach umbrellas. A raft was anchored about thirty yards off-shore but I didn't see a boat.

"Don't you keep your boat out back here?"

Grafalk gave his rich man's chuckle. He didn't share his birds' social indifference. "The beaches here have a very gradual slope—you can't keep anything with more than a four-foot draw close to the shore."

"Is there a harbor in Lake Bluff, then?"

"The closest public harbor's in Waukegan. It's extremely polluted, however. No, the commandant at Great Lakes Naval Training Station, Rear Admiral Jergensen, is a personal friend. I tie my sailboat up there."

That was handy. The Great Lakes Naval Training Station lay on Lake Bluff's northern border. Where would Grafalk keep his yacht when Jergensen retired? The problems the very rich face are different from yours and mine.

I sat in a bamboo chaise lounge. Grafalk opened a window. He busied himself with ice and glasses in a bar built into the room's teak panels. I opted for sherry—Mike Hammer is the only detective I know who can think and move while drinking whiskey. Or at least move. Maybe Mike's secret is he doesn't try to think.

With his back still turned to me, Grafalk spoke. "If you weren't spying on me, you must have been spying on Clayton. What'd you find out?"

I put my feet on the red-flowered cushion sewn to the bamboo. "Let's see. You want to know what I think about Jeannine and what I found out about Clayton. If I did divorces I'd suspect you of sleeping with Jeannine and wondering how much Phillips knew about it. Except you don't strike me as the type who cares very much what men think about your cavorting with their wives."

Grafalk threw back his sun-bleached head and gave a great shout of laughter. He brought me a fluted tulip-shaped glass filled with straw-colored liquid. I sipped it. The sherry was as smooth as liquid gold. I wished now I'd asked for scotch. A millionaire's whiskey might be something unique.

Grafalk sat facing me in a chintz-covered armchair. "I guess I'm being too subtle, Miss Warshawski. I know you've been asking questions around the Port. When I find you up here it makes me think you've found something out about Phillips. We carry a lot of grain for Eudora. I'd like to know if there's something going on with their Chicago operation I should know about."

I took another sip of sherry and put the glass on a tiled table at my right hand. The floor was covered with hand-painted Italian tiles in bright reds and greens and yellows and the table top matched them.

"If there are problems with Eudora Grain that you should know about, ask David Argus. My main concern is who tried to kill me last Thursday night."

"Kill you?" Grafalk's bushy eyebrows arched. "You don't strike me as the hysterical type, but that's a pretty wild accusation."

"Someone took out my brakes and steering last Thursday. It was only luck that kept me from careening into a semi on the Dan Ryan."

Grafalk finished whatever he was drinking—it looked like a martini. Good old-fashioned businessman—no Perrier or white wine for him. "Do you have a good reason for thinking Clayton might have done it?"

"Well, he certainly had opportunity. But motive—no. No more than you or Martin Bledsoe or Mike Sheridan."

Grafalk stopped on his way back to the bar and looked at me. "You suspect them as well? You're sure the—uh—damage took place at the Port? Could it have been vandals?"

I swallowed some more sherry. "Yes, yes, and possibly, although I don't believe it. It's true anyone could empty brake fluid with a little ingenuity—but what vandals carry around a ratchet wrench and a cutting torch just on the off chance that they'll find a car to mutilate? They're much more likely to slash tires, steal hubcaps, or smash in windows. Or all three."

Grafalk brought over the sherry bottle and topped off my glass. I tried to pretend I drank the stuff every day and didn't attempt to read the label. I'd never be able to afford this sherry anyway; what did I care what it was called?

He sat back down with a fresh martini and looked at me intently. He was turning something over in his mind. "How much do you know about Martin Bledsoe?"

I stiffened. "I've met him a few times. Why?"

"He didn't tell you anything about his background at dinner on Thursday?"

I put the expensive glass down with a snap on the tiled table. "Now who is spying on whom, Mr. Grafalk?"

He laughed again. "The Port is a small community, Miss Warshawski, and gossip about shipowners travels fast. Martin hasn't asked a woman out to dinner since his wife died six years ago. Everyone was talking about it. Likewise your accident. I knew you were in the hospital but I didn't know someone had deliberately tampered with your car."

"The *Herald-Star* gave me a front-page story—picture of my poor Lynx with its front missing and everything . . . Gossip about Bledsoe must be buried pretty deep. No one gave me a whiff about his background that sounded as troublesome as you're seeming to imply."

"It is buried deep. I've never told anyone about it, even when Martin left me and I was mad enough to want to hurt him badly. But if there has been a crime committed, if there's been an attempt on your life, you should know about it."

I didn't say anything. Outside, the house cast a lengthening shadow on the beach.

"Martin grew up in Cleveland. Bledsoe is his mother's maiden name. He never knew who his father was. It could have been any of a series of drunken sailors on Cleveland's waterfront."

"That's not a crime, Mr. Grafalk. And scarcely his fault."

"True. That's just to give you a flavor of his home life. He left when he was fifteen, lied about his age, and signed on to sail the Great Lakes. In those days you didn't need the training you do now, and of course there was a lot more shipping—no waiting around union halls hoping to get called up for a job. Any warm body that could haul ropes and lift two hundred pounds would do. And Martin was strong for his age.'' He paused to swallow his drink.

''Well, he was a smart fellow and he came to the attention of one of my mates. A man who liked to help the young men in his charge, not stand on their heads. When he was nineteen Martin ended up in our Toledo office. He obviously had far too many brains to waste just doing muscle work that any stupid Polack could handle.''

''I see,'' I murmured. ''Maybe you could find an opening for me on one of your boats if detective work palls.''

He stared at me for a minute. ''Oh. Warshawski. I see. Don't show your hackles—it's not worth it. The waterfront is filled with Poles strong as oxen but not much brainpower.''

I thought of Boom Boom's cousins and declined arguing the point.

''Anyway, to make a long story very short, Martin was operating in an environment he could understand intellectually but not socially. He'd never had much formal education and he never learned any sense of ethics or morality. He was handling too much money and he siphoned some of it off. I lost a tough argument with my father about prosecuting Martin. I had found him, I had pushed him—I was only thirty myself at the time. I wanted to give him a second chance. Dad refused and Martin spent two years in a Cantonville prison. My father died the month before he was released and I hired him back immediately. He never did anything else criminal that I'm aware of—but if there's some trouble between Pole Star and Eudora Grain or at Eudora Grain itself that involves money, you should know about Martin's background. I'm relying on your discretion to keep it to yourself—I wouldn't want Argus, or even Clayton, for that matter, to know about it if it turns out nothing's wrong.''

I finished my sherry. ''So that was what you meant that day at lunch. Bledsoe educated himself in prison and you

were hinting you could tell people about it if you wanted
to."

"I didn't think you'd caught that."

"Even a boneheaded Polack couldn't miss that one . . .
Last week you were threatening him, today you're pro-
tecting him—sort of. Which is it?"

Anger flashed across Grafalk's face and was quickly
erased. "Martin and I have—a tacit understanding. He
doesn't attack my fleet, I don't tell people about his disrepu-
table past. He was making fun of the Grafalk Line. I was
backing him off."

"What do *you* think is going on at Eudora Grain?"

"What do you mean?"

"You've leaped to a couple of conclusions, based on my
investigations down at the Port. You think there might be
some kind of a financial problem down there. You're concerned enough to reveal a well-concealed truth about Bledsoe. Not even his ship's officers know it—or if they do,
they're too loyal to betray it. You must think something
pretty serious is wrong."

Grafalk shook his head and gave a slightly condescending
smile. "Now *you're* leaping to conclusions, Miss Warshawski. Everyone knows you've been looking into your
cousin's death. And they know you and Phillips have had a
few words together—you just can't keep secrets in a closed
community like that. If there is something wrong at Eudora
Grain, it would have to involve money. Nothing else important could be wrong there." He swirled the olive in his
glass. "It's none of my business—but I do periodically wonder where Clayton Phillips gets his money."

I looked at him steadily. "Argus pays him well. He inherited it. His wife did. Any reason why one of those possibilities wouldn't be good enough?"

He shrugged. "I'm a very wealthy man, Miss Warshawski. I grew up with a lot of money and I'm used to living
with it. There are plenty of people without money who are at
ease with and around it—Martin's one and Admiral
Jergensen another. But Clayton and Jeannine aren't. If they
inherited it, it was an unexpected windfall late in life."

"Still possible. They don't have to measure it in your class to afford that house and their other amenities. Maybe a crabby old grandmother hoarded it so that it would give everyone the least possible pleasure—that happens at least as often as embezzlement."

"Embezzlement?"

"You're suggesting that, aren't you?"

"I'm not suggesting anything—just asking."

"Well, you sponsored them at the Maritime Club. That's impossible for the *nouveaux riches* to crack, from everything I read. Not enough to have a quarter million a year for that place—you have to trace yourself back to the Palmers and the McCormicks. But you got them in. You must have known something about them."

"That was my wife. She undertakes odd charities—Jeannine was one that she's since come to regret."

A phone rang somewhere in the house, followed shortly by a buzz on an instrument I hadn't noticed earlier, set in an alcove by the bar. Grafalk answered it. "Yes? Yes, I'll take the call . . . Will you excuse me, Miss Warshawski?"

I got up politely and moved into the hallway, going the opposite direction from which we'd come in. I wandered into a dining room where a thickset middle-aged woman in a white blouse and blue skirt was laying the table for ten. She was putting four forks and three spoons at each place. I was impressed—imagine having seventy matching forks and spoons. There were a couple of knives apiece, too.

"I bet they've got more besides that."

"Are you talking to me, miss?"

"No. I was thinking aloud. You remember what time Mr. Grafalk got home Thursday night?"

She looked up at that. "If you're not feeling quite well, miss, there's a powder room down the hall to your left."

I wondered if it was the sherry. Maybe Grafalk had put something into it, or maybe it was just too smooth for my scotch-raddled palate. "I feel fine, thanks. I just wanted to know if Mr. Grafalk got home late Thursday night."

"I'm afraid I couldn't say." She went back to the silver. I was wondering if I could beat her into talking with my good arm but it didn't seem worth the effort. Grafalk came up behind me.

"Oh, there you are. Everything under control, Karen?"

"Yes, sir. Mrs. Grafalk left word she'll be back by seven."

"I'm afraid I'm going to have to ask you to leave now, Miss Warshawski. We're expecting company and I've got to do a couple of things before they arrive."

He showed me to the front door and stood watching until I went through the brick pillars and got into the Chevette. It was six o'clock. The sherry left a nice light glow in my head. Not anything like drunk, not even mildly sloshed. Just glowing enough to take my mind off my aching shoulder, not enough to impair my consummate handling of the stiff steering.

14 * Potluck

As I headed back toward the Edens and poverty, I felt as though someone were spinning me around in a swivel chair. Grafalk's sherry and Grafalk's story had clearly been provided for a reason. But what? By the time I got back to Lotty's the sherry had worn off and my shoulder ached.

Lotty's street is even more decrepit than the stretch of Halsted I inhabit. Bottles mingled with crumpled paper cups in the gutter. A '72 Impala drooped on the near front side where someone had removed the wheel. An overweight woman bustled along with five small children, each staggering under a heavy bag of groceries. She yelled at them in shrill Spanish. I don't speak it, but it's close enough to Italian for me to know it was good-natured chivvying, not angry bullying.

Someone had left a beer can on Lotty's front steps. I picked it up and carried it in with me. Lotty creates a small island of sanity and sanitation on the street and I wanted to help maintain that.

I smelled *pot-au-feu* as I opened the door; I suddenly felt good about being here to eat a hearty meal rather than at a seven-course affair in Lake Bluff. Lotty was sitting in the spotless kitchen reading when I came in. She put a marker in her book, took off her black-rimmed glasses, and placed both on a corner of the butcher block.

"It smells great. Anything for me to do?. . . Lotty, did you ever own seventy matching forks and spoons?"

Her dark eyes gleamed with amusement. "No, my dear, but my grandmother did. At least that many. I had to polish them every Friday afternoon when I was eight. Where have you been that they have seventy matching forks and spoons?"

I told her about my afternoon's inquiries while she finished the stew and served it. We ate it with thick-crusted Viennese bread. "The trouble is, I'm going in too many different directions. I need to find out about Bledsoe. I need to find out about my car. I need to find out about Phillips's money. I need to know who broke into Boom Boom's apartment and killed Henry Kelvin. What were they looking for, anyway? I'd been through all his papers and he didn't have anything that looked like a hot secret to me." I pushed an onion around my plate, brooding. "And of course, top of the list, who pushed Boom Boom into Lake Michigan?"

"Well, what tasks can you turn over to someone else—the police, or perhaps Pierre Bouchard? He wants to help."

"Yeah, the police. According to the Kelvin family, they're doing sweet nothing about locating his murderers. I can see Sergeant McGonnigal's point, of course: they haven't got a clue *qua* clue. Trouble is, they refuse to connect Kelvin with Boom Boom. If they did that, they might be able to muscle in and get some real information out of the

Port. But they think Boom Boom died accidentally. Same thing with my crash. They want that to be vandals." I fiddled with my spoon. It was stainless steel and matched my knife and fork. Lotty had style.

"I have a kind of crazy idea. I want to go meet the *Lucella* at the next port she calls in and have it out with Bledsoe— find out what he's been up to and whether Grafalk's telling the truth and whether the chief engineer or the captain could've monkeyed with my car. I know there's stuff I can do down here. But it'll wait three or four days. I want to talk to those guys *now*."

Lotty pursed her lips, dark eyes alert. "Why not, after all? They won't be back here for—what did you say? Seven weeks? You can't wait that long, anyway—their memories will have gone stale."

"The way to do it is to track them down through *Grain News*. It lists contracts and when and where they're to be picked up. That way, Bledsoe's office won't be able to warn him that I'm coming: I like to catch people *au naturel*."

I got up and stacked the plates in the sink, running hot water from the tap.

"What is this?" Lotty demanded. "Your head wound must have been worse than I thought."

I looked at her suspiciously.

"When did you ever clean up dishes within two days of using them?"

I swatted her with a dish towel and pursued my idea. It sounded good. I could get my corporate spy, Janet, to find out how much Phillips earned. Maybe she could even snatch a look at his bankbook, although Lois probably guarded that with her fiery dragon breath. If Bouchard was in town he could find out who this guy was who was interested in buying a share of the Black Hawks. That was the person who'd introduced Paige to Boom Boom last Christmas.

Lotty rubbed Myoflex into my shoulder before I went to bed and fixed me up with a sling to keep me from twisting the joint in my sleep. Nonetheless I woke the next morning barely able to use my left arm. I wasn't going to be able to drive that damned car any place, and I'd planned on taking it down to my cousin's apartment to look at his copies of *Grain News*. The police were through there; as soon as I collected the keys I could go back to it.

Lotty offered me her car, but I couldn't see one-handedly driving a stick shift. I stomped around the apartment, enjoying a first-rate tantrum.

As she left for the clinic, Lotty said dryly, "I hesitate to interfere, but what problems will your rage solve? Can't you do some of your business by phone?"

I stiffened momentarily, then relaxed. "Right, Lotty. Pit-dog Warshawski will be called off."

She blew me a kiss and left, and I phoned Janet at Eudora Grain to see if she could find out how much Phillips earned.

"I don't think I could do that, Miss Warshawski. Payroll information is confidential."

"Janet, wouldn't you like Boom Boom's murderer caught?"

"Well, I've been thinking that over. I don't see how he could have been murdered. Who would want to do it, anyway?"

I counted to ten in Italian. "Someone on your case about the information you've been getting me?"

Not exactly, she explained, but Lois had started asking her what she was doing in the office while everyone else was at lunch. Yesterday she'd come in just seconds after Janet closed the drawer where Mr. Phillips's home address was filed. "If I stay late today, she's sure to hang around to spy on me."

I tapped my teeth with a pencil, trying to figure out some way she could get Phillips's salary without getting into trouble. Nothing occurred to me.

"How often do you get paid?"

"Every other week. Our next paycheck is due Friday."

"Is there any chance you could look in his wastebasket at the end of the day? A lot of people just toss their pay stubs; maybe he does too."

"I'll try," she said dubiously.

"That's the spirit," I said heartily. "One other thing.

Could you call over to the Pole Star Line and find out where the *Lucella Wieser* will be in the next couple of days?''

She sounded more reluctant than ever but copied the information down and said she would get back to me.

Bouchard was out; I left a message with his wife. After that I didn't have anything to do but pace. I didn't want to leave the apartment and risk missing Janet's call. In the end, to pass the time, I worked on some vocal exercises. My mother had been a singer and she had trained me as a musician, hoping I would have the operatic career Hitler and Mussolini deprived her of. That never worked out, but I know a lot of breathing exercises and can sing all the main arias from *Iphigénie en Tauride,* the only opera my mother sang in professionally before she left Italy in 1938.

I was halfway through Iphigenia's second-act entrance, creaking like a windy parlor organ, when Janet phoned back. The *Lucella* would be in Thunder Bay Thursday and Friday. They were unloading coal in Detroit today and would leave there this evening.

''And really, Miss Warshawski, I can't help you any more. I'm calling you now from a pay phone at the 7-11 but Lois was all over me about calling Pole Star. Now that Mr. Warshawski's gone, I'm just back in the typing pool and there isn't any reason for me to do things like that, you see.''

''I see. Well, Janet, you've done a great deal and I appreciate it very much.'' I hesitated a second. ''Do me one favor, though—if you hear anything suspicious, call me from home. Could you do that much?''

''I suppose,'' she said doubtfully. ''Although I don't really know what I would hear.''

''Probably nothing. Just on the chance that you do,'' I said patiently. We hung up and I massaged my sore left shoulder. Somewhere among the hundreds of books that lined Lotty's walls must be an atlas. I started in the living room and worked my way along. I found a pre-World War II map of Austria, a 1941 Guide to the London Underground, and an old U.S. atlas. None of them showed any place along the Great Lakes called Thunder Bay. That was a big help.

Finally I called a travel agent and asked if there were any

flights between Chicago and Thunder Bay. Air Canada had one flight a day, leaving Toronto at 6:20, arriving at 10:12 P.M. I'd have to take a 3:15 flight to Toronto.

"How far away is that, anyway?" I demanded. That was seven hours of travel. The travel agent didn't know. Where was Thunder Bay? In Ontario. The agent didn't know any more than that but agreed to make a reservation on the next day's flight for me. Two hundred fifteen dollars to spend seven hours in an airplane—they ought to pay me. I charged it to my American Express account, tickets to be picked up tomorrow at O'Hare.

I looked for Thunder Bay on the Canadian side of the Great Lakes but still couldn't find it. I guessed I'd know when I got there.

The rest of the day I spent in a whirlpool at the Irving Park Y, the poor person's health club. I pay ninety dollars a year to use the pool and the Nautilus room. The only other people who go there are earnest youths intent on building perfect biceps or catching a game of basketball—no racquet ball courts, no bars, no disco lights, and no hot pink warm-up outfits with designer labels.

15 ✳ The Frozen North

The ticket agent at Air Canada told me Thunder Bay was Canada's westernmost port on Lake Superior. I asked him why it hadn't shown up on my map and he shrugged indifferently. One of the flight attendants was more helpful. On the way to Toronto she explained that the town used to be called Port Arthur; the name had been changed about ten years ago. I made a mental note to buy Lotty a modern atlas as a hostess present.

I checked my small canvas bag through in Chicago, since it contained the Smith & Wesson (disassembled in accordance with federal firearms regulations). I'd packed lightly, not intending to be gone beyond a day or two, just jeans, shirts, a heavy sweater, and underwear. I didn't even carry a purse—just stuck my wallet in my jeans pocket.

After an hour's layover in Toronto's bright modern airport, I boarded Air Canada's Ontario puddle jumper. We stopped five times on the way to Thunder Bay on tiny airstrips which loomed out of open country to receive us. As people got on and off they exchanged greetings and light conversation. It reminded me of a bus ride through rural Louisiana in the freedom-march days; I got just as many covert stares.

At Thunder Bay, the fifteen of us who'd made the final leg of the trip climbed down rollaway stairs into a clear, cold night. We were perhaps six hundred miles north of Chicago, a difference in latitude sufficient for winter to have barely ended.

Most of my fellow passengers were wrapped in winter coats. I shivered across the tarmac in a cotton shirt and corduroy jacket, wishing I had carried my sweater instead of packing it. A husky young fellow with red, wind-whipped cheeks and a shock of black hair followed close behind with the luggage. I picked up my canvas bag and set off in search of a night's lodgings. Thunder Bay boasted a Holiday Inn. That sounded good enough to me. They had plenty of vacancies. I booked a room for two nights.

They told me they would send a car along for me—their regular van was broken. I waited forty-five minutes inside the tiny terminal, drinking a cup of bitter coffee from a vending machine to entertain myself. When the limo finally came, it was a beat-up station wagon which I almost missed until it was rolling away. Then I could read THUNDER BAY HOLIDAY INN painted on its side. I went racing after it, yelling frantically, my canvas bag bumping me in the leg. I longed for the gigantic, impersonal efficiency of O'Hare with its ranks of surly, illiterate cab drivers.

The car stopped fifty feet ahead of me and waited while I came panting up to it. The driver was a heavyset man dressed in a graying white pullover. When he turned to look at me, a pungent draft of stale beer swept over me. The forty-five minutes I'd been waiting he must have spent in a bar. However, if I tried to get a cab I might be there all night. I told him to take me to the Holiday Inn and I leaned back in the seat with my eyes shut, grasping the side strap. It couldn't be any worse than riding with Lotty sober but the memory of my own accident was too fresh for me not to be nervous. We moved along at a good clip, ignoring honking horns.

It was well past eleven when my driver deposited me, intact, and I couldn't find any place in walking distance still open for dinner. The motel restaurant was closed and so was a little Mandarin place across the street. I finally took an apple from a basket in the lobby and went to bed hungry. My shoulder was sore and the long flight had worn me out. I slept soundly and woke up again after nine.

My shoulder had recovered in the night—most of the stiffness was gone. I dressed more easily than I had for days, only feeling a twinge when I pulled the heavy wool sweater over my head. Before going down to breakfast I reassembled the Smith & Wesson and loaded it. I didn't expect Bledsoe to jump me in front of the entire crew of the *Lucella Wieser,* but if he did the gun wasn't going to do me much good with the barrel unattached to the hammer.

I hadn't had much appetite while my shoulder was in pain and I'd dropped five or six pounds. This morning I felt better and sat down to pecan waffles, sausages, strawberries, and coffee.

I was a latecomer in the little restaurant and the middle-aged waitress had time to talk. As she poured my second cup of coffee I asked her where I could rent a car. There was an Avis place in town, she said, but one of her sons had a couple of old cars he rented out if I didn't need anything too fancy. I told her that would be fine as long as they had automatic transmissions, and she trotted off to call her son.

Roland Graham his name was, and he spoke with a Canadian accent, a lilting drawl that sounds as if it has a trace of Scots buried in it. His car was a '75 Ford Fairmont, old but perfectly clean and respectable. I told him I'd only need it until the next morning. The fee, payable in advance in cash, was thirty dollars.

The Holiday Inn was in the heart of town. Across the street was the largest Presbyterian church I've ever seen. A modern city hall faced the motel, but the street behind us had a lot of run-down stores and premises to let. As I got down to the waterfront the stores gave way rapidly to bars and girlie joints. I've often wondered whether seamen really have the primitive appetites port towns attribute to them, or whether they go to sleazy joints because that's the only thing the locals offer.

Finding the *Lucella* turned out to be a larger problem than I'd anticipated. Thunder Bay is an enormous port, even though the town itself doesn't have more than a hundred thousand people in it. But much of the grain shipped by water in North America passes through that port heading east and south, and the lakefront includes mile upon mile of towering elevators.

My first thought had been to stop in at each elevator to see if the *Lucella* was docked there, but the miles of towers made that seem like a waste of time. I did go into the yard of the first one I came to. After bumping around the mud-filled ruts, I found a tiny, green-sided office. But a harassed man inside handling the phone assured me that he didn't have the foggiest idea of where the *Lucella* was; he only knew she wasn't there.

I went back into the town and found the local newspaper. As I'd hoped, it listed the ships that were in port and where they were. The *Lucella* was docked at Elevator 67, the Manitoba Grain Co-op.

There didn't seem to be any logical order to the yard numbers. I was near number 11, but I went past yard 90 without seeing the Manitoba Grain Co-op and wasted time backtracking. I finally found it another two miles down the road, well past the town.

I turned the Ford into the gravel yard, my heart pounding with nervous anticipation. The Manitoba elevator was enormous, some two hundred giant paper towel tubes banked together. Huge though it was, it didn't dwarf the ship tied up on its eastern end. The *Lucella*'s red hulk gleamed sleekly in the late morning sun. Above her, like clouds covering and revealing Mount Everest, hovered a mass of white smoke. Grain dust. The *Lucella* was loading.

The yard was a mess of gravelly mud. In the corners of the elevator, out of the sun's reach, a gray-white residue of winter was still melting. I parked clear of the more obvious holes and picked my way through the mud, the metal shards, pasteboard, and grain clumps making up the now familiar elevator scene.

The Smith & Wesson dug uncomfortably into my side as I climbed the *Lucella*'s ladder to the main deck. I stopped for a minute at the edge of the hardhat area to survey the busy scene and ran a surreptitious finger under the leather holster digging into my diaphragm. Squinting at the whitened figures, I couldn't be sure if any of my quarry were present. I thought I might recognize Bledsoe's stocky body, but it was hard to say.

I went into the pilothouse and climbed the four flights to the mahogany-paneled bridge. Only the first mate, Keith Winstein, was there. He looked up in surprise when I came in. He recognized me at once.

"Miss Warshawski! What—is Captain Bemis expecting you?"

"I don't think so. Is he around? And what about the chief engineer and Martin Bledsoe?" It would be really annoying if Bledsoe had returned to Chicago.

"They're all in Thunder Bay this morning. Going to the bank, doing that kind of business. They won't be back until late afternoon. Not until right before we sail, I'm afraid."

"You're sailing today?" I sat down on one of the mahogany stools. "Your office said you'd be here through tomorrow."

"No, we made good time up from Detroit. Got here a day early. Time is money in this business, so we started loading last night at midnight. We'll finish around four and sail at five."

"Any idea where I can find Bledsoe or Sheridan?"

He shook his head regretfully. "Everyone keeps bank accounts in Thunder Bay because we're here so often. This is a good chance to catch up on personal affairs—I'll be taking off myself for a few hours as soon as the second mate gets back."

I rubbed my forehead in exasperation. "Where do you go from here?"

Winstein was getting a little irritated. "We take this load to St. Catharines, at the other side of the lakes. Why do you ask?"

"What's your route, I mean—do you stop any place along the way where I could get off?"

The first mate looked at me strangely. "If you're thinking of sailing with us, you'll have to clear that with the captain, Miss Warshawski."

"Yes, well, let's assume he's going to give his permission. Where's the nearest place I could get off?"

He shook his head. "There isn't any place on board for you to sleep—Mr. Bledsoe's in the stateroom."

I started to feel my temper rising. "I'm not asking for a place to sleep. That's why I want to get off at the nearest place possible."

"I guess that would be Sault Ste. Marie," he said dubiously. "You could get off when we're at the bottom of the lock. But we won't reach there until three tomorrow afternoon, at the earliest. You'd still have to find someplace to spend the night."

"Oh, never mind that," I said impatiently. "I'll lie down on the couch here in the bridge if I need to. But I've got to talk to the captain and Bledsoe. To Sheridan, too. And I'm damned if I'm going to fly around the country on the off chance of meeting up with them someplace."

"It isn't really my decision," Winstein said pacifically.

"You'll have to talk to Captain Bemis." He returned to his papers and I left the bridge.

16 ✳ Stowaway

I took the Fairmont back to the Holiday Inn, singing "A capital ship for an ocean trip" and "The Barbary Pirates." I repacked the little canvas bag and checked out, leaving a note for Roland Graham with the Ford's keys at the counter. It was one o'clock. If the *Lucella* wasn't sailing until five, I might as well get some lunch.

By the time I'd eaten and found a taxi to take me out to Elevator 67 it was after three-thirty. The midday sun made the air hot enough for me to take off my sweater and stuff it into my canvas bag before once more climbing the ladder to the *Lucella*'s main deck.

They had just finished loading. The heavy grain chutes were being hauled into the elevator from above. Under the second mate's direction, men began operating two little deck gantries to put the hatch covers back onto the hold openings. One man worked each crane, using controls in front of a small seat on the starboard side. He lifted the hatch cover while two seamen steadied it at either end—they are very large, unstable steel lids. Then he lowered the cover while the other two fitted it onto some twenty or thirty protruding bolts. The three would move along to the next cover while a fourth seaman followed behind with an enormous wrench, screwing all the bolts into place.

As I stood watching, I felt the ship begin to vibrate. The

engines had been turned on. Soon the air was filled with their urgent racket. A trail of black diesel smoke drifted upward from the giant funnel. I had no idea how long the engines ran before the ship moved out, but I noticed a couple of seamen at the guy ropes on shore, ready to loose them as soon as the signal was given. I hadn't come back a minute too early.

I felt very keyed up. I knew I was wasting time on deck when I should have been on the bridge confronting anyone who had returned, but I was very nervous and didn't know what to say once I got up there. In my heightened state I thought I saw someone swimming away from the port side of the ship. I moved as quickly as I could past the clutter around the self-unloader but didn't see anything. I stood straining my eyes against the reflecting water and finally saw a figure break the surface twenty yards away, close to the shore.

When I turned back, Bledsoe was just coming on board. He stopped to talk to the second mate, then headed for the bridge without seeing me. I was about to follow when it occurred to me I might be better off just stowing away and presenting myself after castoff. Accordingly, I moved to the back of the pilothouse where a stack of giant oil drums served as both garbage cans and an effective shield from the bridge. I sat down on a metal box, placed my bag against a coil of rope, and leaned back to enjoy the view.

I had momentarily forgotten the figure I'd seen, but now I noticed him—or her—walk out of the water some fifty yards away, on the other side of the elevator yard. A clump of trees soon hid the person from my sight. After that nothing happened for about forty-five minutes. Then the *Lucella* gave two deep hoots and slowly pulled away from the wharf.

Two gray-green troughs appeared at my feet, the wake of the giant screws, and the distance between the ship and the wharf widened quickly. Actually, the ship didn't seem to move; rather, the shore appeared to back away from us. I waited another ten minutes, until we were a good mile or two from land and no one would be disposed to turn around to send me back.

Leaving my bag amidst the coiled rope, I made my way up to the bridge. I loosened the gun in its holster and released the safety catch. For all I knew, I was going up to face one or more killers. A few crew members passed me on my way up. They gave me curious stares but didn't question my right to be there. My heart pounding, I opened the door to the bridge.

Up the flight of narrow wooden stairs. A murmur of voices at the top. I emerged into a busy scene—Winstein was going over charts at the drafting table. A burly, red-haired man with two inches of cigar in his mouth stood at the wheel taking directions from Captain Bemis. "Off the second port island," Bemis said. "Off the second port island," the helmsman repeated, turning the wheel slightly to his left.

Bledsoe stood behind, looking on. Neither he nor the captain turned when I came in, but Winstein looked up from the charts and saw me. "There she is," he said quietly.

The captain turned at that. "Ah, Miss Warshawski. The first mate said you'd turn up."

"Technically you're a stowaway, Vic." Bledsoe gave the glimmer of a smile. "We could lock you in the holds until we get to Sault Ste. Marie."

I sat down at the round table. Now that I was here my nervous tension receded; I felt calm and in charge. "I only have a rudimentary knowledge of maritime law. I gather the captain is complete master of the ship—that he evaluates any crimes committed under his jurisdiction and dispenses judgment, if any?"

Bemis looked at me seriously. "Technically, yes, as long as the ship is at sea. If some crime was committed on board, though, I'd probably just hang onto the person and turn him over to the regular judiciary at our next port of call."

He turned to Winstein and told him to take over the bridge for a few minutes. The first mate finished drawing a line on the chart and then got up to stand by the helmsman. We were going through a channel with a lot of little islands planted in it—humps of earth with one or two trees or a scraggly bush clinging to them. The sun glinted off the gray-green water. Behind us, Thunder Bay was still visible with its line of elevators.

Bledsoe and Bemis joined me at the table. "You're not supposed to come on board without the captain's permission." Bemis was serious but not angry. "You don't strike me as a frivolous person and I doubt you did it frivolously, but it's still a major breach of maritime custom. It's not a crime, per se, but I don't think that's what you were referring to, was it?"

"No. What I really wanted to know was this: suppose you have someone on board who committed a crime while he was on shore. You find out about it while you're at sea. What do you do with that person?"

"It would depend in part on what the crime was."

"Attempted murder."

Bledsoe's eyes narrowed. "I assume this isn't hypothetical, Vic. Do you think one of this crew tried killing someone? Who and why?"

I looked at him steadily. "I was the intended victim. I'm trying to find out for sure that someone here wasn't after me."

For a count of ten there was no sound in the small room but the faint throb of the engines. The helmsman kept his eyes in front of him, but his back twitched. Bemis's jaw set in an angry line.

"You'd better explain that one, Miss Warshawski."

"Gladly. Last Thursday night Martin Bledsoe here took me out for dinner. I left my car in the elevator yard. While we were gone someone cut through the steering controls with a cutting torch and emptied the brake fluid. It was a miracle that when my car crashed on the Dan Ryan I escaped with minor injuries. An innocent driver was killed, though, and one of his passengers is now paralyzed for life. That's murder, assault, and a lot of other ugly stuff."

Bledsoe gave an exclamation. "My God, Vic!" He fished around for something else to say but made several false starts before he could get a coherent thought out. I watched him carefully. Surprise is such an easy feeling to counterfeit. It looked genuine, but . . .

The captain looked at me with narrowed eyes. "You seem pretty cool about it."

"Would it be more believable if I lay down on the floor and screamed?"

Bemis made a gesture of annoyance. "I assume I could radio the Chicago police and get some verification of this."

I pointed to the radio on the port wall. "By all means. A Lieutenant Robert Mallory can tell you anything you want to know."

"Can you give us some more detail on what happened?" That was Bledsoe, finding his voice and his authoritative manner.

I obliged with as much of the accident as I could recall.

"Now what makes you think someone on the *Lucella* might be involved?"

"There's a limited universe of who could have done it," I explained. "Only a few people knew I was down there. Only a few could identify my car."

"How do you figure that?" That was the captain again. "There are a lot of vandals down at the Port and this frankly sounds like vandalism."

"Captain, I don't know what your exposure to vandals is, but I see a lot of them. I don't know of any vandal who goes around with a cutting torch and a ratchet wrench to disable cars. It's a lengthy procedure with a very high risk of getting caught, and there's no point to it. Especially in a place like a grain elevator, which is hard to get to."

Bemis's brow creased. "You think just because the *Lucella* was tied up there we're implicated somehow?"

"You people and Clayton Phillips are the only ones who knew I was down there . . . Captain, I'm certain that my cousin was pushed overboard last month—or underboard, to be literal about it. And I know someone else was killed in connection with my cousin's affairs. The way I see it, the killer is either connected with this ship or with Eudora Grain. Now you've got a big machine shop here. I'm sure you have a couple of cutting torches lying around—"

"No!" Bemis exploded. "No way in hell is Mike Sheridan involved in this."

"How long have you known him?"

"Twenty years. At least twenty years. We've been sailing together a long time. I know that man better than I know—my wife. I see more of him."

"Besides," Bledsoe put in, "there's no reason for Mike—or any of us—to want to kill you."

I rubbed my forehead tiredly. "Ah, yes. The reason. That's the real stumper. If I knew what my cousin had found out I'd know who did the murders. I thought it had something to do with those grain shipment orders, Martin, but you assured me they were perfectly legitimate. But what if it had something to do with the vandalism to your cargo holds? You told me that was what Boom Boom called you about."

"Yes but, Vic, we all need this ship operating to make a living. Why would we put it out of commission?"

"Yes, well, something occurred to me about that, too." I looked at my hands, then at Bledsoe. "What if someone were blackmailing you—something along the lines of 'I'll tell your secret history if you don't give up that load.' "

Bledsoe's face turned white under his windburn. "How dare you!"

"How dare I what? Suggest such a thing—or bring up your past?"

"Either." He smashed the table with his fist. "If I had such a past, such a secret, who told it to you?"

Bemis turned to Bledsoe in surprise. "Martin—what are you talking about? Do you have a mad wife stashed away in Cleveland that I never heard of?"

Bledsoe recovered himself. "You'll have to ask Warshawski here. She's telling the story."

Up to that point I hadn't been sure whether Grafalk had told the truth. But he must have to get that reaction. I shook my head.

"It's just a hypothesis, Captain. And if there is something in Bledsoe's past—why, he's kept it to himself long enough. I don't think it would be very interesting to anyone else these days."

"You don't?" Bledsoe pounced on that. "Then why would anyone blackmail me to keep it quiet?"

"Oh, *I* don't think it's very interesting. But *you* clearly do. Your reaction just now clinches it. What set me wondering was why you smashed a wineglass just because Grafalk made a crack that day about where you went to school."

"I see." Bledsoe gave a short laugh. "You're not so dumb, are you?"

"I get by . . . I'd like to ask you one question in private, however."

Bemis stood up politely. "I ought to look at the course, anyway. . . . By the way, Martin's occupying our only guest room. We'll put a cot up for you in my dining room."

I thanked him. Bledsoe looked at me speculatively. I leaned forward and said in a low voice, "I want to know that you didn't get Sheridan to doctor my car while we were at dinner that night." I saw a pulse start to move in his jaw. "Believe me, I hate to ask it. I hate even to think it. But that was a pretty horrifying experience—it shook my trust in human nature."

Bledsoe pushed back his chair with enough force to knock it over. "Go ask him yourself! I'm fucked if I'll put up with any more of this."

He stormed down the stairs and the bridge echoed with the vibration of the slammed door. Bemis looked at me coldly, "I'm running a ship, Miss Warshawski, not a soap opera."

I felt a violent surge of anger. "Are you, now? I've had a cousin killed and someone's tried to kill me. Until I'm sure your ship and crew didn't do it, you'll damned well live in my soap opera and like it."

Bemis left the helm and came over to lean across the table into my face. "I don't blame you for being upset. You lost a cousin. You've been badly hurt. But I think you're blowing up a couple of very sad accidents into a conspiracy and I won't have you disrupting my ship while you do it."

My temples pounded. I kept just enough control not to offer any grandiose threats. "Very well," I said tightly, my vocal cords straining, "I won't disrupt your ship. I would like to talk to the chief engineer while I am on board, however.''

Bemis jerked his head at Winstein. ''Get the lady a hard hat, Mate.'' He turned back to me. ''You may question the chief. However, I don't want you talking to the crew unless either the first mate or I am present. He'll instruct the second mate to make sure that happens.''

''Thanks,'' I said stiffly. While I waited for Winstein to being me a hard hat, I stared moodily out the rear of the bridge. The sun was setting now and the shoreline showed as a distant wedge of purple in front of it. To the port side I could see a few chunks of ice. Winter lasted a long time in these parts.

I was doing a really swell job. So far I didn't know a damned thing I hadn't known three weeks ago, except how to load a Great Lakes freighter full of grain. In my mind's ear I could hear my mother chewing me out for self-pity. ''Anything but that, Victoria. Better for you to break the dishes than lie about feeling sorry for yourself.'' She was right. I was just worn out from the aftermath of my accident. But that, in Gabriella's eyes, was the reason, not the excuse—there was no excuse for sitting around sulking.

I pulled myself together. The first mate was waiting to escort me from the bridge. We walked down the narrow staircase, me following on his heels. He gave me a hard hat with his name on the front in faded black type; he explained that it was his spare and I was welcome to it as long as I was on board.

''If you're thinking of going down to talk to the chief now, why not wait until dinner? The chief eats dinner in the captain's dining room and you can talk to him there. You won't be able to hear each other over the engines, anyway.''

I looked at him grudgingly, wondering if he was deflecting me from Sheridan long enough to let Bledsoe tell him his version of the story.

''Where's the captain's dining room?'' I asked.

Winstein took me there, a small, formal room on the starboard side of the main deck. Flowered curtains hung at the portholes and an enormous photo of the *Lucella*'s launching decorated the forward wall. The crew's mess was next door to it. The same galley served both, but the captain was waited on at table by the cooks whereas the crew served themselves cafeteria style. The cooks would serve dinner between five-thirty and seven-thirty, Winstein told me. I could get breakfast there between six and eight in the morning.

Winstein left me to go back to the bridge. I waited until he was out of sight and then descended into the engine room. I vaguely remembered my way from the previous visit, going through a utility room with a washer and dryer in it, then climbing down a flight of linoleum-covered stairs to the engine-room entrance.

Winstein was right about the noise. It was appalling. It filled every inch of my body and left my teeth shaking. A young man in greasy overalls was in the control booth that made up the entrance to the engines. I roared at him over the noise; after several tries he understood my query and told me I would find the chief engineer on level two inspecting the port journal bearings. Apparently only an idiot would not know about port journal bearings. Declining further assistance, I swung myself down a metal ladder to the level below.

The engines take up a good amount of space and I wandered around quite a bit before I saw anyone. I finally spotted a couple of hard-hatted figures behind a mass of pipes and made my way over to them. One was the chief engineer, Sheridan. The other was a young fellow whom I hadn't seen before. I didn't know whether to be pleased or disappointed not to find Bledsoe with Sheridan—it would have given a more solid direction to my inchoate searching to see them in cahoots.

The chief and the other man were totally absorbed in their inspection of a valve in a pipe running at eye level in front of them. They didn't turn when I came up but continued their work.

The younger man unscrewed the bottom part of a pipe which came up from the floor at right angles to the overhead valve and then joined it. He stuck a stainless steel tube into the opening, checked his watch, and pulled the tube out again. It was covered with oil, which seemed to satisfy both of them. They tightened up the pipes again and wiped their hands on their grimy boiler suits.

At that point they realized I was there, or perhaps just realized I wasn't a regular member of the team. Sheridan put his hands to my head to bellow an inquiry at me. I bellowed back at him. It was obvious that no one could conduct a conversation over the roar of the engines. I yelled in his ear that I would talk to him at dinner; I wasn't sure he heard me but I turned and climbed back up onto the main deck.

Once outside I breathed in the late afternoon air thankfully. We were well away from the shore and it was quite cold. I remembered my bag resting among the coils of rope behind the pilothouse and went back there to take out my heavy sweater and put it on. I dug out a tam and pulled it down over my ears.

The engines clattered at my feet, less loudly but still noticeably. Turbulent water lifted the stern periodically, giving the *Lucella* a choppy, lurching ride.

In search of quiet I walked down to the bow. No one else was outside. As I walked the length of the ship, nearly a quarter mile, the noise gradually abated. By the time I reached the stem, the frontmost tip of the vessel, I couldn't hear a sound except the water breaking against the bow. The sun setting behind us cast a long shadow of the bridge onto the deck.

No guardrail separated the deck from the water. Two thick parallel cables, about two feet apart, were strung around the edge of the ship, attached to poles protruding every six feet or so. It would be quite easy to slip between them into the water.

A little bench had been screwed into the stem. You could sit on it and lean against a small toolshed and look into the water. The surface was greeny black, but where the ship cut through it the water turned over in a sheen of colors from lavender-white to blue-green to green to black—like dropping black ink onto wet paper and watching it separate into its individual hues.

A change in the light behind me made me brace myself. I reached for the Smith & Wesson as Bledsoe came up beside me.

"It would be easy to push you in, you know, and claim that you fell."

"Is that a threat or an observation?" I pulled the gun out and released the safety.

He looked startled. "Put that damned thing away. I came out here to talk to you."

I put the safety on and returned the gun to its holster. It wouldn't do me much good at close quarters, anyway—I'd brought it out mainly for show.

Bledsoe was wearing a thick tweed jacket over a pale blue cashmere sweater. He looked nautical and comfortable. I was feeling the chill in my left shoulder—it had started to ache as I sat staring into the water.

"I blow up too fast," he said abruptly. "But you don't need a gun to keep me at bay, for Christ's sake."

"Fine." I kept my feet braced, ready to spring to one side.

"Don't make things so fucking difficult," he snapped.

I didn't move, but I didn't relax either. He debated some point with himself—to stomp off offended or say what was on his mind. The second party won.

"It was Grafalk who told you about my youthful misadventure?"

"Yes."

He nodded to himself. "I don't think there's another person who knows—or still cares . . . I was eighteen years old. I'd grown up in a waterfront slum. When he pulled me into the Cleveland office I ended up handling a lot of cash transactions. His mistake—he should never have put anyone that age in front of so much money. I didn't steal it. That is, of course I stole it. What I mean is, I wasn't thinking of stashing away loot and escaping to Argentina. I just wanted to live in a grand style. I bought myself a car." He smiled reminiscently. "A red Packard roadster. Cars were hard to get in those days, right after the war, and I thought I was the slickest thing on the waterfront."

The smile left his face. "Anyway, I was young and foolish and I spent the stuff blatantly, begging to be caught, really. Niels saw me through it, rehired me right out of Cantonville. He never mentioned it in twenty years. But he took it very personally when I set up Pole Star back in '74. And he started throwing it in my face—that he knew I was a criminal at heart, that I'd stayed with him just to learn the secrets of his organization and then left."

"Why did you leave?"

"I'd wanted to run my own show for years. My wife was sick, had Hodgkins disease, and we never had any children. I guess I turned all my energy to shipping. Besides, after Niels refused to build any thousand-footers, I wanted to have a ship like this one." He patted the guy ropes affectionately. "This is a beautiful ship. It took four years to build. Took me three years to put the financing together. But it's worth it. These things run at about a third the cost of the old five-hundred-footers. The cargo space goes up almost as the square of the length—I can carry seven times the load of a five-hundred-foot vessel . . . Anyway, I wanted one very badly and I had to start my own company to get it."

How badly? I wondered to myself. Badly enough to run a more sophisticated scam than he'd thought of thirty years ago and come up with the necessary capital? "What does a ship like this cost to build?"

"The *Lucella* ran just a hair under fifty million."

"You float stock or bonds or what?"

"We did some of everything. Sheridan and Bemis coughed up their savings. I put mine in. The Fort Dearborn Trust owns the biggest chunk of this and we finally got them to arrange a series of loans with about ten other banks. Other people put in personal money. It's a tremendous investment, and I want to make sure it carries a cargo every day between March 28 and January 1 so we can pay off the debt."

He sat down next to me on the small bench and looked at me, his gray eyes probing. "But that isn't what I came out here to say to you. I want to know why Niels brought up the story of my past. Not even Bemis and Sheridan know it, and if the tale had gotten around three years ago, I could never have built this beauty. If Niels wanted to hurt me, he could have done it then. So why did he tell you now?"

It was a good question. I stared into the churning water, trying to recall my conversation with Grafalk. Maybe he wanted to ventilate some of his pent-up bitterness against Bledsoe. It couldn't have been from a desire to protect Phllips—he'd raised questions about Phillips too.

"What do you know about the relationship between Grafalk and Clayton Phillips."

"Phillips? Not much. Niels took him up as a protégé about the time I started Pole Star—a year or two later, maybe. Since he and I didn't part too amicably, I didn't see much of him. I don't know what the deal was. Niels likes to patronize young men—I was probably the first one and he took up a number of others over the years." He wrinkled his forehead. "Usually they seemed to have better abilities than Phillips. I don't know how he manages to keep that office in the black."

I looked at him intently. "What do you mean?"

Bledsoe shrugged. "He's too—too finicky. Not the right word. He's got brains but he gets in their way all the time. He has sales reps who are supposed to handle all the shipping contracts but he can't leave 'em to it. He's always getting involved in the negotiations. Since he doesn't have day-to-day knowledge of the markets, he often screws up good deals and saddles Eudora with expensive contracts. I noticed that when I was Niels's dispatcher ten years ago and I see it now with my own business."

That didn't sound criminal, just stupid. I said as much and Bledsoe laughed. "You looking for a crime just to drum up business or what?"

"I don't need to drum up business. I've plenty in Chicago to occupy me if I ever get this mess unsnarled." I got up. Stowing away on the *Lucella* had been one of my stupider ideas. None of them would tell me anything and I didn't know how to sort out natural loyalty to the ship and each other from concealing a crime. "But I'll find out." I spoke aloud without realizing it.

"Vic, don't be so angry. No one on this ship tried to kill

you. I'm not convinced anyone tried to kill you.'' He held up a hand as I started to talk. "I know your car was vandalized. But it was probably done by a couple of punks who never saw you in their life.''

I shook my head, tired. "There are too many coincidences, Martin. I just can't believe that Boom Boom and the watchman in his building died and I was almost killed through a series of unrelated events. I can't believe it. And I start wondering why you and the captain want me to believe it so badly.''

He stuck his hands in his pockets and whistled silently. "Why don't you step me through your logic? I'm not saying I'll buy it. But give me a chance.''

I drew a breath. If he was responsible, he knew all about it anyway. If he wasn't, there wasn't any harm in his knowing. I explained about Boom Boom's death, the quarrel with Phillips, the search through my cousin's apartment, Henry Kelvin's death.

"There's got to be a reason for it and the reason is at the Port. It has to be. You told me those shipping orders I showed you last week seemed perfectly legitimate. So I don't know where else to look. If Phillips was deliberately fudging the contracts and running Eudora Grain's Chicago office at a loss, that'd be a reason. Although I think Argus would have been on his tail for that a long time ago, especially if he's been doing it for ten years.'' I pushed back the tam and rubbed my forehead. "I was hoping it would be those shipping orders, since that's what Boom Boom was arguing over with Phillips two days before he died.''

Bledsoe looked at me seriously. "If you really want to be certain, you'll have to look at the invoices. The contracts themselves appear fine, but you want to see what Phillips actually paid for the orders. How much do you know about the way an office like that operates?''

I shook my head. "Not much.''

"Well, Phillips's main job is to act as the controller. He should leave the sales to his salesmen but doesn't. He handles all the financial stuff. Now it's his job, too, to know prices and what the market is doing so that when he pays bills he can check on his reps to make sure they're getting the best prices. But he's supposed to stay out of the selling end. He handles the money."

I narrowed my eyes. A man who handled all the money bore further investigation. Trouble was, everything in this damned case bore further investigation and I wasn't getting anywhere. I massaged my stiffening shoulder, trying to push my frustration away.

Bledsoe was still speaking; I'd missed some of it.

"You getting off in Sault Ste. Marie? I'll fly you down to Chicago—my plane is there and I'm planning on going back to the office this week."

We got up together and started back down the long deck. The sun had set and the sky was turning from purple to gray-black. Overhead, the first stars were coming out, pricks of light in the dusky curtain. I'd have to come back out when it was completely dark. In the city one doesn't see too many stars.

17 * Deadlock

Bledsoe and I joined the chief engineer in the captain's dining room, where he was eating roast beef and mashed potatoes. Bemis was still up on the bridge—Bledsoe explained that the captain would stay up there until the ship was out of a tricky channel and well into the middle of Lake Superior. We three were the only ones in the dining room—the other officers ate with the crew. Handwritten menus at our plates offered a choice of two entrees, vegetables, and dessert.

Over baked chicken and broccoli I talked to Sheridan about my accident.

The chief agreed that he had cutting torches of different sizes on board, as well as every possible variety of wrench. "But if you're asking me to tell you if any of them were used last Thursday, I couldn't. We don't keep the tools under lock and key—it'd be too time-consuming to get at them." He buttered a roll and ate a chunk of it. "We have eight people on engine-room duty when the ship's at sea and all of them need to get at the tools. We've never had any problems and as long as we don't I plan to keep free access to them."

No liquor was allowed on the ship, so I was drinking coffee with dinner. The coffee was thin and I poured a lot of cream into it to give it some flavor.

"Could someone have come onto the ship, taken some tools, and brought them back without anyone noticing?"

Sheridan thought about it. "I suppose so," he said reluctantly. "This isn't like the navy where someone is always on watch. No one has to stay on board when we're in port, and people come and go without anyone paying attention. Theoretically someone could go to the engine room without being caught, assuming he knew where the tools were. He'd have to be lucky, too, and not have anyone come on him by surprise . . . At any rate, I'd rather believe that than that one of my own men was involved."

"Could one of your own men have done it?"

Again, it was possible, but why? I suggested that someone—perhaps Phillips, for example—had hired one of the crew to do his dirty work. Bledsoe and Sheridan discussed that energetically. They were both convinced that they'd gotten rid of their lone bad apple when they fired the man who put water in the holds last month.

Sheridan felt great confidence in the men under him. "I know my judgment could be wrong, but I can't imagine any one of those guys deliberately sabotaging somebody's car."

We went on talking long after one of the junior cooks had cleared away the table and cleaned up the galley. Finally the chief engineer excused himself to go back to the engine room. He said I could question the other engineers and the four boilermen, but he didn't think it would do me any good.

As he walked through the doorway, I said casually, "Were you in the engine room that night?"

He turned and looked me straight in the eye. "Yes, I was. And Yalmouth—my first engineer—was with me. We were going over the hydraulics preparatory to starting up the engines the next day."

"Not out of each other's sight all evening?"

"Not long enough to monkey with a car."

He went on out the door. Bledsoe said, "Satisfied, Vic? Is Pole Star clean in your eyes?"

I shrugged in irritation. "I suppose so. Short of launching a full-scale investigation into everyone's movements last Thursday night there's not much else I can do to check up on you guys." Something occurred to me. "You had a security force on board that night, didn't you? Maybe Bemis can give me their names—they'd know if anyone had been climbing around with tools." My villain might have persuaded a guard that he belonged on board: that probably wouldn't be too difficult. But a guard would surely remember someone leaving the ship with a blowtorch and a ratchet wrench. Of course, if Bledsoe was behind the whole business, he might have paid off the guards, anyway.

I drank some cold coffee, looking at Bledsoe over the rim of the cup. "The whole thing turns on money, lots of money. It's in the Eudora Grain contracts, but that's not the only place."

"True," Bledsoe agreed. "There's also a great deal in the freighter business itself, and there's the amount I had to raise to pay for the *Lucella*. Maybe I embezzled it from Niels to pay for my flagship just before I left Grafalk Steamship."

"Yes, and if he suspected that but couldn't prove it, he might want to alert me to the possibility."

Bledsoe smiled genially. "I can see that. You should definitely look into my finances as well as Phillips's. I'll tell my secretary to give you access to my files when we get back to Chicago."

I thanked him politely. All that offer meant was, if he had something to hide, he had it concealed someplace other than in Pole Star's books.

We spent the rest of the evening talking about opera. They'd had a collection of librettos in the Cantonville prison library and he'd read all of them. After he got out of prison he started attending the Cleveland Opera.

"Now I fly to New York five, six times a year for the Met and get season tickets to the Lyric . . . It gives me a queer feeling to talk about Cantonville with someone. My wife was the only person who knew about it—except Niels, of course. And neither of them ever mentioned it. It makes me feel almost guilty when I bring it up now."

Around ten-thirty, two of the crew members came in with a cot and some blankets. They set the narrow bed up under the portholes in the starboard wall, bracing it to the side so it wouldn't slide around with the rocking of the ship.

After they left, Bledsoe stood fiddling the change in his pockets with the awkwardness of a man who wants to make a pass but isn't sure how it will be received. I didn't try to help him out. I liked the way he kissed. But I'm not the kind of detective who hops nonchalantly from bed to bed: if someone's been trying to kill me, it cools my enthusiasm. And I still didn't have total trust in Bledsoe's purity.

"Time for me to turn in," I said briskly. "I'll see you in the morning."

He hesitated for a few seconds longer, scanning my face for encouragement, then turned and went upstairs to the stateroom. I put the Smith & Wesson under the little pillow and climbed under the blankets in my jeans and shirt. Despite the noise of the engines and the lurching of the ship, I went to sleep almost immediately and slept soundly through the night.

The cooks woke me the next morning before six as they started clattering around in the galley next to the captain's dining room. I tried pulling the bedding up over my ears but the disturbance was too persistent. Finally I got up and stumbled up to the next floor where the bathroom was. I changed my underwear and shirt and brushed my teeth.

It was too early for me to feel like eating, even though breakfast was ready, so I went out on deck to look at the day. The sun had just come up, a ball of liquid orange low in the eastern sky. A purple shoreline lay a mile or so to our left. We were going past some more of the small clumps of islands which had dotted the channel as we left Thunder Bay.

At breakfast Captain Bemis, the chief engineer, and Bledsoe were all in affable moods. Perhaps the fact I was leaving soon cheered them up. At any rate, even the captain was gracious, explaining our course to me. We were coming down the southeast coast of Lake Superior leading into the St. Mary's Channel. "This is where the *Edmund Fitzgerald* went down in 1975," he said. "It's the best approach to the St. Mary's, but it's still a very shallow route, only thirty feet deep in places."

"What happened to the *Edmund Fitzgerald*?"

"Everyone has his own theory. I don't suppose they'll ever know for certain. When they dove down to look at her, they found she'd been cut neatly in three pieces. Sank immediately. I've always blamed the Coast Guard for not keeping the channel markings in proper order. The waves were thirty feet high out here that night—one of them must have pushed the *Fitzgerald* into a trough and caused her to scrape against the bottom and snap. If they'd marked the channel properly, Captain McSorley would have avoided the shallowest spots."

"The thing is," the chief engineer added, "these lakers don't have much support through the middle. They're floating cargo holds. If they put a lot of beams through the holds they'd take up too much valuable cargo space. So you get these twenty- or thirty-foot waves out here, and they pick up a ship like this on either end. The middle doesn't have any support and it just snaps. You go down very quickly."

The head cook, a thick Polish woman in her mid-fifties, was pouring the captain's coffee. As the chief spoke, she dropped the cup on the floor. "You should not talk like that, Chief Engineer. It is very bad luck." She called to her underlings to come in and clean up the mess.

Sheridan shrugged. "It's all the men do talk about when there's a storm brewing. Ship disasters are like cancer—the other guy is always the one who's going to get it, anyway." All the same, he apologized to the cook and changed the subject.

Bemis told me we'd be getting into the Soo locks around three o'clock. He suggested that I watch from the bridge so I could see the approach and the way the ship was steered into the channel. After lunch I packed up my little canvas bag for a quick departure: Bledsoe told me we'd have about two minutes to climb over the side of the *Lucella* onto shore before they opened the lock gates and she went on through to Lake Huron.

I checked that my credit cards and cash were in my front jeans pocket and put the Smith & Wesson into the bag. There didn't seem much point in lugging it around in the shoulder holster while I was on board. I stowed the bag next to the pilothouse while I went up on the bridge to watch the *Lucella* slide into the lock. We were now well into the channel of the St. Mary's River, following a slow-moving procession.

"Your position into the locks is determined by your position when you arrive at the mouth of the channel," Bemis explained. "So there's a lot of racing to get into the channel first. We passed a couple of five-hundred-footers earlier this morning. I can't stand tying up here—enforced boredom and everyone gets restless."

"It's expensive to tie up," Bledsoe said sharply. "This ship costs ten thousand dollars a day to operate. She has to make every second count."

I raised my eyebrows, trying to calculate costs in my head. Bledsoe looked at me angrily. "Yes, it's another financial motive, Vic."

I shrugged and walked over to where the helmsman, Red, was turning the wheel. Two inches of cigar stuck out of his pudgy face. He steered off various landmarks without glancing at the tiller. The huge ship moved easily under his hands.

As we drew nearer to the locks, the U. S. Coast Guard

started talking to Bemis on the radio. The captain gave them his ship's name, length, and weight. Of the four locks closing the twenty-four-foot drop between Lake Superior and Lake Huron, only the Poe was big enough to handle the thousand-foot freighters. We would be the second ship into the Poe, following an upbound vessel.

Bemis slowed the diesels to their lowest possible speed. He called down to the engine room and ordered them to put the engines into neutral. Behind us I could see three or four other freighters sitting in the channel. Those farther back tied up at the bank while they waited.

Below us the deck stretched magnificently away. We watched the first mate, Winstein, talking with a group of seamen who would climb down ladders to the sides of the lock and tie up the ship. Theirs was a demanding job physically—they had to keep up tension on the cables as the ship sank and the ropes became slack. Then, just before the gates opened into Lake Huron they would untie the ropes and leap back on board.

We waited about half a mile from the locks themselves. The sun glinted off the water and dressed up the dingy skylines of the twin cities. Canada's Sault Ste. Marie lay to our left, dominated by the giant Algoma Steelworks on the shoreline. In fact, coming up to our current resting place, the captain had steered using different parts of the Algoma plant—off the second smokestack, off the first coal heap, and so on.

After a forty-minute wait the Coast Guard told Bemis he could proceed. As the engines increased their revolutions slightly, a giant freighter passed us upbound, giving one long hoot on its whistle. Bemis pushed a button and the *Lucella* responded with an equally long blast and began to move forward. A few minutes later we were nosing into the lock.

The Poe Lock is only 110 feet wide; the *Lucella*, 105. That gave Red two and a half feet on either side—not much room for error. Slowly we glided forward, bisecting the distance and coming to a halt about twenty feet from the southern gate. Red never once looked at the wheel.

The gates were mammoth wooden structures reinforced with thick steel struts. I turned to watch them swing shut behind us, guided electrically from the bank.

As soon as the gates closed, our crew lowered ladders and scrambled down to the bank. I thanked Bemis for the use of his ship and the chance to talk to some of his crew and turned to go with Bledsoe down to the deck.

Most of the crew came on deck for the passage through the Soo. I shook hands with the head cook, Anna, thanking her in my few words of stumbling Polish for her cooking. Delighted, she unleashed a torrent of smiling Polish on me, which I ducked from as gracefully as I could.

It only takes about fifteen minutes for the lock to empty its two million-plus gallons of water into Lake Huron. We sank rapidly while the men alongside us tightened the cables. As soon as the *Lucella* was level with the lock, Bledsoe and I would hop across the two-foot gap to land. We'd have about thirty seconds before the forward gates opened.

An observation tower on the American side allows tourists to watch the ships as they rise and fall between the two lakes. The May day was still quite chilly and few people were out. I looked at them idly across the intervening MacArthur Lock and then squinted a second time at a man on the lower level. He had a thatch of bright red hair unusual for an adult. The hair reminded me of someone, but I couldn't place him, especially not at a distance of thirty or forty yards. As I peered across the water, he picked up an outsize set of binoculars and focused on us. I shrugged and looked down through the gap between the side of the *Lucella* and the side of the lock where the fetid water was rushing away. The deck was almost level now with the top of the lock. Bledsoe touched me on the arm and I walked back toward the pilothouse to pick up my bag.

I was almost there when I was thrown to the ground. I landed with a thud on the deck, the wind knocked out of me. I thought at first I'd been hit and looked around defensively as I gasped for breath. But when I tried to stand up, I realized the deck was shuddering underneath me. Almost every-

one else had been flung from their feet as well by some
gigantic shock.

The head cook was teetering at the edge of the rocking
ship, groping for the steel cables. I wanted to go to her to
help, but the deck was too unstable; I tried to move to her
and was thrown to the ground again. I watched in horror as
she lost her balance and fell over the side. Her screams were
drowned in a roaring that blocked out all other sound.

We were rising again. We didn't have the buoyancy of a
ship in water, but rocked as if balanced on the air itself.
Sheridan's comment at breakfast came back to me: the *Fitzgerald* being held in the air and snapped in two. I didn't understand what was happening, why we were rising, why
there was no water pushing us up, but I felt vilely sick.

Bledsoe was standing near me, his face gray. I clung to
the self-unloader for support and pulled myself up for the
second time. The crew were crawling away from the open
sides of the ship toward the pilot house, but we could not
help one another. The ship was too unstable.

As we rose, sheets of water rushed up like giant geysers
between the sides of the ship and the lock. They towered
skyward in a thick curtain cutting us off from the land, and
then from the sky. A hundred feet above us the water rushed
before falling in a pounding torrent onto the deck, knocking
me over again, knocking everyone over. I could hear some
of the men near me screaming.

I peered stupidly at the curtain of water, trying to see
through it to the men at the sides with their cables. They
couldn't be holding them, couldn't be restraining the ship as
she rose lurchingly upward, lashing forward and backward
in her concrete confines.

Holding the self-unloader, I struggled to my knees. A
wall of water was pounding the forward gate, ripping panels
from it. Great logs spewed into the air and disappeared
through the sheets of water which still rose on either side of
the ship.

I wanted to shut my eyes, shut out the disaster, but I
couldn't stop staring, horror-stricken. It was like watching
through a marijuana high. Pieces of the lock broke off in

slow motion. I could see each one, each separate fragment, each drop of water spraying loose, knowing all the time that the scene was moving very quickly.

Just when it seemed that nothing could keep us from diving forward and smashing against the rocks in the rapids below us, a great cry sounded above the roaring, the cry of a million women weeping in anguish, an unearthly screaming. The deck cracked in front of me.

People were trying to shout at each other to hold on, but no one could be heard over those screams as the beams wrenched and tore and the ship broke in two. The geysers of water rising above us shut off abruptly. We fell again into the lock, falling forward and down at a great jolting speed, ramming the forward gates and the bottom with a bone-jarring impact. A hatch cover popped free and knocked over one of the crewmen. Wet barley poured out, covering everyone in the middle of the ship with pale gold mud. The deck slanted sharply down toward the crack and I grabbed the self-unloader to keep from being hurled into the center. The broken giant lay still.

18 ∗ The Long Journey Home

The air was blessedly quiet following the roar of the explosion and the screams of the ship; all other sounds carried through it. People were yelling, both on the *Lucella* and on land. In the distance we could hear sirens beginning to wail.

Every few seconds another piece of the deck broke and clattered down the inclined plane toward the gash in the middle.

My legs were shaking. I let go of the self-unloader's side and massaged the aching muscles in my left shoulder. Bledsoe still stood next to me, his eyes glassy, his face gray. I wanted to say something to him, but no words came. An explosion. Someone blew up a sixty-thousand-ton ship. Sixty thousand tons. Sixty thousand tons. The words beat meaninglessly in my brain.

The deck swam up and down in front of me; I thought it was starting to rise again. My trembling legs buckled and I collapsed. I fainted for a few seconds only, but lay on the deck until the swimming in my head passed, then forced myself to my feet. Bledsoe was still standing near me.

I saw Captain Bemis stagger from the entrance to the pilothouse. Red, the helmsman, followed, the two-inch cigar stub still poking out of his face. He walked heavily to the port side of the ship. I could hear him retching behind me.

"Martin. Our ship. Our ship. What happened?" That was Bemis.

"Someone planted explosives on your hull, Captain." The words came from far away. Bemis was looking at me strangely: I realized it was I who was talking.

He shook his head, a jack-in-the-box on a spring; he couldn't stop shaking it. "No. Not my ship. It must have been in the lock."

"Couldn't have been." I started to argue with him but my brain felt flaccid. I wanted to sleep. Disjointed images floated in the gray mist of my mind. The geysers of water towering over the ship. The water changing color as the *Lucella* cut through it. The troughs of water dug by the screws as we left Thunder Bay. A dark figure in a wet suit climbing out of the water.

The figure in the wet suit. That meant something. I forced myself to focus on it. That was the person who planted the charges. It was done yesterday. In Thunder Bay.

I opened my mouth to blurt it out, then swallowed the words. No one was in any state to deal with such news.

Keith Winstein made his way over to us. His face was

streaked with tears and mud. "Karpansky and Bittenberg. They're both—both dead, sir. They were down on the bank with the cables. They must've—must've been—smashed into the side." He gulped and shuddered.

"Who else?" Bemis demanded.

"Anna. She fell over the side. She—she was crushed. She never had a chance. Vergil fell into the hold. Oh, Jesus! He fell into the hold and suffocated in the barley." He started laughing and crying wildly. "Drowned in barley. Oh, Christ!" he screamed. "Drowned in barley."

Focus and energy returned to the captain's face. He straightened and took Winstein by the shoulders, shaking him hard. "Listen, Mate. The ones left are still your responsibility. Get them together. See who needs medical care. Radio the Coast Guard for a helicopter."

The first mate nodded. He stopped sobbing, gave a few last shuddering breaths, and turned to the dazed crew.

"Martin needs some help too," I said. "Can you get him to sit down?" I needed to get away from the crowd on the deck. Somewhere, just out of reach in my mind, important information hovered. If I could just get away, stay awake, force myself into focus . . . I started back toward the pilot-house.

On my way I passed the chief engineer. He was covered with mud and oil. He looked like a miner emerging from three weeks in the pit. His blue eyes stared with horror through his mask of black.

"Where's the captain?" he asked me hoarsely.

"On deck. How are things below?"

"We've got a man with a broken leg. That's the only injury, thank God. But there's water everywhere. Port engine is gone. . . . It was a bomb, you know. Depth charges. Must have been planted right on the center beam. Set off by radio signal. But why?"

I shook my head, helplessly, but his words jarred my mind loose. If it was set off by remote signal, it was done by someone along the bank. In the observation deck. The man with bright red hair and a pair of binoculars. Howard Mattingly, the second-string hockey player had hair like that.

Boom Boom saw him someplace he shouldn't be three weeks ago. Now here he was at the observation deck with binoculars when the *Lucella* blew up.

I forgot the ache in my left shoulder. I needed to find Mattingly. Now. Before he got away. I turned abruptly in front of Sheridan and moved back out on deck. My gun. I wasn't going to tackle Mattingly without the Smith & Wesson. I went back to where I'd left it, to where Bledsoe and the captain were standing.

The bag was gone. I hunted for a few minutes, but I knew it was useless. Two shirts, a sweater, a pair of jeans, and a three-hundred-dollar Smith & Wesson were all lying with Vergil in fifty thousand tons of barley.

"I'm going," I said to the captain. "I've got an idea I need to follow up. Better get one of your junior cooks to get him some hot tea with lots of sugar. He's not doing too well." I cocked my thumb in Bledsoe's direction. I didn't wait for Bemis's response but turned to go.

It wasn't difficult getting off the *Lucella*. She was resting at the bottom of the lock, her deck even with the bank. Clinging to the cables around the side, I swung easily across the two feet between her upraised stern and the side of the lock. As I picked my way up the narrow strip of land separating me from the MacArthur Lock, I passed an emergency crew coming from the Coast Guard and the Army Corps of Engineers. Men in green fatigues, medics, a stretcher crew—a solemn procession befitting a major disaster. Bringing up the rear, of course, was a television news team. They were the only ones who took any notice of me. One of them stuck a microphone under my nose and asked whether I was coming from the ship and what I knew about it.

I shrugged my shoulders in embarrassment and said in Italian that I didn't know any English. Disappointed, the cameramen continued in the wake of the Coast Guard.

The crossway stretched on in front of me, two concrete strips sandwiching a wedge of grass. The wind chilled my sore shoulder. I wanted to run but I couldn't. My legs were leaden posts and would not race for me. I staggered up to the gates closed in front of the MacArthur Lock and made my way across the narrow path on top of them. Beyond me lay the rocks lining the channel into Lake Huron. We were lucky the gates had held.

A tremendous crowd had gathered at the observation deck. It took time and energy to force my way through the crush of people. Mattingly was no longer there.

Before elbowing my way out again, I looked for a minute at the *Lucella*. She was an appalling sight. Bow and stern both stuck up from the lock at jagged angles. A number of cables had snapped from the self-unloader and swung meaninglessly above the remains of the deck. Wet barley oozed from the open cargo holds into a yellow smear across the visible parts of the gaping decks. I strained my eyes at the figures on board and decided that Bledsoe must finally have gone inside. A helicopter had landed near the bow, deploying men with stretchers.

The crowd was enjoying the show. Live disasters are wonderful attractions when you're safe on the other side of them. As we watched, the Coast Guard fished the dead bodies out of the water and a delighted shudder fluttered throughout the observation deck. I turned and shouldered my way down the stairs and across the street to a little coffee shop.

I ordered a cup of hot chocolate. Like Bledsoe and the crew, I'd had a shock and I needed hot liquid and sugar. The chocolate was pretty dismal, made from a powdered mix and water, but it was sweet and the warmth gradually made itself felt inside my numbed fingers and frozen toes.

I ordered another and a hamburger and french fries. Some instinct told me that calories under these circumstances would do me nothing but good. I pressed the plastic mug against my tired forehead. So Mattingly had left already. On his way back to Chicago by car, unless he'd had a private plane waiting for him at Sault Ste. Marie's little airport.

I ate the hamburger, a greasy, hardened black slab, greedily in a few bites. The best thing for me to do was call Bobby and tell him to look out for Mattingly when he got back to Chicago. After all, I couldn't chase him.

As soon as I finished the french fries, I went in search of a pay phone. There was one outside the observation booth, but eight people were lined up waiting to use it. I finally found another three blocks down, in front of a burnt-out hotel. I called the Sault Ste. Marie airport. The one daily flight for Chicago left in two hours. I booked a seat and found a Sault Ste. Marie taxi company which sent a cab over to take me to the airport.

Sault Ste. Marie is even smaller than Thunder Bay. The airport was a hangar and a hut, both very weather-beaten. A few private planes, Cessnas and the like, stood at the edge of the field. I didn't see anything that looked like a commercial plane. I didn't even see any people. Finally, after ten minutes of walking around, peering in corners, I found a man lying on his back under a tiny plane.

He slid out reluctantly in response to my shouts.

"I'm looking for the plane to Chicago."

He wiped a greasy hand across an already grimy face. "No planes to Chicago here. Just a few private planes use this place."

"I just called. I just made a reservation."

He shook his head. "Commercial airport's twenty miles down the interstate. You'd better get down there."

My shoulders sagged. I didn't know where to find the energy to go another twenty miles. I sighed. "You have a phone I could use to call a cab?"

He gestured toward the far end of the dusty building and turned to crawl back under the plane.

A thought occurred to me. "Martin Bledsoe keep his plane here or down at the other place?"

The man glanced back up at me. "It was here. Cappy flew it out about twenty minutes ago."

"Cappy?"

"His pilot. Some guy came along, said Bledsoe wanted Cappy to fly him to Chicago."

I was too tired to feel anything—surprise, shock, anger—my emotions were pushed somewhere far away. "Guy have bright red hair? Scar on the left side of his face?"

The mechanic shrugged. "Don't know about the scar. He

had red hair all right.'' Cappy was expecting the guy—Bledsoe had phoned and told him the night before. All the mechanic knew was he'd given Cappy a course to Chicago. Weather still looked clear across Lake Michigan. They should make it in by six or so. He crawled back under the plane.

I staggered across the floor and found a phone, an old black clunker in the style GTE is ashamed to sell nowadays. The cab company agreed to send someone out to meet me.

I crouched on the sidewalk in front of the hangar while I waited, too weary to stand, fighting sleep. I wondered dreamily what I'd do if the taxi couldn't get me to the other airport on time.

I had a long wait. The cab's honking horn roused me from a doze and I got stiffly to my feet. I fell asleep again on the drive south. We made it to the Chippewa County International Airport with ten minutes to spare. Another tiny terminal, where a friendly fat man sold me a ticket and helped me and two other passengers board the propeller plane.

I thought I would sleep out the flight, but I kept churning thoughts around uselessly during the interminable journey. The plane stopped at three little Michigan towns. I endured the flight with the passivity born of too much emotion. Why would Bledsoe have blown up his own ship? What else was Mattingly doing for him? Bledsoe had blandly offered to let me look at his financial papers. And that meant the real documents were hidden someplace else with fake books available for bankers and detectives. But he had really been in shock when the *Lucella* blew up. That gray face wasn't faked. Well, maybe he just wanted to incapacitate her slightly, to collect enough insurance to meet his financial obligations. He didn't want his pride and joy blown to bits, but Mattingly had gotten hold of the wrong kind of explosive. Or too powerful an explosive. Anyway, he'd way exceeded his instructions.

Why had Bledsoe offered me a ride in his plane if he was turning it over to Mattingly, anyway? Maybe he knew he wouldn't have to make good on the offer. Or, if he expected the *Lucella* to be damaged only slightly, he could have taken off. But then how would he have explained Mattingly to me?

Round and round I went on these useless speculations, giving myself nothing but a headache. At the root of it all, I felt very bitter. It looked as though Bledsoe, who talked to me charmingly last night about *Peter Grimes,* had fooled me. Maybe he thought I'd be an impartial witness to his surprise at the wreck. I didn't like the wound to my ego. At least I hadn't gone to bed with him.

At O'Hare I looked Mattingly up in the phone book. He lived near Logan Square. Late as it was, exhausted, my head pounding and my clothes in ruins, I took a cab straight down there from the airport. It was nine-thirty when I rang the bell of a tidy bungalow in the 3600 North block of Pulaski.

It was opened almost immediately by Howard's young, helpless wife, Elsie. She was struggling with the latter stages of pregnancy and she gasped when she saw me. I realized I must present a shocking sight.

"Hello, Elsie," I said, walking past her into a tiny vestibule. "I'm V. I. Warshawski—Boom Boom's cousin. We met a couple of times at hockey parties—remember? I need to talk to Howard."

"I—Yes, I remember you. Howard—Howard's not here."

"No? You're sure he's not upstairs in bed asleep or something?"

Tears started rolling down her round, girlish cheeks. "He's not here. He isn't. Pierre—Pierre has called three times, and the last time he left a threat. But really, I don't know where he is. I haven't seen him for four days. I thought—I thought he was at—at the Coeur d'Argent with Pierre. But he wasn't and I don't know where he is and the baby may come any day and I'm so scared." She was really sobbing now.

I coaxed her into the living room and sat her down on a bright blue sofa covered with plastic. A stack of knitting lay folded neatly on the veneer coffee table—she had obviously filled her lonely, frightened days making baby clothes. I rubbed her hands and talked soothingly to her. When she seemed a little calmer I made my way to the kitchen and fixed her a mug of steaming milk. Hunting around, I found some gin under the sink. I poured myself a healthy slug of that with a little orange juice and carried the two drinks back to the living room. My left arm protested even this insubstantial load.

"Here: drink this. It'll make you feel a little better . . . Now. When was the last time you saw Howard?"

He had left Monday with a small overnight bag, saying he would be back on Wednesday. Here it was Friday and where was he? No, he hadn't said where he was going. Did Thunder Bay sound familiar? She shrugged helplessly, tears swimming in her round blue eyes. Sault Ste. Marie? She just shook her head, crying gently, not saying anything.

"Has Howard said anything about the people he's been running around with?"

"No," she hiccoughed. "And when I told him you'd asked, he—he got really mad at me. He—he hit me and told me to keep our business to our—ourselves. And then he packed up and left and said he'd better not tell me where—where he was going, because I—I would just—just blab it around to people."

I grimaced, silently thanking Boom Boom for the times he and Pierre had beaten up Howard.

"What about money? Howard had enough money lately?"

She brightened at that. Yes, he'd made a lot of money this spring and he'd given her two hundred dollars to buy a really nice crib and everything for the baby. She was quite proud of that and rambled on about it for a while—the only thing she could brag about.

I asked her if she had a mother or a sister or anyone she could stay with. She shrugged helplessly again and said all her family lived in Oklahoma. I looked at her impatiently. She wasn't the kind of stray I wanted to befriend—if I did it once, she'd cling to me forever. Instead, I told her to call the fire department if she went into labor suddenly and didn't know what to do about it—they'd send paramedics over to help her out.

As I got up to leave, I asked her to call me if Howard showed up. "And for goodness' sake, don't tell him you told me—he'll only hit you again. Just go down to the corner grocery and use their pay phone. I really need to talk to him."

She turned pathetically forlorn eyes to me. I doubted very much if I'd ever hear from her. It would be beyond her powers to deceive her domineering husband even over so simple a matter as a phone call. I felt a pang of guilt leaving her behind, but it was swallowed by fatigue as I got to the corner of Addison and Pulaski.

I hailed a Yellow Cab there to take me crosstown to Lotty's. Five miles on city streets is a slow ride and I went to sleep in the lurching, elderly vehicle about the time we crossed Milwaukee Avenue. The movement of the taxi made me think I was back on board the *Lucella*. Bledsoe was standing next to me, holding onto the self-unloader. He kept staring at me with his compelling gray eyes, repeating, "Vic: I wasn't on the plane. I wasn't on the plane."

I woke up with a start as we turned onto Sheffield and the driver asked me for Lotty's apartment number. As I paid him off and made my weary way up to the second floor, my dream remained very real to me. It contained an important message about Bledsoe but I just couldn't figure out what it was.

19 ✶ Pavane for a Dead Hockey Player

Lotty greeted me with a most uncharacteristic gasp of relief. "My God, Vic, it's really you! You made it back!" She hugged me fiercely.

"Lotty, what on earth is the matter? Didn't you think you'd see me again?"

She put me at arm's length, looked me up and down, kissed me again, and then gave a more Lotty-like grin. "The boat you were on, Vic. It was on the news. The explosion and so on. Four dead, they said, one of them a woman, but they wouldn't give names until the families were notified. I was afraid, my dear, afraid you might be the only woman on board."

By now she had ascertained my disheveled state. She hustled me into the bathroom and sat me in a steaming bath in her old-fashioned porcelain tub. She blew her nose briskly and went off to put a chicken on to simmer, then came back with two tumblers of my scotch. Lotty rarely drank—she was clearly deeply upset.

She perched on a three-legged stool while I soaked my sore shoulder and related the highlights of my adventures.

"I can't believe Bledsoe hired Mattingly," I concluded. "I just don't believe my judgment of character can be so wrong. Bledsoe and his captain roused my hackles. But I liked them." I went on to tell her the same thoughts that had tormented my four-hour ride in from the Soo. "I guess I'll have to put my prejudices aside and look into Pole Star's insurance arrangements and their general financial health."

"Sleep on it," Lotty advised. "You have a lot of different avenues to explore. In the morning one of them will look the most promising. Maybe Phillips. He has the most definite tie to Boom Boom, after all."

Wrapped in a large terry-cloth robe, I sat with her in the kitchen eating the chicken and feeling comfort seep into the worn spots of my mind. After dinner Lotty rubbed Myoflex into my back and arms. She gave me a muscle relaxant and I fell into a deep, peppermint-scented sleep.

The phone dragged me out of the depths some ten hours later. Lotty came in and gently touched my arm. I opened bleary eyes.

"Phone's for you, my dear. Janet somebody—used to be Boom Boom's secretary."

I shook my head groggily and sat up to take the phone by the guest bed.

Janet's homey, middle-aged voice woke me up more thoroughly. She was upset. "Miss Warshawski, I've been fired. Mr. Phillips told me it was because they didn't have enough for me to do, with Mr. Warshawski gone and all. But I think it's because I was going through those files for you. I don't think they would have fired me if I hadn't done that. I mean, there was always enough work before—"

I cut into the repetitive flow. "When did this happen?"

"Last night. Last night I stayed behind to see if I could find out anything about Mr. Phillips's paycheck, you know, like you asked me to. I thought about it, and I thought, really, now, if Mr. Warshawski was killed like you say he was, and if this will help, I ought to find out. But Lois came in to see what I was doing. I guess she was all set to spy on me if I stayed late or stayed after lunch, and then she called Mr. Phillips at home. Well, he wasn't home yet, of course. But she kept calling him, and about ten o'clock last night he called and told me they don't need me to come in anymore and he'll send me two weeks' salary instead of notice. And, like I said, it just doesn't seem fair."

"No, it doesn't," I agreed warmly. "What did you tell her you were doing?"

"Who?"

"Lois," I said patiently. "When she came in and asked you what you were doing, what did you tell her?"

"Oh! I said I'd written a personal letter and I couldn't find it so I was looking to see if it got thrown out."

I thought that was pretty fast thinking and said so.

She laughed a little, pleased with the compliment, but added despondently, "She didn't believe me, because there wasn't any reason for it to be in Mr. Phillips's wastebasket."

"Well, Janet, I don't know what to say. You certainly tried your hardest. I'm extremely sorry you lost your job, and all for nothing, but if—"

"It wasn't all for nothing," she interrupted. "I did find his pay stub just as you thought I might."

"Oh!" I stared at the receiver in disbelief. For once something in this cockeyed investigation had worked out the way I thought it should. "How much does he make?"

"He gets thirty-five hundred forty-six dollars and fifteen cents every two weeks."

I tried multiplying in my head but I was still too groggy.

"I figured it out on my calculator last night. That's ninety-two thousand a year." She paused, wistfully. "That's a lot of money. I was only making seventy-two hundred. And now I don't have that."

"Look, Janet. Would you be willing to work downtown? I can get you some interviews—at the Ajax Insurance Company and a couple of other places."

She told me she'd think about it: she'd rather find something in her neighborhood. If that didn't work out, she'd give me a call back and ask me to set up an interview for her. I thanked her profusely and we hung up.

I lay back in bed and thought. Ninety-two thousand a year was a lot of money—for me or Janet. But for Phillips? Say he had good deductions and a good tax accountant. Still, he couldn't take home more than sixty or so. His real estate tax bill was probably three thousand. A mortgage, maybe another fifteen. Dues at the Maritime Club and the monthly fees for tennis, twenty-five thousand. Tuition, et cetera, at Claremont. The boat. The Alfa. Food. Massandrea dresses for Jeannine. Maybe she bought them at the Elite Repeat shop, or used from Mrs. Grafalk. Still it would take a good hundred thousand net to cover everything.

After breakfast I walked the mile between Lotty's apartment and my own down on Halsted. I was getting out of shape from lying around too much, but I wasn't sure I was up to running yet and I knew I couldn't lift my ten-pound shoulder weights.

My mailbox was bulging. I get the *Wall Street Journal* every day. Five copies were stacked with letters and a small parcel on the floor. I picked up two armfuls and climbed the three flights to my apartment. "No place like home," I murmured to myself, looking with a jaundiced eye at the dust, the magazines strewn around the living room, and the bed which hadn't been made for more than two weeks now. I put the mail down and gave myself over to one of my rare housewifely fits, vacuuming, dusting, hanging up clothes. Having ruined a pantsuit, a pair of jeans, a sweater, and a blouse since I left home, there was less to put away than there might have been.

Glowing with virtue, I settled down with a cup of coffee to sort through the mail. Most of it was bills, which I tossed out unopened. Why look at them just to get depressed? One envelope held a thirty-five-hundred-dollar check from Ajax to pay for a new car. I was grateful for the care of the U. S. Postal Service, which had left that on my lobby floor for any dope addict on Halsted to find. Also, wrapped in a small box were the keys to Boom Boom's apartment with a note from Sergeant McGonnigal saying the police were through with their investigation and I could use it any time I wanted to.

I poured myself more coffee and thought about what I should do. First on the list was Mattingly. I called Pierre Bouchard and asked him where I could find Mattingly if he were in town but not at home.

He clicked his tongue against his teeth. "That I could not

tell you, Vic. I have avoided the man constantly. But I will call around and see what I can find out.''

I told him Elsie was due any day now and he clicked his tongue again. ''That man! What an excrescence he is!''

''By the way, Pierre, does Howard know how to do deep-sea diving?''

''Deep-sea diving?'' he echoed. ''No, Vic, I am telling you, I do not know him well. I do not know his personal habits. But I will ask . . . Oh, don't hang up—I have that name for you.''

''What name?''

''Did you not call Anna before you left town? You wanted to know what man we met at Christmas, when Boom Boom met Paige Carrington?''

''Oh yes.'' I'd forgotten all about that. The man who was interested in buying a few shares of the Black Hawks, the man for whom Odinflute had set up his party. ''Yes. Who was it?''

''His name is Niels Grafalk. Myron says after all he decided not to buy.''

''I see,'' I said weakly. I said nothing else and after a bit Bouchard said, ''Vic? Vic? Are you still there?''

''What? Oh yes. Yes, thanks very much, Pierre . . . Let me know if you hear from Mattingly.''

Though distracted, I took my check over to Humboldt Olds where I bought an Omega, a 1981 red model with fifteen thousand miles on it, power steering and power brakes. I had to sign a finance contract for eight hundred dollars but that wouldn't prove impossible. I'd just bill Boom Boom's estate for a hefty fee when all this mess was cleaned up. If it ever was.

So Grafalk had been interested in the Black Hawks. And Paige had been present at that same party. Now whom had she known? Who took her? It was an interesting coincidence. I wondered what she would tell me if I called her.

Driving in a slight daze, I reached Boom Boom's apartment at three-thirty, parking the Olds in front of a NO PARKING SIGN at Chestnut and Seneca. After two weeks of neglect, which had included a burglary and a police investigation, the place looked far worse than mine had this morning. Gray dust from the fingerprint detectors covered all the papers. White chalk still marked the outline of Henry Kelvin's body next to the desk.

I poured myself a glass of Chivas. I was damned if I was going to clean up two places in one day. Instead, I made a stab at reassembling the papers in their appropriate categories. I'd hire a cleaning crew and some temporary clerks to do the rest of the work. Frankly, I was sick of the place.

I made a tour of the apartment to collect items of interest to me—Boom Boom's first and last hockey sticks, a New Guinea hut totem from the living room, and some of the pictures of him in various hockey guises from the spare-room wall. Once more the picture of me in my maroon law school robes grinned incongruously from the wall. I took it off and added it to the stack under my arms. Once the clerks had gotten the papers to the right people and the cleaners had eliminated all the greasy dirt, I'd get the condo and the rest of his possessions onto the market. With any luck, I'd never have to visit this place again. I slung the items into my trunk and drove off. No one had ticketed me—maybe my luck was beginning to turn.

Next stop: the Eudora Grain offices. I badly wanted to talk to Bledsoe about why Mattingly had left Sault Ste. Marie in his airplane, but I still thought Phillips's finances were an angle worth following up.

Late Saturday afternoon was an eerie time to visit the Port of Chicago. There wasn't much activity at the elevators. The huge ships stood like sleeping giants, prepared to wake into violent activity if disturbed. I eased the Omega into the parking lot at Eudora Grain's regional office and found myself tiptoeing across the blacktop to a side door.

A small bell was set into the wall with a little sign over it reading RING FOR DELIVERIES. I rang several times and waited five minutes. No one came. If there was a night watchman, he wasn't yet on the premises. From my back pocket I pulled a house burglar's compedium of commonly used picklocks and set out methodically to open the door.

Ten minutes later I was in Phillips's office. Either he or

the efficient Lois kept all the file cabinets locked. With an aggrieved sigh, I took out my picklocks again and opened all the cabinets in the room and the three in Lois's desk outside his office door. I called Lotty and told her I wouldn't be in for supper and set to work. If I'd been thinking, I would have brought some sandwiches and a thermos of coffee.

Phillips kept a strange collection of junk in his upper desk drawer—three different kinds of antacids; datebooks going back for six years, most of them without any appointments written in; nose drops; an old pair of overshoes; two broken calculators; and odd scraps of paper. These I carefully smoothed out and read. Most of them were phone messages which he'd crumpled up and tossed in the drawer. A couple from Grafalk, one from Argus. The others were all names I didn't recognize, but I wrote them down in case I ran so far out of leads that I wanted to check them.

The ledgers were in a walnut filing cabinet on the window side of the office. I pulled them out with great alacrity. They were in the form of computer printouts, issued once a month with year-to-date totals and comparisons with prior years. After a certain amount of looking, I found report A36000059-G, payments to licensed carriers. All I needed now was my list of shipping contracts and I could compare the dates and see if the totals matched.

Or so I thought. I went out to Lois's file cabinets and found the originals of the contracts Janet had photocopied for me. These I took back into Phillips's office to lay next to report A36000059-G. Only then did I discover that the ledger recorded by invoice number, not by contract date. At first I thought I could just match totals of individual orders against totals in the ledger; I pulled the Pole Star Line's as an example.

Unfortunately the carriers apparently submitted more than one job on an invoice. The invoice totals were so much greater than the individual transactions, and the number of total invoices paid so much smaller, that it seemed to me that was the only explanation.

I added and subtracted, matching the numbers up every way I could think of, but I was forced to conclude that I wasn't going to be able to tell a thing without the individual invoices. And those I could not find. Not a one. I went through the rest of Phillips's files and all through Lois's and finally through the open file cabinets out on the floor. There wasn't an invoice in the place.

Before giving up for the evening, I looked up the payroll section of the ledgers. Phillips's salary was listed there just as Janet had told me. If I'd known I was going to burgle the place I would never have let her risk getting fired by going through his garbage.

I tapped my front teeth with a pencil. If he was getting extra money from Eudora Grain, it wasn't through the payroll account. Anyway, the ledgers were printed by the computers in Eudora, Kansas—if he was monkeying around with the accounts, he'd have to do it more subtly.

I shrugged and looked at my watch. It was after nine o'clock. I was tired. I was very hungry. And my shoulder was throbbing. I'd earned a good dinner, a long bath, and a sound sleep, but there was still another errand on the day's agenda.

Back in my apartment, I threw some frozen pasta into a pot with tomatoes and basil and ran a bath. I plugged the phone into the bathroom wall and called Phillips's Lake Bluff house. He wasn't in, but his son politely asked if he could take a message.

I lifted my right leg out of the water and ran a soapy sponge over it while I considered. "This is V. I. Warshawski," I said, spelling it for him. "Tell him that Mr. Argus's auditors will want to know where the missing invoices are."

The boy repeated the message back to me dubiously. "You got it." I gave him both my and Lotty's phone numbers and hung up.

The pasta was bubbling nicely and I took it into the bedroom with me while I got dressed—black velvet pants with a high-necked blouse and a form-fitting red and black velvet toreador jacket. High heels and very dangly earrings and I was set for an evening at the theater. Or the end of an evening at the theater. By some miracle I hadn't spilled tomato juice on the white blouse. My luck really was turning.

I got to the Windy City Balletworks just at ten-thirty. A bored young woman in a leotard and stretchy wrap-around skirt told me the performance would end in ten minutes. She gave me a program and let me go in without paying.

The tiny theater was filled and I didn't bother trying to find a seat in the dim light. I lounged against the back wall, taking off my shoes to stand in my stocking feet next to the ushers. A spirited *pas de deux* from a classical ballet was in progress. Paige was not the female dancer. Whoever it was, she seemed technically competent but lacked the special spark with which Paige infused her performance. The whole company appeared on stage for a complex finale, and the show was over.

When the lights came on, I squinted at the program to make sure Paige was, indeed, dancing tonight. Yes, *Pavane for a Dope Dealer* had been performed right before the second act of *Giselle*, which we'd just seen.

I went back out into the hallway and followed a small group down to the door leading directly to the dressing rooms. Rather than accost Paige in her shared dressing room, I sat on a folding chair outside to wait. The dancers began coming out in twos and threes, not sparing me a glance. I'd provided myself with a novel, remembering the forty-five-minute wait here the last time I'd tried talking to Paige, and flicked through the pages, looking up in vain every time the door opened.

Fifty minutes went by. Just as I was thinking she might have left at the end of the *Pavane*, she finally emerged. As usual, her exquisite good looks made me feel a little wistful. Tonight she had on a silvery fur coat, possibly fox, which made her resemble Geraldine Chaplin in the middle of the Russian winter in *Dr. Zhivago*.

"Hello, Paige. I'm afraid I got here too late to see the *Pavane*. Perhaps I can make the matinee tomorrow."

She gave a slight start and then a wary smile. "Hello, Vic. What impertinent questions have you come to ask me? I hope they're not long, because I'm late for a dinner engagement."

"Trying to drown your sorrows?"

She gave me an indignant look. "Life goes on, Vic. You need to learn that."

"So it does, Paige. I'm sorry to have to drag you into a past you're trying to forget, but I'd like to know who took you to Guy Odinflute's party."

"Who—what?"

"Remember the Christmas party where you met Boom Boom? Niels Grafalk wanted to meet some hockey players, trying to decide whether to buy into the Black Hawks, and Odinflute gave a party for him. Or have you blocked that out along with the rest of the dead past?"

Her eyes blazed suddenly dark and her cheeks turned red. Without a word, she lifted her hand to slap me in the face. I caught her by the wrist and gently lowered her hand to her side. "Don't hit me, Paige—I learned my fighting in the streets and I wouldn't want to lose my temper and hurt you . . . Who took you to Odinflute's party?"

"None of your damned business. Now will you leave the theater before I call the guard and tell him you're molesting me? And please do not ever come back. It would make me ill to have you watch me dance."

She moved with angry grace down the hall and out the front door. I followed in time to see her get into a dark sedan. A man was driving but I couldn't make out his face in the dim light.

I didn't feel in the humor for company, even Lotty's astringent love. I gave her a call from my apartment to tell her not to worry. She didn't, usually, but I knew she'd been pretty upset after the destruction of the *Lucella*.

In the morning I went down to the corner for the Sunday *Herald-Star* and some croissants. While the coffee dripped in my porcelain coffeepot I tried Mattingly. No one answered. I wondered if Elsie had gone to the hospital. I tried Phillips, but no one answered there either. It was almost eleven—maybe they had to put in a ritual appearance at the Lake Bluff Presbyterian Church.

I propped the paper up against the coffeepot and sat down to work my way through it. I'd once told Murray the only reason I buy the *Herald-Star* is because it has the most com-

ics in the city. Actually, it has the best crime coverage, too.
But I always read the funnies first.

I was halfway through my second cup when I came to the
squib about Mattingly. I'd almost passed it over. The head-
line on an inner page read "Hit-and-run Victim in Kosciuszko Park" but his name must have caught my eye and I
went back and read the story through completely.

The body of a man identified as Howard Mattingly
was found late last night in Kosciuszko Park. Victor
Golun, 23, of North Central Avenue, was jogging
through the park at ten last evening when he found
Mattingly's body concealed behind a tree on one of
the jogging paths. Mattingly, 33, was a reserve wing
for the Chicago Black Hawks. Police say he had been
hit by a car and carried to the park to die. They esti-
mated he had been dead at least twenty hours when
Golun found the body. Mattingly is survived by his
wife, Elsie, 20, by two brothers, and by his mother.

I counted back in my head. He'd died by two Saturday
morning at the latest, probably been hit sometime Friday
evening, maybe right after he got back from Sault Ste. Marie. I knew I should call Bobby Mallory and tell him to trace
Mattingly's movements from when he got off Bledsoe's
plane Friday night. But I wanted to talk to Bledsoe myself
first and find out why Mattingly had flown home in his
plane.

Bledsoe's home phone wasn't listed in any of the Chicago
or suburban directories. On an off chance I tried the Pole
Star Line, but of course no one was there on Sunday.

I called Bobby Mallory to find out if anything had happened in the Henry Kelvin murder. "I got the keys back and
went down there. The place was pretty grim. You guys
make an arrest yet?"

"You on their payroll or something, Vicki? That family's
bugging us day in and day out. We don't solve crimes faster
for that kind of hassling."

Depends on who's doing the hassling, I thought. But I

kept that comment to myself—I wanted information more than I wanted to hear Bobby scream at me. So I made a sympathetic clucking in my throat.

"I read about that hit-and-run case in Kosciuszko Park. You know, that guy Mattingly used to play with Boom Boom on the Black Hawks. I hope the Hawks have got a good employee benefits plan—the team doesn't seem to be holding up too well."

"You know I don't like you calling up and chatting about crime with me, Vicki. And I hope you wouldn't do it just to get my goat. So it must be you've got some special interest in the case. What is it?"

"No, not that," I said hastily. "But I know his wife. She's a fragile woman—just a child, really, and I don't think this shock'll be too good for her. Her first baby is due any second."

"Yeah, she had it this morning. Between you and me, she's well rid of that specimen. He was a petty grafter, had his hand stuck in everybody's pocket. He owed gambling money, too. If he'd been a starter they'd of had him fixing games."

"You figure one of his creditors got tired of waiting and ran him over?"

"I don't figure anything for your consumption. If I've told you once, I've told you a hundred times, quit fooling around with crime. You'll only get hurt. Leave that—"

"—to the police. They're paid to handle it." I finished with him in chorus. "Make it more like a million times, Bobby. Thanks. Give my love to Eileen," I added as he hung up on me.

Next I tried Murray Ryerson. He wasn't at the *Star* but I found him at home, just staggering out of bed.

"V. I. who?" he grumbled. "It's only eleven in the morning."

"Wake up, sunshine. I want to talk to you."

"Vic, if you knew how long I've waited to hear those words from you. My mother keeps telling me, 'No, she's just using you, Murray. She just wants to worm crime information out of you.' But deep down, I keep believing, in my secret heart, that one day my warmest passions will be reciprocated."

"Murray, your warmest passion, next to beer, is for a hot story. I guess I reciprocate that. Why don't you come up and watch the poor old Cubbies take on the winningest team in baseball and I'll give you an exclusive on the wreck of the *Lucella*."

"What do you know about that?" he asked sharply.

"I was there. I was an eyewitness. I watched the whole thing happen. I may even have seen the man—or woman—who planted the depth charges."

"My God, Vic, I don't believe it. I don't believe you're calling me out of the blue with this. Who was it? Where did you see them? Was it up at the locks? Is this on the level?"

"Certainly," I said virtuously. "Have we got a date?"

"Let me get Mike Silchuck up there with his camera to get a shot of you. Now, let's start at the beginning. Why were you on the *Lucella*?"

"Are you going to come to the game with me or not?"

"Oh, all right. But it's no joy for me to watch Atlanta massacre our faithful boys in blue."

He agreed to meet me at the bleachers at twelve forty-five. Right before he hung up he said, "What do you want from me, Vic? Why the elaborate setup?"

"See you at the game, Murray." I laughed and hung up.

Before leaving for the park I tried Phillips again. Jeannine answered.

"Hello, Mrs. Phillips. This is V. I. Warshawski. I'm a business associate of your husband's. May I speak to him, please?"

He wasn't in. She didn't know when he would be in. I thought she was lying. Under her hauteur she sounded scared. I tried probing a little but couldn't get a handle on it. Finally I asked her what time he'd gone out. She hung up on me.

20 * Unloading

The Braves did clobber the Cubs. Only Keith Moreland, hitting around .345, did anything we could enjoy, knocking a ball into the hands of an eager kid around nine sitting in front of me. However, the day was sunny, if chilly, the crowd enthusiastic, and Murray and I enjoyed a few hot dogs. I let him drink the beer—I don't like the stuff.

Mike Silchuck had taken my picture a few dozen times in front of the ticket counter. Unfortunately all my scars were in places I didn't feel like flashing in the middle of Addison, so they had to be content with a look of noble courage. Murray asked me questions briskly during the first three innings, then spent the fourth phoning his exclusive into the *Herald-Star*.

In the top half of the sixth, while the Braves scored five runs, I asked Murray about Mattingly.

"He's a small-time hood, Vic. What do you want to know about him?"

"Who killed him?"

Like Mallory, he assumed immediately that Mattingly or his wife/mother/brothers were my clients. I gave him the same story I'd told Bobby.

"Besides, even though Boom Boom hated him, he felt sorry for poor little Elsie. I know he used to slip her a few bucks to stretch the housekeeping money, which I guess Mattingly doled out with a grudging fist, since he needed it for his gambling debts."

''Why did she stay with him?'' Murray asked irritably.

''Oh, Murray, grow up. Why does anyone stay with anyone? She was a child, a baby. She couldn't have been eighteen when he married her, and everyone she knows is in Oklahoma . . . Well, let's not get into the psychology of marriage. Just tell me if there are any leads into his death.''

He shook his head. ''He was out of town for three or four days. Elsie doesn't know where he went or how he got there, and the police haven't dug up anyone who can help. They'll question the hockey team, of course, but as far as I can tell most of the guys felt the same way your cousin did.''

So the connection with Bledsoe was still secret. Or the connection with his airplane, at any rate. ''Was he wearing size twelve Arroyo hiking boots by any chance?''

Murray looked at me strangely. ''The footprint left in Boom Boom's apartment? I don't know—but I'll find out.''

I turned my attention to the rest of the game. My hero, Bill Buckner, struck out. Such is life. I kind of knew the feeling.

After the game Murray wandered home with me for something more substantial than hot dogs. I scrounged around in my bare larder and came up with tuna, frozen fettucine, and olives. We drank a bottle of Barolo and put crime behind us for a few hours, while I found out how much exercise my dislocated shoulder was up to.

Murray and I have been competitors on the crime scene, friends, and occasional lovers for several years. Somehow, though, the relationship never seems to develop. Maybe our rivalry over crime investigation gets in the way.

Around midnight the *Star* signaled him on his beeper and he left to deal with a Mafia shooting in River Forest. Beepers are one of the twentieth century's most useless inventions. What difference does it make if your office finds you now rather than an hour from now? Why not give yourself a break?

I asked Murray this as he pulled his T-shirt over the thick auburn curls on his chest.

''If they didn't know where to find me, the *Sun-Times* or

the *Trib* would beat me to the story," he mumbled through the cloth.

"Yeah," I grumbled, lying back in bed. "Americans are afraid that if they unplug themselves from their electronic toys, for five minutes they'll miss out on—everything. Life. Imagine no TV, no telephones, no beepers, no computers, for three minutes. You'd die. You'd be like a beached whale—"

I was working myself into a frenzy over our appalling dependency on gadgets when Murray dropped a pillow over my face. "You talk too much, Vic."

"This is what happened to the girl in *Looking for Mr. Goodbar*." I padded naked after him down the hall to make sure all the locks got closed behind him. "She brings this guy home and he suffocates her with her own pillow . . . I hope you write a definitive exposé of the Chicago mob and get them run out of town."

After Murray left I couldn't get back to sleep. We'd gone to bed early, around seven-thirty, and slept for a couple of hours. Now I felt all the loose ends of the case whirling around in my head like trails of fettucine. I didn't know where to find Bledsoe. It was too late to try the Phillipses again. Too late to call Grafalk, to find out if he had gone to that Christmas party alone. I'd already burgled the Eudora Grain offices. I'd even cleaned my apartment earlier in the day. Unless I wanted to wash dishes twice in twenty-four hours, there wasn't anything for me to do except pace.

About one-thirty the walls started to close in on me. I got dressed and took one of my mother's diamond earrings from the locked cupboard built into my closet. I went out onto Halsted, deserted in the early morning except for a few drunks, got into the Omega, and headed out to Lake Shore Drive. I rode south for several miles, past the Loop, and pulled off at Meigs Field, the small airport on Chicago's lakefront.

The blue landing lights cast no illumination in the thick dark. They seemed like meaningless dots, not part of a human network. Behind the tiny runway lapped Lake Michigan, a dark shape. I felt desolate. Not even a beeper linked me with the rest of the world.

I skirted the runway and stumbled through the weed-grown rocks down to the water's edge, shivering at the nameless menace in the black water. The water slapping at my feet seemed to call me to itself. Let me enfold you in the mysteries of my depths. All the dark things you fear will become your delight. Don't think of drowning, of Boom Boom choking and fighting for air. Think of infinite rest, no responsibilities, no need for control. Just perfect rest.

The roar of an engine brought me back to myself. A two-seater plane was landing. It looked like a living creature, its lights flashing busily, wings flopping for the descent, like a noisy insect settling down for a short rest.

I stumbled back across the rocks to the little terminal. No one was in the waiting room. I went back outside and followed the two men who had just landed into an office. There a thin young man with straw-colored hair and a very pointed nose went over their flight charts with them. They were talking about some wind pattern which had caught them up around Galena and the three had an animated discussion on what might have caused it. This went on for a good ten minutes while I wandered around the room looking at different aerial photos of the city and surrounding countryside.

At last the thin young man pulled himself reluctantly from the weather map and asked if he could help me in some way.

I gave my most ingratiating smile—Lauren Bacall trying to get Sam Spade to do her dirty work for her. "I came in on Mr. Bledsoe's plane Friday night and I think I might have lost an earring." I pulled my mother's diamond drop from my jacket pocket. "It looks like this. The post must have come out."

The young man frowned. "When did you come in?"

"Friday. It would have been around five, I guess."

"What kind of plane does Bledsoe fly?"

I gave a helpless, feminine shrug. "I don't know. It seats about six people, I think. It's new," I added helpfully. "The paint's fresh and shiny—"

The young man exchanged a masculine smirk with the

other two. Women are *so* stupid. He pulled a logbook out of a drawer and ran his finger down the entries. "Bledsoe. Oh yes. A Piper Cub. Came in at five-twenty on Friday. There was only one passenger, though. The pilot didn't say anything about a woman."

"Well, I did ask him specially not to. I didn't want a record that I'd been on the plane. But now I've lost this earring and all, I don't know what I'll do . . . Will Cappy be in this morning? Could you ask him to look for me?"

"He only comes in when Mr. Bledsoe needs him to fly."

"Well, maybe you have a number where I could reach him?"

After a certain amount of hemming and hawing, during which the other two were winking surreptitiously at each other, the young man gave me Cappy's phone number. I thanked him profusely and took off. Whatever gets the job done.

Back home I remembered the memorabilia I'd picked up at Boom Boom's apartment and took them out of the trunk. My left arm continued to heal, despite constant abuse, and the load brought on only minor twinges. With the pile of stuff balanced on my right arm, I fumbled at the door locks left-handed. The New Guinea totem started to wobble. I struggled to save it, and the pictures crashed to the floor. I swore under my breath, put everything down, unlocked the door with both hands, propped it open with my foot, and carried the things properly into the building.

I'd saved the totem, but the glass over the pictures had cracked. I put them on the coffee table and took the frames apart gingerly, knocking the glass into a waste can.

The photo of me in my graduation robes was wedged extremely tightly into the frame. Boom Boom must have put too many sheets of cardboard in to allow the back to fit properly. "You shouldn't have bought such a cheap frame for me, Boom Boom," I muttered to myself. I finally went into the kitchen for a couple of oven mitts. With those on, I forced the frame away from the backing, spilling glass everywhere.

Between the picture and the backing was a thickly folded

stack of white paper. No wonder the photo was wedged in so tightly.

I unfolded the stack. It turned out to be two sheets of paper. One was an invoice from the Grafalk Steamship Line to the Eudora Grain Company. Terms: 10 days, 2 percent, 30 days net, 60 days 18 percent interest. It showed loads by vessel, date of shipment, and date of arrival. The second, written in Boom Boom's meticulous hand, listed six dates when Pole Star had lost shipments to Grafalk.

Boom Boom had also listed the bids. In four lots, Pole Star was the low bidder. I started hunting through the apartment for my bag with the contract copies in it, then remembered I had left it at Lotty's. Not even Lotty could I rouse at three in the morning just to get some papers.

I fixed myself a large scotch and stood at the living room window drinking it. I stared down at the late-night traffic on Halsted. Boom Boom had tried to call me to tell me what he'd found out. When he couldn't get hold of me, he stuffed the papers behind my picture—not for me to find, but to keep anyone else from finding them. He'd thought he'd get back to them, and to me, so he didn't leave a message for me. A spasm of pain contracted my chest. I missed Boom Boom terribly. I wanted to cry, but no tears would come.

I finally left the window and went to bed. I didn't sleep much and what sleep I had was tormented by dreams of Boom Boom stretching his arms out from a cold, black lake while I stood helplessly by. At seven I gave up trying to rest and took a bath. I waited until eight o'clock, then called Bledsoe's pilot, Cappy. His wife answered and called him in from the backyard where he was planting petunias.

"Mr. Cappy?" I said.

"Capstone. People call me Cappy."

"I see . . . Mr. Capstone, my name is Warshawski. I'm a detective and I'm looking into Howard Mattingly's death."

"Never heard of the guy."

"Wasn't he your passenger back from Sault Ste. Marie on Friday night?"

"Nope. Not that guy."

"Bright red hair? Scar on the left side of his face? Stocky build?"

He guessed that sounded like the same person.

"Well, we believe he was traveling under an assumed name. He turned up dead later that night. What I'm trying to find out is where he went when he left the airport."

"Couldn't tell you that. All I know, there was a car waiting for him at Meigs. He got in it and they took off. I was filling out my log forms, didn't really notice."

He hadn't been able to see the driver. No, he couldn't say what kind of car. It was big, not a limo, but it might have been a Caddy or an Oldsmobile.

"How did you come to take this guy home? I thought you were going to fly Mr. Bledsoe down, but you left before the *Lucella* got through the lock."

"Yeah, well, Mr. Bledsoe called and told me he wasn't flying down. Told me to take this guy instead. He said his name was Oleson and that's what I put down on the log."

"When did Bledsoe call you? He was on board ship all day Friday."

He'd called Thursday afternoon. No, Cappy couldn't swear it was Bledsoe. Matter of fact, Bledsoe himself had just phoned with the same question. But he didn't take orders from anyone except the plane owner—so who else could it have been?

The logic of this argument somewhat escaped me. I asked him for whom else he flew, but he got huffy and said his client list was confidential.

Hanging up slowly, I wondered again if it was time to turn my information about Mattingly over to Bobby Mallory. The police could put their investigative machinery into motion and start questioning everyone who'd been at Meigs Field on Friday night until they found someone to identify that car. I looked at Boom Boom's documents on the table next to the phone. The answer to the mess lay in these papers. I'd give myself twenty-four more hours, then turn it over to Bobby.

I tried calling Pole Star. The lines were busy. I tried Eudora Grain. The receptionist told me Mr. Phillips had not yet come in for the day. Was he expected? As far as she knew. I called his Lake Bluff residence. Mrs. Phillips told me tightly that her husband had left for work. So he had come home last night? I asked. She hung up on me again.

I made myself coffee and toast and dressed for action: running shoes, blue jeans, a gray cotton shirt, and a denim jacket. I regretted my Smith & Wesson, lying somewhere at the bottom of the Poe Lock. Maybe when they hauled up the *Lucella* they could fish my gun out of the moldy barley and give it back to me.

Before I took off, the doorbell rang. I buzzed the caller in through the front door and went on downstairs to meet him. It turned out to be a process server—a college student—with a summons for me to attend a Court of Inquiry in Sault Ste. Marie next Monday. The youth seemed relieved that I accepted it so calmly, merely stuffing it into my shoulder bag. I serve a lot of subpoenas myself—recipients range from tetchy to violent.

I stopped at the corner to buy Lotty a bunch of irises and chrysanthemums and zipped up to her apartment in the Omega. Since my little suitcase was also mushed in with fifty thousand tons of barley at Sault Ste. Marie, I stuffed my belongings into a grocery bag. I put the flowers on the kitchen table with a note.

Lotty darling.
Thank you for looking after me. I'm hot on the scent. I'll bring your keys by tonight or tomorrow night.

Vic

I had to keep the keys to lock the apartment door behind me.

I sat at her kitchen table with my stack of contracts and went through them until I found one that matched the invoice I had in hand. It was for three million bushels of soybeans going from Chicago to Buffalo on July 24, 1981. The price quoted in the contract was $0.33 a bushel. The invoice billed it at $0.35. Two cents a bushel on three million bushels. Came out to sixty thousand dollars.

Grafalk had been the low bidder on this shipment. Someone else had bid $0.335 and a third carrier $0.34. Grafalk picked up the bid at $0.33 and billed it at $0.35.

Boom Boom's list of Pole Star's lost contracts proved even more startling. On the forms I'd gotten from Janet, Grafalk was listed as the low bidder. But Boom Boom's notes showed Pole Star as the low bidder. Phillips either had entered the contracts wrong or the invoices Boom Boom referred to were wrong.

It was time to get some explanations from these clowns. I was tired of being shown the old shell game every time I wanted information out of them. I stuffed all the papers back into the canvas bag and headed for the Port.

It was close to noon when I turned off I-94 at 130th Street. The friendly receptionist at Eudora Grain was answering the phone and nodded to me in recognition as I walked past her into the inner office. The sales reps were hanging up their phones, straightening their ties, getting ready for lunch. In front of Phillips's office sat Lois, her bouffant hair lacquered into place. The phone was propped under her chin and she made a pretense of looking at some papers. She was talking in the intense, muttering way people do when they're trying to pretend they're not really making personal calls.

She lifted her eyes momentarily to me as I walked up to the desk but didn't interrupt her conversation.

"Where's Phillips?" I demanded.

She murmured something into the telephone and put her hand over the mouthpiece. "Do you have an appointment?"

I grinned at her. "Is he in today? He doesn't seem to be at home."

"I'm afraid he's away from the office on business. Do you want to make an appointment?"

"No, thanks," I said. "I'll come back." I circled behind her and looked in Phillips's office. There weren't any signs that anyone had been there since me on Saturday night—no briefcase, no jacket, no half-smoked cigars. I didn't think he was lurking outside the window in the parking lot but I went over and peered behind the drapes.

My assault on her boss's office brought Lois, squawking, into his den. I grinned at her again. "Sorry to interrupt your conversation. Tell your mother it won't happen again. Or is it your sister?"

She turned red and stomped back to her desk. I left, feeling pleased with myself.

I headed to the main part of the Port. Grafalk wasn't in; he didn't come down to the Port every day, the receptionist explained. I debated going to talk to Percy MacKelvy, the dispatcher, but decided I'd rather talk directly to Grafalk.

I walked over to Pole Star's little office. The office manager there was harassed but trying to be calm. As I talked to her she took one call from the Toronto *Sun* inquiring into the *Lucella*'s accident and another from KLWN Radio in Lawrence, Kansas.

"It's been like this all morning. I'd like to get the phone disconnected, but we need to stay in touch with our lawyers, and we do have other ships carrying freight. We don't want to miss any orders."

"I thought the *Lucella* was the only ship you owned."

"It's the only big one," she explained. "But we lease a number of others. In fact Martin got so sick of the newspapers he went down to Plymouth Iron and Steel to watch them unload coal from the *Gertrude Ruttan*. She's a seven-hundred-foot self-unloading vessel. We lease her from Triage—they're a big shipbuilding company. Sort of like Fruehauf for trucks—they don't carry much cargo in their own right, just lease the vessels."

I asked for directions to the Plymouth yard and she obligingly gave them to me. It was another ten miles around the lake to the east. She was a very helpful young woman—even gave me a pass to get into the Plymouth plant.

We were into the middle of May and the air was still quite chilly. I wondered whether we were heading for a new ice age. It's not cold winters that cause them but cool summers when the snow doesn't melt. I buttoned my jacket up to the neck and rode with the windows rolled all the way up.

As I moved into steel territory the blue air darkened and turned red-black. I felt as though every movement closer to the mills carried me further back in time to the grimy streets of South Chicago where I grew up. The women on the streets had the same pinched, worn look as they hurried their toddlers along. A grocery store on a corner reminded me of the place at 91st and Commercial where I used to buy a hard roll on my way to school, and I stopped the car to get a snack in lieu of lunch. I almost expected old Mr. Kowolsky to step up behind the counter, but instead an energetic young Mexican weighed my apple and carefully wrapped a carton of blueberry yogurt for me.

He gave me detailed directions on how to find the plant entrance, eyeing me with impartial enthusiasm while he did so. I felt slightly cheered by his guileless admiration and slowly made my way to the steelworks, eating my yogurt with my left hand while I drove with the right.

It was just two o'clock. The plant was between shift changes, so mine was the only car going past the guard station at the main entrance. A beefy young man inspected the pass they'd given me at Pole Star.

"You know where to find the *Gertrude*?"

I shook my head.

"Take the road around to the left. You'll go past the coke ovens and a slag heap. You'll be able to see the ship from there."

I followed his directions, going by a long narrow building where fire danced inside, visible through sliding doors opened to let in the cool air. Slag formed a mountain on my left. Bits of cinder blew onto the windshield of the Omega. Peering through it at the rutted track in front of me, I continued on around the furnaces until I saw the *Gertrude* looming above me.

Great hills of coal framed the lakefront. The *Gertrude* was getting ready to dump her load onto one of them. Hard-hatted men in boiler suits had tied up the ship. As I left the car and picked my way across the pockmarked yard, I could see them turning the swivel top of the ship's self-unloader to position it over one of the smaller coal piles.

Bledsoe was on the ground talking with a man in a dirty gray boiler suit. The two weren't speaking when I came up, just looking at the activity going on above them.

Bledsoe had lost weight in the three days since I'd last seen him. It was shockingly noticeable—he must have dropped ten pounds. His tweed jacket sagged across his shoulders instead of straining as if to contain his monumental energy.

"Martin," I said. "Good to see you."

He smiled with genuine pleasure. "Vic! How'd you run me to earth?"

I explained and he introduced me to the man he was standing with, the shift foreman. As we talked, a great clanking started and coal began moving down the conveyor belt onto the heap below.

"The self-unloader is quite a machine. You ought to watch it in action," Bledsoe said into my ear. He went back to his car and got a second hard hat out of the trunk for me. We climbed up a ladder on the port side of the ship, away from the self-unloader, and Bledsoe took me over to watch coal coming up the wide figure-eight belt from the holds.

The coal came through quite fast, in large chunks. It takes about eight hours to unload the holds with a self-unloader, compared to two days using manual labor.

Bledsoe was clearly tense. He walked around, talking a bit to the crew, clenching and unclenching his fingers. He couldn't stand still. At one point he caught me watching him and said, "I won't relax until this load is off. Every time I move a cargo from now on, I'm not going to be able to sleep until I know the ship has made it in and out of port safely."

"What's the story on the *Lucella*?"

He grimaced. "The Coast Guard, the Corps of Engineers, and the FBI are mounting a full-scale investigation. Trouble is, until they get her out of the lock they won't even be able to see what kind of explosive was used."

"How long will that take?"

"A good ten months. That lock will be shut all summer and it'll take most of next year to repair the gates."

"Can you save the ship?"

"Oh yes, I think so. Mike's been all over it with the guys from the Costain boatyard—the people who built her. They'll take her out in sections, tow her back to Toledo, and weld her back together. She should be running again by the end of next summer."

"Who pays to repair the lock?"

"I don't know, but I'm not responsible for the damned thing blowing up. The army has to fix it. Unless the Court of Inquiry assigns liability to me. But there's no way in hell they can do that."

We were speaking almost in shouts to be heard over the clanking of the conveyor belts and the rattling of the coal going over the side. Some of the old energy was coming back into Bledsoe's face as he talked. He was starting to elaborate on his legal position, pounding his right fist into his left palm, when we heard a piercing whistle.

The noise came to an abrupt halt. The conveyor belt stopped and with it all its attendant racket. An authoritative figure moved over to the opening into the hold and called down a demand as to the cause of the belt's stopping.

"Probably just an overload on one of the side belts," Bledsoe muttered, looking extremely worried.

We heard a muffled shout from the hold, then a young man in a dirty blue boiler suit erupted up the ladder onto the deck. His face was greeny white under its smear of coal dust and he just made it to the side before he was sick.

"What is it?" the authoritative man yelled.

There were more cries coming from the hold. With a glance at Bledsoe, I started down the ladder the young engineer had just climbed up. Bledsoe followed close on my hands.

I jumped down the last three rungs onto the steel floor below. Six or seven hard-hatted figures were huddled over the figure-eight belt where it joined the side conveyors feeding it from the holds. I strode over and shoved them aside, Bledsoe peering around my back.

Clayton Phillips was staring up at me. His body was covered with coal. The pale brown eyes were open, the square jaw clenched. Blood had dried across his freckled cheekbones. I moved the men away and bent over to peer closely at his head. Coal had mostly filled in a large hole on the left side. It was mixed with congealed blood in a reddish-black, ghastly clot.

"It's Phillips," Bledsoe said, his voice constricted.

"Yes. We'd better call the police. You and I have a few questions to discuss, Martin." I turned to the group of men. "Who's in charge down here?"

A middle-aged man with heavy jowls said he was the chief engineer.

"Make sure no one touches the body or anything else. We'll get the police over here."

Bledsoe followed me tamely back up the ladder to the deck and off the ship. "There's been an accident down below," I told the Plymouth foreman. "We're getting the police. They won't be unloading the rest of the coal for a while." The foreman took us into a small office just around to the side of a long shed. I used the phone to call the Indiana State Police.

Bledsoe got into the Omega with me. We drove away from the yard in silence. I made my way back to the interstate and rode the few remaining miles over to the Indiana Dunes State Park. On a weekday afternoon, in early spring, the place was deserted. We climbed across the sand down to the shore. The only other people there were a bearded man and a sporty-looking woman with their golden retriever. The dog was swimming into the frothy waves after a large stick.

"You have a lot of explaining to do, Martin."

He looked at me angrily. "You owe me a lot of explanations. How did Phillips get into that ship? Who blew up the *Lucella*? And how come you're so quick on the spot every time disaster is about to strike Pole Star?"

"How come Mattingly flew back to Chicago on your plane?"

"Who the hell is Mattingly?"

I drew a breath. "You don't know? Honestly?"

He shook his head.

"Then who did you send back to Chicago in your plane?"

"I didn't." He made an exasperated gesture. "I called Cappy as soon as I got to town and demanded the same thing of him. He insists I phoned from Thunder Bay and told him to fly this strange guy back—he said his name was Oleson. Obviously someone was impersonating me. But who and why? And since you clearly know who this guy is, *you* tell *me*."

I looked out at the blue-green water. "Howard Mattingly was a second-string wing for the Chicago Black Hawks. He was killed early Saturday morning—run over by a car and left to die in a park on Chicago's northwest side. He was up at the Soo on Friday. He fits the description of the guy Cappy flew back to Chicago. He exploded the depth charges on the *Lucella*—I watched him do it."

Bledsoe turned to me and grabbed my arm in a gesture of spontaneous fury. "Goddamn it—if you watched him do it, how come you haven't said anything to anyone? I've been talking my head off to the FBI and the Corps of Engineers for two days and you—you've been sitting on this information."

I twisted away from his grasp and spoke coldly. "I only realized after the fact what Mattingly had been doing. I didn't recognize him immediately. As we went down to the bottom of the lock, he picked up what looked like an outsize pair of binoculars. They must have been the radio controls for the detonators. The whole thing only dawned on me after the *Lucella* had gone sky-high . . . You may recall that you were in shock. You weren't in any position to listen to anyone say anything. I thought I'd better leave and see if I could track him down."

"But later. Why didn't you talk to the police later?"

"Ah. That was because, when I got to the airport at Sault Ste. Marie, I found Mattingly had gone back to Chicago on your airplane, presumably under your orders. That really upset me—it made a mockery out of my judgment of your character. I wanted to talk to you about it first, before I told the police."

The dog came bounding up to us, water spraying from its red-gold hair. It was an older dog—she sniffed at Martin with a white muzzle. The woman called to her and the dog bounded off again.

"And now?" he demanded.

"And now I'd like to know how Clayton Phillips came to be on the self-unloader of a ship you were leasing."

He pounded the beach beside him. "You tell me, Vic. You're the smart detective. You're always turning up whenever there's a crime about to be committed on my fleet . . . Unless you've decided that a man with my record is capable of anything—capable of destroying his own dreams, capable of murder?"

I ignored his last statement.

"Phillips has been missing since yesterday morning. Where were you yesterday morning?"

His eyes were dark spots of anger in his face. "How dare you?" he yelled.

"Martin: listen to me. The police are going to ask that and you're going to have to answer."

He pressed his lips together and debated within himself. Finally he decided to master his temper. "I was closeted with my Lloyds representative up at the Soo until late yesterday. Gordon Firth—the Ajax chairman—flew up with him in Ajax's jet and they brought me back down to Chicago about ten last night."

"Where was the *Gertrude Ruttan*?"

"She was tied up at the Port. She steamed in Saturday afternoon and had to tie up for the weekend until they were ready to unload her. Some damned union regulation."

So anyone who could get into the Port and get onto the ship could have put a hole in the side of Phillips's head and shoved him into a cargo hold. He'd just fall down into the load and show up with the rest of the cargo when it came out on the conveyor belt. Very neat. "Who knew the *Gertrude Ruttan* would be there over the weekend?"

He shrugged. "Anyone who knows anything about the ships in and out of the Port."

"That narrows it down a lot," I said sarcastically. "Same thing for who fixed my car, for who killed Boom Boom. I was figuring Phillips for that job, but now he's dead too. So that leaves the other people who were around at the time. Grafalk. Bemis. Sheridan. You.''

"I was up in the Soo all day yesterday.''

"Yeah, but you could hire someone.''

"So could Niels,'' he pointed out. "You're not working for him, are you? Did he hire you to set me up?''

I shook my head.

"Who're you working for then, Warshawski?''

"My cousin.''

"Boom Boom? He's dead.''

"I know. That's why I'm working for him. We had a pact, Boom Boom and I. We took care of each other. Someone shoved him under the *Bertha Krupnik*. He left me evidence of the reason why which I found last night. Part of that evidence implicates you, Martin. I want to know why you were letting so many of your contracts with Eudora go to Grafalk.''

He shook his head. "I looked at those contracts. There was nothing wrong with them.''

"There was nothing wrong with them, except that you were letting Grafalk pick up a number of orders when you were the low bidder. Now are you going to tell me why or am I going to have to go to Pole Star and interrogate your staff and go through your books and repeat that boring routine?''

He sighed. "I didn't kill your cousin, Warshawski. If anyone did, it was Grafalk. Why don't you focus on him and find out how he blew up my ship and forget these contracts?''

"Martin, you're not a dummy. Think it through. It looks like you and Grafalk were in collusion on those shipping orders. Mattingly flew back to Chicago in *your* plane and Phillips's body was found on *your* ship. If I was a cop, I wouldn't look too much further—if I had all that information.''

He made a wrenching gesture with his right arm. Frustration.

"All right. It's true,'' he shouted. "I did let Niels have some of my orders. Are you going to put me in jail for it?''

I didn't say anything.

After a brief pause he continued more calmly. "I was trying to put financing together for the *Lucella*. Niels was getting desperate for orders. The steel slump was hurting everyone, but Grafalk was really taking it on the chin because of all those damned small ships of his. He told me he would let the story of my evil past out to the financial community if I didn't give him some of my orders."

"Could that really have hurt you?"

He gave a wry smile. "I didn't want to find out. I was trying to raise fifty million dollars. I couldn't see the Fort Dearborn Trust giving me a nickel if they knew I'd served two years for embezzling."

"I see. And then what?"

"Oh, as soon as the *Lucella* was launched I told Niels to publish and be damned. As long as I'm making money no one is going to care a tinker's dam about my record. When you need money, they make you sign an acolyte's pledge before they give it to you. When you've got it—they don't care where it came from. But Niels was furious."

"It's a mighty big jump from pressuring you over a few grain orders to blowing up your ship, though."

He insisted stubbornly that no one else cared enough. We talked about it for half an hour or more, but he wouldn't budge. I told him finally that I'd investigate Niels as well.

The golden retriever had departed with her people by the time we got to our feet and climbed back over the sand hills to the parking lot. A few children stared at us incuriously, waiting for the grown-ups to disappear before launching their own reckless deeds.

I drove Bledsoe back to the steel mill, now heavily thronged with Indiana and Chicago police. The four o'clock shift was arriving and I dropped him at the gates. The cops might want to talk to me later, as a witness, but they'd have to find me—I had other things to do.

21 * Fishing Trip

It is easier for a camel to go through the eye of a needle than for a private investigator in blue jeans to see the chairman of a major U.S. corporation. I reached Ajax Insurance headquarters in the south Loop a little after five—traffic had been heavy all the way into the city. I was figuring on it being late enough for me to avoid the phalanx of secretaries who pave the entrance to a CEO's office, but I'd forgotten Ajax's security system.

Guards in the marble lobby of the sixty-story skyscraper demanded an employee identification card from me. I obviously didn't have one. They wanted to know whom I was visiting—they would issue me a visitor's pass if the person I wanted to see approved my visit.

When I told them Gordon Firth, they were appalled. They had a list of the chairman's visitors. I wasn't on it, and they suspected me of being an assassin from Aetna, hired to bump off the competition.

"I'm a private investigator," I explained, pulling the photostat of my license from my wallet to show them. "I'm looking into a fifty-million-dollar loss Ajax sustained last week. It's true I don't have an appointment with Gordon Firth, but it's important I see him or whomever he's designating to handle this loss. It may affect Ajax's ultimate liability."

I argued with them some more and finally persuaded them if Ajax had to pay for the *Lucella*'s hull because they had kept me out of Firth's office I'd remember their names and see that the money came out of their hides.

These arguments did not get me to Firth—as I say, it's easier for a camel to pass through the eye of a needle—but they did bring me to a man in their Special Risks Department who was handling the loss. His name was Jack Hogarth and he came down to the lobby for me.

He walked briskly up to the guard station to meet me, his shirtsleeves pushed up to the elbows, his tie hanging loosely around his neck. He was about thirty-five or forty, dark, slight, with humorous brown-black eyes just now circled with heavy shadows.

"V. I. Warshawski, is it?" he asked, studying my card. "Come on up. If you've got some information on the *Lucella* you're more welcome than a heat wave in January."

I had to trot to keep up with him on the way to the elevator. We were carried quickly to the fifty-third floor; I yawned a couple of times to clear my ears. He barely waited for the elevator to open before plunging down the hall again, through double glass doors enclosing the elevator bank, and on to a walnut and crimson suite in the southeast corner of the building.

Papers were strewn across an executive-size walnut desk. A photograph of the *Lucella* as she lay fractured in the Poe Lock covered a table at one side, and a cutaway picture of a freighter hull was taped to the wood-paneled west wall.

I stopped to look at the photograph, enlarged to about three feet by two feet, and shuddered with remembered shock. Several more hatch covers had popped loose since I last saw the ship and the surfaces pointing steeply into the lock were covered with a thick smear of wet barley.

As I studied it, a very tall man got to his feet and strolled over to stand next to me. I hadn't seen him when I first walked into the room—he'd been sitting in a corner behind the door.

"Shocking, isn't it?" he said with a pronounced English accent.

"Very. It was even more shocking when it occurred."

"Oh, you were there, were you?"

"Yes," I answered shortly. "I'm V. I. Warshawski, a private investigator. And you're—?"

He was Roger Ferrant from the London firm of Scupperfield, Plouder, the lead underwriters on the *Lucella*'s hull and cargo insurance.

"Roger is probably the most knowledgeable man in the world about Great Lakes shipping, even though he operates out of London," Hogarth told me. He added to Ferrant, "Miss Warshawski may know something about our ultimate liability on the *Lucella*."

I sat down in an armchair by the window where I could see the setting sun paint Buckingham Fountain a faint pink-gold. "I'm looking into the accident to the *Lucella* as part of a murder investigation. At the moment I have two separate crimes—the murder of a young man connected with the Eudora Grain Company, and the destruction of the *Lucella*. It's not clear to me that they intersect. However, I was on board the *Lucella* pursuing my murder investigation when she blew up, and that's given me something of a personal interest in the explosion."

"Who's your client?" Hogarth demanded.

"It's a private individual—not someone you'd know. . . . How long does it take to clear up a claim like this?"

"Years." Ferrant and Hogarth spoke in chorus. The Englishman added, "Honestly, Miss Warshawski, it takes a very long time." He stumbled a bit pronouncing my name, unlike Hogarth, who got it right the first time.

"Well, who pays Bledsoe's expenses while he reassembles the *Lucella*?"

"We do," Hogarth said. "Ferrant here handles the hull damage. We pay for the destroyed cargo and the business interruption—the loads that Bledsoe is forgoing by having his ship lying in the bottom of the lock."

"Do you ante up a check to cover the cost of repairing the ship?"

"No," Ferrant said. "We pay the bills as the shipyard submits them."

"And your policy covers Pole Star even though it's clear

that someone blew up the ship, that it didn't just crack due to bad workmanship?''

Ferrant crossed one storklike leg over the other. ''That was one of the first questions we went into. As far as we can tell, it was not blown up as an act of war. There are other exclusions under the policy, but that's the main one . . . Unless Bledsoe destroyed the ship himself.''

''There'd have to be a significant financial advantage to him for doing so,'' I pointed out. ''If he collected the value of the hull and could invest it while he rebuilt the ship, there might be some, but otherwise it doesn't sound like it.''

''No,'' Hogarth said impatiently. ''There isn't any point to ruining a brand-new ship like the *Lucella*. Now if it were one of those old clunkers that cost more to operate than they bring in in revenues, I'd see it, but not a thousand-foot self-unloader.''

''Like Grafalk's, you mean,'' I said, remembering the *Leif Ericsson* running into the side of the wharf my first day down at the Port. ''He's better off collecting the insurance money than running his ships?''

''Not necessarily,'' said Hogarth uneasily. ''It'd depend on the extent of the damage. You're thinking of the *Leif Ericsson*, aren't you? He'll have to pay for the damage to the wharf. That's going to run him more than the cost of repairing the *Ericsson*'s hull.''

Bledsoe had told me he wasn't liable for the damage to the lock. I asked Hogarth about that. He made a face. ''That's another one that's going to tie the lawyers up for a decade or two. If Bledsoe was responsible for the damage to the ship, which in turn damaged the forward lock gates, he's liable. If we can find the real culprit, he's liable. That's what we'd like to do: find whoever blew up the ship so we can subrogate against him—or her.''

I looked a question.

''Subrogate—get him to repay us for whatever we pay Bledsoe. And if we don't find the real culprit, your rich Uncle Sam is going to pay for the lock. He'll probably have to anyway—no one could afford to replace that. They'll just prosecute and send whoever did it to jail for twenty years. If they can find him.'' The phone rang and he answered it. The caller seemed to be his wife: he told her placatingly that he'd be out of the office in twenty minutes and please to hold dinner for him.

He turned to me with an aggrieved expression. "I thought you came by because you had some hot information on the *Lucella*. All we've been doing is answering your questions."

I laughed. "I don't have any information for you now. But I think I may in a day or two. You've given me some ideas I want to play around with first." I hesitated, then decided to go ahead and tell them about Mattingly. I was on my way to the police to let them know, anyway. "The thing is, the guy who probably set off the explosion has been murdered himself. If the police can track down who killed him, they'll probably find the person who paid him to blow up the ship. I'm sure Mattingly was killed to keep him from bragging about it. He was a disagreeable guy who liked to boast about the sleazy things he did."

Getting the inside story on Mattingly cheered up Hogarth and Ferrant, even though it hadn't helped their investigation into ultimate liability much. They put on their suit jackets and walked out of the office with me.

"The thing is," Ferrant said confidentially in his English accent, "it's just cheering to know there may really be a villain out there."

"Yeah," I said as we came out in the deserted lobby, "but what if you find he works for another one of your insureds?"

"You mustn't say things like that," Ferrant said. "You really mustn't. I feel like eating for the first time since I heard about the *Lucella* last Saturday morning. I don't want you to ruin my dinner with horrible suggestions."

Hogarth departed for the Northwestern Station and a train to Schaumburg. Ferrant was staying in Scupperfield, Plouder's apartment in the Hancock Building. I offered him a ride up in my Omega, which was parked in an underground garage nearby.

Before starting it I checked under the hood, looked at the

oil, the brake fluid, the radiator. When Ferrant asked what I was doing I explained that I'd been in an accident recently and it made me more cautious about my car. Nothing seemed to be wrong.

On the short trip up Michigan Avenue to the Hancock I asked him if Scupperfield, Plouder had also underwritten the hull damage to the *Leif Ericsson*. They had; they underwrote all of the Grafalk Line.

"That's how Bledsoe came to us—he knew us from working with Grafalk."

"I see." I asked for his opinion of Bledsoe.

"One of the smartest men in the industry today. It's not a good time to be in Great Lakes shipping, at least not for U.S. carriers. Your government gives considerable advantages to foreign flagships they don't accord to U.S. vessels. Furthermore, old firms like Grafalk have some special legal positions that make it hard for a newcomer to break into the business. But Bledsoe can do it if anyone can. I just hope the wreck of the *Lucella* doesn't put an end to Pole Star."

He invited me to dine with him, but I thought I'd better get to the police with my news about Mattingly. I'd told my tale to Bledsoe, and now to the insurance people. Although I hadn't given Murray Ryerson the name of the man with binoculars I'd seen at the Soo, he was no dummy—he might easily tie it in with my interest in Mattingly. Bobby Mallory was not going to look at me kindly if he read the story first in the *Herald-Star*.

I felt uneasy as I moved my car onto Lake Shore Drive. My life had been threatened two weeks ago. Phillips was dead, possibly because of the veiled threat I'd left with his son Saturday night. Perhaps he'd panicked, threatened to reveal what he knew, and been killed for his pains. Mattingly was dead, probably to keep him from boasting in the locker room that he'd blown up a ship. Boom Boom was dead because he knew that Phillips was fiddling grain invoices. Why was I still driving around? Maybe they thought more people would be killed when the *Lucella* went up. They might have been relying on that to get rid of me and be thinking up some other accident for me now. Or maybe they just didn't believe I knew anything important.

I tried comforting myself with that idea the rest of the way home, but I had known even less when my car was sabotaged ten days ago. It occurred to me as I exited at Belmont that the deaths in this case had been staged as a species of accident: Boom Boom had fallen overboard, Mattingly had been hit by a car, Phillips crushed in a self-unloader. If my car had killed me as it was supposed to, I don't suppose anyone would have gone to great pains to find that the steering control was sabotaged.

I hadn't been able to convince the police that there might be a connection between the night watchman's death and Boom Boom's. They wanted to treat the threat on me as a routine act of vandalism. In other words, the murderer had gauged the psychology of the situation accurately. Now that I was prepared to divulge what I knew about Mattingly, how likely were the police to tie that in with Kelvin and Boom Boom? Not terribly.

I was half tempted to keep the news to myself. But the police have a good machinery for sifting through large crowds of witnesses. If they did follow up on my information, they could find out who picked Mattingly up at Meigs last Friday far more readily than I.

As I parked the car, carefully selecting a spot in front of a restaurant so that would-be attackers would face a maximum of witnesses, I decided I'd keep the story of Mattingly and the binoculars to myself. Just say that he'd flown back in Bledsoe's plane.

22 * Nighttime Chiseler

When I got to my apartment, I saw I was going to have to choose a story quickly. Sergeant McGonnigal was waiting for me in an unmarked brown Dodge. He got out when he saw me walking up the steps to the front door.

"Good evening, Miss Warshawski. Would you mind coming downtown with me? Lieutenant Mallory wants to ask you some questions."

"What about?" I asked, taking out my keys and putting them in the front door.

McGonnigal shook his head. "I don't know—he just asked me to bring you down."

"Lieutenant Mallory thinks I should be living in Melrose Park with a husband and six children. I suspect any questions he wants to ask me have to do with how close I am to reaching that goal. Tell him to send me a Christmas card." Just because I'd been going to see the police voluntarily didn't mean I had to like it when they came to fetch me.

McGonnigal set his handsome mouth in a thin line. "You're not as funny as you think you are, Miss Warshawski. Your fingerprints were found in Clayton Phillips's office. Anyone else, we'd have a warrant and bring them in as a material witness. Because Lieutenant Mallory was a friend of your father's he wants you to come of your own free will to answer some questions."

I was going to have to start wearing gloves if I ever wanted to make it as a burglar. "Very well. I'm coming of

200

my own free will." I opened the front door. "I need to get something to eat first. Want to come up with me to make sure I don't swallow a cyanide tablet?"

McGonnigal made an angry gesture and told me he'd wait in the car. I ran quickly up the three flights to my apartment. The larder was still bare—I hadn't had time to go to the store yet. I settled for a peanut butter sandwich made with the last two pieces of bread in the refrigerator and coffee reheated from breakfast. While I ate, I took Boom Boom's documents and taped them inside a couple of old copies of *Fortune*.

I went into the bathroom and brushed my teeth and washed my face. I needed to feel fresh and alert for a conversation with Bobby. I ran lightly back down the stairs to McGonnigal's waiting car. My shoulder gave me only faint twinges. I realized gloomily that I could start jogging again in the morning.

McGonnigal had the engine running. He took off with an ostentatious squeal of rubber before I even closed the door all the way. I put on the seat belt. "You ought to wear yours if you're going to drive like that," I told him. "Insurance people and police—the two groups who see the most car accidents and the two you never see with seat belts."

McGonnigal didn't answer. In fact conversation flagged all the way downtown. I tried to interest him in the Cubs' chances with Lee Elia and Dallas Green at the helm. He didn't want to talk about it. "I hope you're not a Yankee fan, Sergeant. If you are, you're going to have to arrest me to get me into the same car with you."

His only response was to drive faster. I kept up a monologue on the perfidies of the Yankees until we got to Twelfth Street, forbearing to comment on the fact that he was driving too fast for normal road conditions. He parked the car two feet from the curb and swung himself out, slamming the door behind him. I followed him into the back door of the Twelfth Street station.

"By the way, Sergeant, did you ever find anyone in the Kelvin murder?"

"It's still open," he said stiffly.

Mallory rated a tiny office in the maze making up the homicide division. The back wall was covered with a map of the city, precinct boundaries outlined in heavy black, high crime areas marked in red. Mallory was on the phone when we came in. I went over to look at my neighborhood. We had a very high homicide rate. There were a lot of rapes there, too. Maybe I would be better off in Melrose Park with six children.

Bobby hung up the phone and picked up a stack of papers. He put on his wire-rimmed glasses and started reading reports. "Come over here and sit down, Vicki."

I sat on the far side of his metal desk while he continued reading. "You were at Plymouth Steel this morning when Clayton Phillips's body was discovered."

I didn't say anything and he said sharply. "You were there, weren't you?"

"I thought you were making a statement, not asking a question. Of course I was there—I called the police and I didn't make any secret of who I was."

"Don't get smart with me. What were you doing down there?"

"I put Phillips's body in the hold Sunday morning and I wanted to see people's faces when it came out on the conveyor belt."

Bobby slapped the desk top with his open palm. "Vicki, you're this close to going to jail as a material witness." He held up his thumb and middle finger to indicate a very tiny distance. "Tell me what you were doing down there."

"I was looking for Martin Bledsoe. He owns the Pole Star Line."

Bobby relaxed a bit. "Why?"

"I was on board the *Lucella* when she blew up last week. That's his flagship. Someone put depth charges under her last Friday up in Sault Ste. Marie and—"

"Yes, I know all about that. What did you want to see Bledsoe for?"

"My suitcase fell into the middle of the ship. I wanted to know if they recovered it."

Mallory turned red at that. "You don't go bothering the

owner of a steamship line for that kind of crap. Cut out the horseplay and tell me the truth.''

I shook my head earnestly. "I am telling you the truth. No one else knew anything about it, so I went to see him. You see, my Smith & Wesson was in my case. That cost me three hundred dollars and I can't afford to replace it.''

I knew that would divert Bobby's attention. He does not like the idea of my carrying a gun. He knows that my dad taught me how to use one. Tony believed most shooting accidents were caused by children not knowing anything about firearms. Since he had to keep his police revolver at home sometimes, he made me learn how to clean, load, and shoot it. Nonetheless, the idea of a woman toting around a Smith & Wesson is contrary to all Bobby's notions of a proper lady's life-style. He jumped on that, demanding to know why I had the gun with me on board ship and what I was doing on the *Lucella* anyway.

That was easier ground. I reminded him of my car accident. "You guys wanted to believe it was vandals. I thought it was someone connected with the Port. I went up to Thunder Bay to talk to the captain and the chief engineer of the *Lucella*. Since one of them might have tried to kill me, I took my gun with me.''

We talked about that for a while. I reiterated my belief that Boom Boom had been pushed under the *Bertha Krupnik*. I told him I thought Henry Kelvin, the night watchman in his building, had been killed when he surprised intruders trying to find evidence that Boom Boom had of a crime down at the Port. Bobby wouldn't be persuaded. As far as he was concerned, Boom Boom had fallen in by accident, I was the victim of vandals, and Kelvin had interrupted a routine housebreaking. At that point a stubborn decision to keep the rest of my information to myself overtook me. If they were going to be so damned pigheaded, I would be too.

When Bobby got back to my fingerprints in Phillips's office, I evaded the issue. "What were you guys doing fingerprinting the man's office, anyway?''

"He was killed, Vicki,'' Bobby said with heavy sarcasm.

"We were printing his office and doing everything else to it to find out if he was killed there."

"Was he?"

Mallory drew a doodle on his desk pad. "He actually died of suffocation in the cargo holds. We don't know where he received the head wound—that would have killed him anyway if he hadn't suffocated first."

My stomach turned over. What a terrible death. I didn't like Phillips but I hadn't wished him that kind of end. Although if he had pushed Boom Boom overboard . . . "When do they think it happened?"

"About six Sunday morning. Give or take a few hours. Now, Vicki: I want to know what you were doing in the guy's office. And when you were doing it."

"About six yesterday morning I went down there to talk to him about my cousin's death. When he refused to answer my questions, I became enraged and hit him over the head with that brass thing he's got sitting on the front of his desk."

Bobby gave me such an angry stare, I felt my stomach turn over again. He called to McGonnigal, who was waiting outside the door. "Take down everything she says. If there's one more smart remark, book her as a material witness. I'm getting sick of this." He turned back to me. "When were you down there?"

I looked at the fingernails on my right hand. Time for a manicure. The left was no better. "Saturday night."

"And what were you doing there?"

"If I'd been burglarizing the place, I'd have been smart enough to wear gloves. I wasn't. I was looking for information that might show Phillips led a life of crime."

"Who's your client, Vicki?"

I shook my head. "Privileged information, Bobby."

We talked about that for a while. I still regarded Boom Boom as my client, but I was damned if I was going to tell Bobby that. Lock me up indeed.

"You can't drag a body into the Port without someone noticing you," I remarked at one point. "There's a police guard at the gates. Have you asked them for the names of everyone who came into the Port early Sunday?''

Mallory gave me a withering look. ''We can think of the easy ones too. We're questioning those people right now.''

''Was Niels Grafalk one of them?''

Bobby gave me a sharp glance. ''No. Our guy didn't see him. Why?''

I shrugged. ''Just curious.''

Bobby kept asking why I was down at Phillips's office, what information I had expected to find, and so on.

Finally I said, ''Bobby, you think Boom Boom's death was an accident. I think he was murdered. I was looking for something that would tie Eudora Grain into his death, because it happened at their elevator after he had been arguing with their man.''

Mallory made a neat pile of the papers on his desk. He took off his wire-rimmed glasses and placed them on top of it. That was a signal that the interrogation was over. ''Vicki, I know how much you loved Boom Boom. I think that's making you place too much importance on his death. We see that a lot in here, you know. Someone loses their son or wife or father in a terrible accident. They can't believe it's happened, so they say it's murder. If there's a conspiracy, it makes the death easier to handle—their loved one was important enough for someone to want to kill.

''Now, you've had a rough time lately, Vicki. Your cousin died and you almost got killed yourself in a bad accident. You go away for a few weeks, go someplace warm and lie in the sun for a while. You need to give yourself a chance to recover from all this.''

After that, naturally, I didn't tell him about Boom Boom's documents or about Mattingly flying in from the Soo on Bledsoe's plane. McGonnigal offered to take me home, but in a continuing spirit of perverseness I told him I could find the way myself. I got up stiffly—we'd been talking for over two hours. It was close to ten when I boarded the northbound subway at Roosevelt Road. I took it as far as Clark and Division, then transferred to a number 22 bus, getting off at Belmont and Broadway. I could walk the last half mile or so home.

I was very tired. The pain had come back in my shoulder, perhaps from sitting so long in one position. I walked as rapidly as I could across Belmont to Halsted. Lincoln Avenue cuts in at an angle there, and a large triangle on the south side of the street is a scraggy vacant lot. I held my keys clenched between my fingers, watching shadows in the bushes. At the front door to my building I kept a weather eye out for anything unusual. I didn't want to be the fourth victim of this extremely efficient murderer.

Three DePaul students share the second-floor apartment. As I walked up the stairs, one of them stuck her head out the door. "Oh, it's you," she said. She came all the way out, followed by her two roommates, one male and one female. In an excited trio they told me someone had tried to break into my apartment about an hour before. A man had rung their doorbell. When they buzzed him in, he'd gone past their door to the third floor.

"We told him you weren't home," one of the women said, "but he went on up anyway. After a while we heard him kind of chiseling away at the door. So we got the bread knife and went up after him."

"My God," I said. "He could have killed you. Why didn't you call the police?"

The first speaker shrugged thin shoulders in a Blue Demon T-shirt. "There were three of us and one of him. Besides, you know what the police are like—they'd never come in time in this neighborhood."

I asked if they could describe the intruder. He was thin and seemed wiry. He had a ski mask on, which frightened them more than the incident itself. When he saw them coming up the stairs, he dropped the chisel, pushed past them, and ran down the steps and up Halsted. They hadn't tried to chase him, for which I was grateful—I didn't need injuries to them on my conscience, too.

They gave me the chisel, an expensive Sorby tool. I thanked them profusely and invited all three up to my apartment for a nightcap. They were curious about me and came eagerly. I served them Martell in my mother's red Venetian glasses and answered their enthusiastic questions about my life as a private investigator. It seemed a small price to pay for saving my apartment, and perhaps me, from a late night intruder.

23 ✷ A House of Mourning

I woke up early the next morning. My would-be intruder convinced me that I didn't have much time before another accident would overtake me. My anger with Bobby continued: I didn't report the incident. After all, the police would just treat it as another routine break and entry. I would solve the crimes myself; then they'd be sorry they hadn't listened to me.

I felt decidedly unheroic as I ran slowly over to Belmont Harbor and back. I only did two miles instead of my normal five, and that left me sweating, the ache returning to my left shoulder. I took a long shower and rubbed some ligament oil into the sore muscles.

I checked the Omega over with extra care. Everything seemed to be working all right, and no one had tied a stick of dynamite to the battery cable. Even taking time for exercise and a proper breakfast, I was on the road by nine o'clock. I whistled Fauré's ''Après un rêve'' under my breath as I headed for the Loop. My first stop was the Title Office at City Hall. I found an empty parking meter on Madison Street and put in a quarter. Half an hour should be enough time for what I wanted to do.

The Title Office is where you go to register ownership of buildings in Chicago. Maybe all of Cook County. Like other city offices, this was filled with patronage workers. Henry Ford could study a city office and learn something about the ultimate in division of labor. One person gave me a form to fill out. I completed it, copying Paige Carrington's Astor Street address out of Boom Boom's address book. The filled-in form went to a second clerk, who date-stamped it and gave it to a heavy black man sitting behind a cage. He, in turn, assigned the form to one of the numerous pages whose job it was to fetch out the title books and carry them to the waiting taxpayers.

I stood behind a scarred wooden counter with other title searchers, waiting for a page to bring me the relevant volume. The man who finally filled my order turned out to be surprisingly helpful—city workers usually seem to be in a secret contest for who can harass the public the most. He found the entry for me in the heavy book and showed me how to read it.

Paige occupied a floor in a converted apartment building, an old five-flat built in 1923. The entries showed that there was some kind of dwelling on that site as far back as 1854. The Harris Bank had owned the current building until 1978 when it was converted to condominiums. Jay Feldspar, a well-known Chicago land developer, had acquired it then and done the conversion. Paige's unit, number 2, was held as a trust by the Fort Dearborn Trust. Number 1123785-G.

Curiouser and curiouser. Either Paige owned the thing herself as part of a trust, or someone owned it for her. I looked at my watch. I'd already been here forty minutes; might as well take a little more time and risk a parking ticket. I wrote the trust number down on a piece of paper in my shoulder bag, thanked the attendant for his help, and went out to find a pay phone. I'd been to law school with a woman who was now an attorney on the Fort Dearborn's staff. She and I had never been friends—our aspirations were too different. We'd never been enemies, either, though. I thought I'd call her and give a tug on the old school tie.

It took more than a tug—trust documents were confidential, she could be disbarred, let alone thrown out of the bank. I finally persuaded her that I'd get the *Herald-Star* to come in and suborn the clerical staff if she didn't find the name of the person behind the trust number for me.

"You really haven't changed a bit, Vic. I remember how you bullied everyone during moot court in our senior year."

I laughed.

"I didn't mean it as a compliment," she said crossly, but she agreed to call me at home that night with the information.

While I was wasting dimes and adding to the risk of a ticket, I checked in with my answering service. Both Ryerson and Pierre Bouchard had called.

I tried Murray first. "Vic, if you'd lived two hundred years ago they would have burned you at the stake."

"What are you talking about?"

"That Arroyo hiking boot. Mattingly was wearing them when he died, and we're pretty sure they're a match for the footprint the police found in Boom Boom's place. We'll have the story on the front page of the early editions. Got any other hot tips?"

"No. I was hoping you might have something for me. Talk to you later."

Bouchard wanted to tell me that he had checked around with Mattingly's cronies on the team. He didn't think Howard knew how to dive. Oh, and Elsie had given birth to a nine-pound boy two days ago. She was calling him Howard after the worthless snake. The members of the team were pitching in to make a donation to her since Howard had died without a pension and left very little life insurance. Would I give something from Boom Boom? Pierre knew my cousin would want to be included.

Certainly, I told him, and thanked him for his diligence.

"Are you making any progess?" he asked.

"Well, Mattingly's dead. The guy who I'm sure pushed Boom Boom in the water was killed Sunday. Another few weeks like this and the only person left alive will be his murderer. I guess that's progress."

He laughed. "I know you will have success. Boom Boom told me many times how clever you are. But if you need some muscle, let me know. I'm a good man for a fight."

I agreed with him wholeheartedly—I'd watched him cutting people's heads open on the ice with good-natured enthusiasm many times.

I sprinted back to my car, too late. A zealous meter maid had already filled out a parking ticket for letting the meter run out. I stuck it into my shoulder bag and inched my way across the Loop to Ontario Street, the closest entrance to the Kennedy Expressway.

The weather had finally warmed up slightly. Under a clear blue sky, trees along the expressway put out tentative, pale green leaves toward the sun. The grass was noticeably darker than it had been the week before. I started singing some Elizabethan love songs. They suited the weather and the chirping birds better than Fauré's moodiness. Off the Kennedy to the Edens, past the painfully tidy bungalows of the Northwest Side where people balanced their paychecks with anxious care, up to the industrial parks lining the middle-class suburbs of Lincolnwood and Skokie, on to the Tri-State Tollway and the rarefied northern reaches of the very rich.

" 'Sweet lovers love the spring,' " I sang, turning off onto route 137. Over to Green Bay Road, making the loop around to Harbor Road without a single wrong turn. I went on past the Phillips residence and parked the Omega around the southern bend in the road, away from the house. I was wearing my navy Evan Picone pantsuit, a compromise between comfort and the need to look respectable in a house of mourning.

I walked briskly back along the greensward to the Phillips house in my low-heeled loafers, my legs a little sore from the unaccustomed run this morning.

Once on the driveway, I stopped singing. That would be indecorous. Three cars were parked behind the blue Oldsmobile 88. Phillips's green Alfa. So he hadn't driven himself down to the Port Sunday morning? Or had the car been returned? I'd have to ask. A red Monte Carlo, about two years old and not kept up as well as the neighborhood demanded. And a silver Audi 5000. The sight of the Audi drove any desire to sing from my heart.

A pale teenager in Calvin Klein jeans and an Izod shirt answered the door. Her brown hair was cut short and frizzed around her head in a perm. She looked at me with an unfriendly stare. "Well?" she said ungraciously.

"My name is V. I. Warshawski. I've come to see your mother."

"Well, don't expect me to pronounce that." She turned her head, still holding onto the doorknob. "Mo-ther," she yelled. "Some lady's here to see you. I'm going for a bike ride."

"Terri. You can't do that." Jeannine's voice floated in from the back.

Terri turned her whole attention to her mother. She put her hands on her hips and shouted down the hall, "You let Paul take the boat out. If he can take the boat out, how come I can't go for a stupid little bike ride? I'm not going to sit here and talk to you and Grandma all day long."

"Real charming," I commented. "You read about that in *Cosmopolitan* or pick it up watching 'Dallas'?"

She turned her angry face to me. "Who asked you to butt in? She's back in there." She jerked her arm down the hall and stomped out the front door.

An older woman with carefully dyed hair came out into the hallway. "Oh dear. Did Terri go out? Are you one of Jeannine's friends? She's sitting back in here. It's awfully nice of you to stop by." The skin around her mouth had gotten soft, but the pale eyes reminded me of her daughter. She was wearing a long-sleeved beige dress, tasteful but not in the same price range as her daughter's clothes.

I followed her past the pale blue living room into the family room at the back where I had interviewed Jeannine the week before. "Jeannine dear, someone's come to visit you."

Jeannine was sitting in one of the wing chairs at the window overlooking Lake Michigan. Her face was carefully made up and it was hard to tell how she felt about her husband's death.

Across the room, feet tucked up under her on an armchair, sat Paige Carrington. She put down her teacup with a crash on a glass coffee table at her left arm. It was the first thing I'd seen her do that wasn't totally graceful.

"I thought I recognized your Audi out there," I remarked.

"Vic!" Her voice came out in a hiss. "I won't have it. Are you following me everywhere?"

At the same time Jeannine said, "No, you must go away. I'm not answering any questions now. My—my husband died yesterday."

Paige turned to her. "Has she been after you too?"

"Yes. She was out here last week asking me a lot of questions about my life as a corporate wife. What was she talking to you about?"

"My private life." Paige's honey-colored eyes flicked over me warily.

"I didn't follow you here, Paige: I came to see Mrs. Phillips. I might start staking out your place, though—I'm kind of curious about who's paying those monthly assessments. Astor Place—that's got to run you seven-eight hundred a month without the mortgage."

Paige's face turned white under her rust-toned makeup. Her eyes were dark with emotion. "You had better be joking, Vic. If you try bothering me any further, I'll call the police."

"I'm not bothering you at all. As I said, I came here to see Mrs. Phillips . . . I need to talk to you, Mrs. Phillips. Privately."

"What about?" Jeannine was bewildered. "I answered all your questions last week. And I really don't feel like talking to anyone right now."

"That's right, dear," her mother said. She turned to me. "Why don't you leave now? My daughter's worn out. Her husband's death came as quite a shock."

"I can imagine," I said politely. "I hope his life insurance was paid up."

Jeannine gasped. Paige said, "What a singularly tasteless remark, even from you."

I ignored her. "Mrs. Phillips, I'm afraid I talked to you last week under false pretenses. I'm not from a survey research firm. I'm a detective, and I was trying to find out if your husband might have attempted to murder me two weeks ago."

Her tightly clenched jaw went momentarily slack with surprise.

"My investigations have shown me that your husband had substantial sources of income beyond his salary. I'd like to talk to you privately about it. Unless you want your mother and Ms. Carrington to hear."

At that, her composure cracked. "He promised me no one would ever know." Tears carved two furrows in the makeup on her cheeks. Her mother hurried over with a box of tissues and fussed over her, telling her somewhat confusedly to go ahead and have a good cry.

I was still standing. "I really think we'd better continue this conversation alone. Is there another room we can go to, Mrs. Phillips?"

"What are you talking about?" her mother said. "Clayton had a very good salary at Eudora Grain. Why, when they made him an officer five years ago, he and Jeannine bought this house."

"That's okay, Mother." Jeannine patted the older woman's hand. "I'd better talk to this woman." She turned to Paige and said with sudden venom, "I suppose *you* know all about it."

Paige gave her triangular smile. "I know a fair amount." She shrugged her slim shoulders. "But who am I to cast stones, after all?" She picked up a sweater lying on the table beside her. "Better talk to Vic, Jeannine. If you don't, she'll only come in and burglarize the place so she can examine your bankbooks." She drifted over to Jeannine's chair and kissed the air by her cheek. "I'm going back to the city. I'll see you at the funeral tomorrow afternoon—unless you want me to come up before then."

"No, that's all right, dear," Jeannine's mother said.

"We'll manage fine." She bustled out to the hall behind the elegant younger woman.

I looked after them, puzzled. I assumed at first that Paige must have met Jeannine at some Eudora Grain function when she was dating Boom Boom. But that last exchange made it sound like a fairly close relationship.

"How do you know Paige?" I asked.

Jeannine turned her tear-streaked face to me for the first time since I'd mentioned the invoices. "How do I know her? She's my sister. Why wouldn't I know her?"

"Your sister!" We sounded like a couple of damned parrots. "Sisters. I see." Actually, I didn't see a thing. I sat down. "Did you take her to the party where she met my cousin?"

She looked surprised. "What party was that?"

"I don't know who gave it. Probably Guy Odinflute. He lives around here, doesn't he? Niels Grafalk was interested in buying a share in the Black Hawks. My cousin came up along with some of the other players. Paige was there and she met my cousin. I want to know who brought her."

Jeannine swallowed a sly smile. *"That* party. No, we didn't go."

"But were you invited?"

"Mr. Odinflute may have asked us . . . We get asked to a lot of parties at Christmas. If you want to know who Paige went with, though, you ask her."

I looked at her narrowly: she knew, but she wouldn't tell. I turned my attention to the money. "Tell me about the invoices, Jeannine."

"I don't know what you're talking about."

"Sure you do. You just said he'd promised no one would ever know. I called about them Saturday night—left a message with your son Paul. What did your husband do next?"

She shed a few more tears but in the end it came out that she didn't know. They got back late. Paul had left the message by the kitchen phone. When Clayton saw it, he went into his study and shut the door. He made a phone call and left a few minutes later. No, not in the Alfa. Had someone picked him up? She didn't know. He was very upset and told her not to bother him. It was about one-thirty Sunday morning when he went out. That was the last time she ever saw him.

"Now tell me about the invoices, Jeannine. He was padding them, wasn't he?"

She didn't say anything.

"People would give him bids on Eudora Grain cargoes and he would log the orders at one price but bill them at another. Is that right."

She started crying again. "I don't know. I don't know."

"You don't know how he worked it, but you know he was doing it. That's true, isn't it?"

"I didn't ask, as long as the bills got paid." She was sobbing harder.

I was losing my temper. "Did you know what your husband's salary was?"

"Of course I knew what Clayton earned." Her tears stopped long enough for her to glare at me.

"Sure you did. And you knew ninety-two thousand, however good it looks compared to the other girls at Park Forest South High, or whatever it was, wasn't enough to pay for a boat. This house. Your designer clothes. The kid at Claremont. Those high-ticket cars. The Izod T-shirts little Terri runs around in. Dues at the Maritime Club. Just out of curiosity, what does the Maritime Club run you a year? I was betting twenty-five thousand."

"You don't understand!" She sat up and stared at me with fierce, angry eyes. "You don't know what it's like when all the other girls have everything they want and you're making do with last year's clothes."

This sounded like a real heartache to me. "You're right—I don't. My high school, most of us girls had a couple of dresses we started with as sophomores and wore out the door when we graduated. Park Forest South may be a bit tonier than South Chicago—but not a lot."

"Park Forest South! My mother moved there later. We grew up here in Lake Bluff. We had horses. My father kept a boat. We lived down the road from here. Then he lost everything. Everything. I was a junior in high school. Paige was only eight. She's too young to remember the humiliation. The way people stared in school. Mother sold the silver. She sold her own jewels. But it didn't do any good. He shot himself and we moved away. She couldn't stand the pity people like old Mrs. Grafalk dished out at the country club. And I had to go to Roosevelt instead of Northwestern.''

"So you decided you were going to move back here, no matter what it took. What about your husband? He a Lake Bluffer in exile who made his way back?''

"Clayton came from Toledo. Eudora Grain brought him here when he was twenty-five. He rented an apartment in Park Forest and we met there.''

"And you thought he had possibilities, that he might go all the way for you. When did you find out that wasn't going to happen?''

"When Terri was born. We were still living in that crappy three-bedroom house.'' She was screaming now. "Terri and Ann had to share a room. I was buying all my clothes at Wieboldt's. I couldn't stand it! I couldn't stand it any more. And there was Paige. She was only eighteen, but she already knew—knew—''

"Knew what, Jeannine?''

She recovered some of her control. "Knew how to get people to help her out,'' she said quietly.

"Okay. You didn't want Paige outdressing you. So you put pressure on your husband to come up with more money. He knew he was never going to have enough if he just struggled along on his salary. So he decided to skim something off the top before it ever hit Eudora's books. Did he fiddle with anything besides the invoices?''

"No, it was just the invoices. He could make—make—about a hundred thousand extra a year from them. He—he didn't do it with all the orders, only about ten percent. And he paid taxes on them.''

"Paid taxes on them?'' I echoed incredulously.

"Yes. We didn't want to run—run a risk with the IRS auditing us. We called it commission income. They don't know what his job's supposed to be like. They don't know whether he should be earning commissions or not.''

"And then my cousin found out. He was going through the papers, trying to see what a regional manager does to run an office like that, and he ended up comparing some invoices with the original contract orders."

"It was terrible," she gulped. "He threatened to tell David Argus. It would have meant the end of—of Clayton's career. He would have been fired. We would have had to sell the house. It would have been—"

"Spare me," I said harshly. A pulse throbbed in my right temple. "It was a choice between the Maritime Club and my cousin's life."

She didn't say anything. I grabbed her by the shoulders and shook her. "Answer me, damn you! You decided my cousin had to die to keep you in your Massandrea dresses. Is that what happened? Is it?"

In my rage I had lifted her from her wing chair and was shaking her. Mrs. Carrington came bustling into the room. "What is going on here?" she fussed behind me. I was still screaming at Jeannine. Mrs. Carrington grabbed my arm. "I think you'd better go now. My daughter cannot afford any more upsets. If you don't leave, I will call the police."

Somehow her scratchy voice penetrated and I forced my anger back. "You're right. I'm sorry, Mrs. Carrington. I'm afraid I got carried away by my work." I turned to Jeannine. "Just one more question before I leave you to your mourning. What was Paige's role in all this?"

"Paige?" she whispered, rubbing her shoulders where I had grabbed them. She gave the sly smile I'd seen earlier. "Oh, Paige was supposed to keep track of what Boom Boom was up to. But you'd better talk to her. She hasn't given away my secrets. I won't give away hers."

"That's right," Mrs. Carrington said. "You girls should be loyal to each other. After all, you're all that you have."

"Besides a boat and a condo on Astor Place," I said.

24 * A Question of Policy

I was sick by the side of the road as soon as I got to the end of the drive. Terri rode up on her bicycle, a Peugeot ten-speed, I noticed as I wiped my mouth with a Kleenex. Boom Boom, you did not die in vain if you preserved a French racing bicycle for that girl.

I walked slowly down the road to the Omega and sat in it for a long time without starting the engine. My shoulder ached from grabbing Jeannine and lifting her up.

I had found out about Boom Boom's death. Or proved to myself what I had suspected for several days, at any rate. I felt a sharp pain across my diaphragm, as though someone had inserted a little needle behind it which jabbed me every time I breathed. That's what people mean when they say their hearts ache. They really mean their diaphragms. My face felt wet. I passed a hand across my eyes, expecting to find blood. I was crying.

After a while I looked at my watch. It was one o'clock. I looked at my face in the rearview mirror. It had gone very pale and my gray eyes stood out darkly in contrast. There were days when I'd looked better, but that couldn't be helped. I switched on the engine and slowly turned the car around on the narrow pavement. My arms felt leaden, so heavy I could scarcely lift them to the steering wheel. It would be nice to follow Bobby's advice and go someplace warm for a few weeks. Instead I drove up the road past the Phillips house to the Grafalks'.

The garage was behind the house to the left; I couldn't see the cars to tell if anyone was home. I climbed up the shallow wide step to the front porch and rang the bell. A minute or two passed; I was going to ring again when the thickset maid, Karen, answered. She looked at me grudgingly. She remembered my vulgar interest in Mr. Grafalk's movements last week.

I gave her my card. "Is Mrs. Grafalk in, please?"

"Is she expecting you?"

"No. I'm a detective. I want to talk to her about Clayton Phillips."

She seemed undecided about whether or not she was going to take my card back. I was too worn out from my encounter with Jeannine to put up much of a fight. As we stood there at an impasse, a high, clipped voice demanded of Karen who it was.

The maid turned around. "It's a detective, Mrs. Grafalk. She says she wants to talk to you about Mr. Phillips."

Mrs. Grafalk came into the hall. Her graying black hair was styled to emphasize her high cheekbones, which she had further accentuated with a dark rouge. She was dressed to go out, in a salmon silk suit with a ballet skirt and a flared, ruched jacket. Her eyes were sharp but not unfriendly. She took the card from Karen, who positioned herself protectively between us.

"Miss Warshawski? I'm afraid I don't have much time. I'm on my way to a Ravinia planning meeting. What did you want to talk about?"

"Clayton and Jeannine Phillips."

An expression of distaste crossed her face. "There's not a lot I can tell you about them. Clayton is—was, I should say—a business associate of my husband's. For reasons I have never understood, Niels insisted we entertain them, even sponsor them at the Maritime Club. I tried to interest Jeannine in some of the work that I do, particularly with the poor immigrant community in Waukegan. I'm afraid it's hard to get her to think of anything but her clothes."

She spoke rapidly, scarcely pausing for breath between sentences.

"Excuse me, Mrs. Grafalk, but Mr. Grafalk implied that Jeannine was a protégée of yours and that you wanted to get her into the Maritime Club."

She raised her black, painted eyebrows and opened her eyes very wide. "Why did Niels say that? I wonder. Clayton obliged him on some business deal and Niels sponsored him in the club to show his appreciation. I'm perfectly sure that was the way it happened. Niels keeps what he does with Grafalk Steamship to himself, so I've never known what the arrangement was—in fact I can't imagine being interested in it. I'm sorry Clayton's dead, but he was an insufferable climber and Jeannine is no better . . . Does that answer your questions? I'm afraid I must go now." She started for the door, buttoning on a pair of pale salmon gloves. I didn't know anyone wore gloves anymore. She walked outside the door with me, moving at a good clip on needle-pointed shoes. A woman with less force of personality would have looked absurd in that outfit. Mrs. Grafalk seemed elegant.

As I got into the Omega, someone drove the Bentley up for her. A thin, sandy-haired man got out, helped her into the car, and headed back to the garage behind the house.

Slowly driving back to Chicago, I thought about Mrs. Grafalk's remarks. The business deal must have been connected with the Eudora shipping invoices. What if Phillips had split the difference in the bills with Grafalk? Say he got ninety thousand dollars extra over the price registered on the computer for the shipment and gave forty-five thousand to Grafalk. That didn't make sense, though. Grafalk was the biggest carrier on the lakes. What did he need with penny-ante stuff like that? If Grafalk were involved, the payoff had to be more impressive. Of course, Grafalk operated all those older ships. It cost him more to carry cargo. The amount in the invoices was probably the true price of what it cost Grafalk to carry the stuff. If that was the case, Phillips was really stealing from Eudora Grain—not just pocketing the difference between how much he logged into the contract and the ultimate invoice, but losing money for Eudora on every shipment he recorded when Grafalk was the carrier. What Grafalk got out of it was more shipments in a depressed market in which he had a hard time competing because of his older, inefficient fleet.

Suddenly I saw the whole thing. Or most of it, anyway. I felt as though the truth had been hammered in at me from the day I walked into Percy MacKelvy's office at Grafalk Steamship down at the Port. I remembered listening to him trying to place orders on the phone, and my frustration while we were talking. Grafalk's reaction to Bledsoe at lunch. The times in the last two weeks I'd heard how much more efficient the thousand-footers were to operate. I even had an idea where Clayton Phillips had been murdered and how his body had been carried onto the *Gertrude Ruttan* without anyone seeing it.

A seventy-ton semi blared its horn behind me. I jumped in my seat and realized I had brought the Omega almost to a standstill in the second lane of the Kennedy. No need for anyone to arrange subtle accidents for me—I could kill myself without help. I accelerated quickly and drove on into the Loop. I needed to talk to the Lloyds man.

It was three in the afternoon and I hadn't eaten. After leaving the car in the Grant Park underground garage, I went into the Spot, a little bar and grill behind Ajax, for a turkey sandwich. In honor of the occasion I also had a plate of french fries and a Coke. My favorite soft drink, but I usually avoid it because of the calories.

I marched across Adams to the Ajax Building, singing, " 'Things go better with Coca-Cola,' " under my breath. I told the guard I wanted to see Roger Ferrant—the Lloyds man—up in the Special Risks office. After some delay—they couldn't figure out the Special Risk phone number—they got through to Ferrant. He would be happy to see me.

With my visitor's ID clipped to my lapel, I rode to the fifty-third floor. Ferrant came out of the walnut office to meet me. A shock of lanky brown hair flopped in his eyes and he was straightening his tie as he came.

"You've got some news for us, have you?" he asked eagerly.

"I'm afraid not yet. I have some more questions I didn't think to ask yesterday."

His face fell, but he said cheerfully, "Shouldn't expect miracles, I guess. And why should you succeed where the FBI, the U. S. Coast Guard, and the Army Corps of Engineers have failed?" He ushered me courteously back into the office, which was more cluttered than it had been the night before. "I'm staying in town through the formal inquiry at the Soo next Monday, then back to London. Think you'll crack the problem by then?"

He was speaking facetiously, but I said, "I should have the answer in another twenty-four hours. I don't think you're going to like it, though."

He saw the seriousness in my face. Whether he believed me or not, he stopped laughing and asked what he could do to help.

"Hogarth said yesterday you were the most knowledgeable person in the world on Great Lakes shipping. I want to know what's happening to it with this lock blown up."

"Could you explain what you mean, please?"

"The accident to the lock must be having quite an impact, right? Or can ships still get through?"

"Oh—well, shipping hasn't come to a complete standstill. They closed the MacArthur and the Davis locks for several days while they cleaned debris out of them and tested them, but they can still use the Sabin Lock—that's the one in Canadian waters. Of course, the biggest ships are shut off from the upper lakes for a year—or however long it takes them to fix the Poe—the Poe was the only lock that could handle the thousand-footers."

"And how serious is that? Does it have much of a financial impact?"

He pushed the hair out of his eyes and loosened his tie again. "Most of the shipping is between Duluth and Thunder Bay and ports lower down. Sixty percent of the grain in North America goes out of those two ports on freighters. That's a hell of a lot of grain, you know, when you think of everything that's produced in Manitoba as well as the upper Midwest—maybe eighteen billion bushels. Then there's all that taconite in Duluth." He pursed his lips in thought. "The Soo locks handle more cargo every year than Panama and Suez combined, and they're only open for nine months instead of year round like those two. So there is some financial impact.''

"The cargoes will still come out, but the smaller ships will have an advantage?" I persisted.

He smiled. "Just until they get the Poe Lock back under operation. Actually, there's been a lot of disarray, both in the grain markets and among the Great Lakes shippers since the lock blew up. They'll settle down in a few weeks when they realize that most traffic won't be impaired.''

"Except for the carriers who've converted primarily to thousand-foot ships.''

"Yes, but there aren't too many of those. Of course, grain concerns like Eudora are scrambling to get all their cargoes onto the smaller fleets, even bypassing the 740-foot ships. Grafalk's is picking up a number of orders. They aren't jacking up their rates, though, the way some of their less scrupulous brethren are.''

"How profitable is Grafalk's, in general?''

He looked at me in surprise. "They are the biggest carrier on the lakes.''

I smiled. "I know—I keep being told that. But do they make money? I understand that these smaller ships are unprofitable and they make up his whole fleet.''

Ferrant shrugged. "All we do is insure the hulls. I can't tell you how much freight they're carrying. Remember, though, profitability is relative. Grafalk may not make as much as a firm like American Marine, but that doesn't mean they're unprofitable.''

Hogarth had come in while we were talking. "Why do you want to know, Miss Warshawski?''

"It's not just idle curiosity. You know, no one's come forward claiming responsibility for the bombing—the PLO or the FALN or the Armenians. If it wasn't a random act of terrorism, there had to be a reason for it. I'm trying to find out if that reason included switching cargo from the big freighters to small vessels like the ones in Grafalk's fleet.''

Hogarth looked annoyed. "Not Grafalk, I assure you, Miss Warshawski. Niels Grafalk comes from a very old shipping family. He's devoted to his fleet, to his business—and he's a gentleman.''

"That's a fine testimonial," I said. "It does a lot of credit to your heart. But a fifty-million-dollar ship has been blown up, the North American shipping industry has been thrown into disarray, however temporary, and a lot of business interrupted. I don't know how the courts interpret such a thing, but someone is going to have to pay for that business interruption. Grafalk stands to gain a lot by this accident. I want to know what shape his business is in. If it's doing well, there's less of a motive."

Ferrant looked amused. "You certainly look for the less pleasant side of human nature . . . Jack, you have some idea of the state of the business, don't you? Just look at your records, see how much cargo coverage he's got and what his workers compensation insurance is like.''

Hogarth said mulishly that he had a meeting to get to and he thought it was a waste of time.

"Then I'll do it," Ferrant said. "You just show me where the files are, Jack, and I'll have a look-through for Miss Warshawski here . . . No, really, I think she's got a good point. We ought to follow up on it.''

Hogarth finally called his secretary on the intercom and asked her to bring him five years of Grafalk Steamship files. "Just don't ever let the old boy know you did this. He's very touchy where his family name is concerned.''

Hogarth left for his next meeting and Ferrant made some phone calls while I watched the boats out on Lake Michigan. Monroe Harbor was filling up rapidly with its summer fleet of sailboats. A lot of people were taking advantage of the beautiful weather; the near horizon was filled with white sails.

After some twenty minutes a middle-aged woman in a severely tailored suit came into the office pushing a large wire cart full of files. "These are the Grafalk Steamship files Mr. Hogarth asked for," she said, leaving the cart in the middle of the room.

Ferrant was enthusiastic. "Now we'll see what shape the

business is in. You can't tell that just from the hull insurance, which is all I do for Grafalk.''

Five years of Grafalk history was a substantial amount of paper. We had workers compensation policies, which went on for about a hundred pages a year, showing classes of employees, states covered, Longshoremen's Act exclusions, and premium audits. There was a business interruption policy for each year, cargo coverage, which was written on a per-shipment basis, and inland marine, to cover Grafalk's liability for cargo once it was unloaded from his ships.

Ferrant sorted through the mass with an experienced eye. ''You know, the cargo and the compensation are going to tell us the most. We'll just see the value of the freight he's carrying and how many people he's employing to do it. You tot up those workers compensation policies—look at the final audited statements and that'll tell you how many people he's got sailing for him every year. I'll go through these cargo policies.''

I sat down at a round wooden table and joined him in stacking the papers covering it down on the floor. ''But I thought the whole shipping business was depressed. If he's not carrying much, how will that tell us anything besides the fact that the industry's depressed?''

''Good point, good point.'' Ferrant placed a stack of workers compensation policies in front of me. ''We have some industry statistics—the average load carriers are hauling as a percentage of their available tonnage, that sort of thing. We'll just compare them. I'm afraid it's a rough approximation. The other thing, though, is that we know about what it costs a day to own one of those old clunkers. Now if it's not carrying cargo, there's still overhead—it has to be docked someplace. Unless the ship is in mothballs—which also costs something per diem—you have to have a skeleton crew on board. You need to be able to turn the beast on in a hurry and get to the place where you have a cargo waiting. So we can make a good guess at his costs and then look at these cargoes, here, and see how much he's earning.''

That seemed like a reasonable approach. I started on my part of the assignment, secretly entertained by Ferrant's enthusiasm for the project. He didn't have Hogarth's personal feeling for the insured.

The first page of the 1977 policy explained that Grafalk Steamship was a closely held corporation, principal address at 132 North La Salle Street in Chicago. The summary of the coverage on the declarations page showed Grafalk with fifteen hundred employees in eight states. These included sailors, secretaries, stevedores, longshoremen, truck drivers, and general office workers. Directors and officers were excluded from coverage. The total premium for 1977 was four million eight hundred thousand dollars. I whistled to myself. A lot of money.

I flipped through the pages of state and class detail to the back where the audit of the premium was attached. This section was completed at the end of the year. It showed how many people had actually worked each day by class of job and how much premium Grafalk in fact owed Ajax for 1977. The reduction was substantial—down to three million dollars. Instead of three million hours of work, Grafalk's employees had put in under two million for the year ending then.

I showed this result to Ferrant. He nodded and went back to the cargo policies. I finished the compensation ones, scribbling summary results on a sheet of paper. Ferrant handed me a stack of cargo policies. He was tabulating them by date, total value of contract, and vessel used. We'd compare them later to the tonnage figures of the individual ships.

Hogarth came in as we were finishing the masses of paper. I looked at my watch. It was almost six o'clock.

"Any luck?" Hogarth asked.

Ferrant pursed his lips, his long hair falling over his eyes again. "Well, we have to add up what we've got. Doesn't look good, though. I say, Hogarth, be a sport and give us a hand—don't look so sour. Think of this as an intellectual problem."

Hogarth shook his head. "Count me out. I told Madeleine I'd be home on time for once tonight and I'm already late. I'm going to catch the six thirty-five."

He left and Ferrant and I continued our work, tedious and

uninspiring. In the end, though, it became clear that Grafalk had been using only forty of his sixty-three vessels for the last five years. In fact he'd sold three ships in the middle of 1979.

"He should have sold more," Ferrant said gloomily.

"Maybe he tried and there wasn't a market."

By eight-thirty we'd completed a sketchy analysis of Grafalk's finances. His ships cost about two thousand dollars a day to operate when they weren't sailing, about ten thousand dollars a day when they were. So the total expense to Grafalk each season for running the steamship company was about a hundred twenty million dollars a year. And the total value of the cargoes he was carrying came out to only a hundred million in 1977. Things were a little bit better in '78 and '79 but hadn't improved much the past two years.

"That answers your question all right," Ferrant said. "The lad is definitely losing money." He lined up his stacks of notes. "Odd how much cargo he's been carrying for Eudora Grain the last five years. Almost twenty percent of his total volume."

"Odd indeed," I said. "Of course, Eudora's a big concern . . . Where's Grafalk been coming up with the money to cover these losses? They're pretty staggering."

"The steamship company isn't the only thing he owns." Ferrant was sweeping the policies back into their jackets. "There's a profitable railway that connects the Port of Buffalo with Baltimore—he can unload there and ship by rail to oceangoing vessels in Baltimore. That does very well for him. His family owns a big block of stock in Hansen Electronic, the computer firm. You'd have to see if you could get his broker to tell you whether he's been selling off the stock to pay for this. He's into a number of other things. I think his wife has some money, too. But the steamship company has always been his first love."

We piled the policies back into the cart and left it in the hallway for someone to take care of in the morning. I yawned and stretched and offered to buy Ferrant a drink.

25 * The Old Girl Network

He walked with me to the Golden Glow on Jackson and Federal. It's a place for serious drinkers—no quiche and celery sticks to entice imbibers of white wine on their way to the commuter trains. Sal, the magnificent black woman who owns the place, has a mahogany horseshoe-shaped bar, relic of an old Cyrus McCormick mansion, and seven tiny booths crammed into a space wedged out between a bank and an insurance company.

I hadn't been in for several weeks and she came over to our booth herself for our order. I asked for my usual, a Johnnie Walker Black up, and Ferrant had a gin martini. I asked Sal for the use of a phone and she brought one over to the table for me.

My answering service told me Adrienne Gallagher, the woman I know at the Fort Dearborn Trust, had called. She'd left her home number and a message that I could call before ten

A little girl answered the phone and called her mommy in a shrill voice.

"Hello, Vic. I got the information you wanted."

"I hope they're not trying to fire you or disbar you."

She gave a little laugh. "No—but you owe me some free detective work. Anyway, the condominium is owned by a Niels Grafalk—Vic? Are you there? Hello?"

"Thanks, Adrienne," I said mechanically. "Let me know when you need the detective work."

I hung up and dialed the Windy City Balletworks to see if they were performing tonight. A recorded voice told me that performances were held Wednesday through Saturday at eight; Sundays at three. Today was Tuesday; Paige might be home.

Ferrant looked at me courteously. "Something wrong?"

I made a gesture of distaste. "Nothing I hadn't suspected since this morning. But it's upsetting anyway—Grafalk owns real estate along with everything else."

"You know, Miss War—Do you have a first name? I just can't keep my tongue around your last one—Vic, you're being terribly mysterious. I take it you think Grafalk may be behind the damage to the Poe Lock, since we just spent most of the afternoon proving that he was losing money. Would you mind telling me what's going on?"

"Some other time. There's someone I need to talk to tonight. I'm sorry, I know it's rude to run out on you like this, but I must see her."

"Where are you going?" Ferrant asked.

"To the Gold Coast."

He announced that he was coming with me. I shrugged and headed for the door. Ferrant tried putting some money on the table, but Sal gave it back to him. "Vic'll pay me when she's got the money," she said.

I flagged a taxi on Dearborn. Ferrant got in beside me, again demanding to know what was going on.

"I'll tell you later," I said. "It's too long a story to start during a short cab ride."

We pulled up in front of a massive pale pink brick building with white concrete corners and white-enameled shutters. It was dark now, but black wrought-iron street lamps illuminated the building's facade.

Ferrant offered to accompany me inside, but I told him this was a job I had to handle alone. He watched me as I rang the bell, set in a lighted brass box outside the front door. A house phone was nestled inside the box for communicating with the inmates. When Paige's voice came tinnily through the receiver, I pitched my voice high and told her it was Jeannine. She buzzed me in.

The stairs were carpeted in a rose-patterned blue rug. My tired feet sank gratefully into the pile. Paige was waiting for me in the doorway at the top of the stairs, wearing her white terry-cloth robe, her face not made up, her hair pulled back under a towel as I'd seen her after rehearsal.

"What brings you into the city, Jeannie?" she was saying as my head came in sight. The rest of her sentence died in her throat. She stood immobile with surprise for a second too long. I reached the door as she started to slam it and pushed my way inside.

"We're going to talk, Paige. A little heart-to-heart."

"I have nothing to say to you. Get out of here before I call the police." Her voice came out in a harsh whisper.

"Be my guest." I sat down in a wide armchair upholstered in rust brocade and looked around the large, light room. A Persian rug covered about two thirds of the dark parquet. Gold brocade drapes were looped back from the windows overlooking Astor Street and sheer gauze hung underneath. "The police will be very interested in your role in Boom Boom's death. Please do call them."

"They think it's an accident."

"But you, dear Paige? Do you think it is?"

She turned her face away, biting her lip.

"Jeannine told me this morning your role was to keep tabs on what my cousin was up to. I thought she meant for her and Clayton. But she wasn't talking about them, was she? No, you were keeping track of him for Grafalk."

She didn't say anything but kept staring at a picture on the west wall as if seeking inspiration from it. It looked like a very good copy of a Degas. For all I knew, it was an original. Even with the losses to the steamship line, Niels Grafalk could afford to give his lover that kind of trifle.

"How long have you been Grafalk's mistress?"

Spots of color stained her cheeks. "What an offensive remark. I have nothing to say to you."

"Then I'll have to do the talking. You correct me where I'm wrong. Jeannine and Clayton moved to Lake Bluff five years ago. Niels knew Clayton was fiddling around with Eudora Grain invoices. He promised not to turn him in to Argus if Clayton would start giving Grafalk a preferred position on shipping orders.''

"I don't know anything about the Grafalk Steamship Line.''

"You and your sister are so pure-minded, Paige. You don't want to know anything about where your money comes from, just that it's there to spend when you need it.''

"I scarcely know Niels Grafalk, Vic. I've met him socially at my sister's. If Clayton and he did have some kind of business arrangement, I would be the last person to know about it.''

"Oh, bullshit, Paige. Grafalk owns this condominium.''

"How do you know that?'' she demanded, sitting down suddenly on a sofa near me. "Did Jeannine tell you?''

"No, Paige. Your sister kept your secret. But property titles are a matter of public record in Chicago. I was curious about this place, since I suspect Windy City can't afford to pay you very much. Anyway, where was I? Oh yes, Grafalk got Clayton to give him preferred customer treatment. In exchange, Grafalk helped pave the way for them socially when they moved back to Lake Bluff. Got them into the Maritime Club and all that good stuff.

"Well, of course, you don't like Jeannine enjoying the good things in life alone—and vice versa. So you started hanging out with her around the Maritime Club. Now Mrs. Grafalk's an interesting lady, but she's going at about a hundred knots all day long with her charities and Ravinia and the Symphony Board, and Niels saw you and thought you were just about the most beautiful little thing he'd ever laid eyes on. You saw your chance to get set up in a big way, and three years ago, when Feldspar converted this building, Niels moved you in. Right so far?''

Paige spoke in a low voice. "You are totally insufferable, Vic. You have absolutely no understanding of this sort of thing, or the kind of life I lead.''

I interrupted her. "Jeannine already gave me the heart-breaking details of the Carrington family's slide into poverty and the attendant humiliation. Take it as fact that I'm too vulgar to understand how shattering that must have been to the two of you. What I really want to know is where my cousin fitted into this. You told me a few weeks ago that you two were falling in love with each other. Did you think my cousin was a better prospect in the long run because he wasn't married? Not as much money, but more of it might come to you?''

''Stop it, Vic, stop it. Do you think I have no feeling at all? Do you know what I went through when I learned Boom Boom was dead? I had no choice. I had no choice!'' The last sentence was uttered in a rising cadence.

''What do you mean?'' I was controlling my temper with increasing difficulty. ''Of course you had choices. If you really were in love with Boom Boom, you could do without a lot of things. And he didn't exactly live in poverty, even by Lake Bluff standards.''

Her honey-colored eyes were filled with tears. She held out a hand in a beseeching gesture. ''Vic, Niels pays for everything. This place, all the furniture. My bills at Saks and I. Magnin run me a thousand dollars a month alone. He pays those without question. If I want to go to Majorca for a month in October, he pays the American Express bills. I owe him so much. It seemed like such a little thing to go out with your cousin a few times and see if he had learned anything about the invoices.''

I gripped the sides of the chair to keep from rising up and strangling her. ''Such a little thing. You never thought of Boom Boom as a person, with feelings, or the right to live, did you?''

''I liked Boom Boom, Vic. Please, you must believe me.''

''I believe nothing you say. Nothing. You dare call me insufferable!'' I stopped and checked myself. ''Tell me what happened that day you went sailing. That Saturday before my cousin was murdered.''

She winced. ''You mustn't say that, Vic. It was an accident. Niels assured me it was an accident and the police believe so too.''

''Yes, well, tell me about the sailing trip. Mattingly was

there, right? And Phillips. Grafalk, of course. What was the purpose? Why did you drag Boom Boom up for that?''

"Mattingly wasn't there, Vic. I keep telling you I don't know him. You accuse me of being unfeeling, but I'm not. When I told Niels that Boom Boom had—gotten close to the truth on the invoices, he wanted Clayton to get rid of him on the spot. But I told him not to.'' She lifted her chin and looked at me proudly. "We went up there to see if Niels could persuade Boom Boom to see things their way. On Saturday it looked as though he might. But the next Monday he had a terrible argument with Clayton over the matter, and Niels said it was no use trying to talk to him, in fact that we'd better do something before Boom Boom called Argus. But then—then he slipped and fell and that ended the matter. I was so relieved. I was terrified Niels might do something dreadful.''

It was my turn to be speechless. I couldn't find words that matched my horror and my anger. Finally I choked, "You tried to bribe Boom Boom and he didn't live that way. You vermin just couldn't understand that. You gave him a chance to be corrupted and he refused to take it . . . What about the water in the holds of the *Lucella*? What did that have to do with Clayton and Niels?''

She looked blank. "I don't know what you're talking about.''

"The *Lucella* couldn't take on a load of grain because someone had poured water into her holds. Boom Boom was going to talk to the captain about it before he called Argus . . . Never mind. What about Clayton? Were you with Niels Sunday morning when he put a big hole in the side of Clayton's head?''

She looked at me with gentle reproof. "I don't think you should talk to me like that, Vic. You may not approve of my relations with Niels, but he is my lover.''

I gave a crack of manic laughter. "Me not approve! Christ, Paige, you're a whole separate universe. Why should I give a damn about you and Grafalk? It's what the two of you did to my cousin that I care about. That's what makes your relationship stink.''

Paige looked at her watch. "Yes, well, I don't agree with you. I think I pointed out to you what an obligation I'm under to Niels. He's coming over in a few minutes, too, so unless you want to meet him I'd suggest you leave."

I got up. "One last question, Paige darling. Was it the photocopy of Grafalk's invoice you were looking for in Boom Boom's apartment the day after the funeral? If it was, I've found it. And as for the letter Boom Boom wrote you— 'Beautiful Paige'—I don't think he sent that to the Royal York in Toronto at all. He wrote you the Sunday before he died, didn't he? To tell you he didn't want to see you again. You put it in an old envelope to prove to me that you were writing each other love letters. You knew I'd look at the heading and not read the letter." I choked on a sob and swallowed it. If I stayed any longer the last threads of my self-control would snap.

Paige watched me with dark, angry eyes as I walked across the Persian rug to the front door. For once her exquisite poise deserted her; lines appeared around her mouth and eyes and she looked older.

26 * On the Tiles

Back outside I sat on the stoop, unable to move any farther. Fatigue fogged my brain. The day had started at Jeannine's with confirmation that her husband pushed Boom Boom under the propeller of the *Bertha Krupnik*. Now came the news that her sister had gone out with Boom Boom only to spy on him for Grafalk.

What good would it do Boom Boom if I could prove Grafalk's complicity in his death, or even in destroying the *Lucella* and the Poe Lock? Revenge brings only limited satisfaction, and I didn't feel noble enough to act out of a disinterested sense of justice.

I stood up and looked around vaguely for a cab. A tall figure detached itself from the shadows and crossed the street to me.

"A satisfactory encounter?" Ferrant asked.

"You waiting around for me?" I said. "How about finding me a cab? Speaking as a detective, I guess it was satisfactory. But, as a human being, I can't say it appealed to me much."

"Look, how about dinner and you can tell me about it?"

"Roger, I'm too tired to eat and I don't feel like telling anyone about it."

He trotted over to State Street and flagged a cab there. He helped me inside and followed after.

"Look, you don't have to tell me about the interview, but you'll feel better after something hot to eat and another drink."

I finally let myself be persuaded. He'd been very cooperative about looking into Grafalk's records. If he wanted to hear the gory details of the rest of the case, why not?

We went to the Filigree, a restaurant in the Hanover House Hotel that resembles my idea of a men's club: discreet tables with maroon drapes shielding diners from one another, a fireplace with a high marble mantel, and elderly waiters who seem to ooze a vague distrust of women diners: do they really appreciate the fine old vintages they're drinking?

You go to the Filigree for steaks. Over a thick-cut T-bone and a bottle of Château St. Georges (1962) I felt myself reviving.

"Earlier this evening you said you weren't really concerned about the locks or the freighters—that you were involved in this from a personal standpoint. What is that?"

I explained to Ferrant about my cousin and the problems down at Eudora Grain. "I was just visiting the woman he was dating the three months before he died. Her name is Paige Carrington. She's a talented dancer, maybe not New York quality, but quite good. She is exquisite, the kind of woman you gawk at but who appears too perfect to touch. Anyway, it seems she's been Grafalk's mistress for a number of years. He arranged a party at which she could meet my cousin—said he wanted to buy some shares in the Hawks and asked Guy Odinflute to hold a party for him and the team. Boom Boom was always included in that kind of function and Grafalk saw to it that Paige had an invitation too.

"Well, my cousin was easily as susceptible as the next man. When Paige made a dead-set at him, he responded— probably with enthusiasm. She's that type of person. And she spent the next three or four months tracking what he was doing at Eudora Grain.

"When it became obvious that Boom Boom had discovered the extent of the problem there and was planning on blowing the whistle to Argus—Eudora's chairman—Paige's tender heart was touched: she got Grafalk and Phillips to try to buy off my cousin. Instead, they knocked him off."

I drank some more wine and slumped back in my seat. I'd only been able to eat half the excellent steak.

I gestured with the wineglass. "This whole business with the freighters and the locks looks like something separate altogether. I wouldn't even be interested if it didn't seem to tie in with what happened to my cousin." I finished my wine and poured myself another glass. At this rate I was going to be mildly sozzled; after the day I'd had, it felt good. Ferrant ordered a second bottle.

"I've got a couple of problems right now. One is, although Jeannine Phillips as good as told me that her husband pushed Boom Boom off the wharf, I don't have any proof. She didn't come out and say it in so many words, and nobody witnessed the drowning. I do have some skeletal proof about what was going on at Eudora. I could send that to Argus, but all it would do is discredit Phillips. Even if they could make the tie-in with Grafalk stick, it doesn't prove anything more criminal than taking kickbacks."

The waiter took my plate with a contemptuous glance at

the unfinished steak as the wine steward opened the second bottle of St. Émilion for us. Like many very thin men, Ferrant ate a great deal—he'd consumed a sixteen-ounce sirloin while we talked, along with oysters florentine, the special potatoes Filigree, and a platter of beefsteak tomatoes. He ordered chocolate cheesecake; I passed on dessert and had some more wine.

"The one thing I might be able to get Grafalk on is murdering Phillips."

Ferrant sat up in his chair. "Go on, Vic! Grafalk murder Phillips?"

"He was last seen alive around one o'clock Sunday morning. The police figure he was in the holds and suffocated by 8:00 A.M. at the latest. So between one in the morning and eight in the morning someone bonked him on the head and got him onto a Great Lakes freighter. The police have a guard on duty at the entrance to the Port. Not that many people enter the Port that late at night, and they have a pretty good list of who came in. I'm sure that they've been through those people's cars quite thoroughly. If one of them had driven Phillips's body into the Port, they'd have nailed him for it. But they haven't made an arrest."

"Maybe the murderer brought him on board in a plastic bag and no blood got on his car . . . Was Grafalk at the Port that night?"

"He didn't drive down there."

"What'd he do—fly?"

"Don't think so—a helicopter would be pretty noisy."

"Then how did he get there?"

"Good heavens, Roger, I'm ashamed of you. You come from this island country, famous for four centuries of naval prowess. It ought to be the first thing to leap to your mind."

His brow creased. "By boat? You must be joking." He thought it over. "I suppose he could. But can you prove he did?"

"I don't know. The evidence is so circumstantial—it's going to be hard to sell people on it. For instance, you. Do you buy Grafalk as master criminal?"

He gave a half smile. "I don't know. We proved the figures on Grafalk this afternoon. And yet—that's a big jump to stuffing someone into a freighter to die . . . What about Bledsoe?''

I shook my head. ''Bledsoe was up in the Soo and his plane was down in Chicago. Not only that, someone sent his plane back down here in such a way as to implicate him for a different murder.''

I wondered what the waiters would do if I curled up on the plush cushion and went to sleep. I yawned. ''The trouble is, if I can't convince you, when you believe the financial evidence, I know I'll never convince the cops enough to swear out a search warrant. It's a big step, going to look at a rich man's yacht. They have to be real convinced before they do something like that.''

I leaned back in the seat and closed my eyes, still holding the wineglass. ''He can't get away with it,'' I muttered to myself. But it looked as though he might. Even with blowing up the *Lucella*, because nobody knew where the depth charges came from. If only I had evidence, someone who'd seen Grafalk and Phillips at his boat Sunday morning—or some bloodstains on the foredeck of Grafalk's yacht.

I opened my eyes at Ferrant. ''I need to get some proof. And the cards are not going to be stacked all his way. They just can't be. Even if he is as rich as Rockefeller.''

On this dramatic statement I got up from the table and walked with careful dignity to the front door. The maître d'hôtel also gave me a scornful glance. Not only can women not appreciate the great vintages, they swill them disgustingly and get revoltingly drunk.

''Thank you, my good man,'' I said as he held the door open for me. ''Your contempt for women will bring you more pleasure than any paltry tip I could give you. Good night.''

In the lobby of the hotel was a pay phone. I walked over to it, carefully avoiding the Greek columns haphazardly dotting the floor, and tried to call the Great Lakes Naval Training Station. The operator and I went a few rounds before I got my meaning across and she found a number for me. The phone rang twenty times or so, but nobody answered. A grandfather clock by the front door showed that it was close to midnight.

Ferrant was standing nearby holding my handbag, which I'd left at the table.

"Who's defending the country at midnight?" I demanded as I took my bag from him. "If nobody answers the phone, how will they ever know the Russians are attacking?"

Ferrant took my arm. "You know, Vic, I think you should wait till morning to get your proof."

"If I wait until morning he'll get away with it," I protested stubbornly. "Get me a cab!" I yelled at the doorman.

"Where are you going?" Ferrant demanded.

"Back to my car. Then out to Grafalk's boat. I'm going to get proof."

The doorman looked at us uncertainly.

"Are you getting my cab?" I called at him. He shrugged and went outside with his whistle.

Ferrant followed me into the chilly night. He kept trying to take my arm and I kept pushing him aside. When the cab came I climbed in and told the driver to take me to my car.

"Yeah, well, where is your car?"

"In the garage," I mumbled, and fell asleep.

27 ✳ On Board the Dragon Ship

When I woke up, my head pounded uncomfortably and I felt sick. Bright sunlight was coming in through a window, blinding me. That didn't make sense—I sleep with heavy drapes pulled across my windows. Someone must have broken in during the night and opened my curtains.

Holding my head with one hand, I sat up. I was on a couch in a strange room. My shoes, purse, and jacket were lying on a glass-topped coffee table next to me with a note.

Vic

I couldn't get you to wake up long enough to tell me your address, so I brought you back here to the Hancock. I hope you find your proof.

R.F.

I staggered across the room and out into a carpeted hallway, looking for a bathroom. I took four aspirin from a bottle in the medicine chest and ran a hot bath in the long yellow tub. I couldn't find any washcloths on the shelves, so I soaked a heavy hand towel in the water and wrapped it around my head. After about half an hour in the water I started feeling more like me and less like a carpet after spring cleaning. I couldn't believe I'd gotten that drunk on one bottle of wine. Maybe I'd drunk two.

I wrapped myself in a dressing gown hanging on the back of the bathroom door and went on down the hallway to find a kitchen, a small but completely equipped room gleaming in white and stainless steel. A clock hung next to the refrigerator. When I saw the time I put my head next to the face to see if it was still running. Twelve-thirty. No wonder Ferrant had left me to go downtown.

Puttering around, I found an electric coffee maker and some canned coffee and brewed a pot. Drinking it black, I recalled last night's events—the meeting with Paige and dinner with Ferrant. I dimly remembered trying to call the Great Lakes Naval Training Station. The reason why came back to me. Sober, it still sounded like a good idea.

Using a white wall phone next to the stove, I tried the Station again. This time a young man answered. I told him I was a detective, which he interpreted as meaning I was with the police. Many people think that and it helps not to disillusion them.

"Niels Grafalk keeps his private yacht at the Training Station," I said. "I want to know if he took it out early Sunday morning."

The young sailor switched me down to the dock, where I talked to a guard. "Mr. Grafalk handles his boat privately," the guard told me. "We can call around and try to find out for you."

I told him that would be great and I would call again in an hour. I put my clothes back on. They were smelling rather stale by this time. I was short a corduroy pantsuit, jeans, and two shirts as a result of this case. Maybe it was time for new clothes. I left Ferrant's apartment, rode the elevator down to the ground, and walked across the street to Water Tower Place, where I treated myself to a new pair of jeans and a red cotton shirt with a diagonal yellow stripe at Field's. Easier than going back to my apartment at this point.

I went back down to the Loop. I hadn't been in my office since the morning I talked to Mrs. Kelvin, and the floor inside the door was piled with mail. I looked through it quickly. Bills and advertisements—no solicitations from millionaires to find their missing husbands. I dumped the lot in the trash and phoned the Naval Station again.

The young sailor had exerted himself to be helpful. "I called over to Admiral Jergensen's office, but no one there knew anything about the boat. They told me to call Mr. Grafalk's chauffeur—he usually helps out when Mr. Grafalk wants to sail. Anyway, he wanted to know why we were asking, so I told him the police were interested, and he said the boat hadn't been out on Saturday night."

I thanked him weakly for his help and hung up. I simply hadn't anticipated that. Calling Grafalk. At least they had said police and not given my name, since I'd never told the sailor who I was. But if there was evidence on the boat, they'd be at pains now to get rid of it.

I debated calling Mallory but I couldn't see how I could convince him to get a search warrant. I thought about all possible arguments I might use. He still believed Boom

Boom and I had been victims of separate accidents. I was never going to be able to convince him Grafalk was a murderer. Not unless I had a sample of Phillips's blood from Grafalk's yacht.

Very well, then. I would get the sample. I went to a safe built into the south wall of my office. I'm not Peter Wimsey and I don't carry a complete police lab around with me, but I do have some of the rudiments, like chemicals to test for the presence of blood. And some self-sealing plastic pouches to put samples in. I had a Timothy Custom Utility Knife in there, so I took that along. With a three-inch blade, it wasn't meant as a weapon but a tool, its razor-honed blade ideal for cutting up a piece of deck or carpet or something containing the evidence. My picklocks and a magnifying glass completed my gear.

I emptied everything out of my shoulder bag, put my driver's license and my detective ID in my pocket with some money and stuck the detective equipment in the zippered side compartment. Back to Grant Park for my car, which cost me fifteen dollars to retrieve. I wasn't sure I was going to remember all my expenses for submitting a bill to Boom Boom's estate. I needed to be more methodical in recording them.

It was after four when I reached the Edens Expressway. I kept the speedometer at sixty-five all the way to the tollway. Traffic was heavy with the first wash of north-bound executives from the city and I kept pace with the cars in the fast lane, not risking a ticket and the delays that would bring me.

At five I exited onto route 137 and headed toward the lake. Instead of turning south on Green Bay for Lake Bluff, I went on to Sheridan Road and turned left, following the road up to the Great Lakes Naval Training Station.

A guard was on duty at the main entrance to the base. I gave my most vivacious smile, trying hard not to look like a Soviet spy. "I'm Niels Grafalk's niece. He's expecting me to join a party down at the *Brynulf Nordemark*."

The guard consulted a list in the booth. "Oh. That's the private boat the admiral lets the guy keep here. Go on in."

"I'm afraid this is my first time up here. Can you give me directions?"

"Just follow this road down to the docks. Then turn left. You can't miss it—it's the only private sailboat down there." He gave me a permit in case anyone asked me any questions. I wished I was a Soviet spy—this would be an easy place to get into.

I followed the winding road past rows of stark barracks. Sailors were wandering around in groups of two or three. I passed a few children, too. I hadn't realized that families lived on the base.

The road led down to the docks, as the guard had said. Before I reached the water I could see the masts of the ships sticking up. Smaller than the lakes freighters, covered with turrets and radar equipment, the naval ships looked menacing, even in the golden light of a spring evening. Driving past them, I shuddered and concentrated on the road. It was pitted from the heavy vehicles that routinely used it and the Omega bounced from hole to hole past the line of training ships.

About a hundred yards farther down, in splendid isolation, sat the *Brynulf Nordemark*. She was a beautiful vessel with two masts, sails furled neatly about them. Painted white, with green trim, she was a sleekly lined boat, floating easily against the ropes that fastened her to the dock. like a swan or some other water bird, natural and graceful.

I parked the Omega on the boat's far side and walked out on the little jetty to which the *Brynulf* was tied. Pulling one of the guys slightly to bring her over to me, I grabbed the wooden railing and swung myself over onto the deck.

All of the fittings were made of teak, varnished and polished to a reflecting sheen. The tiller was set in a gleaming brass base, and the instrument panel, also teak, contained a collection of the most up-to-date gadgets—gyro compass, wind gauges, depth sounders, and other instruments I couldn't begin to understand. Grafalk's grandfather had bought the yacht, I recalled—Grafalk must have updated the equipment.

Feeling like a caricature of a detective, I pulled the magnifying glass out of my handbag and began to scrutinize the deck—on hands and knees, just like Sherlock Holmes. The tour took some time and I failed to discover anything remotely like blood on the highly polished surface. I continued the inspection along the sides. Just as I was about to give up on the deck, I spotted two short blond hairs caught in the starboard railing. Grafalk's hair was white, the chauffeur's sandy. Phillips had been a blond, and this was a good spot for his head to have banged as they dragged him off the yacht. Grunting with satisfaction, I took a pair of eyebrow tweezers from my purse, plucked out the hairs, and put them in a little plastic bag.

A small flight of stairs next to the tiller led to the cabin. I paused for a minute, hand on the wheel, to look at the dock before I went down. No one was paying any attention to me. As I started down the stairs my eye was caught by a large warehouse across the road from me. It was a corrugated Quonset hut, dingy like the other buildings on the base. Plastered with red triangles, it had a neatly lettered sign over the entrance: MUNITIONS DEPOT, HIGH EXPLOSIVES. NO SMOKING.

No guard patrolled the depot. Presumably, if you had clearance to be on the base at all, you weren't likely to rifle the munitions. Grafalk passed the dump every time he went sailing. His chauffeur probably had the tools to get past the lock on the large rolling doors. As a friend of the admiral's, Grafalk might even have gone in on some legitimate pretext. I wondered if they kept an inventory of their explosives. Would they be able to tell if enough depth charges were gone to blow up a thousand-foot ship?

I went down the short flight of stairs where a locked door led to the living quarters. It was after six and the sun was starting to set. Not much light made its way into the stairwell and I fumbled with the picklocks for several minutes before getting the door open. A hook on the wall clipped to another hook on the door to hold it open.

The one thing I'd forgotten was a flashlight. I hunted for a light and finally found a chain connected to an overhead lamp. Pulling it on, I saw I was in a small hallway, carpeted in a green that matched the boat's trim. A latched door at my right opened into a master bedroom with a king-size bed, mirroed walls, and teak fittings. A sliding wardrobe door opened on a good collection of men's and women's clothes. I looked at the women's outfits doubtfully: Paige and Mrs. Grafalk were both thin and short—the wardrobe could have belonged to either.

The master bedroom had an attached bathroom with a tub and a sink fitted with gold faucets. It didn't seem too likely that Grafalk and Phillips would have fought in there.

I went back out to the hallway and found two other bedrooms, less opulent, each with sleeping for four, on the port side. A dining room with an old mahogany table bolted to the floor and a complete set of Wedgwood in a handsome breakfront was next to them on the port side of the bow. Next, in the very tip of the bow, was a well-equipped galley with a gas stove. Between the master bedroom and the galley on the starboard side was a lounge where the sailors could read or play bridge or drink during inclement weather. A shallow cupboard unlatched to reveal several decanters and a good collection of bottles. The scotch was J & B. I was disappointed—the first sign of bad taste on Grafalk's part. Maybe Paige selected the whiskey.

Unless Phillips had been knocked out on deck, my guess was he had been hit in either the lounge or the dining room. I started on the lounge as the more hopeful place. It contained a leather-covered card table and a desk, a number of chairs, a couch, and a small fireplace with an electric fire in it.

The lounge floor was covered with a thick, figured green carpet. As I surveyed the room, trying to decide where most efficiently to begin my search, I noticed that the pile in front of the little fireplace was brushed back at a different angle than the rest of the rug. That seemed promising. I skirted around the brushed area and began inspecting it with my glass. I found another blond hair. No blood, but a strong smell of cleanser, something like Top Job. The carpet was still faintly damp to my touch, although it had been three days since Phillips's death. I smelled other sections of the rug, but the odor of cleanser and the damp only came from the section in front of the fireplace.

I pulled myself to my feet. Now the problem was going to be to get the police up here for a more formal search. Their equipment could detect whether blood stuck to the rug in microscopic quantities. Maybe the thing to do was to cut off a bit of the pile and get them to examine it. If there were blood on it, they'd be more likely to want to see where the rug fragments came from. Using my Timothy Custom Knife, I cut a small section of fibers from the place where I'd found the blond hair.

As I put the fabric into a clean specimen bag, I heard a thud on the deck. I sat quite still and listened, straining my ears. The cabin was so well paneled, you couldn't hear much above you. Then another, gentle thud. Two people had boarded the boat. Navy children playing around the docks?

I stuck the specimen bag in my pocket. Holding the knife firmly, I went to the door and turned out the light. I waited inside the room, listening. Through the hallway I could hear a faint murmur of male voices. These were grown-ups, not children.

Footsteps moved overhead, toward the bow. At the stern an engine turned over and caught. The boat, which had been floating aimlessly with the water currents, started vibrating and then began moving slowly backward.

I looked around for a hiding place. There was none. The card table and the couch offered no protection. Through the porthole in the lounge's starboard wall I watched a destroyer slide by, then the gray concrete of a breakwater, and finally a small white channel marker, its light flashing green as it swung around. We were out of the channel into the open lake. Straining my ears near the door, I heard the sharp slapping noise of wind on canvas: they were raising the sails. Then more voices, and finally a footstep on the carpeted stairs.

"I hope you're not going to play hide-and-seek with me, Miss Warshawski. I know this boat much better than you do." It was Grafalk.

My heart pounded sickeningly. My stomach turned over. I felt short of breath and too weak to speak.

"I know you're here—we saw your car on the quay."

I took several diaphragm breaths, slowly exhaling on a descending scale, and stepped into the hallway.

"Good evening, Mr. Grafalk." Not the world's greatest line, but the words came out without a tremor. I was pleased with myself.

"You're a very smart young woman. Knowledgeable, too. So I won't point out to you that you're trespassing on private property. It's a beautiful night for a sail, but I think we can talk more easily down here. Sandy will be able to manage the boat alone for a while now that the sails are up."

He took my arm in a steely grip and moved me back into the lounge with him, turning the light back on with his other hand.

"Do sit down, Miss Warshawski. You know, you have my heartfelt admiration. You are a very resourceful lady, with good survival instincts. By now you should be dead several times over. And I was impressed with the reconstruction you gave Paige, quite impressed indeed."

He was wearing evening clothes, a black suit tailored to his wide shoulders and narrow hips. He looked handsome in them, and there was an expression of suppressed excitement in his face which made him appear younger than he was.

He let go of my arm and I sat in one of the leather-covered straight-back chairs next to the card table. "Thank you, Mr. Grafalk. I'll have to remember to ask you for a reference the next time a client inquires."

He sat down facing me. "Ah, yes. I fear your clients will be deprived of your services soon, Miss Warshawski. A pity, since you have the brains and the skill to be of help to people. By the way, who are you working for now? Not Martin, I hope."

"I'm working for my cousin," I said levelly.

"How quixotic of you. Avenging the memory of the dead Boom Boom. Paige says you don't believe he fell under the *Bertha Krupnik* by accident."

"My parents discouraged a faith in Santa Claus at an

early age. Paige never struck me as terribly naive, either—just reluctant to face facts which might upset her comfort.''

Grafalk smiled a bit. He opened the latched liquor cupboard and pulled out a decanter. "Some Armagnac, Vic? You don't mind if I call you that, do you? Warshawski is an awkward name to keep repeating and we have a long conversation in front of us . . . Don't blame Paige, my dear Vic. She's a very special person, but she has these strong needs for material possessions that go back to her early childhood. You know the story of her father?''

"A heartrending tale," I said dryly. "It's amazing that she and her sister were able to go on living at all.''

He smiled again. "Poverty is all relative. At any rate, Paige doesn't want to jeopardize her current standard of living by thinking about anything . . . too dangerous.''

"How does Mrs. Grafalk feel about the situation?''

"With Paige, you mean? Claire is an admirable woman. Now that our two children are through school she's thoroughly absorbed in a variety of charities, all of which benefit profoundly by Grafalk backing. They claim the bulk of her attention and she's just as pleased to have mine diverted elsewhere. She's never been very interested in Grafalk Steamship either, unfortunately.''

"Whereas it has Paige's breathless attention? That's a little hard for me to picture, somehow.''

"You're sure you don't want any Armagnac? It's quite good, really.''

"I'll take your word for it." My stomach warned me against putting any more alcohol on top of last night's St. Émilion.

He poured himself some more. "Paige is in a position where she has to be interested in what interests me. I don't mind knowing I've bought her attention—it's quite intense and delightful whether bought or volunteered. And I'm afraid the steamship line is the thing I care most about.''

"So much that you killed Phillips and Mattingly, got Phillips to push my cousin off the wharf, and blew up the *Lucella Wieser* to protect it? Oh yes. I forgot Henry Kelvin, the night watchman in Boom Boom's building.''

Grafalk stretched his legs out and swirled the brandy in his glass. "Technically, Sandy did most of the damage. Sandy's my chauffeur and general factotum. He planted the depth charges on the *Lucella*—quite a diver. He was a frogman in the navy, served on my ship in World War II. When he was discharged I hired him. Anyway, technically, Sandy did the dirty work."

"But you're an accessory. The law holds you equally responsible."

"The law will have to find out first. Right now, they seem extremely uninterested in me."

"When they have the evidence that Phillips received his head wound here in this lounge their interest will pick up considerably."

"Yes, but who's going to tell them? Sandy won't. I won't. And you, I'm afraid, aren't going to be with us when we return to port. So you won't."

He was trying to frighten me and succeeding rather well.

"Phillips called you Saturday night after he got my message, didn't he?"

"Yes. I'm afraid Clayton was cracking. He was a smart enough man in his way, but he worried about details too much. He knew if you told Argus about the invoices his career would be finished. He wanted me to do something to help him out. Unfortunately, there wasn't much I could do at that point."

"Why'd you kill him, though? What possible harm could it do you if word got out that you'd been involved in some kickbacks in assigning cargoes? You own the controlling interest in Grafalk Steamship—your board can't force you to resign."

"Oh, I agree. Unfortunately, even though we hadn't involved Clayton in the—uh—mishap to the *Lucella*, he knew my feelings toward Martin too well. He suspected I was responsible and threatened to divulge that to the Coast Guard if I didn't protect him with Argus."

"So you smashed a hole in the side of his head—What'd you use? One of these andirons?—and sailed him down to the Port. Putting him on the *Gertrude Ruttan* was a macabre touch. What would you have done if Bledsoe hadn't had a ship in port?''

"Used someone else's. It just seemed more poetic to use one of Martin's. What made you think of it?''

"It wasn't that difficult, Niels. The police patrol that facility. They were questioning everyone who'd been down there between midnight and six Sunday morning, inspecting their cars, too, I'm sure. So whoever put the body in the holds had to get to the ship without going by the police. Once I realized that, it was pretty easy to see it must have come by boat. A helicopter would have attracted too much attention.''

It pricked his vanity to have his great idea treated lightly. "We won't run those risks with you, Vic. We'll leave you a couple of miles offshore with a good strong weight to hold you down.''

I have always feared death by drowning more than any other end—the dark water sucking me down into itself. My hands were trembling slightly. I pressed them to the sides of my legs so that Grafalk couldn't see.

"It was the destruction of the *Lucella* I couldn't figure out at first. I knew you were angry with Bledsoe for leaving you, but I didn't realize how much you hated him. Also, the Eudora shipping contracts I looked at puzzled me. There were quite a number of orders last year which Pole Star gave up to Grafalk Steamship. For a while I thought you two were in collusion, but there wasn't any financial advantage to Bledsoe from the *Lucella* being blown up. Quite the contrary.

"Then he told me Monday that you'd pressured him while he was financing the *Lucella*—you knew he'd never raise the money if word got out on the street that he'd been in jail for embezzling. So you promised to keep it to yourself if he'd give you some of his shipping contracts.

"That explained the water in the holds too. Once the *Lucella* was financed, you could tell the world and be damned, as far as he cared. He started underbidding you—considerably—and you got Mattingly to bribe one of the sailors to put water in her holds. So she lost the load, and in a rather expensive way.''

Grafalk wasn't so relaxed now. He drew his legs up and crossed them. "How'd you know that?" he asked sharply.

"Boom Boom saw Mattingly there. He wrote Pierre Bouchard that he'd seen Mattingly under odd circumstances. I thought it must have been up here on the *Brynulf*, but Paige told me Mattingly didn't go on that expedition. The only other really odd place for my cousin to have seen him was down at the Port. It bothered Boom Boom enough to try to get Bouchard to trace Mattingly, and he wouldn't have done that for something trivial . . . But what I really want to know, Niels, is how long Grafalk Steamship has been losing money?''

He got up with a sudden movement that knocked his brandy glass over. "Who told you that?"

"Niels, you're like an elephant on a rampage. You're leaving a trail of broken trees behind you and you think no one else can see them. You didn't have to tell me Grafalk Steamship was the only thing you really cared about. It was obvious the first day I met you. Then your fury with Bledsoe for deserting you was totally irrational. People leave jobs every day for new jobs or to set up their own businesses. I could see you might feel hurt if you gave Bledsoe his big chance. But, my God! You acted like King Richard when one of his barons broke the oath of fealty. Bledsoe didn't work for Grafalk Steamship—he worked for you. It was a personal betrayal when he left you.''

Grafalk sat down again. He picked up his glass and poured some more Armagnac; his hand wasn't quite steady.

"Now you're a relatively smart man, and you don't need money. Not personally. There wasn't any reason for you to get sucked up in Clayton's scheme for your personal gain. But there was if your steamship company needed help.

"My first day down at the Port I heard your new dispatcher on the phone trying to get orders. He just couldn't get his bids down low enough. You're operating this antiquated fleet. When the *Leif Ericsson* ran into the wharf, Martin Bledsoe asked if that was how you were planning on getting rid of your old ships. That was when you needled him about his prison background. He reacted violently, and everyone's attention was diverted. But you *did* need to get rid of your old ships. Martin hadn't been able to persuade you to build the thousand-footers, and you were stuck with these unprofitable clunkers.''

He swept the brandy decanter from the table with a violent movement and sent it flying against the starboard wall. It smashed and a shower of glass and Armagnac sprayed my back.

''I never thought they'd be profitable!'' he shouted. ''They're too big. There weren't many ports that could handle them. I was sure they were a passing fad.'' He clenched his fists and his face took on an angry, brooding look. ''But then I started losing orders and I just couldn't get them back. And Martin! Goddamn him to hell! I saved him from prison. I gave him his life back. And how did he thank me? By building that damned *Lucella Wieser* and flaunting her under my nose.''

''Why didn't you just build your own at that point?'' I asked irritably.

He bared his teeth at me. ''I couldn't afford to. The steamship company was overleveraged by then. I'd mortgaged a lot of my other holdings and I couldn't find anyone to lend me that kind of money.

''Then I found Phillips and his pathetic wife and I saw a way at least to get some orders. But last fall your damned cousin started nosing around. I knew if he got onto the truth we were all in trouble, so I sicced Paige on him.''

''I know that part. Spare me a rerun—these sentimental stories make me gag . . . What made you blow up the *Lucella*?''

''That crack of Martin's—had I deliberately run the *Ericsson* into the wharf? At first I was wishing I could blow up my whole fleet and collect the insurance. Then I had a better idea. Get rid of the *Lucella* and close the upper lakes to the big ships at the same time. I can't keep the Poe Lock shut forever. But I've got three of those bastards stopped up at Whitefish Bay. They'll have to trundle tiddlywinks between

Thunder Bay and Duluth for the next twelve months and there's no place big enough for them to dock for the winter up there.''

He laughed crazily. ''I can carry a lot of freight this summer. I should be out of the woods by next spring—I'll be able to start capitalizing some new freighters next year. And Martin should be wiped out by then.''

''I see.'' I felt tired and depressed. I couldn't think of any way to stop him. I hadn't left a trail of my investigation. I hadn't even told anyone about the documents taped in my old copies of *Fortune*.

As if reading my thoughts, Grafalk added, ''Paige told me you had those invoices Boom Boom threatened Clayton with. Sandy went over there early this morning—no kids with bread knives to get in his way. He had to tear the place up a bit, but he found them. Pity you weren't there. We wondered where you were.''

The anger had subsided in Grafalk's face and the look of suppressed excitement returned. ''And now, Vic, it's your turn. I want you to come on deck with me.''

I pulled my utility knife from my back pocket. Grafalk smiled at it tolerantly. ''Don't make it difficult for yourself, Vic. I assure you, we'll kill you before you go overboard—no unpleasant drowning for you.''

My heart was beating faster, but my hands were calm. I remembered a day many years ago when Boom Boom and I had taken on a gang of South Side bullies. The excitement in Grafalk's face made him look like one of those twelve-year-old punks.

Grafalk started around the table for me. I let him follow until he was behind it and my back was to the door. I turned and ran down the hall toward the bow, slashing through my shirt sleeve with the knife as I ran. I cut the surface of my arm and blood rolled down it to my hand.

Grafalk had expected me to head for the stairs and I gained a few seconds. In the dining room I whirled and kicked the china cabinet with the Wedgwood in it. Glass shattered across the room and cups and saucers fell from their perches with the rocking of the vessel and crashed to the floor. I ran behind the table and wiped my bleeding arm on the drapes.

"What are you doing?" Grafalk bellowed.

"Leaving a trail," I panted. I scraped the knife across the mahogany table and rubbed my blood into the scratches.

Grafalk stood momentarily transfixed as I cut chair fabric. I opened the shattered doors to the china closet and swept the rest of the Wedgwood out, ignoring glass fragments that cut my arm. Grafalk recovered himself and lunged for me. I slid a chair into his path and backed into the galley.

The gas-burning stove stood there and a mad idea seized me. I turned on a burner and a blue flame flared up. As Grafalk came through the door at me I tore a curtain from the porthole and dropped it on the burner. It caught fire immediately. I brandished it in front of me like a torch, whirled it around, and set the other galley curtains on fire.

Grafalk came at me in a diving tackle and I jumped out of the way. He fell, heavily, and I ran with my torch back to the dining room where I set the drapes on fire. Grafalk tore after me with a fire extinguisher. He started spraying at me and the curtains. The chemical stung my lungs and partially blinded me. Holding my shirt over my face, I ran back down the hall and up the stairs to the deck.

Grafalk ran at my heels, spraying the fire extinguisher. "Stop her, Sandy. Stop her!"

The sandy-haired man looked up from the tiller. He grabbed at me and tore a piece from my new shirt. I ran to the back of the boat. It was dark now and the water was black as the *Brynulf* cut through it. Running lights from other boats winked in the distance and I screamed futilely for help.

Grafalk charged onto the deck toward me, his face a maniacal mask, fire extinguisher gripped in front of him. I took a breath and jumped overboard.

28 ✳ The Fire Ship of Wodin

The black water was very cold. It washed the chemical from my aching face and I trod water for a few seconds, coughing to clear my lungs. For a minute I panicked, thinking of the depths stretching beneath me, and I took in a mouthful of water. Sputtering, choking, I forced myself to relax, to breathe deeply.

I kicked off my running shoes, then reached into the water and pulled off my socks and shirt. The *Brynulf,* under full sail, was moving at a good clip and had gone some thirty feet past me.

I was alone in the icy water. My toes were numb and the water hurt my face. I might last twenty minutes—not enough to swim to shore. I looked over my shoulder. The yacht started to turn. Firelight flickered through the starboard portholes. A searchlight lit up the water and Grafalk quickly picked me up. I tried not to panic, to breathe naturally.

The boat continued to come toward me. Swimming on my back, I saw Grafalk at the bow, a rifle in his hand. As the *Brynulf* came alongside, I took a breath and dove under the keel. I pushed my way along underneath until I came out the back. The engine wasn't running—there were no chopping propeller blades to slice me.

Something slapped against my face as I surfaced. One of the ropes used for tying the boat was trailing in the water. I seized it and let the *Brynulf* tow me while Grafalk scanned the water with the searchlight. He turned it toward the stern.

His face appeared at the side. The rifle pointed at me. I was too numb to dive.

A blinding flash came, but not from the gun. The galley fuel must have exploded. The shock knocked me loose from the rope and deflected Grafalk's arm. A bullet grazed the water near me and the yacht moved away. A hatch cover blew off and a small fireball flew at the tiller.

Bits of the yacht broke off and floated past me. I seized a spar and leaned on it, kicking doggedly. My left shoulder ached from the cold.

The *Brynulf* continued to move away from me, her sails still catching the wind while Sandy struggled with them, finally letting them go so they hung limply. The yacht then floated in a little circle about fifteen yards from me, moved by the heat of the fire.

Grafalk appeared next to Sandy. I was close enough to see his shock of bleached white hair. He was arguing with Sandy, grabbing him. They struggled in the flickering light. Sandy wrenched himself free and leaped overboard.

Grafalk shook his arms in fury. Walking to the stern, rifle in hand, he searched the water and found me. He pointed the rifle and stood there for a long minute, sighting me. I was too frozen to dive, too frozen to do anything except move my legs mechanically up and down.

Suddenly he dropped the rifle over the side and raised his right arm in a salute at me. Slowly he walked toward the flaming tiller. Another explosion came, this one jarring my numb arms. It must have stove in the side, for the yacht began to sink.

I thought I saw Wodin, who cares nothing for murder, come for this out-of-time Viking to carry him off in his dragon-ship pyre. As the *Brynulf* went down a sudden gust tore loose a flaming shard from one of the sails and sent it over my head. It lit up the black fearsome water around me. Wodin was calling me. I clung to my spar, gritting my teeth.

Strange hands pulled me from the water. The spar was locked in my fingers. I was babbling of gods and dragon ships. There was no trace of the *Brynulf*.

29 ✳ The Long Good-bye

We sat on a stone terrace overlooking Lake Michigan. The water, pale blue under a soft summer sky, lapped gently at the sand below us. A green canvas awning protected our faces. The May day was bright and clear, although the air was cool out of the direct light of the sun. I buttoned my green serge jacket up to my chin.

Claire Grafalk inspected the brass and teak trolley. I could see a bottle of Taittinger poking over the side of a silver ice bucket. Some salmon, something that looked like a duck sliced and reassembled, and a salad were the only items I could identify without peering too greedily.

"Thank you, Karen. We can take care of ourselves." As the stocky maid disappeared up the path toward the house, Mrs. Grafalk deftly uncorked the champagne and poured it into a tulip glass.

"I don't drink myself, but I enjoy serving champagne—I hope you like this."

I muttered something appreciative. She poured water for herself and handed me a plate, creamy bone china with her initials on it twined in a green and gold wreath. She was wearing a gray shirtwaist dress with a scarf neck and a strand of heavy pearls. Her high cheekbones were covered with the circles of rouge which were doll-like yet somehow elegant and endearing.

She perched her head, birdlike, on one side, eyeing me questioningly but not talking until I had filled my plate. I sipped the champagne and ate a little cold duck. Both were excellent.

"Now. I must hear what happened. The papers gave only the sketchiest accounts. What happened to Niels's boat?"

"There was an accident in the galley and the hull caught fire." This was the answer I had given to the police and to Murray Ryerson and I wasn't going to change it now.

Mrs. Grafalk shook her head vigorously. "No, my dear. That won't do. Gordon Firth, the chairman of Ajax, came to visit me two days ago with a most extraordinary story about Niels. He had a young Englishman with him, Roger Ferrant. Mr. Ferrant says you and he discovered that Niels was running Grafalk Steamship at a loss and had cause to suspect him of blowing up Martin's ship."

I put the champagne glass down.

"And what do you want me to tell you?"

She looked at me sharply. "The truth. I still have to deal with this matter. I am still Niels's chief heir; I shall have to dispose of the remaining assets of Grafalk Steamship somehow. Martin Bledsoe would be the ideal person to take over the company. He and I—were good friends a number of years ago and I still have a special spot for him. But I must know the whole story before I talk to him or to my lawyers."

"I don't have any proof—just a chain of suggestions. Surely you don't want to hear a lot of unsubstantiated allegations. The police or the FBI or the Coast Guard may find proof of wrongdoing. But they may well not. Wouldn't you prefer to let the dead bury the dead?"

"Miss Warshawski. I am going to tell you something that no one besides Karen knows. I expect you to respect my privacy—but if you don't, it doesn't matter that much. Niels and I have lived as two neighbors for over a decade." She fluttered small, ring-covered hands. "We gradually grew apart. It happens that way, you know. Then he became more and more obsessed by Grafalk Steamship. He couldn't think about anything else. He was bitterly disappointed that our son wasn't interested in the steamship company: Peter is a cellist. Our daughter is a thoracic surgeon. When it became

clear that no one of his name lived to care about Grafalk
Steamship, Niels removed himself emotionally from the
house.

"I have paid little attention to Niels in the last several
years. Nevertheless, it became quite clear to me that he was
growing more and more erratic over the past eight or nine
months. I invited you up here for lunch because you struck
me as clever and intelligent the day we talked. I think you
can tell me what Niels was doing. You were not a social acquaintance of my husband's. I don't believe you were his
mistress—"

She paused to look at me sharply. I couldn't help laughing, but I shook my head.

"Yes. You don't have the look about you. Now. I want to
know why you were on Niels's boat and how it came to burn
up."

I took another swallow of champagne. If anyone had the
right to know, Claire Grafalk did. I told her the whole tale,
beginning with Boom Boom's death and ending with the icy
waters of Lake Michigan. I glanced at it, involuntarily shivering.

"And how did you get out? Someone rescued you?"

"Another sailboat came up. They were attracted by the
fire. I don't remember it too clearly."

"And the evidence of Clayton's death?"

I shook my head. "I still have the plastic pouches with his
hair and the carpet scraping. I think I keep them because
they give some reality to the whole episode, not because I
want to use them."

Her head was still perched on one side. She reminded me
of a robin or a sparrow—not cruel, just impersonal.

"But you don't want to prosecute?"

"I talked to Mrs. Kelvin. She's the black woman whose
husband was killed in Boom Boom's apartment. I figure she
and I are the chief mourners—Jeannine doesn't count." I
stared unseeing out at the lake, remembering the conversation with Mrs. Kelvin. I spent two days in the hospital re-
covering from the shock of my near drowning; she came to

see me late on the second day. We talked for a long time, about Boom Boom and Henry Kelvin, and love.

"Niels and Sandy are both dead, so there's no one left to prosecute. Legal action against your husband's estate would bring no pleasure, only sully the memories of two heroic men. We have no interest left."

She didn't say anything but nibbled with delicate energy on a petit four. I drank some more champagne. The food was excellent, but reviewing my time in Lake Michigan brought knots to my stomach. It looked so peaceful now under the May sun, but it is not a tame lake.

"The United States Government may try to prove a case against Grafalk Steamship. It will really depend on their proving that your husband engineered theft of the depth charges and all the rest of that. With Sandy and Howard Mattingly both dead, there aren't any witnesses. And as long as he gets the *Lucella* floating again, Martin doesn't want to push it too hard. I think the investigation will go on quite a while, but they're never going to be able to fix blame for blowing up the *Lucella*. Not unless Admiral Jergensen decides to testify that your husband stole the explosives. He doesn't seem to want to right now."

Bledsoe had been around once or twice. He figured out most of the story when he read about the accident to the *Brynulf*. I went drinking with Bledsoe one night while I told him the rest. His lovemaking matched his kissing. That had helped, but I knew the nightmares would last a long time.

Claire Grafalk looked away from me and said in a flat voice, "Niels left Paige Carrington a condo on Astor Place."

I drew a sharp breath. Paige was the spot that still hurt, the little needle in the diaphragm every time I thought of her. "I was wondering how she'd be able to afford that. Of course, she still has those monthly assessments to keep up. They're not cheap."

Mrs. Grafalk still didn't look at me. "She's in London now with Guy Odinflute."

"Do you mind so much?" I asked gently.

Tears sparkled briefly in her bright eyes, but she gave a

twisted smile. "Do I mind? Niels has been dead to me for many years. But once—it was different. For the sake of the man I once loved, I would have liked to see her mourn."

About the Author

Sara Paretsky is the author of INDEMNITY ONLY and DEADLOCK. Like V. I. Warshawski, she lives in Chicago.

LA JOIE DE VIVRE!

by
Janine Boissard